BORN IN FIRE

Also by K.F. Breene

FIRE AND ICE TRILOGY (DDVN World)

Born in Fire

Fused in Fire

Fused in Fire

MAGICAL MAYHEM TRILOGY (DDVN World)

Born in Fire

Raised in Fire

Fused in Fire

DEMIGODS OF SAN FRANCISCO

Sin & Chocolate

Sin & Magic

Sin & Salvation

DARKNESS SERIES

Into the Darkness

Braving the Elements

On a Razor's Edge

Demons

The Council

Shadow Watcher

Jonas

Charles

Jameson

Darkness Series Boxed Set, Books 1-4

WARRIOR CHRONICLES

Chosen

Hunted

Shadow Lands

Invasion

Siege

Overtaken

BORN IN FIRE

BY K.F. BREENE

Contact info:
www.kfbreene.com
Facebook: www.facebook.com/authorKF
Twitter: @KFBreene

CHAPTER 1

THE STICKY-SWEET NIGHT embraced me like a satisfied lover. Raucous laughter crowded in close as idiots strolled up Bourbon Street with their green plastic drink holders fashioned after grenades. A little girl broke away from her parents and ran toward me, stopping much too close and snatching a string of pink beads off the street.

She looked up at me with clear blue eyes sparkling with excitement. “Pink is my favorite color!”

I stared back at her, struck mute. Only the naive would pluck beads off Bourbon Street. There was no telling what sweaty chest those had been on. I didn’t want to kill her dreams, though. She was so excited as she stood there, clutching the plastic string in a small fist.

Seeing that she was expecting some sort of reply, I blurted out the first thing that came to mind. “So is mine.”

She flashed a giant smile before turning at the calm call of her mother.

With a gaping mouth, I stared after her.

So is mine?

Pink was most certainly not my favorite color. I didn't hate it, but being caught dead in it would be a horrible way to go. *Black* was my favorite color, if I had to choose. It hid stains. I could spill food or blood on it, and no one was the wiser. You certainly couldn't do that with pink leather. No way. Everyone would gasp and point.

A very important question assaulted me: why wasn't that kid afraid of me?

I glanced down at my black army boots, made for kicking in teeth. Paired with my black leather pants, decorated with scuff marks and four parallel lines from when a mark had tried to rake me with his claws last month, I looked fierce. A bad mama-jama. *Right?*

I had a freaking gun strapped to my leg! And if, for some reason, that wasn't hardcore enough, then surely the sword strapped to my back should've made that kid hesitate in approaching, grimy pink beads or no. Sure, this was NOLA, where anything goes, but still, my outfit should've at least panicked the mother.

My job hinged on the fact that I was terrifying, dang it!

Intent on getting to the bottom of this, I adjusted my bra. A catcall came immediately. I swung a glare toward the source, a man in his early twenties loitering in a bar doorway.

He took a step toward me with a drunken smile, displaying the unmistakable swagger of idiocy.

I'm not the kind of girl sane men hit on, bro.

In a power stance, I faced him dead on, letting my glare amp up until I was sure *crazy* sparkled within my eyes. The man flinched. His drink slopped out of his plastic cup and down the front of his shirt. He didn't notice. Instead, he started sidestepping back into the bar, his smile twisting into a grimace.

Good sign. That made me feel better.

Clearly, any kid brave enough to pick beads up off this street wasn't worried about an armed bounty hunter.

She reminded me a little of myself.

With a glance back at the girl, who took a running leap and splashed into a puddle, I continued on my way to the edge of the French Quarter. I had a mark to pick up and money to collect. Soon it would get unbearably hot in New Orleans, and Mama needed air conditioning.

I turned a corner, away from the half-flooded, busy street. Clouds still spotted the sky above, blocking out stars in patches. The earlier deluge of water from the spring storm would hopefully continue to seep into the storm drains, making my hunting ground more pleasant to navigate. Wet boots really put me in a bad mood, and I refused to wear galoshes. I had to have a *little* pride in my badassery.

Tourists and partygoers dotted the way ahead, this month a little slower for visitors. When summer revved up, the jeering crowds would flood the street. It would be my cue to avoid the area.

Up ahead, jazz clattered out of a bar. A man backed out of my way and I caught sight of Red, a resident were-dog.

Yeah. He turned into a *dog.* A nondescript brown one, at that. His style points in the were-community were seriously lacking, hence his position as a snitch for Roger, the alpha of a bunch of sub-packs spread out across North America. When a magical person without a pack wanted information in this area, torturing Red was a great way to get it.

Red caught sight of me as I stalked down the sidewalk.

"No way!" He turned to flee, straight into a large group of drunk tourists. His escape route cut off, he threw a panicked look out at the street, where a police car was rolling by, before hunching down against the wall.

The man was pure comedy.

I stopped near him with a grin, just to see what he'd do next.

He threw up his hands to block his face. "I don't

know anything. Nothing is going on, I swear!"

I patted him on his bony shoulder. He flinched with each touch.

"I'm good this time," I said, scanning the way ahead. "I don't need any information."

"I've heard that before. Then something goes wrong and here you come, looking for secrets."

"That's your own fault." With a last pat, I headed away. "Friends shouldn't keep secrets from each other."

"You're not my friend," he yelled at me.

That wasn't very nice.

I turned and scoured him with a half-assed glower. He skittered in the other direction.

I really shouldn't pick on the poor guy, but he was a thorn in my side, always helping those infuriating shifters track my whereabouts. Half the time they showed up to dog my footsteps, no pun intended, watching my movements for some clue as to what my magic was. What *I* was, basically. My scent told them something was up with me, but they couldn't find a reason to haul me into the Realm, the magical world basically run by the elves, to question me. That meant they skulked around, trying to catch me doing something wrong. Their presence made people skittish, and my marks, who were usually up to no good and already skittish, often found somewhere else to be.

The shifters represented the elves in the human

world, policing the magical people to ensure our kind was kept secret. I sometimes worked for the other type of law enforcement, a human-world office funded in secret by the U.S. government that operated with the same goal—keeping all things magical from the humans. One would think the two factions would combine forces, but for whatever reason, that didn't happen. Instead, the two groups were always at odds with each other. Hence my eternal annoyance with the shifters.

No sooner had I reached my destination, the Purple Bear, than Jimmy, the manager, said, "I don't want no trouble in here tonight." He stood at the doorway of the bar, warding away underage partygoers with his perma-scowl. "It's a slow night and I don't want no one leaving."

"This one will be real easy, Jimmy, don't you worry." I patted him on the arm. Unlike Red, Jimmy did not flinch. "Grab and bag. No big deal."

"You say that every time."

"And it would be true every time if it wasn't for outside influences."

He sniffed. "Who you looking for?"

I scanned the dimly lit interior. Four people sat at the bar. Two were on their own and hunched over their drinks, and the other two were rehearsing for the horizontal ugly dance, hands all over each other.

"A small, wiry fella." I shifted to the side of the door

when two girls staggered closer. Jimmy reached for their IDs. "Balding. Brown eyes. He has a tattoo of a yeti on the side of his neck. Yesterday I was told he'd be in here to meet a buyer. Don't ask what he's selling—I have no idea."

"A yeti?" Jimmy shoved the ID back at the first girl and took the ID of the other. The girls giggled for no reason.

"Yeah. An abominable snowman. You seen him?"

Jimmy returned the second ID and jerked his head for the women to enter. They giggled again, still for no reason. "I seen a short, balding man. Didn't notice no tattoo. He walked through 'bout a half hour ago. I'd leave that one alone, if I was you."

"Why is that?" I shifted so I could scan the booths. "The music tonight sucks, by the way. Did you lose a bet?"

"Becau—" He cut his explanation short and glanced inside. "That's the best I could get last minute. The normal gig canceled an hour before they was supposed to be here. I had to get a human band, and I don't have many connections on that front."

Jimmy was a merman, which had shocked the hell out of me. I constantly wanted to ask how procreation worked, since they did it in mermaid form, what with the fins and the man parts and all that, but he was very closed-mouthed about it. All I knew was that he disappeared for a month out of the year to frolic in the ocean. Also, he hated when I used the word *frolic*.

Especially while smirking.

"Why'd they cancel?" I asked, eyeing the first booth of people, an older couple wearing beads and laughing.

"Same reason you should call it a night and walk away. We got vamps. They came in out of the Realm."

I pulled away from the door—reflex. "Out of the Realm? What level are they?"

"Middle or higher. And an elder. He walked in earlier like he owned the world. He ain't the type to mess with, Reagan, even for you. Seems like they have an interest in your mark."

I swore silently and stared out at the street. "How do you know? Did they make a move?"

"Because I know. And no, they didn't. Not yet. Been vamp sightings all over the place, though. Them little furries are in a tizzy."

He meant the resident shifter pack, probably. Mostly wolves and one badger. They were always the first respondents to vamp sightings in this area—under the Realm jurisdiction, anyway. My branch didn't respond until something actually happened.

"The little furries don't have enough power to move in and chase the vamps away." Jimmy pulled up his britches. "That should tell you something about what's going on. I'd go after someone less noteworthy."

"Or…" I scratched my chin in thought. "I could bag him, hold him, and negotiate for a larger payout."

Jimmy's lips turned downward, and his brow furrowed. "Or you could bag him, hold him, and get eaten by vamps."

"Don't be silly. Vamps are just cuddly creatures that want a hug."

Ignoring his protest, I slipped into the bar and immediately against the wall. Moving fast, I made it to the corner with the broken light fixture. Nice and shadowy. From there I had a full view of the first two booths and their inhabitants.

Baldy was sitting in the middle booth with a girl. She glanced around the bar with moving lips, her eyes wary. A forgotten beer sat at her elbow. Baldy sat opposite, his eyes on the strap of the handbag resting on her shoulder. He licked his lips in anticipation.

What are you selling?

It didn't matter to my job in the least, but I was curious what would get the vampires all worked up. Elders seldom acted directly, preferring to send their minions. So it was extraordinary for one to not only leave the Realm, but to actually follow a mark into a bar.

I glanced at the last booth, seeing a shoulder. The person sat with his or her back to the divider, on the other side of Baldy. My waist bumped the wood of the bar as I edged over until the person's hair came into sight, cropped close and styled with mousse. Probably a man.

"What can I get you?" the bartender asked, leaning against the bar.

"I'm good. I won't be here long. Actually..." I reached into my pocket for a five. One of my last. "What's the guy at the end drinking?" I pointed to the far booth.

Wariness crossed her bold features. "Just a beer, but it's full. He doesn't want company."

The head in the last booth turned a fraction, his awareness now encompassing me, the chick who wanted to buy him a drink. Abnormally great hearing confirmed he was the vampire, and the fact that he could hear me over the racket of the band meant he was old.

Very old.

Well then, everyone was accounted for, elder included.

I shrugged. "His loss." I pretended to think for a minute. "I'll have a beer. I'm waiting for Prince Charming. I sure hope he's rich. I hate working."

The bartender's face screwed up in confusion as I stuffed my money back in my pocket. Without giving her a chance to ask what I wanted, or if I actually planned to pay for my drink, I took off toward the middle booth. I grabbed Baldy and yanked him to his feet.

"What the—"

I punched him so as to daze him, which made people much easier to transport, and threw him over my shoulder. The woman shrieked, but I ignored her. I wasn't here for her, and whether she realized it or not, I was doing her a favor.

With my mark bouncing on my shoulder, I rushed for the door. A man entering the bar jumped out of the way. I darted a glance behind me as I ran out. No one exited the last booth.

Good news.

Baldy started to struggle. I threw another punch at him, and he went slack.

"Dumb move, girl," Jimmy said.

"What's he selling?" I yelled over my shoulder, already moving again.

"Blood."

Blood?

Jogging now, I hastened through the streets. If Jimmy was right, I needed to outrun the vamps. Middle- or high-level vampires could move fast, organize faster, and box me in. If five or more joined forces, they could kill me. That was not the ideal situation.

I turned a corner and had to put on the brakes. A group of people collected on the sidewalk in front of a convent. A ghost tour.

“Great work, Lou!” I shouted, saluting her. To the group, I said, “Best guide in the city!” She loved her fanfare.

Lou gave me a bow, then pointed at the man starting to struggle on my shoulder. “Looks like that one is trying to get away.”

“I got it.” I hesitated long enough to punch him again, which was pretty awkward considering his face was hanging over my back, and knocked him out. If only he’d stay unconscious, my life would be a lot easier. “Resident vamp. Nothing to it.”

“Just dramatics, folks.” Lou turned back to her crowd. “She loves the theater. As does her boyfriend, there.”

Lou was good to me. I saw her on the streets often.

“She’s really strong…” one of the tour patrons said.

“She works out a whole lot, yes. Hence the display. She plays a vampire in the local theater, actually. So she has to be strong.”

All lies. I could thank my genetics for my abilities.

I hurried on. When I was nearly out of sight of the tour, a mere two blocks from safety, a shadow stepped gracefully into my path. I recognized the haircut, the large shoulders and unfaltering confidence. The elder had caught up. Crap.

I cut right and ran diagonally across the street, dodging a car. Another shadow stepped out, not as suave, but with smooth enough movements to give me a racing heart.

"Captain, we have a problem," I muttered, looking for another escape route. Graceful and elegant shadows stepped out all around me, perfectly synchronized.

"Oh look, she's putting on a show for us!" I could hear the worry in Lou's voice. She knew I was up shit creek with a broken paddle.

Haircut walked toward me, slow and purposeful. Confidence radiated out from him like a weapon. He was much too calm for my taste. He didn't think I was a threat.

Being that he was upwind, he probably also thought I was human.

"Drop the man," he said in a velvety-smooth voice.

"Look." I stopped in the middle of the street. "I'll make a deal with you. I'll—"

"I do not make deals." He stopped ten feet from me. His minions stayed back, though perfectly placed to box me in. All ten of them. So that wasn't good.

"Interrupting someone is rude." I shifted so I could drop Baldy at a moment's notice. "I need to turn him in for the money. Just him, though. You can have whatever he is selling."

"I will have him *and* what he is selling. You are outmatched and outnumbered. Drop him and scamper away, girl. This does not concern you."

"Do you know how hot it gets in New Orleans in the middle of summer? The humidity will kill you. I need air conditioning, man. Work with me on this one, and everyone walks away."

He laughed, a sexy sound that tightened my lady bits. Stupid elder vampires.

A spell came out of nowhere, one of the minions shooting it at me from its small rubber casing.

I dropped Baldy, ripped out my sword, and sliced through the stream of white. My blade unraveled the magic, the spell's power level strong but no match for mine. I sheathed my sword and turned to the elder. I didn't plan to hand over my mark and lose my payday, but if I could escape without killing one of these buggers, thereby putting a huge price on my head, I would. Dare to hope.

I rushed forward, aiming for the elder. As if on cue, the minions charged forward, tightening their blockade around me, lightning fast and smooth as silk. Claws outstretched on the end of their human-looking fingers. Lips and gums turned black as fangs elongated. The predators were showing themselves, and *these* predators were upper-middle level, at least.

Crap-tastic.

Lazily, the lead vamp slashed. Claws sprang from his hand as it sailed toward my face.

Holy tater tits, he was powerful.

I bent backward, *Matrix*-style, before straightening back up and punching him in the face. His head whipped back as his expression turned to shock.

Yeah, I'm fast and super strong. Surprise!

I rocked a punch to his middle, another to his face, and then paused. That rhythm-breaking hesitation had him flinching, as though another strike had come. I followed with a kick. Faster than before, he blocked with his shin. Bone met bone.

It hurt like the bejeebus!

I struck for his middle next, but he was onto me. He dodged and swung claws toward my neck. I shifted out of harm's way and struck again, watching the elder's minions out of the corner of my eye. A spell rocketed toward me. I ripped out my sword, sliced through it, and made another lunge at the lead vamp. My blade cut through his designer shirt right before he slashed.

I bent out of the way of his strike. I slapped him across the face. Not punched. Slapped. Because I knew how to piss people off, and angry people made mistakes.

His eyebrows lowered over his deep-set eyes. I braced for his retaliation. His minions responded from an unseen cue. They pushed in, readying for severe violence, I could tell. Considering how old they were, and how plentiful, there was no way I could get out of this without ending up dead or worse. He was way better prepared.

I clenched my jaw and stepped back, throwing up my hands. "Fine. Take him."

He relaxed, his muscles no longer pushing at his dress shirt, and stared at me. The minions kept creeping forward, which wasn't happy news.

Still he stared.

"Here." I gestured at Baldy. "Take him. I give up." Still the minions came. "Is this going to get messy?"

"Will she escape?" Lou asked in a theatrical voice. Hopefully the onlookers missed the underlying terror in her tone. "Or will he bite her neck?"

There was no way this critter would get anywhere near my neck.

Animal shapes jogged out from the sides, behind the vampires. An onlooker gasped.

The wolves had shown up. It was the first time I was happy to see them. If they could just distract the vamps long enough for me to grab the mark and make a run for it—*another* run for it, I guess—that would make my night.

"They are fighting on public streets," I yelled, backing up to stand right next to my mark. "That violates the...*thing* you are paid to uphold..." Yelling about magic in public would also be a violation of the magical decree, and the last thing I wanted to do was give the shifters an official reason to take me in.

The lead vampire, still assessing me, tilted his head

slightly. A grin worked at his lips. I had no idea what he found so amusing.

A fierce snarl erupted from the side. A wolf lunged at a vampire minion. The other shifters ran in, ready to take down the gathering.

Sensing my golden opportunity, I snatched up Baldy and threw him over my shoulder. Before I could turn and run, clawed hands reached for me. I slashed with my sword, nicking a minion's arm. A wolf lunged, his jaws snapping at my knee.

"I'm the good guy," I said in a harried voice. "I'm on official business!"

Baldy's body was ripped away.

Clutching at air as I turned around, I was just in time to see the lead vampire toss Baldy at his minion. The other vampire caught him like a doll. Before I could even open my mouth to say, "Hey!" the lead vampire had given me a poignant stare and then bolted away at an awe-inspiring speed. He was one old-ass vampire.

The rest of the vampires took off, not even sparing a kick for the animals trying to kill them. Wolves took up the chase. In a moment, the streets were bare of all things magical except me and my sword.

There went my air conditioning.

"Crap," I said softly as someone started hesitantly clapping. The rest of the onlookers joined in, applauding me losing my mark. It was not an awesome end to the night, that was for sure.

I stashed my sword and gave the onlookers a bow. Lou would smooth everything over.

As I started walking, one question nagged at me: what were vampires doing coming after my company's marks? Vampires were supposed to get clearance for things like that.

A thought struck me that I couldn't shake.

Suddenly, I knew *exactly* what was going on.

CHAPTER 2

I BURST INTO the office early the next morning with a chip on my shoulder and a hole in my bank account. Cubicles dotted the floor in systematic rows, one of the many reasons I wouldn't succumb to being a paid employee of this establishment. In front of me was an aisle leading through the best of the best, my competitors in the bounty-hunting gig and the A-list of the Magical Law Enforcement office. The ones who got all the jobs I wanted, leaving only the insanely dangerous marks for me.

Okay, fine. I'll admit it. I wished I were in a position to get a regular paycheck from a comfy job. I'd deal with cubicles for a little security, but that option was denied to me.

"Look who it is. Miss I-Can-Bring-In-Anybody." Garret, the man who constantly taunted me for being an outcast, rolled to the edge of his cubicle and laughed. "I heard you screwed the pooch last night. Useless."

Nearing his cube, I caught the edge of his chair with my toe and thrust my hips forward, shoving. His chair rolled backward so suddenly that he tipped out and tumbled onto his face.

"Not entirely useless," I said with a smirk, continuing onward.

Snickers filled the floor as I reached the large corner office. The covered windows and closed doors didn't exactly scream *welcome.* Neither did the underpaid receptionist who sat out front.

"He in there?" I asked her.

"You need to make an appointment," she said in a bored voice.

"Will do." I kicked the door. The hinges tore free. Wood groaned as the door fell inward, crashing to the ground and wobbling.

Captain John Lox looked up, startled. After seeing me, his expression mellowed. He leaned back in his chair.

"So you don't think I can bring in a mark, is that it? You have to resort to the vampires to do it?" I stepped on the door on my way into the office.

He threaded his fingers together in his lap, studying me. His gaze flicked to the chair facing his desk, a silent invitation for me to sit down and speak about this calmly.

I grabbed the chair, picked it up, and threw it at the doorway.

I missed.

The chair hit the frame and ricocheted, hurling back in my direction. I dodged it, then stumbled on the edge of the fallen door.

This confrontation wasn't playing out how I'd hoped.

"You owe me ten grand," I barked, trying to regain control of my intimidation tactics. Humor sparked in his eyes.

After a silent beat, he said, "Come again?"

"You owe me ten grand," I repeated slowly.

"You got the mark?"

"I did not. You know why."

His brow furrowed and he shifted, his chair squealing under his weight. "The bloodsuckers got him first."

I rolled my eyes. "Bloodsuckers? Really? Every vampire TV show *ever* called—they want their catchphrases back."

"Vampires suck blood. Hence the term."

"Use a little originality. They screw like rock stars, too. So why don't you call them rock-star screwers?"

"Besides the clumsiness of that phrase, rock stars are mortal. They couldn't possibly screw as well as vampires."

"Whatever. Regardless, yes, the vampires got the mark. They brought enough people out of the Realm to organize the effort. The shifters couldn't compete with that kind of power, but they knew the vampires were around. Which means there is no way you didn't. Being that you didn't give me a heads-up, what do you think that says to me?"

"I have no idea."

I cracked my neck in frustration. "Clearly you are covering your bases again."

"I did that *one time.*"

I glared at him.

"Fine, twice. I didn't realize you found out about the second." He leaned against his desk and spread his hands in front of him. "They didn't tell me they wanted the mark. The first I heard of it was this morning, when the mark's head was delivered in a cooler."

I crinkled my nose at that visual. "So much for me getting him back," I muttered. "You expect me to believe you didn't know about a mass entrance of old vampires? Give me a break."

"I don't care what you believe. That is the truth. I'm no happier than you are. That mark was supposed to come in alive. The bounty is void. But…" A flash of confusion crossed his features. "I did get a note. It was taped to my office door when I got in this morning." He reached into his drawer, extracted a piece of paper, and pushed it across the desk. "The head arrived via parcel, so the note was delivered independently. We checked the security cameras, but we didn't see anyone deliver it."

I grabbed the note. "Come on, everyone knows vampires don't show up on film or video."

"Not everyone. Humans, for example, don't even know they exist."

I flipped the note open. "You know what I meant."

"The video didn't show any doors opening or things moving around. One second, the door was clear, and the next, the note was on it. Why not leave the head at the same time?"

I scanned the note as my heart sank into the abyss of my body, which somehow didn't stop it from thumping manically. I met his assessing stare. "The leader was an elder. He could open and close a door between frames. Getting past your shoddy security wouldn't be a problem for him. He brought a host of upper-mid levelers last night. I'm sure he had his people attend to the head." I shook the note. "And in answer to this—" I huffed. "No. Hard no. No way. Not on your life."

"It wouldn't be on my life. It'd be on yours."

My clenched fists matched my jaw. "How the hell did you get this position?"

"Stating the obvious really goes a long way. Idiots tend to ignore the thing staring them right in the face."

I put a boot on the door, a little reminder of the destruction I was capable of. "Are you calling me an idiot?"

"Again, just stating the obvious. Do you want another case?" He tapped a brown file on the edge of his desk. "Eight hundred bucks, dead or alive. Unless you take a desk job, I'm afraid this is all I have."

"I can't take a desk job." I stuck out my hand. "I don't have legit paperwork for the Brink. You know that."

"You merely have to buy some. *You* know *that*."

"With what? My beatbox broke, so I can't take to the curb for money."

"I don't know what any of that means."

I flipped open the file and my heart sank even lower. The thing felt like it was trying to squeeze into my boots. "All this risk for a measly eight hundred?"

"He only bothers the magical community. A couple of his neighbors got together to raise the money. It isn't on the government's dime, so I can't send my people. It's either you or no one."

I groaned and dropped the hand holding the file. "Why not the shifters?"

"They have their hands full with the vampires. That's what they said, anyway. Word is, they tried, but lost two of theirs. This is heavy magic, and they don't have that kind of arsenal. Neither do I, if you want to know the truth. This guy has dabbled in the dark arts. He'll throw hexes at you that you might not be ready for. Word of caution."

I shook my head and tapped the folder against my

leg, thinking about the vampire's note. "I have to eat," I said vaguely.

Pity crossed his features for a brief moment, but was wiped away immediately. "That's all I've got, kid. Sorry about the vamp trouble. Ain't nobody got time for that."

I blew out a breath.

A silent beat. "So, you going to do it?" he asked.

We both knew he wasn't asking about the file.

I glanced at the note again. I didn't know. I said as much.

"In addition to that note, I got the official notice of a bounty." The captain nodded toward his computer screen. "They're doing it by the book, though the actual mark is not yet known. There's a catch, though. If you accept the bounty, they'll be assigning you a vamp partner."

"Wait." I let my confusion show on my face. "What?"

"Together, you'll track down the mark, bring him in alive, and collect the bounty. You will take half. The vamp will take half."

"They're going to take back half of the bounty they put up? That doesn't make sense."

"It's our system. Otherwise, they'd have to personally hire you. This way they're doing it through us."

"Why bother?"

The captain smirked. "Working through us means the wolves have to leave them alone. They're using you and my department as a get-out-of-jail-free card. It's pretty clever, really."

I shrugged. "With the power I saw last night, the wolves wouldn't stand a chance. Not unless they pulled in bigger numbers from other parts of the country."

"Which they'd do for a chance to take out an elder. Roger would be all over that."

I swore under my breath. "Still. Why me? Why not Garret?"

"I have no idea. Maybe something you did last night impressed them."

"Doubtful." I scrubbed my fingers through my hair before redoing my ponytail.

"So…you going to do it?"

"How much?" I asked, thinking of running away and joining a circus instead. It would make more sense than my life.

"Your cut would be fifty grand."

The muscles in my jaw went slack. A wash of tingles worked down my body. That was a lot of money. That would let me disappear for a good long time. I needed that.

"I don't know," I said honestly, defeated. "Have you ever heard of anyone going into the vampires' lair and coming out alive?"

"No. But then, I've never heard of anyone being invited, either."

"I was more commanded than invited."

"People don't boss you around. That's an invite if anything is."

He knew me well.

"The elves don't have jurisdiction within that lair." I bit my lip. "Anything could go on in there."

The captain tapped his fingers against his desk, something he did when he was working out a problem. "Does he need your help, or is he curious about you? Maybe he's testing you. There is no way to guess what a vampire that old is really up to."

"You're sure it was the elder?"

He nodded slowly, his eyes surveying me. "He probably wants to know if you're magical, and if so, what breed you are."

I'd come to the same conclusion. "I should've showered to get rid of the weird stench," I joked.

The captain's gaze turned piercing. He'd said it once and never repeated himself: I looked human but didn't smell it, I was chock-full of powerful magic, and most people would guess, correctly, that I was a hybrid of some sort, but I wasn't a type that had ever been catalogued before. He'd ended his analysis with, "Reagan, that doesn't add up. People notice."

No, it did not add up. Yes, people did notice. Luckily, as long as I kept to myself, meaning no magical BFFs or drunken gabfests about my ancestry, I would be in the clear.

After a moment, he huffed and glanced beside me. "I'm going to have to dock you for that door."

"It wasn't me. It was the one-armed man."

He nodded thoughtfully. "Actually, I bet it was the vampire. They are damned clumsy, aren't they? Surely he knocked it off the hinges when he was putting up that note." He nodded decisively. "I'll write that up."

I couldn't help a smile. "You're an asshole, but you're my asshole."

His grumpy expression turned quizzical. "Is that from a movie?"

"I feel like it is, but…I'm not really sure, to be honest. Fits, though, no?"

"Too touchy-feely for my taste. Now get out of here. And leave Garret alone when you walk past. Every time you break one of his body parts, we get behind."

"Hire better people."

"Buy some papers."

I glanced back at the note one last time as I walked from the room, the folder tucked under my arm. I needed to think on that. I also needed to plan a course of action for bringing in the idiot terrorizing one of the few solely magical neighborhoods within the city. So much to do…

Fifteen minutes later, I sat down on a barstool.

"Hurricane, please." I rapped my knuckles on the bar as the bartender walked away to make me a drink mostly consisting of turpentine and artificial flavoring. Other bars made a fruity drink high in alcohol that the tourists loved. Not this bar. They tried to peel the eyebrows off your face.

Just what I needed to take the edge off.

I shifted, trying to get comfortable. The stool clunked to the right, uneven.

"Do you live around here?"

I glanced over to find a twenty-something guy slumped in the stool next to mine. Glazed-over eyes and a strange lean said he didn't know what he'd gotten himself into with the hurricanes.

"Yeah," I answered. "You?"

He shrugged and visibly tried to play it cool. The result was a dangerous sway in the other direction. "I'm in town for a few days. Just taking it in, you know?" He leaned over the bar. His tongue wandered out of his mouth until it bumped off the straw in his drink. He corralled the straw between his open lips before taking a sip like a giraffe eats leaves, grossly floppy.

"Is that tasty?" I asked sarcastically, nodding toward the drink.

He released the straw and licked his lips. A cock-eyed, drunken smile slid up half his face. The other half was probably numb from the alcohol. "Yeah. Killer."

I figured there was about a ninety percent chance he'd end up half-naked and facedown in the gutter with beads littering his back. Grimacing, I pulled out the file. My drink arrived as I was perusing the magical misdeeds of my new mark, which all seemed like high-powered hexes gone slightly wrong.

"Power-drunk mage," I muttered to myself, looking at his handiwork.

"Mage. Is that, like, Warcraft or…" The man swiveled in his chair until his knees bumped off mine, clearly attempting to face me.

I pushed his leg, turning his body back toward the bar. "There you go. That's better. Just ride that stool, cowboy. Keep straight and hold on. It's going to get worse before it gets better."

"Ha ha ha!" He wiped his mouth. "But, like, a mage. That's cool, right?" He might have attempted a thumbs-up, but only succeeded in pointing at himself with his thumb.

I sucked down a quarter of my drink.

"Whoa. Careful. I don't know if anyone told you"—his burp turned into a small groan—"but these drinks are strong." A finger wobbled into my peripheral vision.

I batted his hand away. "I'm a local. I know how this shit works."

"I know. How this *shit*. Works." He nodded dramatically and slumped toward the bar. "Ha!"

I looked for the bartender, who was perched in the corner looking out at the bright day through the distant door. A little wave brought his eyes toward me.

I threw a thumb at the man next to me before putting that digit to my head, indicating his intoxication level.

The bartender shrugged. "Let's see how he does."

A little sport on a slow day. Fair enough.

I pored over the contents of the file, preparing myself. A touch skimmed my back and a face closed in for my throat.

A shock of fear washed over me. The next instant, my fist smashed into the guy's nose, throwing his head back. I'd already grabbed the hand on my back, and now I twisted it, bending his body toward the ground. He rolled off the barstool and crashed to the floor like a clump of wet paper towels.

"Oh shoot." I dramatically grimaced. "Sorry about that, guy. But really, you shouldn't try to invade a girl's space without approval. That's a dick move, right there. Stuff like that gets you hurt. Obviously."

Face toward the floor, he threaded his hands behind his head like the ceiling was falling down. "Please don't hurt me."

The bartender hurried closer, looking over the bar with a smile plastered on his face. "Hey, bud. You okay?"

"I definitely tweaked his wrist," I murmured. "I wasn't thinking."

"Serves him right." The bartender leaned on the bar for a better look. "Good reactions, though. Fast."

The drunk guy's hands relaxed to the floor. His breath evened out into a slow, deep rhythm.

"Did he pass out?" a woman down the bar asked, leaning backward to see around me.

"He passed out!" the bartender said with glee.

The woman turned to her friend. "I told you these drinks were intense. Didn't I tell you?"

Somehow she seemed to have missed the fist he'd taken to the face.

I gingerly sat down and vaguely gestured at the body on the ground. "Should someone pick him up, or…?"

The bartender shrugged. "Probably."

No one moved to lift him.

Like everyone else, I decided it wasn't my problem.

Back to my notes—I went over a few more particulars before closing up the file and finishing my drink. I grabbed my duffel, which held my sword, a pack of throwing knives, and a nine millimeter I called Daisy. Wearing the full arsenal at night was one thing—I'd saved a cop's life from a drugged-out tourist a few years ago, and he'd spread the word that I was good people.

The police feigned blindness under the cover of darkness. But in the daytime, when it was easier to see what was strapped to my body, I dinged all kinds of danger bells with the visiting folk. For that reason, I only kitted myself out in daylight in dire emergencies.

"Wish me luck," I said to the bartender as I headed for the door.

"Thanks for the tip." He collected the five off the counter.

He wasn't great at listening to direction.

The glare of the sunshine made me squint as I stepped out of the bar. I threw up a hand to block the rays and struggled to get my phone out of the small leather pouch around my waist.

There was a Lyft car nearby, so I ordered it and waited until it worked around the block. I slipped into the back and froze as the clanking of my weapons gave away what was in the duffel.

"Where ya headed?" The bearded driver showed me a pleasant smile in the rearview mirror.

I pointed at my phone. "I put the coordinates into the app…"

He leaned toward the dash where his phone was stationed. "There it is. Okay, then." He pulled away from the curb, almost hit a pedestrian, swore under his breath, and away we went.

"Good day so far?" he asked.

I mumbled something to the tune of "fine." My thoughts had strayed back to the vampire's note. Short and sweet, penned in an elegant hand, it had read: *I require a bounty hunter. Reagan Somerset. Send her to me. I'll make it worth her while.*

It hadn't said anything about a partner. Maybe they'd try to stick me with a new vamp that would lose its head and try to latch on to my neck. I'd then be forced to kill it, which might stress my relationship with the poster of the bounty, somewhat.

The real question was: was this a trick to get me into the Dungeon, a name everyone but them used for the vampire's lair, so they could check me out?

"This is it, right?" The driver turned in his seat to look back at me, and that was when I realized we were stopped in front of a dilapidated house overrun with weeds.

"Yes. Thanks." My bag clinked as I climbed out of the car.

Small houses fairly close together stretched down the street. All but one had perfectly manicured, brownish-green lawns—all the weeds trimmed, if not pulled—straight welcome mats in front of the doors, and pruned bushes. No beads hung from the power lines. In their desire to fit in with the humans, they completely stuck out.

I eyed the sore thumb, the kind of house I might

expect in this area. The breeze rattled leaves across the ground. Weeds grew like a disease, choking the sides of the cracked or crumbling walkway leading to a weathered door with peeling paint. I noticed a blackened area charring the dirt in the front yard—any hint of grass was long gone. Beside it were shells, a bone, and some feathers sticking to a clump of something no longer living.

Sacrifice, probably, intended to boost the power level of a spell. I hoped it wasn't one I would soon be running into.

Dare to dream.

With my eyes on the house, I bent to my bag and pulled back the zipper. My sword greeted me. I strapped it on, followed by my knives and gun. Once done, I walked the sidewalk in front of the house, feeling the vibration of magic. Somewhat powerful but straightforward. No flair, and no complexity.

Next door, curtains ruffled in a window. I was being watched.

Busybody.

I thought back to the file again. Had it said anything about the magical nature of the people in the neighborhood? I couldn't remember, but if they were mages, or even witches, they'd expect me to coat my blade with a spell. Few, if any, mages could pump raw power into a weapon and then use it to unravel a spell. Which meant

I needed to put on a show to hide my abilities. So annoying.

I dug into the leather pouch and extracted an empty casing. Pinching it together so no one would know it had already been used, I held the ball near my sword. It was an effort to keep myself from looking around guiltily as I muttered a few curse words. That would pass for spell casting, I hoped.

Once done, I dropped the casing and surged fresh power into the sword. My blade passed through the spell, steaming. Nothing to it.

Before I could charge forward, the front door burst open. A spell gushed out, sizzling the air.

I dove to the side and rolled onto the mage's dirt yard. Hopping up quickly, I ran at him, sword held in front of me.

"Melt!" he bellowed—or something similar, anyway. I wasn't paying much attention to the words.

A stream of crystalized blue rushed toward my face.

Holy balls!

I pushed more of my magic into the blade and sliced through the middle of the stream. The hex crackled as the magic fell away and slithered along the ground. Snakes boiled up, hissing. One struck at me and hit my leather boot. Fangs didn't puncture my skin, thank god.

"What the hell kind of magic are you practicing in there?" I stomped through the vipers, keeping my blade juiced up. Another stream of magic came at me, frosty blue this time. He was losing power. That was good news for me.

I dug my hand into my leather pouch and pulled out another rubber casing, this time with a spell inside. I didn't have many of these, since they were expensive, but the ones I did have were powerful.

I cracked it open and threw it at him. Nothing happened at first, then a starburst of pure white light exploded against his chest. The spell burned through his clothes and met his skin with a sizzle. I bet that hurt.

He screamed and dodged into his house, most likely heading for more magic.

CHAPTER 3

I RAN AFTER him. "Don't do anything stupid...guy!" I probably should've paid more attention to his name.

Black rings stained the brown carpet throughout the dingy interior. Yellowed wallpaper peeled away from the walls. Bedsheets with tears and holes hung over the windows, streaming weak light in odd patterns through the dusty air.

"This place looks like a meth lab," I mumbled as I paused in the entryway.

"They've come before." His voice bounced off the walls and crawled along the floor. "In twos and threes, they've tried to take me alive. They've tried to take me dead. But I am Chartross the Almighty. No one will stand in my way!"

I stuck a finger in my ear and wiggled while extending my jaw. My ears popped, breaking the spell that had amplified his voice. *That's better.*

"That was a very showy spell, Chartross the Almighty. Let's have a look behind the curtain, shall we? I bet I'll find a little man with a plastic ring from a cereal box. Is that what you are, Big C? Seen one case, seen 'em all."

Something crunched under my boot. A piece of chalk lay crumbled in the middle of an unfinished pentagram. The carpet had been ripped away, revealing the discolored hardwood underneath. Unfamiliar characters had been scrawled near each point, along with stick figures contorted in extremely uncomfortable looking positions.

"I think you've got the wrong idea about how to make a circle, buddy." The house rumbled. Miniature statues, all naked, rocked on the small table next to me. The smallest two fell over and spun across the tabletop until they finally clattered onto the floor.

A gun in one hand and my sword in the other, I peered into the nearest doorway. Small piles of garbage littered the corners. A funky smell tickled my nose. More patches of carpet had been peeled away, and shapes were drawn in paint or blood in each open patch. A hole had been blasted through one of the walls. Movement caught my eye. I could just make out the side of a face through the gap, and from the angle, it was clear his body was facing the door of the room he was in.

Criminals were rarely very bright.

A voice echoed through the house, the words sounding like gibberish. The walls shook and the floor rolled as waves of magic washed through the house. The power level was mediocre, but the spell itself seemed intricate and advanced. I'd never run into that dichotomy.

I leaned away from the door and looked down the hall, ignoring the arch of the living room behind me. At the back of the house, I glimpsed the kitchen. Before that, sharing the wall to my right, there was another door, this one shut. I knew what lay behind Door Number Two, and only a fool would traipse in willy-nilly.

I was only a fool when there were no other options.

Thanks for the hole in the wall, Big C. Now that I know where you are, it'll be easy to extract you.

To throw him off my scent, I walked toward his door with heavy footsteps, stopping five feet away. "This is not the way to make friends, Big C. Come on out and we'll talk it through. There's no reason why we can't compromise."

There was eight hundred dollars' worth of reasons why we couldn't, actually, but who needed details?

"You insignificant human!" His spell-encased voice boomed through the house and wrapped around my head, stealing my breath. My lungs started to burn, lacking oxygen.

I didn't bother cutting through the spell. I let him pour his power and focus into it, sapping his energy even more. It would be a painful few minutes for me, but since I didn't need oxygen to live, it would be worth it.

I quickly backtracked and ran into the first room. My feet thundered across a spot of hollow wood.

Mental note: see if there is anything cool hidden in the floor.

I kicked away a small black pot. Liquid sloshed out. Smoke rose into the air and one of the few remaining patches of clean carpet started to burn away. I sheathed my weapons and bent to look through the hole in the wall. My mark stood in front of a large cauldron. Purple steam curled above the metal lip and wound around his body. The look and feel of the spell said it was his try at body armor. The casting was all wrong, though. Both the color and the way the spell moved said it wouldn't fully solidify.

The character of this mage was starting to come into focus. He worked magic he didn't fully understand, with power he couldn't totally harness. Self-taught, probably, and not very intelligent. No wonder he harassed his neighbors—he couldn't keep his creations under control. Doofus.

I braced one hand against the wall and punched through with the other. His head snapped up and he flinched toward me. I curled my fingers around his shirt and dragged him closer to the wall. His body hit wood and he grunted.

"Wrong entry point, Big C," I wheezed. I might not need air to live, but it turned out I did need it to talk. The things you learned.

Annoyed, I ripped out my sword and cleared away the sticky suffocating spell before yanking him toward the wall again. His head banged off the hard surface. That would hurt.

"Let's work together, Big C, and this'll go a lot smoother. I will be taking you out of here, and I'd like to do that with you still alive. It's your call."

I ripped chunks of wood out of the wall, making the hole bigger. He seemed relaxed.

When did marks ever relax when I had a hold of them?

"Don't do whatever it is that you are planning to do, buddy," I said. "It won't work out well for you. Trust me on that one."

"Telco matzo burn!" he shouted.

A blast of heat surged through the hole and raked across my face.

There went my eyebrows.

Like a live thing, the blistering fire crawled across my skin and ate away a strap of my tank top. I should've worn leather on my torso. Trying to get home half-naked wouldn't be awesome.

The house rumbled. The floor splintered with the

pressure, and bits of the ceiling rained down.

I kicked a larger hole in the wall as the heat of my magic surged through me. I grabbed him with both hands, easily ignoring the dying blast of fire. He didn't have the power to sustain it.

I wrangled him through the hole, finishing the job with a fast jerk. The fire sputtered out and the house sagged onto its frame, creaking and squealing as it settled.

Uh oh. That wasn't a good sign.

"You okay, Big C?" I let go of him, and he crumpled to the floor.

Definitely not a good sign.

Hoping he was just knocked out, I put two fingers to his neck. No pulse.

"Dang it." I straightened up, my hands on my hips. I hated when I accidentally killed the mark.

I kicked the wall in a temper. My foot went through to the other side and hooked on a jagged piece, stuck.

"Flippity-shit, double damn it!"

Would nothing go right?

Forcing myself to calm down, I twisted my foot and delicately brought it back through the wall. Breathing heavily, I stared down at the lifeless body. "How'd you work up that kind of fire, huh, Big C? That's a rare spell. Not many mages know how to do it. Or so I was told."

Silence met my question.

Of course it did…I had bloody killed him. A human's body was so fragile. I dealt with non-human types so often that I sometimes forgot to be careful.

I blew out a breath into the silence. Cracks and breaks in the wood made for a very uneven floor surface. How he had planned to live in this house after his weapon-spell went off? But then, the criminally insane rarely thought ahead.

Remembering that hollow area I'd heard earlier, I tapped the spot in front of me with my boot. It sounded solid. I kept trying until I found the location, then bent to run my hand just above the floor.

A pulsing sort of magic vibrated across my palm. A defensive hex, surely.

I didn't bother using my sword as a medium this time. With no one to witness and then possibly tell on me, I was free to openly use my unique sort of magic.

Fire sprang to life along the floor, but it wasn't wild, like the kind the mage had created with a spell. This was concise, as hot as liquid magma, and completely controlled. A blast of it would melt a normal person's skin off. Not even leather would survive. I knew from experience. While my skin was fireproof, I'd once ruined a perfectly good pair of pants.

Glowing red-orange flame ate through the section of floor in a matter of moments. I clenched the air over the fire and pulled my fist away, shifting the fire into the air for a moment as I surveyed what was in the hole.

A leather-bound book with some sort of ancient scrawl greeted me. "Well hel-lo, gorgeous." A defensive hex throbbed around it, promising a blast of pain should anyone touch it.

I lowered the fire back into the hole, increasing the power but decreasing the heat. Too hot and I was liable to make the spell explode. Something else I'd learned the hard way.

My fire peacefully ate away at the magic. I extinguished the flame and drifted my hand over the hole again, making sure all the active magic was gone. The coast was clear.

The leather cover was smooth to the touch. I lifted the book, feeling the solid weight of it, and opened the cover. Familiar characters and the musty smell of aged paper made my eyes flutter closed and a smile grace my lips. This old volume was sure to contain some excellent spells. This was where he'd probably learned about magical fire, body armor, and whatever he'd done to make his house rock around like a holiday party. I often studied a similar book, though I'd never attempted any of the spells. Or really any magic performed by mages, having spent so long perfecting my own, which didn't exist in any books.

Where had he gotten this text, I wondered? It must've been a recent acquisition, or he would've been terrorizing his neighbors some time ago. Thankfully, he'd chosen to hoard the book rather than share it, or we might've had a citywide epidemic of mediocre mages running amok. The humans would've noticed the magical community for sure.

I glanced around, deciding that a great use of my time, while in the house of this dead man, was to poke my nose into other nooks and crannies. It wasn't like he'd mind, and I thoroughly enjoyed treasure hunting.

After placing the book in an unmolested part of the room for safekeeping—it blended nicely into a trash pile—I set out through the house, waving my hands in front of me like a blind man, feeling for magic. I repeatedly tapped the floor with my toe, including in the carpeted areas, and checked his shelves and even under his bed. Finally, I looked on his computer, grimacing as I went through his browsing history. The man had some odd tastes, and not a lot of magically relevant information.

Almost giving up, I checked the refrigerator, found a can of soda, and then tapped the floor as I had a drink.

Tap-tap-tap-tonk.

I paused with my foot hovering over a discolored section of linoleum.

On closer inspection, I had another winner.

No magic vibrated my palm, so I peeled back the square of flower-patterned linoleum, which likely hadn't started out that horrible brown color, and stared down at what lay beneath it—a square of particle board with a small hook in it.

The lack of a protective spell should've been my first clue that something was amiss.

I lifted the floorboard to a spray of green goo. I flung myself away, but not in time. Liquid slashed my cheek and splatted on the side of my neck. It immediately started to burn, and not in that great way fire did. This felt more like acid.

"Mother-trucker!" I grabbed a kitchen towel off the counter and wiped the stuff off. The pain lessened into a throb before morphing into a cold sensation seeping into my skin.

I still didn't feel magic, which meant this stuff was naturally made.

I had no knowledge of natural crap.

In a panic, I rifled through his cupboards for potions or books on poison or a cookbook, *anything* that might give me some hint as to what he'd made.

The cold burrowed deep into my neck. That was probably bad. The neck was an extremely vulnerable area.

I tore back through the house, aiming for the magical book. Maybe he had notes in there, or a big star marking the kitchen booby trap.

Before I made it halfway down the hall, the front

door cracked open.

I dove, rolled, felt a poke of wood in my back, and yanked out my gun. Killing a random person would be bad news, especially if they were human—the human police would be all over it—but hopefully the gun would scare them away. Otherwise, I'd shoot, torch the place, and run. Which was why I didn't have paperwork. A person with no records of any kind was hard to identify.

"Freeze!" I shouted in a deep voice, trying to sound like a cop.

"Oh!" A big-bosomed woman jerked to a stop in the doorway, throwing up her hands. "Don't shoot."

"This is a crime investigation," I lied, my focus back on my neck.

"You're the bounty hunter, right? The one I saw outside?" The woman peered through the gloom, staring vaguely.

Just my luck. I was in peril, and a blind person was the only one available to help me find a written spell.

"I'm the bounty hunter, yes. I'm a little busy right now, actually. If you'll just—"

"Is he dead?" she asked quietly.

"Unfortunately, yes. Hazard of the trade." I crawled to my feet and felt my neck. To my fingers, my skin felt perfectly normal, but the cold was eating down into my chest now.

Before I could dash for the spell book, a flare of light stopped me short.

I reeled back and covered my eyes, adjusting. It wasn't until then that I realized why she hadn't looked directly at me—only a select type of magical people could see in the dark. I was one of those people, but given that there wasn't a spell for it, at least not that I knew of, mages generally were not.

Big C had been able to see in the dark! I hadn't noticed because I'd had other things on my mind. *How?*

My burning curiosity made it even more annoying that I'd accidentally killed him.

"How could you get anything done—Oh no!" The woman dropped the sheet she'd just ripped off the window and rushed toward me. "That's going to leave a mark, dear."

"What is?"

"Here. Quickly. Into the garden." She half dragged me behind her, which was pretty impressive given the difference in our strength levels. She had the drop on me when it came to pushiness.

"I am really impressed," she said conversationally as we reached the kitchen. "I didn't think anyone would be able to help us." She walked me out of the back door, into a well-tended herb garden. Unlike the front yard, this place saw a lot of loving care. "I've tried a few others. It didn't end so well for them. When his house started shaking, I thought that was it for you. Here we are."

She released my wrist and bent to a plant. After ripping off a leaf, she stuck it into her mouth and chewed. Moments later, she smeared the wet pulp onto my cheek.

I grimaced. "I could've chewed that myself."

The numbness from the slash line receded with cold, tingling pain.

"He became very powerful," she said before sticking more plant into her mouth.

"I really don't mind chewing it…"

"Crazy, but very powerful." She took out the pulpy mess and reached up to smear it on my neck. "It was mostly in spurts, though, his increases in power. One day, heightened power. The next, back to normal. He wouldn't say why."

I prevented myself from flinching away from the green spit-wad being spread on my neck. My face felt better now. That was worth the ick factor of having this woman's saliva on my skin.

"Unlike those shifters, you came prepared." She stepped back and analyzed her handiwork.

"Not all that prepared. I got sprayed with freezing goo." My cheek started to itch.

A brief nod and she was scrutinizing me as a person. "I haven't seen you before, but you seem experienced. It would take someone powerful to outmatch John. Are you a mage?"

"No. Just a do-gooder." I stopped myself from itching my face. "When can I take this stuff off?"

"A few more minutes." Her eyes narrowed as she assessed my pouch. "That is a small fanny pack. You can't have much in the way of supplies in there…"

"This is not a fanny pack. It is a *pouch.* A very cool pouch. The nineties are over, okay? I know that." Garret's constant taunting was ringing through my head. He liked to make fun of my pouch to no end.

I adjusted it so it was off to the side a little. "I'm not a mage, like I said. I don't need supplies."

"But I saw you cast spells."

"I bought those spells. That's standard procedure, even for me."

Her brow furrowed suspiciously. I was a terrible liar.

I opened my pouch and dug out an empty casing. "Here. You can have that." I put it into her hand. "Nothing unusual about a non-mage using a mobile spell. I'm just like any other bounty hunter."

I barely stopped myself from itching my cheek again. "Not that I'm vain or anything, but is this going to scar?" I pointed at my cheek.

"I think I got to it in time." She minutely shook her head. I could tell the wheels were still turning regarding my ability. Time to go.

"Right, then. Thanks for this." I waved my finger across my face. "I need to grab a few things, including Big C"—she'd just said his real name, but I'd already forgotten it—"and head out. I have rent to pay. You know how it is."

I headed to the kitchen first, because I wanted to see what was in that hole. That green goo wasn't magical, but it was still a defense. He was protecting something.

She followed closely behind me. "How is someone as skilled as you not permanently employed by one magical faction or another?"

"I like to keep my options open." Back on the dirty linoleum, I stayed as far back as I could and peered into the hole, just in case. It was too deep, though—I'd have to get closer to see anything.

"Forgive me for saying…" She edged around me so she could see my face. "But bounty hunters are usually hiding from something. What are you hiding from?"

"You watch too much TV."

She eyed the thin, holey curtains, then my face again, squinting in the low light.

Dang it! The darkness. I kept forgetting. This was why I didn't work with other people.

I snatched the curtain and ripped it off. Light flooded into the kitchen. "I am definitely hiding from something. Coworkers. They get in my way. Have you ever met Garret in the New Orleans Magical Division?" I paused and ducked my head closer to the mouth of the hole before quickly pulling it back. Nothing spat out at me. "He is no picnic, let me assure you."

"No man is an island," she said.

I bent forward again, for a little longer, before pulling back. The hole held something canvas coated in green goo, containing small bumpy-somethings. Dropping my hand right above it, I could feel various currents of magic, mostly mediocre in power.

If that danged hole hadn't been so deep, I would've felt the magic a lot sooner, and wouldn't have had a run-in with the goo. Nor this inquisitive, chatty lady.

Too bad kicking a dead body was in bad taste.

I hunted through Big C's drawers until I found some tongs. "Men aren't islands because they want someone to do all the domestic stuff for them." I peeled back the canvas, realizing it was a sack. "They leave their islands for the promise of a lazier future. But there are a bunch of women islands. We'd rather be alone than take on the role of life secretary and housemaid." Or so my mother had always said. I wouldn't know.

"I suppose you have a point. If my ex-mother-in-law had raised her son to lift a finger, I might still be married," she groused.

"Reason number two for being an island—I don't care." I opened the bag and found what I'd expected, a bunch of various-sized casings in good condition.

Thank you for the cache of mediocre spells, Big C. I will use them in your memory.

She laughed. "Honesty is good. I can support honesty."

"Awesome," I muttered. I grabbed a paper bag from under the sink and emptied the spells into it, the transfer a bit awkward what with the goo and kitchen utensils. I didn't want to touch that stuff again. I didn't need another spit bath.

"You're taking his spells?" I could hear the uncertainty in her voice.

"Finders keepers, Ms…."

"You can call me Margaret."

"Great. Finders keepers, Margaret. With mediocre risk comes mediocre treasure." I bunched the top of the paper bag to keep everything in, abandoning the goo-covered sack.

"You're really capable, which is good, because I should warn you that he had friends." She hurried after me as I stalked down the hall. "I'm not sure I mentioned that on the listing with the agency."

"You're not sure, huh?" I stopped in front of the bedroom door and stuck my hand out. "Stay here."

I could tell she was trying to see what I was doing in the bedroom and, judging from her squinting, having a hard time of it. I grabbed Big C by the back of the shirt and carried him over to where I'd hidden the book. Concealing my movements behind Big C's bulk, I slid the book into his shirt.

"What are you doing?" she asked.

"Minding my own business." I tucked his shirt in to keep the book put, then hoisted him up and draped him over my shoulder, thankful for the daylight outside, which would mean no vampire could come and steal my mark.

"Wow. You're strong." It sounded like another accusation.

"I think there was a vampire in my lineage somewhere…"

"Vampires can't breed."

"You know what I mean." I pushed past her and hesitated at the mouth of the living room.

"No, I'm not sure I do," she said, still watching. "Oh heavens, is that him?"

"The vampire thing was a joke, and yes, it is. I don't cart dead people around when I go on jobs." After a quick decision, I set Big C on his stomach so he was still hiding the book, and darted for his laptop. Weird porn searches aside, the machine was pretty new, and I'd make good use of it. Once it was stowed in its computer bag and slung over my shoulder, I bent for Big C again.

Margaret started, giving me room, her eyes somewhat glassy. Clearly she'd known him before he'd gone crazy, and now she seemed to feel a bit squishy in the middle from his passing. But I didn't have much sympathy for someone who'd tagged a bounty notice with *dead or alive.* She'd made her bed, and I'd help her lie in it.

I started for the door. "All right, then. Have a good one."

"Wait, you're taking his computer?"

"Evidence," I mumbled as I hastened down the steps.

At the sidewalk, I grabbed my duffel bag. I would put my weapons and everything into it later. I didn't want to give Margaret time for more questions.

With a body on my shoulder that, happily, wasn't leaking blood, I quickly headed down the street. I went a couple blocks away, making sure I wasn't followed, before stopping by a sprawling bush. I set the dead body on the ground and jabbed my app for Lyft, the ride-share service that made my life so much easier. That done, I stowed all my weapons and rearranged Big C so he looked like he was lounging near the plant. Finally, I sat down next to him, really hoping the person whose yard we were crashing wasn't home. That'd be an awkward conversation.

When the driver pulled up, I hopped to my feet and opened the back door.

"Can you pop the trunk?" I asked innocently. "I

have a couple bags." Thank heavens Lyft drivers never helped with the bags.

"Yeah, sure." He bent for the button.

I moved quickly, picking up the body and stashing him in the clean trunk. I followed that up with my duffel and pushed down the lid. I slid into the back seat, adjusted my seared tank top so a nipple didn't accidentally pop out, and waited.

"Hi," the driver said, glancing back at me, also waiting.

"Hi. I've loaded the destination." I pointed at his phone.

"Right, yes." He studied his phone to communicate his knowledge of the coordinates before glancing back again. "Is the other guy coming too, or…?"

"What other guy?"

Confused, the man turned his girth in order to check the back seat, and then looked out the passenger window. "Oh. Wasn't there someone laying in the grass?"

"No?" I made a show of looking out the window. "Where? Just where I was sitting?"

"That's…" His brow furrowed. "That is so weird. I could have sworn you had someone laying next to you when I pulled up. I thought maybe he was drunk or sleeping or something. Ha! But yeah, he's gone. Wow. That's a trip."

"I hope it wasn't a ghost." I rubbed my arms and gave a dramatic shiver. "Yuck." I pulled my tank top up again. I had a sneaking suspicion I'd flashed Margaret without knowing it.

The car pulled away. "That's crazy. I really thought I saw someone. Like, a solid form, too. I specifically remember thinking—"

The ride consisted of various ghost stories and his growing certainty that he had, in fact, seen a ghost.

At the office, I took the body out of the trunk, set it on the street behind the car, really hoping the guy didn't randomly back up, and picked up my duffel. I stepped to the side and waved. "Thanks again. Hope you don't see any more ghosts."

He waved, laughed, shook his head, and took off.

I grabbed the body quick-like and hurried to the side, but there was a flash of taillights in my peripheral vision. He'd seen me in his rearview, and now, instead of a ghost, he'd always wonder what he'd transported in his trunk.

I threw the body over my shoulder and stepped into the safety of the magical division. "And *that's* how you get a dead body across town without calling the removal service," I said with pride.

The removal service was pricy and took forever. This was definitely the faster, cheaper option if it could be pulled off.

As I started toward the dead mark drop-off area, my good mood drained away. The time for procrastination was coming to an end. I needed to decide if I'd go to the Dungeon. Sure, there was a big payoff at the end, but it might be a trap. Once I went through the vampires' doors, I'd be at their mercy.

CHAPTER 4

A COUPLE HOURS later, I sat on the porch in front of the run-down house I rented. I was just high enough to see over the wall of the St. Roch cemetery across the street, but the real viewing pleasure was through the gate directly in front of me. Being a little off the beaten track and in a tough neighborhood, my neighbors and I didn't see as many tourists stopping through. We did, however, see a lot of thrill-seekers and wannabe witches.

I loved when, like now, the sun drifted toward the horizon and the shadows elongated, eating up the light. In this confusing time between day and night, I got to watch the magical people, or humans trying to be magical, creep between the gravestones with their supplies. They'd draw circles or pentagrams on the ground, among other things, and mutter spells on the breeze. Occasionally, I witnessed a great possession by a voodoo priestess or priest, and ate popcorn as they slithered along the ground, or spoke in unfamiliar tongues. I loved New Orleans. All manner of magic was expressed here—the traditional and the not so much. The hobbyist and the believer. I saw it all come through, and usually enjoyed it.

The exception, of course, was when idiots tried to summon demons. It happened every so often, and usually the culprit had no idea what they were messing with.

Once I had watched a coven of witches correctly call a level-one demon. The thing had been loosely trapped, and it was working on breaking free when they finally sent it back. With such little power, it wouldn't have done much damage, but it surely would've ripped through one or two of the casters before it weakened and disintegrated.

I'd had a long day before witnessing their idiocy, but that sort of deed shouldn't go unpunished—so I'd ducked across the street and hidden among the gravestones. When the witches were ready to leave, I jumped out at them with a snarl and a knife.

"How could you summon my kind and *send it back*!" I'd yelled, thumping and thrashing at them in turn. "I am the master of this domain. You are insignificant humans. *Rawr!*"

I only said the word "rawr." I couldn't summon the energy to actually growl.

They didn't notice the lack of effort. Half of them even dropped their witch kits, as I call them, with their sage and their chalk and candles, and ran like hell.

Demons don't laugh like humans do—they give a dry cackle more than anything—but I couldn't contain belly chuckles as they sped out of the graveyard. It had almost made the effort worth it.

I softly chuckled to myself, remembering, and leaned further into my chair. Tonight all was quiet. Peaceful.

My thoughts drifted to the elder vampire, and the note he'd left in Captain Lox's office. Tall, muscular, powerful—he moved like the world was a stage and he was the diva, arrogant as all hell and coated with a thick layer of ego. I bet it was bugging the hell out of him that he didn't know what I was.

Or maybe he did.

Elder vampires had been around a *long* time. They'd survived some pretty troubled eras and seen all manner of things. It was quite possible this vampire would be resourceful enough to piece together the clues of my heritage. I was a secluded sort of person, with a strong overhang of mystery, but being that I needed money, I wasn't a recluse.

I blew out a breath, thinking that possibility over.

It would be pretty hard to get *all* my details, though. Captain Lox would know some, the agents at the office would know a little, my neighbors would know a few things, and the shifters a bit more, but out of all of those people, only the agents might actually talk to a vampire. I didn't have any birth records, and something that annoyed the captain to no end, no paperwork, so…

No, he didn't know about me. He couldn't.

What about if I was in his lair? Could he sort it out then?

I scratched my chin, thinking through the options.

He could bite me and taste my blood, but would that tell him anything?

I bit my lip, not sure. They were wily, elders, so there was definitely a chance he could figure it out and run straight to the bank, i.e. my father, but a good chance? I wasn't so sure. The shifters hadn't been able to, and they'd been sniffing around for a while.

Literally.

"Your eyebrows've gone missing again." Mince, a thick guy who had taken too many punches to the face in his boxing career, and had the nose to show for it, stalled by the steps to my porch.

I fingered the smooth skin where my eyebrows were supposed to be, and then the singed remnants of my bangs. "Yeah. Got too close to an open flame."

"Looks like you stuck your face in an open flame. How come you never get a burn on your skin?"

"Sunblock. You wouldn't know, since you have a natural deterrent."

He frowned at me. "That has got to be the stupidest

thing I've ever heard. Because I'm black, I can't get burnt? Are you dumb?"

"No, Mr. Sensitive, I'm kidding."

He huffed and looked away, probably waiting for his flash of annoyance to wear away. I could irritate the most patient of people. Misdirection was my superpower.

"You taking tonight off?" he asked, turning back.

"Don't know. Just pondering that now."

"Your boss doesn't mind your random hours, huh? I got let go for all that."

"You know that I work for myself. I make my own hours."

"Ah yeah, that's right. I get you confused with that white girl down the way."

I didn't know how. She was ancient and wrinkly, using a walker for her every outing, while I was twenty-four and scrappy. We were pretty different.

He nodded at the bag by my feet containing my new book. I'd brought it out here to have a look through it, but the issue with the vampires had sidelined my focus. I'd have to come back to it later.

"What's in that?" he asked

I rose. "Something I stole today. I have to get it checked out."

"Need any of my contacts?"

"Nope." I took the paper bag by the flimsy handles.

A nicer bag might've drawn attention. "The only electrical device I got was a computer, and it didn't have a password. Unless you know someone who's knowledgeable about three-hundred-year-old books..." I turned toward the screen door.

"Stealing smart person stuff, huh?" Mince leaned against the weathered railing. "Yeah, I got someone. He ain't cheap. Charges a consulting fee. He can help you find a buyer, though."

I froze with the screen door half open and turned back. "You know someone who specializes in really old books?"

He shrugged. "When you ransack a rich man's house, sometimes you get rare books. Or so I've heard."

I shook my head. "You need to get a real job. You're going to get pinched someday."

"Says the girl with a bag full of stolen goods."

"That's different. I killed the guy first."

"Whoa." He raised his hands and backed away. "I didn't hear that. I did not hear that. Just let me know if you need my guy, okay? Keep the rest of your business to yourself." He walked away shaking his head.

Sometimes I forgot how crazy I sounded.

I dropped the bag in my room so I'd remember to put it in my version of a safe, and then headed to the fridge. Mostly bare. I needed to go shopping.

Sighing, I closed it up again and looked around my

tiny residence. Rent was cheap, so that eight hundred dollars would cover it, but the money wouldn't stretch over all my bills. I'd have the same problem next month. If I'd taken Baldy in, the money would've kept me out of sight for a while, not to mention kept me cool in the hot summer months.

I scrubbed my fingers through my hair and got myself a glass of water. Sinking into the couch, I pondered the bounty notice. Fifty grand. What I wouldn't give for that kind of money…

That vamp probably knew it, too. As far as the magical community went, I was the only full-time, independent bounty hunter in the area. I got all the high-risk and high-paying jobs because no one else would take them. Without that payout, I was broke. If the vamp knew anything at all, he would know I was poor. That stealing that mark had put me in the hole.

Suddenly, anger boiled through my body.

That vamp had stolen my livelihood, and now he was suckering me into working for him. Probably just for his personal entertainment, too. I wouldn't put it past him. Everything was a game to the elders, and people were just strategy. I should say no, thereby giving him the bird. I should. And maybe I would…right after I punched him in the face.

I INFORMED THE captain that I'd meet with the vampires,

and no more than an hour later, after I'd scarfed down a quick meal of frozen food and secured the book in my safe, I received an email on my new computer regarding how to get to the Dungeon. Not having a printer, I wrote all the info down before strapping on my weapons.

I stepped out into the night with my game face on.

"Going to work after all, huh?" Mince wasn't far from my porch.

"Are you stalking me?"

"Nah. A couple kids wandered into the cemetery. That old loon Smokey went in after them. I figured I'd watch from a distance to see if anything happened. Smokey probably thinks they're witches or some shit. He's nuts." I had no idea who Smokey was by name, but if he haunted the area, chances were I'd know him on sight. "I figured I'd get some game time in while I waited." He held up his phone.

"You're too old for computer games."

"A person is never too old for computer games. I'm good, too. Those little ten-year-old bastards don't know who they're dealing with."

"Watch my house," I said, bouncing down the steps.

"Maybe," he mumbled.

I rolled my eyes and started to jog. All my weapons bounced on my person, which was annoying, but I was too impatient to walk. That would give me time to think, and I didn't want to talk myself out of that fifty grand and punching a smug vampire in the mouth.

This was a terrible idea.

"La. La. La. La. La," I sang to myself, and ran faster.

I made it to the gate in no time and slowed as I approached the white, wavy line cutting vertically through the air. As a rule, I didn't spend much time in the Realm. My mom had always warned me away from the watchful eyes of nosy magical people.

Summoning my courage, I pushed through. Electricity surged through me as the tear in the fabric of the universe checked my body for the pass: magic.

The black sky in New Orleans shifted to the burned-orange of dusk as I emerged in the Realm. A tiny breeze ruffled my hair, perfectly pleasant. A bench sat off to the side, meant for those with only a little magic. Crossing was extremely taxing for them, but not for me, so I hurried along my way.

Light gold filaments drifted through the nighttime air, swirling as I walked. My boots scraped the cobblestone pathway. Eternally blooming flowers lined the edges, the sweet smell and lovely colors adding to the pleasantness of the temperature.

I reached a fork, checked my directions, and took the road less traveled. That made sense—no self-respecting person paid house calls to the vampires.

I was an idiot.

As far as I knew, the Realm was as expansive and diverse as the Brink. The elves lived in a huge castle of some sort (I'd never seen it) surrounded by a metropolis, but there were also giant stretches of woods and wilds, and equally as many towns and villages. In parts, various groups of magical people lived together in relative harmony, compromising and adapting to everyone's differences. In other parts, the magical groups more or less isolated themselves.

The other interesting thing about the Realm was the travel ways, which was the only reason I'd visited in the past. Minute for minute, time in the Realm was the same as the Brink, but the distances you could travel within that minute changed. In relation to the Brink, I could enter from a gate in New Orleans and exit in France within an afternoon if I chose the right paths. Or it could take a whole day to go five miles at a fast run, something I'd learned the hard way.

In addition, some of the travel ways were magically enhanced to speed up travel within the Realm. You walked along as normal, but the towns and cities whipped by like you were in a train or fast car. It didn't take me long to realize I was on one of the special paths. As I walked, turning occasionally, patches of wilds whipped by, shaggy and forlorn. The effect was mind-boggling. I didn't see any gates leading back into the Brink, which was probably why it was a fast track, but it was still crazy. And though it felt like it took all night, light did not illuminate the horizon. Nor did either of the two moons shift in the sky.

No, I did not go to the Realm often. It freaked me out a little.

Nearing the end of the directions the captain had sent me, which had apparently been posted with the bounty notice by a vampire named Darius, I wound around a bend and found two things. The first was that the cobblestone path ended abruptly—as did the lovely flowers on the sides. Clearly the magical path was finished. I was on my own.

The second item of interest was the massive cluster of rocks directly in front of me. Large and jagged, the smallest could crush a skull, and the larger ones loomed over me.

"'Scuze mer!"

The deep, booming voice made me jump. I whirled around and was confronted by a stone crotch. There was no definition or dangling bits—just an apex between huge stone legs. Looking upward, I gaped at the face of a giant man made of stone.

"How do you reproduce?" I blurted.

Of all the questions I could've asked.

A big hand swung down, swatting at me.

I dodged, whipping out my sword. "Good gracious, what's your problem?"

"Move!" He swatted at me again.

"How about a *please*?" I stepped to the side, ready to dodge a kick.

"What you here from?"

"Your grasp of the English language is excellent. Tell me, who's your teacher?"

"Who brought you from?" He bent at the waist to survey me, creating a crack in his stomach instead of a crease.

"Your questions are bending my brain, man. My turn for a question: is that crack going to heal?"

"Who brought you here from?" He picked up a rock in a huge hand and threw it. It smashed into others without a sound. Shards flew into the sky.

I kicked a rock next to me. It made the expected thud. I hadn't heard the rock-man coming, though. With his size and weight, that should've been impossible.

"I do not understand this place," I muttered, eager to get back to the Brink, where things made sense. "I'm going to see a vampire called Darius. He requested my presence. I came from the Brink." I hesitated for a moment. "Did any of those statements answer your question?"

The rock-man swung a big foot and kicked a rock next to him. It silently bounced off a boulder and came rolling toward me. I dove out of the way. Still no sound other than what I was making.

I jumped to my feet, ready for action and dreading it at the same time.

The rock man stalked forward. As he did so, he constantly kicked out, reconfiguring the rocks violently. They smashed into each other, all plenty big enough to squish me if I were in the way. Silence reigned.

"I do not like this place at all." I worried my teeth against my bottom lip.

Now or never.

I hurriedly picked my way through, paying attention to my direction and keeping an eye out for movement. My goal was not to end up between two huge rocks.

When I made it out, thankfully unscathed, I turned back to see if any other giants were on my heels. There weren't any, but I realized my jaunt through the silent rock garden had been planned. It cropped up in the middle of mostly desolate land with the main path right through. Other, smaller paths went around.

A test.

Well, I would definitely take those on the way back.

Continuing on at a normal pace, which I no longer fancied that much, I finally saw the end point. An enormous wrought-iron gate with decorative scrolls. Beyond it, a mound. In the mound, a door.

Nothing else.

A gate, a mound, and a door.

As expected, the vampires' lair was entirely below surface, and while it probably only had a couple other exits, they'd be equally as minimal. I was about to be trapped inside a hole with hundreds, if not thousands, of vampires.

CHAPTER 5

I APPROACHED THE door slowly and tucked my directions into my leather pouch. I moved my palm over the heavy metal door. No spells to keep out intruders, not like that was a surprise. I tried the handle. It shook, but didn't open. Locked.

A lock was plenty. Who in their right mind would be stupid enough to force their way in?

This was one of those times that I was a fool.

I jump-kicked, putting all my power behind it. My foot banged into the door. Metal squealed and the side of the door bent inward. I kicked it again, busting it and sending it swinging.

"Knock, knock," I said, strolling in.

My eyes quickly adjusted to the darkness.

My directions had ended at *knock,* so I waited a moment to see if anyone would come for me. Given how quickly some of those buggers ran, I didn't wait long. The absence of a greeting party meant I was on my own.

No problem. I was used to wandering around dead

people's houses.

I walked forward, eyeing the huge, finely worked stone walls with intricate detailing. If this were Middle Earth, I'd be in a dwarf stronghold.

The main path sloped downward gradually. Other, smaller paths, which I might even call trails, led away every so often on either side. I kept to the larger path in case I had to fight. I was, quite possibly, the only thing in this whole place that could serve as food. I didn't want to end up in that position, no matter how pleasurable it might be.

One foot in front of the other, further down I went, my footfalls silent, matching my surroundings. An intruder was in their midst, and no one had come out to check on me. That was suspicious.

Another ten feet down, I felt eyes digging into my back. Not much further and the press of bodies surrounding me grew until it was almost a palpable pressure. I couldn't *see* anyone, though. Columns climbed up the walls to either side, with empty spaces between. The paths led away, bare. But it *felt* as though the place was packed.

Nervousness crawled up my spine and then skittered across my skin. Adrenaline pumped into my bloodstream. A move had to be made, I felt it.

Trusting my instincts, I grabbed a throwing knife from the harness around my leg, spun, and threw. It flew high and straight, up into the stone platform between the columns. A flicker of movement gave someone away, a hand shooting out of nothing and vanishing just as quickly.

The sound of my knife hitting a hard surface never came.

"Caught you peeking." I tsked. "That's not nice, you know. Guests should be welcomed, not stared at by lurkers."

I felt more than heard shifting. Knew without proof that my watchers were uneasy with my complete lack of fear. Villains were all the same after a while.

"Can I have my knife back, please?" I asked, starting forward again.

The flicker of movement came from the same area. The knife flew through the air, end over end, in my direction. The throw was a little short. I had to jog forward to snatch it out of the air, a feat I probably wouldn't have been able to duplicate a second time. Luck be a lady.

"Thanks." I saluted with it before putting it away, extremely uncomfortable that I couldn't see the watchers, though they could clearly see me. "Say, you guys wouldn't happen to know where Darius is, would you?"

Silence answered my question, eerie in such a grand space packed with bodies I couldn't see.

I kept moving as the pathway narrowed. The columns lining it pushed in closer, and with them, invisible vampires who could pluck a knife out of the air. I'd put some heat on that throw, too. It didn't bode well for my odds of dominating in a fight.

Flickers of movement came from the left. I glanced over in time to see an arm disappear to the side. The scrape of feet on rock hinted that the vampire I'd spied wasn't as old and graceful as the one that had invited me.

Pace even and body language unaffected, I continued acting as though I were out for a Sunday stroll.

"I can hear you breathing," someone taunted from above in a raspy voice.

"Dude, don't be *that guy*," I said, not looking up. "No one likes the creepy guy."

Footsteps sounded behind me and echoed around the walls. I patiently awaited an attack. Nothing happened.

I kept moving, my breath even, my senses on high alert.

Metal scraped against the ground, loud and obvious. Someone wanted attention.

"Yes, Timmy, I hear you. You don't have to shout." I kept walking, not looking back or to the sides. Ignoring their intimidation tactics. Bullies hated that.

"You smell delicious," a woman said from directly above me in a thick, lust-filled voice.

She had a good sniffer, I had to give her that. The columns were right beside me now, but the platform was still at least thirty feet up. That was a long distance for my smell to travel.

"That means a lot, coming from you," I said, careful not to pick up my pace, even though I was a bit worried that someone would soon want to see if the smell matched the taste.

"We're going to peel your skin off and lick your bones clean," someone else called.

"Good grief, that escalated quickly," I muttered. "I'm bored. Do I have much further to go?"

As if I'd voiced a command, vampires filed out in front of me, clogging the way. Black gums sported elongated fangs. As I watched, claws extended from their fingers, which turned long and bony. Their bodies widened, ripping the fabric of their clothes until the destroyed garments slid to the ground. Skin, once all shades of human-colored, melted into the gristly green of younger vamps, slower and weaker than their older counterparts. They hunched and hissed at me, swampy and gross.

It was the vampire fighting form. Like when shifters turned into animals, vampires could become swamp monsters to gain speed, strength, and magical power. The fact that they'd ruined their clothes to show me their power look meant this was part of the show.

Another intimidation tactic.

"Ah, look, wee babies." I laughed. "How'd it feel, going to bed with a beautiful vampire and then waking up to this? Ugly stuff. Did you guys freak out? I totally would've."

One stepped out from a trail to my right, jerky and much too close. "Ew." I curled my lip and scrunched my nose. Also for show. "Don't get slime on me; these are new pants."

"They are in their most perfect form," someone said in a haughty tone from above.

"Yeah, keep on telling them that, bro. See if it helps." I put my hand to the side of my mouth like I was whispering secret knowledge. "Do yourself a favor, everyone. Keep practicing the control of your human form. There is no way the guy up there walks around looking like a swamp thing. Not that I can verify that, since he's hiding in the darkness like a coward."

A sheet of some kind fluttered down from the platform. It had been used to render the vampire invisible somehow. A pasty mustard-green monster, with long, matted hair falling over its bony shoulders, stepped forward on bowed legs. Its skin sank between its ribs. At the end of its stringy arms curved large, razor-sharp claws.

"Good Lord." I held up my hand to shield my eyes. "Put it away, man!"

"Show the proper respect, little girl, or you will meet a most unpleasant fate."

"Don't pretend you have any say in what goes on down here. Your gross, hanging balls show your age, and they aren't nearly low enough for you to be an elder." I had no idea if that was true, but I was pretty sure the colors went from green, being newer, to the pasty white-green of the elders. I had no idea why it dipped into yellow and mustard in the middle levels, only that I'd seen some monster forms like this guy's. He wouldn't be too fast or skilled.

A newbie on the path in front of me jerked, which turned into a stilted walk forward. Black took up its eyes, banishing the whites. Saliva dripped from its fangs, something that happened when a vamp was about to feed.

Newbies didn't have much control over their need for blood. This all might unravel in the next few moments.

I stared at it, ready for action. "If you lose control and try to bite me, I will kill you. Do you understand me?" I raised my voice. "Do you all understand me? I'll play nice until you go for my neck. Then vampires will die. That is the only warning you'll get."

Laughter crowded the space above me. They wouldn't be laughing when I fulfilled my threat.

More sheets fluttered away and sailed toward the

ground. I half wanted to rush over and grab one. Those would be really handy on the job.

Someone grabbed the hungry newbie and pulled it to the side. The throng of monsters parted in front of me, revealing a naked vampire in human form blocking my way. Huge and rippled with muscle. His fangs were elongated, distending his jaw, and his eyes were wells of black. Not handsome like many of the others, it looked like his face had been hit with a bat a few times. Nothing else had changed yet, meaning he had some control. When he stepped forward, though, showing a jerky movement, I realized that while he might not be a newbie, he wasn't far from it. His control to keep from biting me and draining me dry would be slippery, at best. A fight would bring out his urges that much more.

Not to mention he was a mammoth of a man.

He had been sent to kill me. Or try, anyway. Clearly this was a test.

"Well holy-moly, look at you. You're a big mother-trucker." I whistled. The vampires around me made a circle, either trying to keep me from running, or excited for the fight. Probably both.

"It's a lovely day in the neighborhood..." I sang as I took out my sword. I paused. "I am supposed to kill you, right? We aren't getting ready for a thumb war?"

"Oou're aun insif-icat ooman!" Meat-grinder Face said.

"What's that? You've got fangs in your mouth…"

"Fight to the death," a lovely voice rang out, musical and cultivated.

"And that is why the human form is so useful. Communication." I ripped out my gun, sighted, and shot. The bullet tore through the big vamp's chest, just missing his heart.

Dang it. That was almost cool.

I shot him in the legs. Mostly.

He crumpled to the ground with a roar.

I slammed my gun in its holster and ran forward. The huge vampire roared again as his body changed. He flailed and then pushed himself upward, roaring a third time.

"You're angry, we get it." I kicked him in the face, flinging him away from one of his planted hands. I swung down with my sword. It hacked into his neck a fraction, not even making it a quarter of the way through.

"Holy shiznit—what are you made of, iron?" I hacked down again as his tree-trunk arm lashed out. I dove over it and rolled back onto my feet, pushing the circle of vampires wider.

Meat-grinder staggered to his feet, and I could see that his neck was already trying to stitch itself back together. This one healed at an incredible rate, even for a vampire. I saw now why they'd chosen him.

His fist came around, fast. I ducked and thrust forward, stabbing him through the stomach, a nonlethal area. He staggered back instead of bending over it, so I hammered a foot into his balls. He bent in time to meet my fist's upward swing. His nose smashed, sending a gush of black blood over his face. I leapt onto his chest like a spider monkey, helping his backward fall. His arms windmilled, but there was too much momentum.

Timber!

I rode him down until his back hit the ground. Nimbly, I hopped off, planted my feet to either side of him, and stabbed down with everything I had. The blade pierced his chest, prompting a monstrous sort of squeal. Thick black sludge oozed out of his chest while his body started to disintegrate.

Panting, I took a cloth from my pouch and wiped off my blade. I dropped the cloth on the body, since it had to be cleaned up anyway, and started forward, continuing down the path again.

A stringy vampire in its fighting form hissed at me as I passed by. When I didn't react, it leaned toward my neck.

I turned and thrust my sword through the vampire's gut. Its eyes rounded and the hiss turned into a howl. It staggered backward, holding its stomach.

"Don't do that." I shook my head at it and took out another cloth—I'd brought several.

The vampires above me, which had been right at the edge of the platform to watch my fight, turned almost as one and began clearing out. The minions around me continued to dog my steps, irritatingly close.

"While I have your ear," I said conversationally, trying to keep my rage at bay. I really wanted to go on a vampire-killing spree. "Am I going the right way?"

"For a while longer," someone mumbled. He grunted a moment later, probably from an elbow to his ribs.

I sneaked a glance behind me and saw a very attractive guy about my age. "Resisting the swamp-thing look, huh? Are you new to all this?"

He nodded before scowling, clearly annoyed he'd answered again.

We continued on, all my new friends and me, until the air smelled heavy and moist. We were deep underground, probably amidst the oldest vampires who had ever walked the Realm or the Brink.

The surroundings had become almost catacomb-like those last few hundred feet, but they opened up again and spread out into a huge chamber fit for a king. At the far wall was a massive table with ornate chairs seated around it. A beautiful chandelier made of crystal, gold, and probably diamonds hung down in the middle. Nothing was on the table at the moment, but it made me wonder what typically adorned it when the vampires met. I knew they didn't have to eat food, but had no idea if they did it anyway as sort of an homage to their former life.

The flock of newbie vamps shifted their flight pattern to the right. I dutifully stayed within the haphazard circle, just to keep everything moving, until we came to a throne-like chair against a heavily decorated wall. Gold and precious gems adorned the stately seat, and beside it were two lesser chairs with a smidgen less finery.

"Wow," I muttered. "Who gets the little chairs? And don't say wives, because that's just messed up."

"Wait here," one of the newbies said. My new friends drifted to the side of the chamber.

I continued to look around, noticing a crown sitting on a cushioned stool against the far wall. I wasn't great at Brink history, but I'd bet that was real. Next to it was a chest filled to the brim with gold coins and large hunks of precious gems. It looked like pirate treasure, but it had probably been taken from some monarch. Along with that crown.

"You guys are way better thieves than I am," I whispered in awe.

My eyes ate up all the jewels and regalia around me. It was endless, staged in clusters that were designed for flaunting. I noticed the newbies staring at it, too, with wide eyes and sometimes gaping mouths. They seemed just as impressed as I was. Newbies clearly weren't often allowed down in the spacious room. It made sense, then, why all the finery was on display. Vampires did love to show off.

"Miss Somerset," came a deep voice I recognized.

The vampire from last night stalked into the chamber. His wide shoulders swung with each confident step. Behind him came two other vampires, their faces vaguely familiar, which meant they'd probably made an appearance last night as well.

"May I call you Reagan?" He took the throne-like chair, and I couldn't help a smirk, the words *compensating for something?* on the tip of my tongue.

"Yes," I said instead, trying to regain control of my expression.

"What happened to your face?"

"My eyebrows melted off from the warm welcomes you guys gave me." My response was met with a blank stare. "That was sarcasm…"

He continued to look at me, his gaze rooted to mine.

"Now it's getting awkward," I mumbled.

"As you probably know, I am Darius. I summoned you here." A slippered foot swung up and braced on his silk-clad knee. He leaned back in relaxation, but his eyes didn't soften as he took me in, his gaze traveling from my head down to my toes. He noticed my weapons and the way I held myself, and even paused on parts he had no business checking out.

Preventing myself from shifting uncomfortably, I waited him out. Finally, when every creature in the room was inhumanly still, he said, "Your smell is abnormal."

"Wow. You're a real lady-killer, huh? Mr. Charming."

"I have never had an issue attracting members of the opposite sex," he said before returning to his assessment.

Clearly he'd been handsome before being changed. That explained the confidence, and certainly the arrogance.

Turning into a vampire enhanced a person's appearance, so an eight on a one-to-ten scale would be bumped up to near perfect. Not everyone started out hot, though, like Meat-grinder Face. No one had probably warned him a three would only get bumped up to a five. That was probably the reason for all the roaring. Always being the ugly guy, no matter how strong, had to gall.

"You are deformed," Darius said, his gaze on my cheek.

"And you're an asshole. Now that we've pointed out each other's flaws, can we move on?"

His brow furrowed as a figure strolled out from the side of the room. I hadn't noticed a body in that location a moment before, nor had I seen the flip of a camouflaged sheet. This vampire was sneaky, and that usually meant dangerous things.

He walked toward the trio of thrones. Slowly. Purposefully.

His eyes didn't sweep my body like Darius's had. Instead, his intense black gaze stayed rooted to mine, glimmering with intelligence and humor.

My jaw dropped.

Whereas Darius was super handsome with the natural ability to melt panties, this new guy was…

There were no words.

No words.

He was absolutely the most attractive person I had seen in my entire life. Ever. In his human life, he must've been a ten, hands down. Now, off the hotness scale. They didn't make numbers for how gorgeous this former person was.

If I hadn't been rendered simultaneously on fire and mute, I would've sidled toward him and slapped him a high five. Then sketched a selfie (since he wouldn't show up in a picture).

"Hello, Reagan," he said in that lovely, musical, and cultivated voice that had instructed me to fight to the death a few minutes ago. "I've heard so much about you. Please, will you have a seat?"

Newbies walked forward with a large chair inlaid

with gold. It had to weigh a ton, given how the vampires were struggling. They set it down right behind me, bowed, and backed away quickly.

I had no idea who the new vampire was, but there was something regal about him. Something so old world that I felt like I should probably bow, too.

"It seems you've found yourself between a rock and a hard place," he said. And smiled knowingly.

CHAPTER 6

ADRENALINE SURGED THROUGH my body. Those words, teamed with his knowing smile, were not doing kind things to my fight-or-flight reflex.

"You are depleted of funds and my associate has taken your recent mark," the vampire went on. "We've put you in a tight spot, as they say."

The breath left me in a relieved gush. I quickly regrouped. "Yes, it seems you have."

"What luck, that we find ourselves in need of a bounty hunter such as yourself. I've been told that you not only move quickly and with great skill, but you have a working knowledge of magic. Is this true?"

I frowned, because they wouldn't have seen much of my powers on display last night. I didn't like the idea of vampires spying on me, even if they'd just looked at my records from the office. "Yes."

"Might I also assume that you work entirely for yourself, and do not sell information to third parties?"

"To be honest, I've never been in the position to sell information, so I really have no idea."

"Ah, but you have." He smiled again, a thing of perfection. It almost made Darius look plain.

I squinted, trying to parse his remark. I'd dealt with a lot of sensitive cases, but none of them had imparted useful information. Often, the marks babbled about how they could enrich my life until I knocked them unconscious for some peace and quiet. I delivered them, signed some papers, and went about my day.

"I see," he said, taking my silence as an answer. The vampire took a few graceful steps and lowered himself into one of the secondary thrones. His choice of a seat of lesser height and grandeur did nothing to diminish his regal appearance. Darius was sitting higher physically, but for reasons I couldn't pinpoint, I knew he was lower in hierarchy. "We have a sensitive matter you might be able to help us with. But first, I must know. What is the smell, Reagan Somerset, which reaches many of the vampires in this vast chamber?" He looked around those gathered. "Strangely, the young ones are not affected similarly. Those of us who are older, however…" His gaze flicked into the shadows. I followed his look, but saw only empty space.

I needed to get me one of those sheets!

"Male and female alike, we are driven half mad with desire." The vampire's dark gaze hit me again, intelligence and fire. "You know your effect; I can see that. Tell me, what is it? I must know."

"Perspiration and a little deodorant." Or, in this case, a *lot* of deodorant working very hard.

A smile lifted his shapely lips. "You have secrets, Reagan, do you not?"

"All girls have secrets."

"And so they do." His manicured nails tapped the armrest. "You are filled to the brim with extremely potent magic. I can feel it, tickling my skin in the most pleasing of ways."

"That's swell," I replied dryly.

"You are aroused. I can see it in your enlarged pupils. Smell it oozing off your body."

"Ew. All due respect, please stop."

"You will not act on it; I can see that. Does our nature repulse you, Reagan?"

I could tell he was playing games, trying to see what made me tick. It was starting to get on my nerves. If he wanted my sassiness to come out and play, I'd just cut right to it.

"Your nature annoys me." I adjusted my sword. "Look, your…friend stole ten grand out of my hands last night, then added insult to injury by posting a job he *knew* I had to take. That's some bullshit right there. Don't further aggravate me by dancing around with sexual crap and asking stupid questions. While I wouldn't make it out of here alive, I'd make sure you didn't, either. If you don't believe me, lob me a challenge."

A feral sort of smile curled his lips. It was predatory, ruthless, and blood-chilling. Fangs were bared all around me, and the quiver of shifting forms crowded the room. Fear I couldn't help iced my spine. I breathed through it, keeping my blood rich with oxygen. I'd move faster that way. Hit harder.

One thing was certain—this vampire was extremely important to their hierarchy, and they didn't like me talking smack to him. That was good to know.

He stared at me in a way that made my bones wobble and knees threaten to knock. I stared back, trying to keep those issues from showing on my face.

He leaned back slowly.

As though someone had snapped their fingers, the intense pressure that had been squeezing me released from the room. Apparently I wouldn't be dying today.

I barely kept from sighing in relief.

"What is it you need from me?" I asked in a loud, clear voice, amazingly not shaking.

"Why, your services, of course." The vampire's smile was back to pleasant, as though his joke was funny. He didn't seem to mind that no one laughed. "We have a sensitive issue that requires the aid of a magical person. While we could enlist a number of mages, certain issues render us hesitant to do so."

"Meaning, you have no idea who you can trust?"

His eyes crinkled at the corners. "Just so. You would be required to work with one of ours"—he nodded toward Darius—"and to visit an area of the Realm not many walk away from. The knowledge of such a place is only entrusted to a very few. Once you have seen it, you are tied to us, forever. If we ever suspect that you are not loyal, we will bleed you dry."

He paused. The large chamber fell into silence.

I closed my mouth with a click. Despite this vampire's unreal beauty, he wasn't rainbows and sunshine.

"So..." I began, trying to formulate words around my desire to turn around and walk away. "Once I see this place, I'll be watched by you, forever. Any *hint* of my not being a team player, including a small, drunken slip-up that would only mean something to you, would result in a pleasurable sort of death?"

"Ah. Our bite causes you pleasure. I thought I smelled human on you."

"Yes. About my question?"

He spread his hands. "Please. We are reasonable. We will not watch you constantly. We will merely keep an eye on you to ensure our secret is safe."

"And when you say loyal," I went on, "are you implying that I'm supposed to be your cheerleader with all your crazy political stuff? Because I'm not about to stand up to the elves. No way. Nor do I want to be labeled a menace by the shifters in the Brink. More so than I am now, anyway."

"Loyal to our secret, then. Darius will only reveal what is absolutely necessary regarding the case. Nothing more. You will be a protector of that truth. Your loyalty will be tied solely to…the inhabitants."

Inhabitants?

"Right." I drew the word out, hating my burning curiosity about what the vampires were hiding. It wasn't worth my life or freedom. I needed to be sure about this decision.

"I need to mention that this bounty will be fraught with danger," the vampire continued. "However, you will receive bonuses for every enemy of ours that you kill or turn over to us, to the tune of five thousand dollars. As a gesture of good faith, I will include the capture of your recent mark in that sum. This is in addition to, and paid separately from, the bounty we placed with your office."

"Hmm." They were holding money in front of me like a carrot to a donkey.

"Have no fear," the vampire said. "Darius will be with you every moment. He is our strongest in combat and our most magically proficient. He'll ensure you come to no harm."

"Given what I saw, you will only occasionally be in grave peril," Darius said, his voice deep and gruff compared to the music of the other vampire. I liked him better for it. It felt more human.

"Only occasionally? Well, that's comforting," I replied.

"Yes, I have heard you are exceptionally capable." The other vampire nodded at me.

I couldn't tell if he'd caught my sarcasm or not.

"So…to sum up." I braced my hands on my hips. "Taking this job will earn me a bunch of money, but I'll have a vampire mark burned into my skin, I'll have to hang out with Mr. Arrogant twenty-four-seven, and there will be at least a few situations that might kill me."

The unnamed vampire smiled. "Who doesn't love a challenge?"

I blew out a breath. "Well, listen, the danger I could handle. The money I would gladly take. I might even consent to ignoring Darius's presence for an extended period of time, since he's nice to look at. But the prospect of future ties to vampires make this a no-go for me, sadly. You lot are fickle, nowhere near reasonable, despite your assertions, and not to be trifled with. I'd be a fool to tie myself to you, money or no. Thanks for the walk on the wild side, but I'll be showing myself out." I'd be trying to rob some gold while I did it, too.

I gave him a thumbs-up and stood. Before I could take a step, he said, "I will increase the bounty and buy you a house anywhere you choose. Choose a place in the Brink without property taxation, live among humans, and you'll never have to work again. A slip-up to a human will be nothing, as you know. It is the magical community we are worried about."

I tried to keep my feet moving, but they were pretty much rooted to the ground after that offer. It sounded like a dream. The problem was that vampires didn't generally die, which meant I wouldn't outlive them. Since I probably wouldn't die either, at least for a very long time, I would eventually run out of money. That path led back to the bounty-hunting game and the magical community.

I shook my head. "Sounds great. But no, thanks. You can find someone else."

"She is cautious," the vampire said to Darius in a low hum. "You were correct—she's perfect."

"Nope. Not going to happen." I made my way around the extremely expensive and probably stolen golden chair, scratching a little to see if any gold would flake off. What could I say, I was an opportunist. Behind, a wall of swampy vampires stood in my way. "Please have the decency to change back. I'm not used to this display of gross."

"What will it take, human?" Darius asked.

"I've already said—I will not be tied to vampires." I half turned back. The smaller chair sat vacant. "What the hell? Where'd the other guy go?"

"I can make it so you are not tied to us." Darius rose

and took a step forward, ignoring the questions.

"How?"

"I will keep from you that which is secret. First, you will study the entrance point of the secret place, but will venture no further. After that, we will head to the Brink. Your dealings with us will be limited to this contract."

I squinted at him. "Why didn't you make that offer in the beginning?"

"Forging bonds is in our interest. Doing that with fear of death has shown to work the best."

"Clearly not, since you can't trust mages."

He blinked quickly, clearly surprised by my comment. *Truth bomb!*

"What about the money?" I asked, skeptical.

"How much more do you require?"

"Thirty grand." It was a knee-jerk reaction. I'd really been asking if all that money was still on the table, but I wasn't about to decline getting more. "But I will settle for another fifteen."

He nodded.

Don't do the happy dance. Don't do the happy dance. Stop that foot from moving!

"No forced loyalty?" I reiterated.

"No. We will settle for a contractual relationship."

"What about you?" I asked.

"What about me?"

"I don't mean to be rude, but I don't want to be with

you the whole time."

"Of course you do." His brow furrowed. "All female humans do, and many males."

"Good gracious. How does the weight of that ego not crush your spine?" I shook my head in wonder. "But no, Mr. Suave, I don't want your company all the time. In fact, I'd rather you give me directions and bugger off. I work best on my own."

"Foolish," he scoffed. "You would die in the first day. I will give you privacy for toiletries and other human functions. Will that ease your mind?"

"Wait." I held up a hand. "You're planning on being with me *all the time*? Like…in the same room?" I chuckled. "That's not going to happen."

"It's settled, then." He stalked toward me with an outstretched hand.

"You have a listening problem." I hid my hand behind my back so he couldn't grab and shake it. "I won't be sharing rooms with you. When I'm off-duty, I'm *off*-duty."

"Of course. Let us begin. Time is wasting." He loomed over me with his hand held out. Granted, he was only a head taller, but it seemed like so much more, what with the broad shoulders and all the muscle.

I took a step back. "Tonight? Don't I get time to sleep?"

"When you are ready to fall from exhaustion, I will

give you something to revive you."

"Not your blood, I hope." I eyed his hand, which had changed position. He was no longer looking to shake, but now directing me to the side of the room as if the shake had already happened.

"I didn't mean my blood, no, but I would be willing."

"I'll bet you would. A few swap-a-roos and you could leave that mark on me. I have no idea why you're trying so hard. I'm the best bounty hunter in the area, but certainly not the best in the nation."

"Vlad is eager for an alliance with you. Come."

My legs went numb and I stumbled, no longer trying to stand my ground about the rooming situation. All I could focus on was that name.

"That was *Vlad*?" I whispered. Having Vlad's attention was very bad news. Very bad. Probably the worst news of the day, actually.

"Yes. I relayed my experiences from our meeting yesterday. Naturally, he wanted a meeting of his own. His offer speaks volumes of his hopes for you."

Pressure squeezed my chest. "I'm confused."

"You are human, at least in part. That is to be expected."

"This partnership between you and I isn't going to work, I can already tell," I said on autopilot. My lips were numb and my mind was blank.

Vlad was, quite possibly, the oldest living vampire in existence. He played with Brink nations like children played with toys. The guy was a constant, *constant* thorn in the elves' side, and was whispered about in the magical community.

I'd almost turned him down. That would have been worse than agreeing to work for him. Probably.

I swallowed down the lump in my throat. Darius had said he wouldn't tie me to the vampires. I had to make sure that was true.

We walked into a tunnel off the main hall. It looked more like an arched-ceilinged hall from another era. The walls resembled that of historical palaces, lined with candleholders and oil paintings wrapped in large, gaudy frames. The soft glow of candlelight illuminated the way.

"You guys have really put some work into this place," I said, my voice a little strained. "This is great." I ran my finger along the wall. Painted stone.

"Where did you think we lived, in a pit?" he scoffed. I didn't mention that the appearance of their entryway was pretty close. "We had thought to welcome you with light." He gestured to accentuate his comment. "Were you using magic to see in the darkness?"

"Yes?"

"You are lying. It seems you have a very rare ability." He glanced back at me. "Only humans bonded to vampires have such an ability. Yet your name is not in our records."

A mental light bulb blazed through my thoughts. Big C hadn't been using magic after all—he must've been bonded to a vamp.

I grimaced as I eyed an interesting ivory plaque that hung on the wall. "What happens when a human bonded to a vampire is killed?"

"The killer is hunted down, questioned, and then justice is meted out. We protect those who are bonded to us."

"You aren't protecting them all that well," I muttered. At his glance, I added, "If they're being killed, I mean."

"Our bonding practices are extremely selective." We came upon a fork in the tunnel. On the left, the light cut out. Within the darkness moved shapes, graceful and languid, not hurrying. One was moving toward us and stopped, looking out. Waiting.

I wondered if she knew I could see her staring at me.

The soft glow of candlelight continued down the hallway to the right, where Darius led me.

"Each potentially bonded subject is scrutinized by a middle-level vampire or higher, for what they can offer us." Darius gestured at the wall, silently drawing my eyes to an oil painting of a woman holding a girl. It was probably by a well-known artist, given how valuable everything looked and the fact that he was pointing it out. Not like I could tell. I didn't speak art. "Only the very best, or very influential, are noticed. This is not limited to magical people—humans are bonded equally as often. The selection is then presented to three elders, who must approve of the union. Often the bond is denied. Those who are approved are then entered into our records. The vampire holds the responsibility of guarding their bonded."

We reached another intersection in the hall, and Darius again led me right. "Magical people aren't as guarded as thoroughly as humans, of course," he continued, "since they are usually selected by their magical prowess. Powerful mages, or the leader of the east centaur pack, as examples."

I hoped he didn't hear my gulp. "So, does the individual vampire hunt down the perpetrator, or is there a team of you..."

"Whatever is necessary."

"And, just out of scholarly curiosity, how long does it take for vampires to learn of their bond...person dying?"

"They feel it when it happens. Shortly thereafter, they will go about finding out who did the deed."

"Ah." It would seem I'd already tied myself to vampires. "Do any of you ever bond someone in secret?"

"Yes, of course. Often it is a pet, or a strategic move. When found, the vampire and bonded are both killed."

"Ah, sure. Of course." So there was hope that I'd killed an illegal bond-mate, and then would only have one vampire after me.

"While you are involved in this investigation, you are protected from the follow-through of these rules," he said. "In that time, your bond-mate may apply for your bond. I am sure it would be accepted. When this investigation is complete, you will have nothing to worry about."

He thought *I* was an illegal bond.

I huffed out a laugh. "I haven't had any vampires hanging off my neck, I can assure you. Well…except for that one time, but I was college age. That doesn't count."

He stopped in front of an iron door with a large cross stenciled into it. After turning, he stared down into my eyes. I could tell he was trying to read me.

"Question," I said, my curiosity now running rampant. I didn't know much about vampires, and this seemed like a great time to learn. "Does iron affect you? Like…burn you or whatever?"

His brow furrowed. He swung his hand back and placed his palm on the door. I listened, but couldn't hear a sizzle.

"Let me see?" I waited while he complied, staring at

me all the while. His hand was silky smooth. "Not one for manual labor, I see. Or does roughness smooth out when you become a vampire?"

"Both. You do not have a bond-mate?"

"No. Question: do crosses burn you? I see one on the door, but you didn't touch it—Ah, okay. So crosses stenciled on doors do not burn. You can remove your hand again, thanks. How about crosses on a person? Let's say I had a cross blessed by a priest, and then I whipped it off and pushed it against your cheek. Would that leave a mark?"

"We are wasting time. Tell me what allows you to see in the dark."

"We're wasting time because you're a narcissist and only think your questions matter, is that it?"

"Yes. Tell me."

I had to hand it to him: he was honest. "I'll show you mine if you show me yours."

His exhale would've fluttered my bangs if I'd had any. "Come. I need to get a few supplies." Face glossed over with annoyance, he dropped his insistence on learning my secrets and pushed the heavy door inward.

A pulse of magic drew my eyes to the door handle. I ran my hand in front of it. A potent spell pushed back at me. I reached a bit closer and received tiny, invisible pinpricks of pain. The spell was a nasty one.

"Does this work on vampires?" I asked, pulling my

hand away. Then I rolled my eyes. “Pretend I didn’t ask that—”

“Who else would be this far into our domain?” he asked, incredulous.

“Sorry! I spat out the question before I thought it through.”

“I was led to believe you were intelligent.”

“I didn’t think it through, okay? Give me a break. It’s been a long day.” I finally pulled my attention away from the large door and felt a surge of adrenaline. This was his private quarters. I could not believe what I was seeing.

CHAPTER 7

LIGHT FILLED THE chamber, dancing off a crystal chandelier hanging above a round table with fragrant flowers in the center. Behind that was a huge four-poster bed topped with a canopy that swooped down, attached to the posts by tasseled ropes. On each side hung wall-to-floor paintings depicting people from Roman times pointing or fighting or just idling around half-naked. Oil paintings and other artsy items littered the other walls, many in gilded frames. A desk sat in a corner, off to the side of a massive marble fireplace.

Where does the smoke go? I wondered vaguely.

Vases that were probably priceless decorated the mantelpiece, along with golden candelabra. The other side of the room housed a quaint area for sitting and chatting, complete with velvet couches and a marble coffee tabletop supported by golden-looking scrollwork. That style was mimicked in the dining area, a large room off to the side, accessed by grand double doors that currently stood open.

"Vampires eat, then?" I heard myself ask, blinking

at decor that had to cost a bloody fortune and currently existed a long ways underground. "How the hell did you get all this down here?"

"I am ready." He came away from a gold-looking cabinet on the other side of his ridiculously huge bed with a sword strapped to his back and a leather satchel draped cross-wise on his body. The two leather straps made an X across his broad chest.

I tapped the leather pouch surrounding my hips. "This baby makes it so you don't have supplies hanging off you like a donkey."

"It is still hanging off you, just in a different place. Donkey." He sniffed in humor. Or was it disdain? It was hard to tell with him.

"Anyway, this place is sure something." I waved my hand through the air, encompassing my surroundings. "I'm impressed. Why the light, though, if you see in the dark?"

"Light makes everything shine and sparkle. The room is much more magnificent that way."

"So you're vain, then." I smiled at him. "That's all you had to say. You're vain, and light helps demonstrate your glory. Got it." I surveyed his satchel, which was nearly full to the brim. Vain, and had a bunch of money for spells. That, or he had a bond-mate to make them for him.

"Do you have a bond-mate?" I asked, following him

out of his private quarters.

"No. The press of duty to protect that mate is too steep of a price to pay for any benefits I might acquire."

"Yet you offered it to me, in so many words."

"To bind you to us. Vlad would approve. His approval would be worth any inconvenience. Not to mention that my duty, currently, is to protect you in this endeavor. At the end of this affair, should you not prove to be the asset we'd hoped, I'd merely kill you. The short-term torment of a bond-mate dying would be worth the regained freedom."

"Very logical, Watson. One problem. Vlad does not a group of elders make."

"Vlad is *the* elder on which our whole faction hangs. He rarely gets involved in such trivial matters. That topic is left to other competent overseers, such as myself."

"So you are an elder."

"Of course." He reached the door, turned the handle, and pushed it open while stepping to the side—all with a sort of flourish that didn't exist in this century. It was fun to watch, but the whole rigmarole was time consuming.

"I hope this gentleman thing is only for non-combat times, or you're going to kill us both." I straightened up as I went through the door. His presence seemed to require good posture.

"I am not a simpleton, Reagan Somerset. A left just there."

"So, back to you, something I know you love talking about. What about holy water? And you never answered my question about the blessed crosses."

"There are many religions in the world. Vampires are not a product of any of them. As such, their murmurings do not affect us. Neither do their trinkets. A right here, please."

"Yet you have a huge cross on your door."

"It was because of religious-fueled hostility that I was made. I now embrace the irony of it. Your turn—another right followed quickly by a left. What is your unique scent? I've never smelled its equal. Are you fae? I have heard they have an unusually delicious scent, though I have never smelled it."

"You've never smelled a fae?" We came to another door. My palm was nearly on the handle before I felt the magic. I yanked my hand back. "What's this all about?"

"I wondered if you would kill yourself. Alas." Darius stepped forward and palmed the handle. A quick turn and thrust, and the door swung open on well-maintained hinges.

"Look." I held up my hand and stopped. Turning to face him, I refused the urge to take a step backward due to our proximity. "I am part human, and as such, I get tired. When I get tired, I make mistakes. If you are planning to constantly test me, this isn't going to work. I'm not asking for a partnership by any means, but I do need a heads-up if you know a death trap is lurking. Savvy?"

He analyzed me for a moment. "I will take up my duty as soon as you make it to the surface."

"Something you might've hinted at *before* we set off." I slouched and continued up the way. He no longer deserved my good posture.

"You have admitted a few times that you are only part human. Yet you have not volunteered your specific type of magic. What are you hiding?"

"Whatever it is, it's none of your business. Which way?" I waggled my finger between right and left at the next intersection. The walls in this area weren't lined with stone, showing instead the raw substance from which they were carved, which may have been dirt, but was just as likely to be magical mud of some kind. "Do the elders and important folk not travel up this way?"

"How else would we get out? Go right."

"Another way, presumably. Why didn't you do up the walls?"

"When leaving, we usually travel at much faster speeds, so there would be little point in decorating the areas inhabited by new vampires."

"Welcome to vampirism. Sorry about the lodgings." I trudged up the steeper incline, feeling the burn in my thighs. "This is the *worst.*"

"You are out of shape and lacking muscle tone."

"Don't hold back for my sake. Let the truth bombs roll." Magic fizzled around me, running along the walls and stretching across the floor. I slowed, closing my eyes to cut out one of my senses. That made it easier to use the magical sense. "I imagine you know what this magic is?"

"Yes. You've sensed it late. I am losing hope in your abilities."

His attitude was really starting to get on my nerves.

Without another thought, I ripped out my sword, pushed magic through it, and sliced along the wall. The dirt—or magical mud—parted like canvas, revealing wriggling worms within. The magic coating the wall snapped like a cord before blinking out. The fizzle from a moment before dulled until it was a memory.

"How do you like me now?" I said with a little swagger.

A strange sound reverberated up the halls. I tilted my head, not able to place the weird sort of *thrushing.* Blood pumped through my veins. My fight reflex thundered, making me grip the handle of my sword tighter and mentally notice the weight of the gun on my side. Yet another sense, probably passed down from my father's side, told me of danger rushing my way.

"I tripped an alarm," I muttered as Darius stepped

gracefully to the side. "With friends like you..."

A blur of movement came at me, a middle-level or greater vamp, judging by the speed. I launched forward, closing the distance, sword already slashing. It ripped open the chest cavity. The creature—because it was in monster form—screamed in a bloodcurdling way and flung itself to the side.

Another blur came right up behind it, claws out but in human form. Jaw extended, showing the teeth, able to rip through flesh like its claws could. I tugged out my gun and shot the creature in the face. Its head whipped back and its body followed, showing me the bottoms of its feet.

As I continued to run past it, I stabbed down into its stomach. It squealed and clutched at the offending spot.

Another vampire, slower, ran along the wall. In creature form but slightly jerkier than the others, it had its hands out like a ghoul. I started to chuckle—I couldn't help it. The thing looked like a prancing monster.

I stowed my gun, bent low, and swiped. My blade tore through a protective spell and then the creature's leg.

"Oh shit!" I grimaced. "I didn't mean to sever the thing; I just meant to give you a deep cut. Sorry about that."

Scratching sounded behind me. I whirled and

slashed, reopening the quickly closing gash in the first vamp. My strike barely missed its heart. It clutched at its middle and staggered backward, its creature face a mask of shock, its lips forming an O around its ghastly fangs.

"Enough!" Darius shouted.

Movement slowed then stopped further down the hallway. I could barely see shapes lurking there. The three wounded vampires around me picked themselves up. One hopped, staring down at its severed limb.

"Seriously, I'm really sorry about that," I muttered. "I hope you can put it back on…"

"She left you three alive on purpose," Darius said in disgust. He sauntered away from the wall and continued upward. "Come up with a better defensive strategy. This one was truly lacking."

"Good job, Reagan," I mumbled, knowing he could hear. "By the way, thanks for not killing my minions. Oh, no problem, Darius. I do what I can."

He ignored me.

As we left the carnage behind, Darius took over leading. Clearly I'd passed the last test, though I had a feeling the attack hadn't been planned. I could've gotten around that spell without disabling it. I wondered if he knew that.

"We may be confronting rogue vampires during this investigation," Darius said as the tunnel walls pushed in on us. "They should be killed as quickly as possible. You seem familiar with the easier ways to kill us—cut off the head, or destroy the heart. You do not need to use wood or metal for these things, as you clearly know. Sunlight is the easiest, of course. The older we get, the longer we can stay out in direct sunlight, but even someone my age can only last a half-hour before disintegration. I can remain in indirect sunlight for a few hours, I believe. Maybe longer—I haven't tested that in decades. It is horribly painful.

"The last, least common way to kill a vampire is hellfire. Only a few magical beings can create that kind of fire naturally, and few mages have enough power and know-how to create it magically. A certain type of fae is one of those natural beings, from royal lineage, which is why I have always kept my distance from that group. We have allied ourselves with most of the other wielders of hellfire so that we may watch them closely."

"Why not have the fae in alliance so you can watch them?" I asked as we reached a door.

Darius barely twitched his fingers before the lock magically disengaged.

Being predators of humans, vampires assumed a lot of heightened traits, like vision, hearing, and strength. Basically, they were the lions of the cat world. Part of being predators had to do with sneaking up on their prey. Since humans slept inside locked dwellings, somewhere along the line, vampires had developed the magic to circumvent any padlock or deadbolt. Needing to invite a vampire inside your house was pure myth.

The door swung open by itself. He stepped back and swept his hand toward the exit. “Please. After you.”

A girl could get used to this. I glided through like an idiot, pretending I was a princess. The night embraced me softly. I breathed in a wonderfully sweet smell drifting on the breeze.

“The elves have a firm hold on the fae.” Darius stepped out beside me and closed the door. “They are out of our reach. As far as I know, however, fae cannot see in the darkness.”

“I’m not fae.”

He’d probably figured that already. “Unlucky,” he said. “They are privileged within the Realm.”

“Why unlucky? If I were fae, you wouldn’t be my friend. Then who would you ambush with rock-men and mostly hidden underground spells?”

He sniffed. I had no idea what that meant.

“I thought I was down there for longer.” I checked my watch. It said nine o’clock, the same time I’d entered the Realm.

“We live in eternal night. It is our natural habitat, after all.” He gently touched the small of my back while holding out his other hand, ready to escort me like a guy out of a Jane Austen book. “Please.”

"What era are you from?"

"You can hardly expect me to reveal my past if you are unwilling to reveal yours."

"I did expect that, yes." I patted my weapons and tuned into my surroundings. The lightheartedness of the moment dried up as the great wide world of the Realm stretched out before us. We took up a path that led parallel to a long string of mountains, blocking the northern way.

"You can move faster than a human when fighting. Is that also true of walking?" Darius asked, his stride perfectly matching mine. He was only hinting at rushing me. Very polite.

"Not really, for reasons I don't understand. It seems like battle is the only time I can increase my speed to non-human proportions."

"And your strength?"

"Strong like a bull." I made a fist and flexed my bicep. "Always."

"Your sword?"

"Is lovely, don't you think?" The height of the grass around us increased as we walked, hiding boulders and pitfalls. We stayed to a solid dirt track that slowly rose above the surrounding area, big enough for three people to walk abreast—or one normal person and one wide-shouldered Darius.

"It is magical?" he asked.

"Of course. Normal swords can't cut through spells."

"Normal magical swords can't cut through spells either, unless a counteractive spell is fed to the blade before each interaction. You did not use a counteractive spell, and there is no way you could've guessed what to pre-load it with."

"No one likes a know-it-all, Darius. Just so you know."

I felt his glare beating against my temple, but he didn't ask for more information. I got the feeling he was tired of being turned down. It probably wasn't something he had much experience with.

A glimmer at the base of the grasses alongside us suggested we were heading into swamplands, which made the raised dirt path necessary unless we wanted to slip on rubber boots. Another mile, and my suspicion was confirmed by the soggy mud at the edges of the path and the standing water leading away from it. Very few mud islands rose above water level, which meant the path we were on was man- or mage-made.

Near us, a line of grass moved in a wave, indicating something at its base was traveling the same way we were. Judging by the waves it was making, the creature, probably a water serpent, was mighty big. Four feet? Five?

"How close is the next solid path that leads this

way?" I asked.

"A mile up we will intersect a path that leads down from the north. A mile after that, we will intersect a path that leads up from the south. There is a path that leads to our destination from the west. Only two paths, this size, go in. They are closely monitored."

"By that thing in the water, or something on two legs, or..."

"By vampires," he said. "We always post sentinels. One will be stationed at each intersection, and there will be a third at the entrance of the enclosure. The serpent is just one of a great many dangers lurking in those waters."

The serpent continued to dog our steps, later joined by another on the other side.

"Do those fairly giant serpents eat people?" I asked, surveying the water lapping the bottom of the raised dirt path, which was now basically a continual mound rising about two or three feet from the water. Though I couldn't see how deep the swamp got in some places, I bet that those rubber boots would have to be mighty big to keep a person dry.

"Their poison is more deadly than any Brink snake." Darius glanced at the serpent on my side, much too close to the path for my comfort. One drunken misstep, and I'd be riding it. I edged closer to him. "Larger, as well. They hunt, feeding on their spoils.

They do not often show themselves above water."

"Their size means they've had plenty to eat," I surmised, scanning the grassy waters beyond. "Staying near this path—two of them doing it, even—suggests we're easy kills. If someone were to wade in, they'd be taken down. I doubt a boat would be disturbed, though."

"The boat would need to be left somewhere. In that event, our sentinels would surely notice it."

"Magic can trick the eye. With a good enough spell caster, a boat would be easy to stash. You'd be surprised how many houses go unnoticed. Right in the middle of town! It's crazy."

"Do you notice them?"

"No. I notice the magic surrounding them."

Another raised path cut through the grasses to the left. It intersected ours, forming a large, circular dirt area, safely elevated from the creatures within the swamps. No one stood watching.

"How many vampires have I missed over the years who were hiding under one of those sheets?" I murmured, sweeping the area with my gaze. "You'd think they'd at least block my view, making a small disturbance to the plane. It's like no one is standing there."

"No one *is* standing there." One of Darius's large hands covered my shoulder, stopping me. "Can you see any magic?"

"I sense or feel the magic, and no." I shrugged off

his touch and walked forward, hands at my sides, my mind on my weapons. None of my senses went off. The area between the two intersecting paths felt empty and void.

"There's nothing," I said when I got to the center of the circle. I held my hands wider and focused, feeling for any residual magic. A moment later, I shook my head and dropped my hands. "Which doesn't mean no spells were cast here—it just means it didn't happen within the past few hours. Otherwise, I'd still feel traces. Unless it was really weak magic, and then the last hour. The power of the magic used determines how long afterward I can feel its properties."

Darius stared at me for a beat too long.

"What?" I asked, strangely self-conscious and not sure why.

"I have never, in all my years, seen someone do as you are doing, Reagan." His stare was getting awkward again. "I have worked with a lot of mages. I have talked to a lot more. No one has this ability."

"No one that you know of. I've been hanging out in New Orleans for some time. And look, you just met me. You should really get out more. Socialize. It'd do you good." I talked a good game, but I was hunching for all my worth, trying to hide my burning face.

"Something is not right about you."

"Takes one to know one, eh? I'm rubber, you're

glue…"

His brow furrowed and he glanced out to the side, looking into the distance. A moment later, his gaze dropped, scouring the ground. He roamed the outside of the circle and then surveyed the way we'd come. "There are no tracks."

My focus snapped back to the situation. I checked out the ground, cursing myself for being distracted. It didn't take me long to realize he was right, and I should've seen that right away. Besides ours, it looked as though the path had never been used.

I bent down and put my palm flat to the ground. It only succeeded in making me look stupid. "Do you know who was supposed to be sentry?"

"Specifically? No. I can find out, but I would need to travel back to do so. With your speed, it would take too long, and I do not wish to carry you on my back."

"Like a donkey?" I smirked, noticing the serpents had vamoosed. The waters were completely still. Time to take a peek. "Hold the back of my shirt, would you? I want to take a look, and I'm always worried I'll accidentally jump."

"What—?"

I laughed, because his voice—always so perfect, so unfazed—was a little shrill.

"I don't have vertigo or anything," I said patiently, "but if I stop at the edge of something, I have a strong sense of losing my balance and falling. While falling into a few feet of water wouldn't normally bother me, there are huge serpents down there. I'd rather not take any chances."

"Vertigo."

"You really do hate listening, don't you? No, it's not vertigo. I don't get dizzy, and never actually *lose* my balance, either—it's the *what if* factor that bothers me."

Seeing that he didn't get it, I gave him a few examples. "What if I get too close and a gust of wind pushes me over? What if I faint and fall off the side? What if I suddenly decide to jump and don't have time to talk myself out of it? See what I mean? If there's something stable to hold on to, I'm fine. If there's nothing, I get scared I'll fall off the edge."

"I could push you off. How am I a stable item?"

"Give me a break. There is no way you'd go against Vlad's wishes and kill me." I grabbed his hand and felt a jolt of electricity crackle between us. I scowled. "Stop that."

"That was your doing. I do not have that reaction with others."

"You probably do, you're just too busy moving in on their neck to notice."

After a beat, he said, "Possibly."

"We have got to be the worst detective team alive," I mumbled, moving his hand to the center of my back.

"Now hold on like a security rope, please. I don't want to end up in that swampy water. It's a strange phobia, but it's mine."

At the edge of the circular path, I looked down into the waters. Only the very tops of the grasses poked above the surface, meaning this area was at least four feet deep. Nothing stirred.

"You are not leaning," he said, annoyed. "What is the point of my holding on to you if—"

A mouth full of teeth launched out of the water and straight for my face.

CHAPTER 8

BEFORE I COULD flinch out of the way, I was yanked backward and surrounded by thick arms. My feet left the ground and then I was swinging through the air. Darius let me go before I could struggle free, dropping me like a stone. My butt hit the dirt and my teeth chattered.

The serpent chomped at the air a second time before dropping back into the water with a splash, red body with black fins disappearing into the murky waters. Darius hadn't so much as reached for his sword.

"Why didn't you kill it?" I asked, out of breath and climbing to my feet.

"It protects the waterway. Why kill free labor?"

He had a point.

"Has no one ever looked over these waters before?" I asked.

"Maybe they were drawn to something special in you." Darius threw me a dark look.

"I sure hope not, because I don't want one of those as an enemy."

"It is an enemy confined to the black swamps of Sector Three of the Realm. I hardly think that it is an enemy worth thinking about."

He had a point. Again.

"Okay, well, your sentinel is missing." I dusted myself off and adjusted my weapons. "Magic was likely used to disguise any tracks, but it was either done a long time ago or the spell was weak, because it left no lasting effect on the area. Or on the jumping serpents, for that matter. So, we're left with a few scenarios. Shall I lay them out?"

"That is your job."

"I still owe you a punch in the mouth for stealing my mark. Know that." I schooled my annoyance. "The options are as follows." I ticked off a finger. "Your sentinel is in on it and is now carrying out your enemy's plans." I ticked off another finger. "Your sentinel *isn't* in on it and is therefore dead. The killer could've easily tossed the body into the swamp before wiping away the footprints and, presumably, the black goo vampires leave behind when they die." I dropped my hand. "Or the sentinel who was supposed to be on duty slept in, or was killed elsewhere, leaving time for someone to clear away the old footprints in order to track our movements."

"Track our movements?"

"Well…yeah. Hasn't anyone ever staged a trap for

you?"

His brow rumpled.

"Really?" I prodded. "*No one* has tried to get you to a certain place so they could attempt to kill you? Ever?"

"Once. Which led to this life."

"I'm not talking about the act of changing you into a vampire."

"Neither am I."

I looked at him askew, questions filling my head. We didn't have time for the detour into his history, though.

"Okay, fine." I tossed up my hands. "Well, let me assure you, I have plenty of experience with traps. I'm not well liked in the magical criminal circuit. Our prints are the only ones on the path, so there is a real possibility someone is watching us. They know which direction we've traveled, and from the spacing of the prints and their depth, they'll know how fast we're going and roughly how heavy we are. That is a lot of information for someone who cares."

"What would they do with that information?"

"Combine it with other information they'll be gathering. In the past, I've had marks watching me to make sure I didn't get too close to their operations. As soon as I did"—I slapped my hands together like a bear trap—"attacked. Some of them tried to get me before I got them. A few times it was because someone had taken a hit out on me. Once, a stalker wanted me for himself. That guy was whack-a-doo. A human, too. Boy, did he pick the wrong girl."

"Please." He did that *touching my back and directing me* thing.

"Anyway." We continued along, and this time I paid more attention to my surroundings. "Has the path always been this even?"

"Even, yes. As smooth as a Brink sidewalk, no. I should've noticed."

A while later, I saw another intersection, this time from the south. The circular area in the middle was just as bare as the last one had been. A French word floated on the breeze. Judging by the tone, it was a swear word.

"No vampire covered in a camouflaged sheet?" I asked quietly.

He didn't answer, but his glower said *no*.

We made it to the circular area. "Hold my back again, please."

I felt his fist close around the belt of my leather pouch.

"No, not there." I tapped his hand upward. "What if the belt breaks free and I fall in? It's old. Grab clothes."

"Something is wrong with you."

"I know. You've said."

He did as instructed.

Hands out, ready to grapple with a serpent launching into the air, I looked around the edges of the circular area. The sides of the path were rocky and pocked with plenty of imperfections. The water gently lapped against the edges, cutting a groove that hadn't been fixed.

"They've only smoothed out the top," I whispered, not sure why, but my intuition thought it was a good idea.

I made my way around the edge and almost straightened up when something caught my eye. I waved Darius's hand away before bending for a closer look.

"How is this—"

"*Shhhh!*" I looked around for a boogeyman.

"How is this different enough for you not to need my help?" he whispered.

"Because I'm crouching near the ground. Trust me, this all makes sense in my head." Quick as I could, I snatched an item off the surface of the water that had been rolling against the side of the raised area. The water disturbed a fraction of a second before that mouth exploded out of it again, aimed for my face.

"Holy bastard!" I rolled to the side and hopped up as the creature hit the raised area. Calmly, Darius kicked it in the head, sending it back into the water.

"That thing was waiting for me, did you see that?" I pointed at the water, no longer whispering. I let out a breath, backing up until I reached the middle of the circular area. "They're smart. Thank God they don't have legs." Breathing heavily, I sat down with my elbows resting on my knees. I brought up the item and smiled to myself. It had been worth it.

"Recognize this?" I held up the magical casing for Darius to inspect. When he reached for it, though, I pulled it back. "Not so fast. I'm not giving you all the leverage. Steal my mark once, shame on you. Steal my evidence twice, shame on me."

His eyes fluttered and he shook his head. "This must be another circumstance that only makes sense..."

"Exactly." I stood and held it up for his inspection, ready for grabby hands.

His gaze roamed the rubber orb before flicking back to me. His eyes, fairly close, were the color of honey, with green specks swimming through. If he didn't scowl at me so much, I'd remark on how pretty his peepers were. "Not one I recognize."

"What does that mean in the scheme of things?"

"I oversee the purchase of spells for our entire faction. I often work directly with the most powerful mages, and know the style of the casings my subordinates handle. As you must know, most mages mark their spells in case they fall into another's hands—"

"You mean, in case someone steals them."

"I find it strange that that casing is not marked. It

has a certain style, yes, but nothing more."

"What kind of an idiot would mark a casing they planned to use against a vampire? Do you hear yourself?"

Anger flashed in his eyes. "Most mages buy casings in bulk. They order them with their markings. If they didn't think the evidence would be found, since not many people dangle their heads above large serpents, they would have no need to prepare specialized spells and casings."

I sighed, because even though I should've expected an argument like this, it was still tiresome. "I'll just leave you with this: there are a great many mages in the world, and most of them don't have the money to buy individualized anything. They certainly don't have the money to buy in bulk."

"It seems we travel in different magical circles—"

"What gave you that idea, Mr. Golden Chair?"

"—but we can agree that finding the user or maker of that casing is a start."

All that build-up to a simple, logical conclusion. It would be a long case.

I cleared my mind and felt along the smooth rubber. "Do your people ever buy or steal spells without your knowledge?" I dug another empty casing out of my pouch and compared the two. The one I'd just found was larger and sturdier, with thicker rubber and a glossier exterior. That indicated a more volatile spell, which I relayed to him.

"I agree. And yes, occasionally they procure spells from an unauthorized dealer, when the need arises. Often the casings are kept, however, all marked, so we can keep track of who is using what. I make it my priority to make note of them all."

I just could not believe he had never seen a casing without a marking. That said volumes about the people he dealt with—and how little he'd seen of the magical world's underbelly.

Volumes.

"Regarding making a note of the casings," I said, "we can assume your memory is…"

"Photographic."

"Of course. Why wouldn't it be, what with all the other things you have going for you?"

"I am ready to dangle you over the water again." He stared down at me, utterly serious.

Laughter bubbled up from my middle. "I get that a lot."

He looked at his feet. "Smoothing dirt doesn't seem like it would require a volatile spell."

I stared at the two casings. If I put the new one in the pouch, I'd have to show Darius all my spent spells. That would just amount to a lot more questions, like *why do you have a bunch of empty casings in your spell pouch?*

I slipped the old one into its home, to be used as a fake spell down the road, and put the new one into my pocket. "It doesn't make sense, does it? Could be an old specimen, I guess, that just didn't make it to you."

"Pity we didn't look harder at the other site." He glanced back that way, then at me. "Keep walking forward. Don't fall in the water or look over the edge. I will be right back."

"Wait—"

He sped off like a motor was strapped to his back.

After taking a glance at the still waters, I did exactly what he'd said. Onward I walked, lost in thought about the many enemies I'd managed to accrue in such little time, all without the benefit of a bounty. At least the vampire who'd bonded that crazy mage would have to wait until Darius and I figured out whatever this riddle was. The mage's friends, however…

"Another."

I jumped and struck. My fist glanced off Darius's muscled side before he danced backward, his brow furrowed.

I palmed my chest, trying to still my heart. "You scared the bejeebus out of me."

"You need to pay better attention to your surroundings."

If it wouldn't stroke his ego, I'd mention something

about his utterly silent advance, amazing speed, and daunting quickness. I was doing him a favor by withholding that information, surely—otherwise the guy's ego would swell so large that he'd never have friends.

He held out his hand. When I reached for the proffered token, he pulled it away and tsked. "Finders keepers."

"Mature." When his hand advanced again, I inspected the orb, the same as the one I'd found. "Still, there's the question of the sentinels. Did they use the spells? Or did the magic user kill them or trick them into leaving their posts?"

Without warning, I snatched at the casing. Darius yanked it away just in time, leaving my fingers to glance off his closed fist.

"Only turtles would be jealous of your speed." Darius tucked his prize away.

"I was close. Admit it," I said, continuing on.

"This was the same magic user. The pellet was discarded in roughly the same way. Tossed after use. Mages do it a lot. Witches and warlocks do not."

"Witches don't throw down their used casings?" That was something I'd never noticed.

The terrain slowly began to change. More land patched the waters with taller, thicker reeds. In the distance, the mountain loomed larger, spilling its trees onto the flatter, hopefully dryer, land.

"Witches and warlocks seem to be more earth conscious. When one has less power, he or she must reach for any source at their disposal to make up for that which is lacking."

"I bet you're a hit with all of them, hmm?" I shook my head. "By the way, many men use the term *witch*. It's gender neutral these days, like mage. Something about negative connotations with the term *warlock* in the Spanish Inquisition days..."

"That doesn't concern me."

"Oh yes, a real hit."

"Not far now." He motioned in front of us at a wall of trees. I could barely make out a small, rickety wooden fence separating the suddenly wooded area from the swamp. Water closed the wooded area off into an island; the raised path we were on was the only dry way in.

Closer still, I squinted at what looked like a boot at the edge of the trees and the water, off to the right after the path met the island. From the angle it was splayed on the ground, it looked as if it still contained a foot. Problem was, I didn't see the leg attached.

Darius stuck his hand out in front of me, surveying the same thing. After a moment, he dropped his limb. "I think we will soon find the answer to our latest question."

My attention stayed on that boot as we drew closer

to the end of the raised path. I could barely see where the land bowed strangely—not something you'd see in the Brink. "He's got one of those sheets on, doesn't he?"

"She. That is a woman's boot."

I rolled my eyes—it looked like a normal combat boot to me. "Don't tell me you're a fashionista, too. How do you possibly find the time?"

"It is important to change with the times so as to remain undetected among humans," Darius said. "I always pay attention to fashions of the day, and patterns of speech. It is how I am still alive after all these years."

That made sense. Another point to him. So annoying.

Right where the path met the island, still about ten feet from where that boot lay off to the side, a vibration of magic jiggled my bones and stopped me dead. I held up my hand for Darius to stop beside me before taking out my sword.

"Do you feel that?" I asked in a hush.

I raised my palm to face the magic, inviting the currents to run through my blood so I could hear their song. That would lead me back to the nature of the spell, then to the type, and finally to the purpose. That was the goal, anyway. When a powerful mage was behind the wheel, he could disguise his intentions.

I bent to feel the area near my feet. The magic thinned down near the ground, not forming a root as it should have. "Our mage either got lazy, or isn't as experienced as his power level suggests. This wouldn't trap someone, though. This blockade was placed independently from whatever has that boot. Though the distance alone should've told you that."

Slowly, with a steady hand, I slid my palm along the ground. Razor-sharp pain sliced into my skin, the edges of a nasty spell catching the top of my hand. I sucked in a breath and gritted my teeth, waiting to see if the spell manifested into magical knives or some other horrible thing. When it didn't, I continued pushing my hand forward until the pain moved up toward my wrist. I held it, wondering if this would evolve into a physical reaction of some kind. Still nothing. Just a barrier.

"Three inches thick, or so." I pulled my hand back slowly. "The edge of it, which is frayed because the spell wasn't properly rooted, hurts like the devil. That seems to be about it. I can't tell if it's a tripwire of some kind. Not yet, anyway."

I eyed the path, and then the water off to either side. The memory of that gaping mouth with the sharp rows of teeth flitted through my mind. Those serpents were onto me—at least the one was—and they knew I liked to hang out over the water. I had to make this quick.

"I need to reach right, Darius. Help."

He knew the drill, and quickly realized he'd have to be a more active participant this time.

I leaned over the side, feeling his strength holding my weight. "Pull me in," I said, watching the water. I leaned over the left side of the path as well, feeling how far that spell went. "Okay, lift me up."

His long fingers curved around my ribcage and glanced off my breasts.

"Dude," I said, shaking him off as soon as I could. "Not cool."

He didn't comment, clearly only concerned about my analysis and not my personal boundaries.

I scowled in thought, remembering the bite of the spell. The gap at the bottom. "This was done by a powerful mage who has good control over his magic, but lacks experience. A younger person, maybe, or someone without the proper training early on. The feel of the currents suggests a darker sort of magic—the type that gains energy from sacrificing, calling on demons, that sort of thing. Not all of those things are bad, mind you. Some religions exist peacefully while using those practices, but I'd bet this guy is after personal gain. This spell…is not peaceful. I came across another mage whose magic felt like this just a day or two ago, depending on how long I've been in this place. Could be coincidence, but given your problem and my involvement, I'd bet not."

"Who is this other mage? We should speak with him."

"Oh. Uhm." I drew the sound out. "I accidentally killed him, actually. That was my bad."

"How can you be sure this mage is male?"

I shrugged. "I'm not. I just deal with guys a lot in my trade. When they go crazy, they really let that freak flag fly. The mage I accidentally killed is proof of that." I blew out a breath and stepped back, looking to the side, around the barrier spell, at the boot. "The spell over there is keeping the vampire from melting away like you all normally do when you die. Of course, she could just be asleep, but it's obvious she's intended to act as bait."

"Bait?"

"Yeah. I mean, she's clearly on display. We saw her from a ways out—any vampire would've. So you'd hurry to check on her, not notice the clear barrier spell before smacking into it, and whammy, bad day."

"Given that the other sentinels are nowhere to be found, it's doubtful one was left alive. This mage wouldn't want to leave behind a live witness."

There was that, yeah.

"Up until now, someone has been getting in and out without making their presence known," he continued. "But now, sentinels are missing and a wall of magic has been thrown up to block our entrance. Our enemy is stepping up his game."

I held up my hand, something I did when I needed to think and people were talking to me. "With this much power, he could've used a boat those other times and easily disguised it. That's the most logical explanation for how he got in. These new developments of hiding his tracks, possibly killing sentinels, and creating a barrier could mean that he's in a hurry. Like maybe he's trying to head us off and had to navigate on foot. Maybe also that he is watching us, seeing how we deal with all this. He could even be trying to ambush us to prevent us from finding anything. There's no way to know yet."

"Watching us doesn't fit."

"Not really, no. Do a lot of vampires know you were going to investigate this?"

"This specifically? No. What lies in this place is not common knowledge, even to vampires. We choose carefully who guards this paddock, and the vampires are all at least upper-middle level. However, Vlad's involvement and my role in the investigation will signify something big is going on."

"And our mark will see the writing on the wall."

"Easily."

"Okay. So you've got some loose-lipped vampires tipping off our mark. While you were playing *dodge death* with me, he was running ahead and blocking our way into this place. And he did a good job. I'm not sure who you would've gotten to break through this."

"That I trust? No one."

"Aw. Doesn't that just make me feel all warm and cozy inside." He opened his mouth, and I held up a finger to stop him. "Yes, I know, you're only using me because I'm expendable, and you can't afford to kill your precious, expensive mages. Relax. I know the score."

I bet *he* didn't know the score, though. I wasn't nearly as easy to kill as he probably thought. Especially when I knew the hammer was about to drop.

"Hacks," I said, back to thinking about the problem in front of me. "They're probably charging you an arm and a leg for their bulk ordering and the marks on their casings. I bet you showed them the golden chair and they immediately thought *sucker*."

"Are you finished?"

"Stalling? Not really." I blew out a breath and stared at the waters. "No way to get in by going around. That serpent will attack, I have no doubt."

"One jumped up for me when I retrieved the other casing. I wouldn't be surprised if the carcasses of the other sentinels were dangled over the water for the serpents to dispose of. When you dangled yourself over, the creatures probably thought it was feeding time again."

I grimaced. "I am not having warm thoughts about this mage we are dealing with." I looked at the spell and motioned him forward. "Do me a favor. Bend down and slide your hand along the ground. Slowly."

Those honeyed peepers were trained on me for a long moment before he bent and did as instructed.

I guessed he did trust me a little.

The top of his hand started to sizzle, then peel. Webs of black lines flowed over his skin. The muscles in his arm started to tremble and his hand shook, but he didn't make any other sign that it hurt, nor did he withdraw.

"Holy crap, man, take your hand away!" I yanked at his sleeve.

He shook his hand out and watched as his skin regenerated. Wide-eyed, I stared back at the empty space, which hosted a much nastier spell than I'd realized.

"They aren't heading me off—they are heading you off. You'll want to watch your step more than usual." I pushed power into my blade.

Darius stood slowly, his face the terrifying mask of a predator. "They should hope to catch me."

"They hope to kill you, it looks like. But whatever. Okay. How do you want to do this? I can most likely cut this spell down, but that will let them know you have powerful help. Right now, they are just planning for you. I'm a wild card, and spells like this, while they hurt, don't affect me as strongly. That helps us now, but if they figure out my deal, they'll tailor their attacks a little better. That would definitely hinder us down the road.

"The alternative is sneaking under this thing with a little know-how from me. Call it magic cat-burgling. They'll never know."

His eyes trained on my face for a few beats too long. "Sometimes, you seem so naive, almost useless, in your approach. Other times, like now, you are truly eye-opening, Reagan Somerset. It's like beholding a goddess. I almost can't believe you've touched down in the world of mortals."

Heat crawled through my cheeks, and I blinked way too much. I did not see that coming.

"Right," I said, unsure how to reply because, despite the really sweet part of that comment, half of it was a bitch slap. "Awesome." I cleared my throat. "So anyway, about the spell…"

"Cut it down and then I will set a spell. How they take down my spell will tell me a great deal regarding their magical style."

Excitement ran through me. I'd used spells conjured by others, and been attacked more times than I could count, but I'd never seen someone meticulously formulate an info trap out of purchased magic, like I knew Darius would.

"What type of counter-spell will you be working?" he asked.

"Oh. Uh…" I drew out the sound, half looking down at my pouch. The more powerful the spell, the harder it was to break. Getting the correct opposing magic just right, usually in the form of a counter-spell, could make the difference between a dead spell, or a dead spell breaker.

Of course, my magic didn't work like that. It just ate through spells. I was the world's master key to all the magical locks within a mighty large power spectrum. Mine was a very specific skill set that I could not advertise.

When I worked alone, I didn't have to bluff.

I really missed working alone.

"I'm just going to…" I took out a casing and pretended to break it against my blade while moving to shield my movements. "I have this spell here which should subdue the volatile magic…" My voice drifted away into mumbles.

He leaned forward to ask another question, but before he could get it out, I steadied myself and struck, aiming to tear through the thick, gooey magic as fast as possible. My blade sliced in and slowed. The working was much more intricate and intense than it had appeared. The mage had disguised the real meat of the thing, which was now sucking the power from my sword. Once depleted, the spell would attach to me like a leech, stealing my life with each beat of my heart.

Hell's doorbell. This was very tricky spell working.

Straining with effort, sweat beading on my forehead, I pushed more power into my sword. It slogged through, fighting. Losing. Only halfway to the ground, its power was almost depleted.

Tapping into my life force, where I could store magic like a battery, I pumped more into the sword. My sword turned an angry shade of red, and black tendrils ran through the wall, crystallizing it.

My arms were quivering, but my shining blade was once again making progress. Breathing hard, knowing the spell needed direct contact with my magic—not through the sword—I summoned a tiny bit of fire. It flicked along the bottom of my blade, hopefully not noticeable to the nosy parker looking over my shoulder, and seeped into the spell. The fabric of the spell tore, little by little at first, then faster as I bled in more fire. My toes tingled and spikes of pain jabbed my eyes and temples. My power was almost out.

"Blood would be good about now," I said through a clenched jaw, squeezing my eyes shut against the pain and putting everything I had into the sword, cleaning out the corners of my body and wringing myself dry.

"My blood can help revive you, not lend power," Darius said, his face suddenly close but his voice so far away.

"Almost." The word fell from my lips, vague and wispy. I should've risked using more of my direct power in front of Darius. The decision to protect my secret might've been my undoing. "Almost." The last of the power gushed from my blade. The spell unraveled in a *whoosh*. Metal snapped. I saw black.

CHAPTER 9

"THAT'S BETTER. YES, drink," a deep, sexy voice urged me. A strong arm held me tightly against a rock-hard body. "*Drink.*"

The sweetest elixir I'd ever tasted dripped past my lips and exploded on my tongue. I couldn't even describe the flavor, only that it was the best thing I'd ever had the pleasure of tasting in my entire life. Joy and adrenaline surged through my core, blossomed in my middle, and blasted into all the dark, depleted magical wells inside my skin. My life's force filled up and overflowed, a feeling that made me want to laugh manically. Even my skin felt healthier. My head fuller. My nails stronger.

The dripping stopped and I groped wildly for more, finding a smooth face and latching my palms on to the cheeks. I claimed the full, warm lips, which quickly moved against mine. Passion rose up between us. A moan welled in my throat. But as good as it felt, the taste of that delicious, lifesaving decadence was missing.

I pushed away. Sunlight danced in my eyes, but I

didn't have to squint. The most beautiful man, with gorgeous honey eyes, gazed down at me. His muscular arms held me on his lap as we sat in the middle of a bright green meadow. Wildflowers danced and played in the soft breeze, their movements like laughter. His hard, pulsing heat pushed against my butt.

Ten feet from where we huddled together, two bodies entwined as one, stood a cream-colored, regal animal. Light glowed from around it, and rainbows flickered when it moved.

"No fucking way." I blinked a million times it seemed like, laughing, or maybe crying, from joy as I beheld the most glorious animal that had ever walked the Brink or the Realm. "Am I tripping on acid?"

"In a way."

Oh man, that voice was sexy. Perfectly tuned for my listening pleasure.

Speaking of pleasure…

I leaned my head back as kisses trailed down my neck, making me shiver. When Darius sucked in the sensitive skin on my neck, I twisted so I could wrap my legs around his middle. His hardness was now right where I needed it. If it weren't for these danged clothes, he could enter me. Over and over.

"Taste me," I groaned as a fang trailed along my artery. "Take me, Darius."

His fingers snaked through my hair and he made a

fist, clutching tightly. His other hand hardened at the base of my neck, trapping me in his hold. A surge of desperation overcame me—a need so strong that I was panting with desire.

"Yes," I cried, gyrating against him. "Yes. Harder."

He shook me a little, proving his dominance. Ready to claim what was his. In contrast, his lips glided softly across my fevered skin, leaving a trail of scorching wetness.

This seemed so right in the presence of that great animal. Mating. Bonding. Celebrating life.

What the hell?

Shock, fear, and—most importantly—reality bitch-slapped me.

Have I gone fucking crazy?

I tried to struggle away, but Darius wouldn't release his hold. The dull, delicious ache of fangs pressed on my skin, ready to puncture. "Don't you fucking dare, Darius!"

I slapped my hands to the sides of his face and dug my thumbs into his eyes. His grip loosened. He flinched away. I used the space to my advantage by hooking my arms under his and ripping them upward, flinging his hands off. I hopped up and wobbled across the meadow, patting my body to make sure my weapons were in place. Once I was far enough away, I turned back and prepared to physically fight the man while I mentally fought his effect on me.

Darius rose slowly, the bulge in his pants prominent and a little smile tickling his lips. "My, my. What layers you have, my lovely Reagan. So much passion. So much fire. Come. Let me taste you."

The shiver racing across my body turned into a heebie-jeebies dance. "Stop it. Did you feed me blood? Or what was it, and when does this acid trip wear off? Because I'm seeing things."

Those delicious eyes glimmered with sex and mischief. My core pounded so hard that I wondered if it would dislodge from my body and skitter across the field.

"I am quite aroused, Reagan. Vampires my age usually only feel this way when we are feeding, and we only feed once in a great while. I should've been sated for months. But instead, I am harder than I can remember being. I want to be inside you, Reagan, while tasting the sweet nectar of your veins."

"Awesome. Great info. Thanks for sharing." I swatted at my arms to stop the tingles. Then squeezed my nether region for the same reason.

He walked toward me slowly—prowling, almost. Graceful and beautiful, his body was like a dance. An erotic, sexy—

I dug my thumbs into the corners of my eyes and backed up. "Make this stop. Please."

"Whatever for? You were enjoying it as much as I was."

"Look, dude, I will literally take out my gun and shoot you in the heart right now. Okay? I'm saying no. No means I'll kill you if you don't stop stalking me like a feral cat trying to make kittens. Back off." I rubbed my eyes and blinked them open.

A smile drifted up his face, but he halted. "As you wish, *ma biche*—"

"Is that derogatory?"

"—but I will think on that moment for decades to come."

"You need to get out more. Seriously. It wasn't that hot."

"You know that it was. I can still smell your desire."

"Gross." I put my hand up to stop the insanity. "What happened?"

"I felt you gyrating against my—"

"Not that part! After I blacked out, I mean."

His smile brightened. "Come back to me, Reagan. Let me taste you, as you commanded."

I ripped out my gun. "Really? That the road you want to take?"

"I want to slide my—"

I pulled the trigger. A slug dug into his leg.

Shock covered his features and he faltered before regaining balance on his good leg. He did not call out.

There was no sign of pain in his expression. Instead, his sparkling sexual heat dimmed. His features smoothed out, arrogance and disinterest taking over.

I ignored the twinge of regret. Ignored it, and vowed to knife it out of myself if I had to.

He nodded once. It almost seemed like a thank-you.

Mental note: green light for shooting Darius in the leg to prevent sexy times and possibly fall under his enchanting vampire spell.

"You lost consciousness when your blade split in two," he said, back to business. "Luckily, you had just made it through the last of the spell. I rushed you in here to see if I could get help. The mistress of the island, this great beast, took your measure, and found you worthy. She lowered to give you her life's blood so that you could heal." Darius regarded me warily now. "It had an immediate effect on you, and you had a…strange effect on me. I apologize. I lost control."

"You're a vampire and therefore bloodthirsty. Don't stress. Shooting you was strangely gratifying."

"I am an elder, and therefore *not* bloodthirsty. The unicorn blood enhances your allure. You call to me, more so than before. It is…unnerving."

I waved my hand in the air, trying to wipe away the crazy. "You have issues, I get it. But—*What?*" I rubbed my eyes, blinked, and stared at the regal animal. It had pranced backward when I shot away from Darius's warm, hard… "Dang it. *Stop.*"

"What?" Darius asked.

"Nothing." I stared at the animal, a larger version of a Brink horse with shining cream…fur, almost. Silky-smooth fur, like velvet. The twinkle of rainbow when the animal moved had diminished, but it still seemed to shine in an ethereal way. On its head, like all the myths throughout time, protruded a vicious-looking horn with a point.

"This isn't real," I said, staring up at the clear, golden-orange Realm sky. No sun shone down on us, but the light was bright enough that Darius should be a smoldering wreck. "How are you even alive? This has to be some sort of hallucination."

Darius bowed to the animal, received a horse nod in return, and waited while the animal regarded me.

"It is not my place to teach you civility, but the mistress saved your life. A *thank you* wouldn't go amiss." Darius waited for me patiently.

I kicked the ground and left a divot. I pinched my skin and felt the pain.

I regarded the animal again, which was looking at me with shining black eyes. It neighed, so much like a horse that the two must be related, the only thing separating them being magic, size, and a horn.

"If it gave me blood, where's the wound?" I crossed my arms, having made my last effort to prove this was all in my head.

The horse stamped its foot before turning. A small drip of red graced its neck, coming from a tiny wound.

"Lucy, you have some 'splaining to do," I muttered to Darius before I blew out a breath. I spoke to the horse. "I assume you can understand me, since you just turned, so…thank you. Really. You did save my life. I wouldn't have been able to come back from that. I'd depleted my power too much."

The great animal neighed, and small flashes of rainbows surrounded it. It bowed, that fierce point leveled toward me, and suddenly I felt a little faint. Something told me the animal had an extreme vicious side, and that it would use its glorious horn in battle to gouge its opponents. Considering its great size and—I imagined—incredible strength, that would be a mighty warhorse. Not to mention an intelligent one. With delicious and helpful blood.

"Does it let people ride on its back?" I couldn't help but wonder.

The unicorn puffed out breath and turned, prancing away in all its majestic glory.

"Don't be ridiculous. Would you ask that of a minotaur?" Darius scoffed.

"Um, *yes*. Why, do they have a thing against giving people rides?"

Darius stared at me. Clearly that was a yes. Also,

probably silent name-calling.

"Can we talk about this for a second?" I sat down and hunched over my knees. "Was that really a unicorn? A unicorn! The fabled animal that has always existed in myth."

"As you saw, yes, though they call themselves something different. Don't ask what it is. They alone choose to whom they will reveal their true name. It bestows a sense of power and sight on any graced with the good fortune."

"Let me guess, you've been graced."

"No. Only Vlad that I know of."

"Ah. Fine. So why isn't it common knowledge that they're real?"

"This is the secret Vlad spoke of. This is the knowledge you must protect with your life, and we will need to change the contract to reflect that. You are now tied to them, and through them, to us. Should you ever attempt to reveal this knowledge—"

"Yes, yes, death by pleasure. I know." I shook my head, because who could think of contracts at a time like this? "But…*how* have you possibly kept this secret? Unicorns, man! *Unicorns.*" I shook my head again. "I'm blown away. I am simply blown away."

"Given that there are thousands of myths about them, Brink-wide, the secret isn't wholly kept."

"But everyone thinks they aren't real."

"They also think vampires aren't real."

"The Brink does, but the Realm knows better."

"Yes, true." Darius gave me a slight bow. "When a vampire vows to protect something, he does it with everything he has. We have made such a vow to these animals. As of right now, our oath is being called into question. Someone has not only broken into this land on multiple occasions, but has imprisoned one of these creatures and bled her dry. That is unacceptable. Vlad has assigned me to find this person, and great honor will come to me if I succeed. Given that the mistress herself just saved your life, hopefully our objective is as important to you as it is to me."

"Even if it isn't, very few people could've gotten through that spell like I did. Our mark will be coming for me." I dropped my head to my hands. "Quite the pickle you've gotten yourself into, Reagan. Forming a line of people who want to bring you down."

"Who else wishes you harm?" A strange ruthlessness filled his voice. It almost sounded possessive.

I shrugged it off. "Doesn't matter. Okay, time for a quick question-and-answer segment. First, why are you still alive in the sunlight? I thought that was a no-no."

"I am in no danger. It is not real sunlight, merely magic. Unicorns are our exact opposites; they thrive in the glow of sunshine, and their spirit and power diminishes in the dark. We have altered our territory in the

Realm to continually stay in darkness, so that they may stay in constant magical light. For that, they have deigned us worthy. Our loyalty to them, and our vigilance to make sure they are kept secret and protected, has created a partnership. They allow us a certain amount of blood to make a special brew. This brew is integral to our future."

"You're talking about the turning potion used to create new vampires." His look turned flat. "Come on. Everyone knows you guys use one. That's not secret."

"The ingredients are."

"Clearly. Fine. But why are they excited about being trapped on this island? Why don't they want other magical creatures to know they exist?"

"Do you recall how it felt to ingest their blood?"

A surge of joy filled my body. The craving to run after the beast and latch on to the wound in its neck took hold of me. I turned away and shut my eyes, fighting the desire that had come out of nowhere.

"The closest thing to that feeling is the Brink drug heroin," Darius said in a cool tone, striding toward me. "But that craving doesn't come close to the residual desire for unicorn blood. Magic has great perks, but with it comes great pitfalls." His hand landed on my upper back and slowly ran down my spine. Tingles erupted, but I didn't shrug him off. The craving for unicorn blood slowly subsided. "Our blood counteracts the desire. I thought our blood and theirs would be sold as a pair, but when I apprehended that mage the other night, only unicorn blood was in his possession."

"You're saying that vampires have loose lips somewhere, but they might not be in on it."

"It is too early to tell."

"But you could be, essentially, hunting one of your own."

"Yes."

"Well, if we are, let's hope they aren't as old and fast as you, huh?" I stepped away from him. "I don't want any of your blood."

Hunger flashed in his eyes. "Let's wait and see." The next moment, confusion bled through his expression. He minutely shook his head. "I apologize for how that sounded. I meant, if you need more of their blood, you might need something to reduce the craving."

"Nice save. How's the leg?"

"The bullet has worked its way out."

"Happy, happy." I redid my ponytail. "So if knowledge of unicorns was widespread, they'd probably be hunted and destroyed in a mad panic to consume them. Do the elves know about them?"

"The royal cabinet do. They are happy with this arrangement."

"Of course they are. They don't want a bunch of magical people running amok, trying to get high. That would be the easiest way for them to lose control." I took a last look around the lovely meadow. "Let's get to work."

He nodded and led us to the right.

"Did you leave your trap or whatever you'd planned?" I asked as we stepped into the trees. Another of those majestic animals, though not as big, stood off to the side, watching us. All I could see was that horn, though. It looked gilded and lethal, over a foot long, and with a dullish point that you'd surely feel as it rammed through your middle.

Not like you'd miss many things, dull or otherwise, that rammed through your middle.

"I decided saving your life was top priority," he said in a matter-of-fact sort of way.

"Thanks," I muttered, a little embarrassed. This was unfamiliar territory.

A soft rustling caught my attention as we wandered through a patch of dense trees. A colt—or whatever unicorns called their young—peeked its head through a leafy bush, its horn nothing more than a tiny nub. As I walked, it wobbled out, its legs shaky.

"Holy smokes, stop the presses." I halted and felt a silly smile crawl across my face. At half my height, it was not little by any means, but the critter still seemed brand new. "Look how *cute*!"

Before I knew what I was doing, I had walked toward it with my hand out. “Hello!”

It wobbled toward me, its legs bending awkwardly and threatening to give out.

“No! Don’t!” Darius shouted.

Before his blur of movement could intercept, the colt’s nose rubbed against my palm and then fell toward my body. I wrapped my arms around its neck and laughed with glee. The memory of the blood wasn’t controlling me, though—I was just enjoying some cuddle time with a seriously cute animal.

“How adorable is this?” I laughed again and backed off. “But where is your mama, little baby?”

“You should be dead. It is forbidden to touch their young.” Darius stalked toward the bush. He paused for a moment, and then said, “Come here, Reagan.”

The way he said it, deep and vicious, raised the small hairs on the back of my neck. I gently pushed the baby, who was trying to nuzzle my stomach, and joined him. As I peered over the hedge, a blast of anger rose up through me.

A unicorn stood in mid-stride, frozen in space. The residual items of birth trailed along the ground from the animal’s glistening backside. It looked as though it had birthed its baby, walked a few feet, and then gotten snared in a spell.

“And now we know how the unicorn was bled dry,” I said, reaching for my sword. My hand grasped emptiness. "Crap."

"Can you break the magic without your sword?"

Not without revealing what I was. "Keep that little baby away."

"We are forbidden to touch them."

"I might not be able to get Mama free. How many do you want to lose to this magical trap, one or two?"

I barely heard his soft growl of annoyance before he took up space between the colt and me. "Get away, small creature. Do not touch me."

"That's…one way to do it." I closed my eyes, once again feeling the vibrations of the magical currents. They didn't reach out for my touch, and certainly didn't swirl around my fingers. Instead, they kind of buzzed right where they were.

I stepped back and looked at the sky. "It seems like a simple enough freezing spell. I've seen these used on people, though with much less power. The thing is…" I cranked my neck, wishing I had my sword. "The way it was done, I am positive this is the same guy who cast the other spell. It has less power, though. Significantly."

"Did he not mask the power of the other?"

"He wasn't masking the power so much as the type of spell. It was harder to break through than I was expecting." I analyzed it further, wanting to be as sure as I could. "He clearly laid this spell like a snare, waiting for something to walk into it. But I have no way of seeing if there's a defensive situation disguised in it."

"There isn't. No, little creature, I am not to be touched! Begone, silly thing." He flinched away from its seeking nose. It stomped the ground with its foot, then wobbled toward him. He contorted his body so its seeking nose couldn't touch his hip, then his waist. He looked like he was playing Twister standing upright. Finally, he sighed in exasperation when it nuzzled his stomach, and then dropped his hands to his sides, relenting. "Any defense woven into a freezing spell would result in the trapped victim dying. If she died, her blood would quickly turn black and unusable, like ours does. Can you get her out? I have something that might help, but if he used even a fraction of the power he used in his other trap, my spell won't be enough."

I waggled my fingers in the air and bit my lip, thinking. In short, yes, I could. And I should, because this was a life-for-a-life situation. Without a powerful mage or me, this unicorn, and probably the little baby that needed its mother's milk, was as good as dead.

I owed them this. The problem was that I might end up giving my life as payment for their help.

CHAPTER 10

"WHAT'S THIS HELP you have?" I asked with a sigh.

He pulled back the flap on his satchel and peered inside. Instead of digging around like I would've, he reached in and plucked out the item. He stepped through the bush, followed by the colt, and handed over a small, light green orb.

"Keep that colt away from the spell," I hollered with a shock of fear.

He shepherded the creature away.

"Okay, then," I said, holding the spell between my finger and thumb to analyze it. "Very disco. Why is it green?"

"We have our mages color-code the spells so we can easily identify their properties."

"Organized." I didn't need that, of course. I could *feel* the spell's properties. Also, I rarely had the luxury of too many spells in my possession. Still, I loved the idea. "Can you get some with sparkles?"

He leveled me with a glare. *No, then?*

"Not a big push of power in here." I rolled it behind my fingers as I eyed the spell. There was nothing for it—without the sword to act as a medium for my power, I'd have to apply it directly. I would basically be handing Darius the key to figuring me out.

The unicorns were putting me in a tight spot.

"Look, Darius, I'm going to need you to look away."

"No."

"I'm not asking. If you want my help, then you need to let me do this. I can't work with your eyeballs scratching at the back of my head."

"If you succumb to the magic—"

"That'll be immediate without a sword. I'm about to wrestle directly with it, spell to spell. If I lose, there is no coming back. So…off you get."

He took a deep breath, staring at me. It was a reaction I hadn't seen yet. I had no idea what it meant.

Slowly, he shook his head before eyeing the unicorn. "Okay."

"Lovely. Go play in the meadow with little Max."

"This is a female."

"Little Lucy, then."

I studied the spell around the unicorn and pinched the casing between my pointer finger and thumb. "Do I throw this, or gently let it go about its business?" I called.

"Use it like a normal spell casing."

Impossible. This one actually had a spell in it.

After a glance behind me to make sure he wasn't in eyesight, I dropped the casing into my pouch and rubbed my hands together. Time for real magic.

Palm aimed toward the unicorn, I swept my hand through the air. Fire sprang up, outlining the spell. I stepped back and created a thin wall of fire in front of me in case something went wrong and the spell exploded.

Focusing now, I felt the spell with my fire, managing the heat and intensity until it was happily eating away the magic like fuel. Not sensing any changes in the spell's properties, I amped up the flame, burning away the magic.

"It is working?" Darius asked.

I jumped and ripped the wall of fire away. A glance behind said Darius had kept his word—so far, anyway—and wasn't peeking through the hedge.

I let out a haggard breath and clutched at my rampaging heart.

"Yes, it's really helping. Thanks." After another glance behind, I quickly threw up a veil of fire and refocused on my task at hand.

I pushed the fire down toward the ground, where the spell wasn't properly rooted, eating away the fringe. The air around the unicorn pulsed with color and light, making me smile, before it changed. Like a piece of paper consumed by flame, the spell oxidized before blackening and flaking away. The last traces of it sputtered before losing the fight and unraveling. Cold air gushed outward, ruffling the leaves and smacking harmlessly into my wall of fire.

I ripped the fire away, letting it shrink to nothing in midair. Heat pulsed through me, a glorious feeling. I wished I could use my true magic all the time.

The unicorn neighed, loudly, and stamped its foot. It swung that vicious-looking horn my way.

"Holy crap!" I bent, then dodged a hoof striking out. "You snapped out of that way faster than a human would." It bit down at me, missed, and swung its head again. That brutal horn sliced the air right next to my face.

"Darius! Help! Darius!" I ducked away, but nearly caught a hoof in the chest. I dove and rolled, not sure what to do. I couldn't very well fight the thing—if I did it harm, a whole faction of old vamps would come for me.

"I saved you," I yelled, throwing my hands out. "I'm a good guy."

It reared, clearly having no desire for discussion.

I threw myself back as Darius popped up by my side.

"What the hell took you so long?" I demanded, feinting like a boxer.

"I am here," he said, putting a hand up. It took me a moment to realize he wasn't talking to me. "I am here. Calm now. Your *solino* is safe. I brought Reagan to help you."

Lucy wobbled through the brush, already much sturdier on her new legs. She gave a soft neigh and ambled toward food.

"This doesn't look like it happened long ago," Darius said quickly, putting a hand to my shoulder and backing us up. "We caught it early. That was lucky. Let's leave now before she smells our scent on her newborn."

When we crossed the meadow without being chased down, I asked, "Why didn't the colt—or *solino*, I guess—run into the spell with her?"

"Size, probably, wouldn't you think? A snare is only so big."

I nodded, because yes, it did make sense—and I should've known that. Fatigue was dragging at me. Despite the pick-me-up of unicorn blood, using so much power in so short a time, not to mention sleep deprivation and hunger, had drained me. I felt weak and shaky.

I barely made it to the other side of the small island, which only took an hour's walk. Despite my current issues, though, it wasn't a big place for animals that size. I said as much to Darius.

"The Island of Eternal Light stretches north to

south, mostly. It is not overly wide." Darius nodded at a fierce-looking vampire, the first living sentinel we'd seen. "We found a magical snare and rendered it useless. Get a team and patrol the island. If you find anything, send word."

The vampire nodded but didn't head out. Apparently he'd get to it when he was good and ready.

Darius directed me back the way we'd come. "There is nothing more to see here at present. We'll continue on to the Brink and start collecting more information."

"Are you serious?" I trudged alongside him.

"What is the matter?"

"You must think humans are really clumsy if my stiff-legged lurch rings *normal.*"

"You're tired?"

"So tired I can't think of a sarcastic response to that question." My toe hit a rock, and I stumbled. Darius's hand shot out, steadying me before I fell on my face. "Thanks. Are you going to send in a replacement for that sentinel?"

"No. To use that entrance, the mage would have to go through land the elves closely watch. Only a fool would try to get by them."

"Why, what will the elves do?"

"Question them. I will carry you."

"So...only fools would get themselves into positions where they would have to provide answers?"

He bent and scooped me up into his arms. I didn't complain, because if I did, chances were he'd throw me over his shoulder. "Have you spent so little time in the Realm?"

"Very little time. Almost none, actually."

He put on a burst of speed that made me clutch his shoulders and nearly squeal in delight. Thrilling, running so fast. I wished I could do it.

"Elves are not a species to trifle with, even for us. They are brutal, when they want to be. Extremely powerful. It is never wise to put yourself in their path."

"They rule the Realm, though. If they are oppressive, why don't people rise up?"

"How often do people in the Brink rise up?" He ducked under a branch and swerved around a group of unicorns munching grass. "When you are on the correct side, the elves are fair, usually."

"Which side is the correct side?"

"The one that bows to them."

"Which side are you on?" I could already guess the answer.

He slowed as we reached the other side in record time. Gently, he put me down and waited until I was steady before stepping away. "Vlad's."

"My guess is, Vlad doesn't bow."

"Of course he does, as do we all—when we have to. That is why we still exist. But we won't bow forever. The elves want to rid this Realm of the temptation of the unicorns, and, with them, us. They have not acted yet, but they will. When they do, we will be ready." He looked down at the visible boot. He'd left the bait, his own kind, to save me. "Can you tell if she lives?"

"Well…I don't know about *lives,* since she's a vampire, but…" I grimaced at his straight face. Not the time for that sort of joke. "The short answer is…maybe."

I wiped the back of my hand across my forehead and walked closer to the boot. Immediately, I could tell that it was a form of the freezing spell the mage had used on the unicorn, but with a burning type of twist, making it more powerful. I had this mage's number now. After saying as much to Darius, I added, "If she's alive, she won't be for long. I'd wager her skin was blackening like yours did after you touched the first spell. The mage froze her before she died."

"This mage knows us well." Darius looked into his satchel.

"If he's partnering with a vampire, then of course he does."

"There is a difference between being told our traits, even seeing them, and knowing how to work a spell to freeze us at the exact right moment. He must know that it is taking everything in my power not to try and rip into that spell to see if she still lives."

"I wouldn't advise that."

"My point exactly. This is the perfect bait, as you said. He is dangerous, this mage."

"Okay. Let's find him, then."

Darius nodded and motioned at the path where the barely lingering residual magic was the only thing left of the barrier spell I'd taken down. "Wait there."

I really didn't want to.

Like a sulky teenager, I trudged onto the path of death where that overanxious serpent was probably still waiting for me to dip a toe in the water. I sat in the very middle with shifty eyes, half terrified the thing would catapult out and attach its face to mine. I didn't have the energy to fight it off.

Muttering caught my attention, and I looked Darius's way in time to catch him cracking open the final capsule in his cocktail. The spell sifted down onto the ones he'd already opened and crystalized, partially blocking the way. The other vampire probably knew how Darius worked, and would know how to edge around the area.

"Will the trap do anything besides getting to know the mage's magic, which I already have a pretty good handle on?" I asked, rising.

"I altered my plans for this spell, given your extraordinary senses." I half preened at the compliment. He didn't give them out often. Not without a slap in the face to accompany them. "The goal of this mix of spells is to attach a piece of tracking magic to the mage." Darius picked me up again. Without warning, he started running. I did squeal this time, with a huge smile on my face.

"How do you hope to—"

"I am right here, Reagan. There is no need to shout."

"Sorry. With all the wind whipping by us, I didn't know if you'd hear. Anyway, how do you hope to attach it?"

"The spell is an intricate offensive one that should explode when another magic worker comes in contact with it."

"One of those, huh?"

"Intricate, I said. I created it from a lot of different spells, so it should take hardly a moment for someone of higher-caliber magic to disable it. He will laugh at me, surely. I am hoping his ego masks his ability to notice smaller details, like that tracker."

"If there is anyone who knows about egos, it's you." I laughed.

"Do humans find you humorous?"

We passed the first circular area. I could still see the disturbance of our tracks. That was a good sign. "Yes. Well, they don't laugh out loud, but I'm pretty sure they laugh inside."

A little over a minute later—by my rough timekeeping—we were passing the other circular area. "Wow. You really move. I'm starting to get a little jealous."

"We need to plan what is next," Darius said, ignoring me.

"Easy. Get those casings checked out and ask around about an extremely powerful mage. The latter should be easy. There is no way that much power has gone unnoticed."

"I can arrange a meeting with my most trusted contact."

"No." I shook my head as we neared the Dungeon. "If he hasn't told you anything by now, he either doesn't know or is holding back—believe that. No, you hired me for a reason. This is what I specialize in. I can think of a dozen people to shake information out of. But first I need sleep."

"You will sleep in my chambers while I attend to some business."

I sure hoped that bed was as comfortable as it looked.

CHAPTER 11

"DID YOU LEAVE your house in this state?" Darius asked from beside me as we stood on the sidewalk in front of my home.

My brow furrowed as I stared at my front door. It had been ripped off the frame, and leaned against the chairs on my front porch. The screen lay in my yard among the weeds, the metal framing twisted.

"Yes, I left my house with my front door torn off," I said dryly. "Why, isn't that normal?" I rubbed my eyes and sighed, because up until that point, I'd been nice and relaxed. My nap in the most comfortable bed ever made had been refreshing, and while the protein bar I'd dug out of my pouch wasn't the stuff of dreams, it had taken the edge off my hunger. Darius had even carried me back to the Brink gate because he was in a hurry. This was not the welcome home I had hoped for.

This had been the first stop because I'd insisted on getting ammunition and changing, and thought I'd check Big C's computer. Given Big C's boost of magic and being in the mage community at all, I couldn't help but wonder about his possible connection with the mage we were chasing. Maybe the computer would have something of use. I hadn't checked all the files when I'd looked on it earlier.

Something occurred to me. "Did you question that mark of mine you stole? He was selling blood, right? Did he tell you where he got it?"

Darius's shift was small but relayed his annoyance. "He was still unconscious from your efforts. We did not realize until it was too late that he didn't have enough magic to cross into the Realm."

"So you killed him."

He shot me a glare. "It could not be helped."

"You don't have to tell me." I threw up my hands. "I get it. Accidental death is a real bummer in my trade."

In the distance, thunder rolled, promising showers. Cloud cover hid the moon, forcing the streetlights to work harder. Judging by the lack of people wandering around, I estimated that it was late in the night. I had no clue what day it was or how much time I'd spent in the Realm.

Black loomed within the doorway of my house. There was no telling if the person—or people—were still inside.

I inhaled and wondered which of my two recent enemies had paid a visit: the friends of that crazy mage, looking for his spells or vengeance, or the vampire who'd bonded him, looking for plain vengeance.

"I wouldn't go in there if I were you." Mince wandered over, cutting through my reverie. He nodded at Darius. "Hey, man."

Darius stared at the newcomer, not returning the salutation.

Mince gestured toward the house, a half-eaten apple in his hand. "A few guys busted in there a while ago. I bet they're still in there somewhere."

"Did you call the police?"

"Do I look stupid to you? If I called the police, people would think I was a snitch. I ain't no snitch."

"How would people know you called the police if you made an anonymous call?"

"Anonymous call..." He made a face like that was the biggest farce he'd ever heard. He took a bite of his apple.

"Can you at least give me a little information instead of standing there like you're waiting for a show to start? What'd they look like? For example, were any of them graceful and good looking? Like...too good looking..." That drew Darius's attention. I was careful not to look at him.

Mince thought for a moment. "Two of 'em were smaller types. Useless. I'd take them down in a second. One was a bigger dude. Kind of fat, but you could tell by the way he walked that he could take care of himself.

That's the one I would look out for."

"But were they good looking?" I asked.

"How would I know if they was good looking?" The crunch of his apple competed with a distant train whistle blowing.

"Were they carrying anything? Help me out, Mince. I want to know what I'm dealing with."

"Well, if you keep standing here, they'll be out to deal with you soon enough." Mince shifted. "The smaller ones had bags. The cross-body kind. Kinda big, too. I remember wondering what they had inside. Kind of ratty, those bags. Their clothes were pretty nice. They looked like their wallets would be worth grabbing."

"Not rich, though. Not like him." I hooked a thumb toward Darius.

"Oh no. No way."

They were most certainly mages, then. Mages who clearly thought I wasn't a threat. I'd taken out their friend on his home turf, so they'd decided breaking and entering my house was a good idea.

Clearly I wasn't dealing with the brightest bulbs in the ceiling.

I felt the emptiness where my sword should be. I could take them down quick-like with my magic, but I'd risked revealing myself to Darius once already, I couldn't hope to get away with it again.

I glanced down at his satchel, stuffed with all the

spells I could want. Spells that were color coded and marked, of all things. The only thing in my house that Mr. Money Bags couldn't provide was that computer, and frankly, there were other ways to get information. Risking my life, or worse, my freedom, wasn't worth an untested short cut.

"Right, then." I rubbed my hands together. "Let's leave them to it."

"You aren't going to go in there?" Darius asked in disbelief.

"I wouldn't." Mince took another bite of his apple. "Seems like they should've noticed you standing out here, though. Maybe they went out the back."

"They probably did notice us," I said. "But I'm with him." I indicated Darius. "They have to know what he is. And they'll know that you're a human. I mean, you know, a law-abiding citizen." I nodded at Mince. "They aren't coming out here to force the issue. No, if they noticed us, then they're probably waiting in there, in the shadows or behind something, staring out at us."

"Oh shit…" Mince gave a little hop, like a cartoon turkey vulture, and started sidestepping down the sidewalk. "I'm not trying to get messed up in that. Have a good night."

"He is a coward," Darius said, staring at the darkened doorway.

"No he's not, he's smart. He doesn't want to get involved. Neither do I. Let's follow his lead."

"You cannot leave strangers in your home."

"I don't have proof they're even in there."

"Someone is in there. I saw movement not long ago."

"Well then, I hope they enjoy my horrible couches. C'mon. You can buy me breakfast."

"Reagan, we can't—"

"Look," I said in a loud voice. "I know who they are, and I know what they want. They can keep looking, for all I care. They won't find it. If they're smart, they'll bugger off. Otherwise, I'll meet them soon enough, and they'll go out the same way their friend did."

I stared into the gaping door and then shifted my gaze to the windows, hoping it looked like I was looking at someone, before turning and stalking off. Darius stayed where he was for a moment. He didn't switch his gaze from the doorway, which told me that he saw something I didn't, like a hiding mage. After a moment, he followed me, catching up immediately.

A moment of silence passed between us.

"Do you plan to tell me who that was, and what they are after?" Darius finally asked.

"You know that mage I accidentally killed? Well, I took some of his spells, and his cronies want them. Or else those guys were his friends. I really have no way of knowing. This is all hearsay from a nosy neighbor. Do you have a working watch, or some other way of knowing how long we have until you need to scurry into cover?"

"I don't scurry."

"So you say…"

"I don't need a watch to know when dawn is coming. I can sense it. We have four hours, and then we will stay at my residence in the French Quarter. You're sure you want to leave those men in your house? I can easily remove them for you."

"If they are who I think they are, there would be no *easily*. They probably have spells at the ready. Spells you wouldn't be able to outrun. While they might even be good to question, without my sword, things would be very dicey. I need an arsenal or a new sword before I deal with people like them. We should get some breakfast and regroup—decide the next step."

"We don't have time for breakfast. Your longer-than-usual sleep has delayed our plans."

"Longer than usual?" I narrowed my eyes at him. Rather than reply, he pulled a phone out of his pocket and typed a few words into a text message screen. "Tell me you haven't been standing outside my windows and watching me sleep. Because that's creepy, and I don't hang out with stalkers."

"You are not human, therefore you shouldn't have to sleep as long as a human does. That you did sets us severely behind."

"That does sound logical, but you should've asked to make sure. Your bad." A black Lincoln Town Car turned slowly around the corner up ahead. The streetlights shone in the rolled-up windows as it crept toward us, an urban shark. "That doesn't look good. That car is a little too nice for a drive-by in these parts, but it could still happen." I grabbed his arm, ready to pull him away.

"It is my man. He will take us to our next destination."

"Oh." I relaxed. I probably should've figured that. "What is our next destination if it isn't breakfast? I need some food."

The car stopped by the curb, allowing a dilapidated truck to get around him. Darius stepped forward and opened the rear passenger door. He stood to the side and held out his hand, ready to help me in. I let him before scooting across the bench seat so he could slide in after me. Instead, he closed the door.

I scooted back and noticed the dark, piercing gaze in the rearview mirror. While vampires didn't show up in cameras or video, for some reason, they did have a reflection in mirrors and water and what not. It was one of those unexplained things I had never bothered to dwell on.

"Hi," I said.

The eyes were trained on me for a moment longer

before drifting down to the road in front of him. Another vampire, this one not much younger than Darius.

"Do you always travel with mid-level and upper-mid-level vampires?" I asked Darius once he'd settled into the car.

He closed the door. "Of course, unless I have a new child. And only then when I am teaching or checking on her."

Creating a child, for vampires, meant giving their blood to finish the transformation from human to vampire. It made the newbie "theirs."

"Her? Never him?"

"In the last couple hundred years I have found that human males of a certain wealth and influence greatly rebuke any change they are not accustomed to. Any hardship causes them to whine and moan. It is most vexing."

"I assume the females also come from backgrounds of wealth and prestige so you can take their fortune. Are they any different?"

"They are usually beautiful, use their beauty to secure a powerful man, and usually allow said man to dictate their lives. Within reason, of course. In general, I find guiding female children much easier, with a higher rate of success."

"They can control themselves better."

"Generally, yes." He entwined his fingers on his lap, the visual of patience. "Do you need more of an arsenal?"

"I have to commission another sword. We need to put the order in pronto. I need bullets, as well. I'd hoped to stock up at my house. Like I said, food would be nice. You'll have to lend me money, obviously, since you took the mark that would ensure I could keep eating."

He didn't respond to my dig.

We spent the next handful of minutes navigating the streets of New Orleans, heading over to the Garden District for God knew what. I asked Darius a few times, but the car remained silent. Which was particularly aggravating, since we really should've been heading to place the sword order.

Finally, we pulled up at a gorgeous mansion with a huge front of manicured lawns and lovely flowers. A tire swing dangled from a branch, drifting back and forth lazily. I wished I could've been there in the daylight to see the marvel that was the gardens.

"Come," Darius said as he exited the car. The driver did as well, his dark gaze flicking to me before he climbed out of his seat.

I reached for the handle and met empty space. My door had already swung open. Darius stood beside it, reaching down to help me out.

"Wow. I feel like a princess." I took his hand, warm

despite the myth that vampires always ran around with the temperature of iceboxes. He gave me a slight bow as he helped me stand before closing the door.

"This way," he said, directing me to the front door.

"Are you going to tell me what this is about?"

"No. Stop asking. It is extremely annoying."

"You act in such a gentlemanly way, but you say such dickish things. How do you manage the dichotomy?"

"With aplomb." He paused as his man knocked on the door.

The door opened, spilling light across the wooden porch and up the leg of a rocking chair that sat empty and to the side. An older man with padding around the middle peered out through the screen. Seeing who awaited him, he beamed, his smile crinkling his face.

"Well, hello," he said, opening the door. "Hello, hello. Good to see you, good to see you. I'm so glad you could stop by. Please. Come in, come in!" He pushed at the screen door, opening it a crack.

Darius's man grabbed it and pulled it wide, allowing us to enter.

As I stepped closer to the older man, I could feel the residual magic pulsing from him. Its vibration calmed me, relaxing my muscles and putting me at ease. It was almost like a homey feeling in chemical form.

I let my hand drift to my gun and stepped aside

quickly, giving myself space. I didn't know why he was making a spell equivalent of Xanax, but I didn't want to get blasted with it and then have to fight.

"Mr. Durant, so good to see you." The man ushered Darius into a grand foyer with marble for days and lovely green plants on stands that looked like columns. In contrast, he wore shabby pants covered in burned holes and colored splotches. His T-shirt had a hole at the bottom, also appeared to have been burned, and there were more stains on it than there was white. "Mr. LaRay. Hello."

Mr. LaRay, our driver, didn't acknowledge the salutation, and stood just inside of the doorway with his hands clasped in front of him.

"Yes." The older man turned his gaze on me. His eyes crinkled in the corners with his continual mirth. "And you must be Ms. Somerset. Such a pleasure."

I glanced at Darius and got a minimal nod. He must've alerted this man that I was coming.

"This is Mr. Banks," Darius said. "He will be assisting you this evening."

"Assisting me?" I got another nod, but no further explanation. What else was new?

With a half-confused frown, I offered the man a smile and a "Hello." I didn't offer my hand. I'd learned the hard way that one should never touch a mage who recently performed magic. You never knew what cooties might suddenly explode across your skin. That had been an exciting lesson followed by a horrible rash.

The man's hand lingered in the air for a moment before he clapped. "Yes, yes. Come, come. I think I have just the thing."

He led the way back into the hollow of a finely put-together house with rooms galore and lots of areas to lounge. A big staircase curved away right, with a sweeping banister that Mary Poppins would ride down in style. The porch at the back was a large affair with a table and chairs sprawled around a closed-up umbrella. We crossed the deck and then a large section of plush grass.

I didn't realize, before that moment, that grass could be plush. I'd been in my fair share of parks, but this was the sort of gardening miracle that made me slow and wish for a sunny day.

"Can I come here without you?" I asked Darius.

"Do you know this mage?" he asked.

"No. But his house is fantastic, and it would be even better in the—"

"Oh I'd love to have you," the man interrupted as he trampled through a patch of flowers. I tried to pick my path much more carefully. "You would fit in here expertly, I can tell. Here we are."

We had arrived at a large wooden shed in the corner of the property that matched the man's clothing. He tugged on a rusted metal handle and pulled the squealing door open. Light washed over his face and body.

"Just in here, now." He hurried in.

"I'm not going in there," I said as a wave of magic rolled out.

Darius lightly touched my back and leaned in close, his version of a private conversation. "I have been in there many times, Reagan. I vow that you will come to no harm."

The driver, who had trailed behind us, took up residence near the door, apparently providing security.

I pushed Darius away. "I'm not someone you or your man need to protect, Darius. You opening doors and feeding me grapes and wine—yeah, I'm in. Trying to coddle me on my home turf? That'll get you punched. You do you. Let me do me. You go in if you want. I'm not."

He stared at me for a long moment. "I will go in," he said, "and bring it out."

"It?" But it was too late. Darius had already stalked into the shed that may or may not have been purchased from the Unabomber. The thing did not fit with the house at all.

I felt eyes boring into the side of my head. I swung my gaze toward the driver. "No one told you staring's rude, huh?" He continued his unwavering gaze with a straight face and body. "No compute?"

He ignored me. While still staring.

"Were you creepy before you became a vampire, or is this a recent development?" I asked.

"Oh no! Let me show her myself," I heard from the opened shed door. Mr. Banks hurried outside with a pained expression, trying to shrug off Darius's attempts at grabbing a long blade from him. "No. You couldn't understand what it is I have made. Don't touch it. She needs to be the first." He stopped in front of me and thrust forward a sword.

"Nope." I took a step back. "You can't expect me to take whatever you give me. You must know that."

Impatience covered his face. He shook the sword at me. "It is ready to pair. You must be the first to hold it."

"Besides you, obviously."

"Yes." He shook it. "Obviously."

"This is a replacement for the sword you lost," Darius said with wary eyes as he looked at the weapon.

I felt my confusion cross my face. "My sword took two weeks to make. When was this called in?"

"While you were sleeping," he replied.

"I loved that movie." I shook my head at the blade being offered me. "I've lost track of time, but I haven't lost track of *that* much time. The kind of sword I use couldn't possibly be ready this quickly."

Mr. Banks scoffed. "Ignorance." He shook the sword. "The fundamentals of the sword are easy. We have several on hand. It's the magical composition that requires finesse, and my missus is a master. She can create a spell to feel out the user's magic and mesh the two together. If the sword marries to you, it will only work for you, and it will work better than any sword prepared for you by the hacks you usually work with. If this one doesn't marry, we'll try another. Simple. She has loaded three swords, per Mr. Durant's instruction, but I have dozens ready."

Swallowing down my hesitation—he seemed legit, if excitable—I let my hand hover over the blade. The vibration was pleasant, but too warm. Too…sticky. It made me uncomfortable.

I shook my head and took my hand back. "No."

Mr. Banks scowled, annoyed, before confusion stole his expression. He analyzed me, looking over my face, my body, and the things I carried before shifting back to my eyes. There was a strange moment of gravity between us, like he recognized me. A smile drifted onto his face and excitement sparked in his gaze.

He stepped away. His eyes flicked at Darius before he minutely nodded. "Let me just get the missus. She is best suited for clients such as yourself, Ms. Somerset."

I watched him set down the sword, smash a few more flowers, half run across the grass, and go back into the house.

"What kind of dog and pony show is this?" I asked,

strangely nervous. Darius's uncharacteristic look of confusion told me I wasn't getting any answers from him. The driver, whose name I honestly couldn't remember even though it had been less than ten minutes since I'd heard it, was staring at the house where Mr. Banks had disappeared, his scowl a permanent fixture.

After an amount of time that had me shifting impatiently, and the vampires go unnaturally still, which probably wasn't good, an older woman came trundling out of the house. She had a stocky body, a hair net, a shiny sort of robe that must've been hard to find, since it was so odd, and fists at the end of her arms. Instead of crossing the grass like Mr. Banks seemed to favor, she took the path, with him trailing after her.

When she reached me, she wore a bulldog expression. "So. You don't trust me, huh?" She looked over my face.

"This is my wife, Callie," Mr. Banks said, pushing in close so he could get a good look at me too.

"No," I said flatly, answering her question and inching back. "Which you should be accustomed to."

"I'm not, actually." She sniffed, blinked at me a couple times, nodded as if she was agreeing with something, then walked toward the shed. Mr. Banks followed her.

"What is going on?" I mouthed to Darius, ready to

pack it in and take off. I'd never seen mages act so weird around me. They were usually comfortable in my presence because I understood magic but couldn't cast—they didn't think I was a threat. These two were studying me, like they knew a secret about me.

Considering the enemies I'd recently accrued in the mage world, and the things I'd done in Darius's presence, that didn't bode well.

"No, Dizzy, the red one," Callie shouted from inside the shed. She stalked out, rolling her eyes. "I hate being in that place. He loves chaos. It's how he thinks best. I can't *stand* it. I need order."

"So you stuck him in the shed out back?" I asked, taking a step in the direction of the house.

"*Which* red one?" Dizzy—clearly Mr. Banks's nickname—called out.

"The red hilt. Deep silver blade. The *red* one! You know which one. You spent a month on the thing."

"*Oh!* That's the silver one."

Callie scoffed and threw up her hands. "Suddenly he calls them by the color of their blades and not the hilts." Focused on me again, she said, "In answer to your question, absolutely not. Do you think I want this God-awful shed dragging down the look of the garden? No, honey. He has a wing dedicated to the sort of chaos he loves. He won't use it. Prefers this ramshackle disgrace for a workstation. Insisted it be nearly falling down, too."

"I think better in it," Dizzy said as he came out holding another sword. "The house is too walled in. I need nature."

His wife rolled her eyes again.

He held up a smaller sword with a red hilt, an expectant expression on his face.

I did the same thing as before, assessing the magic. This one was better, more pleasant, with a good killing edge, but it seemed…distant, somehow. Unimpressed.

"Magic with emotion," I murmured as I handed it back to her. "That's a new one for me."

The woman leaned in as a sparkle lit up her eyes. Her lips tweaked upward at the edges, threatening a smile. "Tell me, did you have a mother who practiced around here?"

Pain flicked at my heart, as it always did when someone mentioned my mother. Equally as common was the expression of longing that Callie wore. Everyone who'd known my mother loved her. They couldn't help it. She just had a *way* about her.

"Yes," I said. "She died five years ago. Did you know her?" I was terrible with names, but great with faces, and I hadn't seen this mage before. She might've known my mother before I was born, but I doubted she'd seen much of her since. We hadn't talked to many people, mostly just vendors or shop owners, and we hadn't invited friends over. She'd hidden me until I was old enough to hide myself, and twenty-four years was a long time to still miss someone you used to know. It made me nervous, like these mages did in general.

"A long time ago, yes. You look so similar, but even more beautiful, if that were possible. Except for the eyebrows, of course. Those are ghastly. I wish I could say I feel her in you, but I can't. You're much too powerful for that, aren't you? Did she know you could feel magic like you do?"

"Yes. She helped me hone it."

"Very rare, that trait," Callie said softly. "Very rare. Only a handful of mages in the world have that talent. You got it from your father, right?"

I bristled. She was right; it was a very rare trait. And yes, I did get it from my father. He wasn't a mage, though.

"I wouldn't know," I said calmly, despite my frantically beating heart. "I never knew him."

"Of course not." She looked like she was about to go on, but her eyes flicked to Darius again, and her mouth shut with the click of teeth.

Fear such as I'd never known washed over me. I glanced at the hilt of the sword she was holding, ready to take it up should she move to capture me, because I was almost positive this woman knew who my father was. Not the story my mom told strangers, but the *real* man. He'd been the love of her life until she realized that love wasn't real. That it was mostly magic. Magic, a handsome face, a delicious body, charm, and great sex. But as soon as my mother learned there was life in her, my father's draw on her dried up. The love of her child took over, and she kicked his ass to the curb.

She'd admitted all this to me on her deathbed, sexual ability and all. I'd had no idea how to take the news. Talk about awkward farewell speeches.

I'd vowed to achieve what my mother had died for—a long life of freedom. And it had been going fine, until these danged vampires had gotten involved.

"No wonder she was hiding you," Callie said, her eyes shining despite her bulldog expression. "Didn't want the Mages' Guild to get a hold of you."

I scoffed, watching her body language, and monitoring Dizzy to make sure he wasn't working on a spell. "Right. Like they have a pot to piss in."

She barked out a laugh. "They create more bad mages than good, I'll give you that. They can push their weight around when they see trainable talent, though."

"I'm not trainable."

"Of course you are." She scowled at me. "Curse breakers are headstrong, but they can still be taught."

CHAPTER 12

THE TENSION THAT had surrounded me like a bubble deflated. I relaxed. "I'm not a curse breaker. I don't even know what a curse breaker is. I think you're remembering the wrong person."

She made a sound like "pouf" and waved me away. "Dizzy, less magic. Almost none. Get the old sword."

"Which old sword?" He accepted the reject sword she handed back to him and then paused in the entryway of his shed.

"The *old* sword. The black one."

"*Which black one?*" he yelled.

"The one with silver in the hilt. The red hilt, with silver—"

"That's the *red* one!" He grunted and stalked into his shed.

"The man needs a better system. Trying to talk to him is a nightmare." Callie wiped a hand across her face. "I swear, I want to wring his neck. He gets me so worked up."

My grin was probably rude, but I couldn't get rid of

it. “Are you both mages, then?”

“You know we are. You can feel our magic, can’t you?”

“It’s polite to ask.”

She waved me away again as a sound like a metal avalanche filled the shed. Swear words rode the breeze, but finally Dizzy emerged. His shirt had three new rips, his arm had a line of red an inch long, and his leg was bleeding.

“He doesn’t have a ladder in there,” Callie said, crossing her arms over her chest. “He piles the swords on a shelf, so when he tries to get one down, he drops them all on his head. Men. They never learn.”

“How often do I get these down?” Dizzy demanded, a sword in hand. It sounded aggressively rhetorical. He stopped in front of me with a sheen of sweat on his forehead, breathing heavily. “This is the one. I can feel it.” He held it out.

The sword was absolutely gorgeous. A delicate line of silver shot through the red leather hilt, curled around onto the black blade, and then straightened into a line toward the point.

“He got that one from a garage sale,” Callie said, standing beside me and staring at the blade. “Or was it a swap meet?”

“EBay.” Dizzy wiped his palm on his shirt. “Great stuff on eBay.”

"Yes. He prepares them with the fundamentals of magic, and I weave in the spells." Callie motioned me toward the blade. "See if it will work. No one else can even touch it. Except us, of course, because we made it magical."

"Why can't anyone else touch it?" I asked, holding my palm over the blade.

"Too hungry. In the field, we call these types of swords magic conductors, but they aren't. They feed off your magic, then store it for your future use. They're magical lockers for certain types of magic. Storage. Did the person who made your last sword take your magical measure before making it?"

"Yes," I said. "He is one of the best."

She huffed. "Maybe for your paycheck. That instrument, which we have, of course, only accurately gauges certain types of magic. Witches and mages would mostly get accurate readings. But even though you're similar to a very powerful mage, your power is fundamentally different. You would simply register as high power. You probably had to push your magic into the sword he made you because it wasn't hungry enough to siphon it out of you."

"I have heard of instruments that siphon power." Darius stepped closer and leaned into my space protectively. I tried to push him back with an elbow. He nudged my elbow out of the way. "They are dangerous.

That is not why we are here."

Callie's brow furrowed as she looked at Darius. When her gaze switched to me, it was assessing. "That is why this sword is still in our possession," she said. "A local hack who stares into crystal balls for tourists visited me one afternoon. She insisted on tea, and when I told her I didn't have time—she's a serious whack-job, this lady—she forced her way in and started making tea herself.

"After she made a nuisance of herself, I finally agreed to sit down for a cup with her. A moment later, she went into a trance and laid out the type of sword I had to make. Make, keep, and store. She described the sword itself in detail, as well as the properties I should put into it. I knew for a fact that no one would be able to use a sword that hungry. It would bleed the holder dry and keep looking for more. I didn't voice my refusal, of course. You shouldn't argue with crazy; it can get dangerous.

"Anyway, she finished her spiel, rose, and knocked her cup onto the floor like the low-class hack she is. She was pretending to be in her trance still, but I didn't get this house by being an idiot. Without another word, she left. I hate that woman. I really do. I haven't talked to her since, even when she's been in the same room at the magical women's rum mixer."

She gestured toward the sword. "This was delivered

later that same day. It matched her description perfectly, down to the last detail."

"I'd actually ordered a different one," Dizzy said, looking down at it. "This was a mistake. I asked Callie to help me send it back—"

"He *still* doesn't know how to process a return. How, I don't know, because we've done it a million times—"

"—but she insisted we keep it. After I heard the story, it was hard not to agree. And here you are."

"You've just said that it siphons too much power." Darius touched the small of my back, still leaning in too closely. "It is too dangerous, and you are wasting my time."

"This is why I leave vampire clients to Dizzy," Callie muttered to me. She patted my arm. "You had to push power into the other sword you used, right?"

"Yes. That's how my power works."

"No. That is how your power works with the wrong instrument. What about portable magic storage?"

"The casings don't work for me. My magic eats them away."

"Typically, yes, that's what I would expect. I have one that might hold up, though. I can make more as well. He can afford it." Callie hooked a thumb toward Darius. "Eventually you'll meet someone who has more power than you." She gave a pregnant pause, and shivers coated my body. For the second time, I wondered if she knew the truth about my father. And if so, how soon before she'd try to sell me out and I'd have to kill her.

"You'll need the extra boost," she finished. "Try the sword."

"Be cautious here," Darius said, still acting like an umbrella. Perhaps this was the real reason why he didn't want a bond-mate—his level of protection was stifling.

"How do you not have more problems with your children rebelling? This is ridiculous." I elbowed him again.

He pushed my elbow away. "My children have some sense."

"They became vampires, and you think they have sense?" I muttered, my hand near the hilt. A feeling of friendship stole over me, almost like the sword welcomed my touch and was inviting me closer. Taking a deep breath, I complied.

The second my fingers wrapped around the leather, I felt the minimal suction. My arm acted like a straw, drawing forth the magic from the rest of my body. With very little effort, I stopped the flow. It required no fight—less effort than pushing magic into my other sword.

I put it into my scabbard, a little loose-fitting, then drew it out again. Light and agile, it was an improvement over the last one. The magic was still stored inside, not that it should've gone anywhere in that small span of time.

"Seems to work." I shrugged. "It's light and pretty, too. So that's nice."

"*Voila.*" Callie patted my arm. "Let Reagan test it, Dizzy. I'll go get the little brooch. It's ugly as sin, but it's great for heavy magic users, trust me."

"Are you sure this is a good idea?" Darius asked as Dizzy headed into his shed.

A cooling sensation spread through me as I let the sword take more magic. When the magic depleted from my body and the sword began to draw on my life force, the cold turned into frost, highly unpleasant. I cut off the draw, and the feeling subsided.

"Seems like there is a built-in warning." I made a duckbill with my lips and waved the sword, nearly nicking Darius with the tip. Finally, he stepped back. "It's really nice. Like the Cadillac of blades."

"Cadillacs break down," Darius said.

"Helpful."

"I love mine," Dizzy said, holding a small sphere between his thumb and forefinger. "My Cadillac, I mean. I don't have a sword. That I use. Anyway, the car has lasted a long time. Callie insists I get a new one, but mine works just fine. Ready, Reagan?"

"For what?"

"To test it out, naturally." He threw the casing at the ground and hastened backward. It cracked like an egg. In a few seconds, a twenty-foot-high, ferocious green dragon grew from a puff of smoke. It roared, a sound that shook the ground.

"Oops. Shoot. That's going to wake the neighbors." Dizzy rushed into his shed.

Darius ripped a spell out of his satchel, pinched it, and spoke it alive. A red blob flew up and fluttered open, unfurling into a large, flat surface that hung over half the backyard, dragon spell and all, before draping down. He was trying to diminish the sound for the neighbors. It did nothing to block out the sight, I didn't think. Hopefully no one would peek out their windows and catch sight of the giant mythical beast in their midst.

The creature stomped at me. I dodged easily but didn't stab. I was feeling out the vibrations from the spell, learning how it was constructed. It had a hefty amount of power and incredible finesse, clearly created by two masters. What I wouldn't give to afford their designs on a regular basis. It would make my life so much easier.

The tail swung around, long and thick, with three-foot-long spikes on the end. I jumped over it, rolled to the side, and ducked under the return swing. The thing didn't have a pooper, but otherwise the dragon looked remarkably real. Solid, with colors that stayed in the right areas.

"Reagan, we are short on time." Darius lazily avoided a stomping foot.

"It's a bit slow, this dragon, isn't it?" I touched the leg and felt a painful zing through my arm.

"It's made to distract," Dizzy yelled as he came out of his shed. He noticed the spell Darius had thrown. "Oh." He ducked back in, yelling, "If an opponent thinks the creature can be beaten, he will engage because of the size. If he thinks it cannot be beaten, he will resort to extreme measures to find a way around it. Or run. So you see, a large beast, that looks real, is a better—"

"We understand," Darius interrupted. "Reagan."

"Yup." I let the tail smash into me, and was rewarded with a very solid hit that hurt like the bejeebus. I rolled backward onto my head, sword still in hand, before hopping to my feet. "I thought it might pass through me."

"We do not create weak spells, young lady," Dizzy said disapprovingly, outside his shed again.

"Now I know." I ducked under a smashing foot and hacked into the leg, not even thinking about enacting the magic within my sword. Much to my delight, it still worked. The sword sliced through the spell, tearing it open and burning the edges. The blade glowed a soft blue.

"The sword is designed to sense any extreme temperatures and show a color connected to the opposite spectrum. That crazy crystal ball reader said we should incorporate that," Dizzy said. "Clearly your magic is made up of extreme fire and heat."

Yes, it was, and now everyone knew. Darius had gained another piece of the riddle. *Thanks, Dizzy.*

"Of course…" Dizzy's eyes crinkled. "I don't think you'll fight the same person often enough for them to catch on. Or you wouldn't be your mother's daughter."

The dragon unraveled like a sweater before finally puffing out, leaving a big pile of residual magic that wafted sulfur.

"The smell is intended to be a further distraction once the dragon has been taken down," Dizzy said, reading my mind. Or maybe my scrunched-up face.

Darius held up his used casing and spoke what sounded like Latin. The red spell shimmering above us sparkled before folding back into the casing.

"Oh, that's handy," I said. "And a money saver. Do you have to speak Latin to use it?"

"This one, yes. Which is why very few people steal my best spells." He tucked it into his satchel. "It's doubtful those who do will be able to use them. I will not be angry if they are returned."

I narrowed my eyes at him. I doubted he knew that I

had pocketed the spell he'd given me in the unicorn paddock, but he'd clearly noticed the ones I'd used my five-finger discount on in his chamber. I mean, they were just sitting there, staring at me as I made my out. "That was a dig at me, wasn't it?"

"Yes," he said.

"I got a call about the noise," Callie said to Dizzy as she made her way out of the house.

"Sorry! I'd forgotten about the sound." Dizzy shrank a little and glanced at me. "I didn't used to put sound in them."

"You should put fire in it, too," I said, touching the blade with my finger. It was way too nice for the likes of me.

It's all about who you know.

"Here, honey. You'll have to push magic into this, but it should hold it for you." Callie handed me a strange-looking brooch fashioned to look like a big beetle with a lion's head.

"Never wear that in my presence," Darius said. "Keep it out of sight."

He'd get it pinned to his back when he wasn't looking so everyone would laugh at him, that was what he'd get.

"Will you be needing any more spells?" Dizzy asked Darius.

"How many of those swords do you possess?" Darius pointed at my blade, which I hadn't put away yet. It was too new and shiny to hide.

"None like that, but we could make some." Dizzy glanced at Callie.

She shrugged and nodded. "Full payment up front." At Darius's shrewd look, she crossed her arms over her chest. "She is the only one I know who can use a blade like that. I would be making it specifically for her. I don't plan to waste my time simply because vampires can't be trusted. Money up front."

"And a brooch that isn't so hideous?" Darius hadn't reached for his wallet. Assuming he had one.

"How many?" she replied.

"As many as would be necessary in the event that she encounters a spell much stronger than she can comfortably handle."

"Since when are vampires worried about the wellbeing of humans?" She turned on me quickly. "Tell me you didn't bond the shrewdest vampire in existence!"

"I'm not an idiot." I shrank away from her scowl. Thunder clouds rolled across Darius's face.

"A sword can create a bond with the handler," she said, relaxed now. "But a brooch is too small. Anyone who got their hands on it could use it. For some people, that isn't a big deal. But for Reagan, that could have extremely damaging consequences."

Those threads of fear resurfaced. She was right

about my power, but was she guessing, or did she know?

"For that reason," she went on, speaking to me, "You need to take care of them, or your power can be used against you. Not to mention analyzed. So two small magical containers would be all I'd advise."

"Fine," Darius barked. He checked his watch. "Get two more in motion. Charge the card on file. I will have my assistant review the charge. I expect a discount for the bulk order."

"You'll get no discount, or you'll get no supplies." Callie gave Darius her bulldog expression.

"That's what you get for not using *please*," I murmured.

Darius threw his hard gaze at Dizzy. "I would like a handful of distraction spells, delivered to Reagan now. Then a dozen more, styled to look like various creatures, color coded. My people will supply you with the colors, as usual. Make the dragon breathe fire."

"I'm…not sure I can do that." Dizzy scratched his head.

"C'mon, honey, let's heal your face." Callie tugged me along behind her.

"Oh. Do we have time?" I glanced at Darius. He gave me a nod before following Dizzy into his shed. That wasn't the answer I'd hoped for. I wasn't sure I wanted to be alone with this woman.

"I hate dealing with that vampire," Callie said as she pulled me toward the house. "Which is why I usually don't. He makes me want to kick him." She huffed as we entered through the door. "Right, honey, down to the brass tacks." She still hadn't released my wrist, and was now yanking me toward the stairs. "Do you know about your father?"

"I don't think I am who you think I am," I said, guarded. "I'm not a curse breaker. I don't even know what that is."

"You didn't tell that fool of a vampire what you are, did you?" At the top of the stairs, she saw my hesitation. "I knew your mother. I knew her when she met your father. I helped her after she kicked your father out. I know what danger you are in, which is why I agreed to cut all bonds until you were old enough. She died before her time, and I lost sight of you. You took her teachings to heart, which is good. But because of that, we've lost valuable time."

This time I didn't resist when she pulled me down the hall.

"I loved your mother like a sister," she continued. "We all did, those of us who knew her well. We didn't like that she tried to disappear. I was the only one powerful enough to confront her about it. Lord almighty, she gave me a good magical wallop, I'll say that much. She had great offensive magic. I got through, though. I got to meet you." She smiled and touched her hand to her heart before directing me down the hall. "Such a little cutie, you were. I couldn't have kids myself, but I do love them. I got to hold you and rock you—Mother Nature is the most magical of us all. It is wise to use her for guidance."

Touching moments made me uncomfortable.

I scratched my arm and contemplated making a run for it. Curiosity stayed my feet, however. My mother had never told me someone else knew about me. We'd always been alone. I said as much.

"Your mother and I agreed that your identity should be a secret. At least until we assessed your magic. When it turned out you had a good deal of your father in you, keeping you secret became a necessity until you mastered your various gifts. I didn't visit your mom because I am always surrounded by busybodies and power seekers. If someone followed me, it would've put you both in jeopardy."

Callie sat me down in front of a huge vanity. It didn't surprise me to see that all the little boxes and serums were perfectly organized. A massive bed sprawled out behind us, one side ruffled and the other crisply made. An open door on the other side led to a bathroom and a giant bathtub.

"I wondered if she would eventually turn you over to the Mages' Guild." Callie assessed my face. "They would want to claim you, and in doing so, protect you. But she was probably right in her choice. They'd seek to use you. Maybe even trade you. They've gone horribly corrupt. They don't have a presence around here, thank God."

"When I was old enough to look after myself, I tried to get her to join the world of the living again." I shrugged. "By that point, she said there was nothing for her anymore. She was happy with the life we had, working on her magic, seeing if she could create a spell I couldn't break apart."

"I bet that was a challenge for her." She leaned closer to my forehead. "Burned your eyebrows away, huh? And how'd you get the scratch?" She thumbed my cheek.

"A plant-based sort of goo. I wasn't paying enough attention."

"Ah. No problem. I can fix this in a jiffy." She pulled one of the containers toward her and took off the lid.

"My mother was excellent with healing magic. I didn't inherit the ability."

"Not many do." She waved her hand around. "Hence the big house. Rich humans pay me to smooth facial lines and cure hangnails. Vanity pays, dear, which you'll learn readily enough from that vampire out there. He's as vain as…" She let the words trail away. "Don't trust him, by the way. I'm sure you know that."

"Obviously."

"And while he is gorgeous, and undoubtedly has great techniques in the bedroom, it's not worth it. Think with your head."

"I know this."

"It doesn't hurt to be reminded. A man that fine can wear on the logic, don't I know. I got mixed up with one of them when I was in college. Time of my life. Getting away wasn't so easy. Had to kill him and cover it up." I jerked back in shock. "Hold still, honey. I only want to put this salve on the trouble spots."

"You killed him because you didn't want to stop seeing him?"

"It was the only way, I assure you. He wanted to bond me, of all things. I was extremely naive and powerful, a great combination for a predator. Thanks to the advice of an old biddie like myself, I got out. Otherwise I would've been lost to him. He didn't want me to leave, of course. This might sting a little."

I sucked in a breath—it felt like acid was eating away my cheek. "This is helping me, not disfiguring me, right?"

"Let me work." She blew on my cheek. "It took a combined effort of a few of my friends to trap and kill him, but we managed. It was hairy there for a little bit. He almost broke free. But my friend—a dainty little thing—rushed him with a stake. She saved the day. We covered it up and no one knew. Or else they didn't care. I assume you are excellent at killing vampires?"

"At killing everything."

"Yes. Your mother told me she'd teach you to fight. She was fierce. Had been training since she was little. This will feel better. Here you go."

A cool liquid calmed my burning skin.

"I was five when she enrolled me in a martial arts studio," I said. "She lied on all the documents. Paid in cash. I have no idea where she got the money."

"Me. Don't wrinkle your eyebrows, or I'll miss and give you a hairy forehead."

"You?"

"I was the middle man, actually. She made her potions and spells in the woods, shipped them to my warehouse for distribution, and I saw that her customers got them. It was no hassle, and since I had my own setup as well, no one was the wiser."

"You did all that for her?"

"I got something in return, don't you worry. She was a better healer than I am. I learned plenty, bought supplies from her—it wasn't just goodwill. Otherwise, she would've cut me off. Okay, there you go. Back to normal."

I turned to look in the mirror. Except for the singed bangs, which could be swept to the side, I looked like myself again. "Wow," I said. "That was quick work."

"I've been doing this a long time. Flesh and hair problems are easy. So is making a vampire disappear without a trace." She tapped the side of her nose with her forefinger. "You know, just in case you sample the sexual waters and get stuck in them." She gave me a knowing look.

Gross.

I hopped out of the chair. "Thanks."

"And sweetie," she said quietly, her eyes flicking sideways toward the door, "I know it doesn't need saying, but if you want to continue living life as you know it, you'll keep your true gifts a secret. Better to be a bastard than to be dead or under someone else's control."

"Maybe I won't actually call myself a *bastard,* but..."

"Smart girl." She threw her arms around me for a tight hug. "There has been so much business, I haven't let this sink in. What a treat! We've stayed in the area, hoping to catch wind of you again. I wondered if it was you when I heard about a particularly effective bounty hunter, but no one at the Magical Office would tell me anything. We had no way of knowing you were still around here."

She stepped back and smiled, staring at me with glistening eyes.

"Yes, well..." I tried to wriggle away, feeling intensely awkward.

"I wondered if I would recognize you when I did see you," she said. "And look, here you are. I absolutely do. There is so much of your mother in you, amplified by your father's good looks. He was a stunner. We were all very jealous when he gravitated toward your mother."

"You were probably relieved when you found out what he was."

"I can't get pregnant, honey. I would've used him and let him go, like I should've done with that vampire."

I sidestepped away. "Okay, then. That's… I'll get going."

"Yes, of course. That vampire of yours is probably planning which village to pillage."

She waved her hand as we neared the door. Magic fizzled away. She'd placed a ward and I hadn't even noticed. Very good at finesse indeed. I'd definitely need to get some spells from her after Darius paid me.

I walked out of the room and immediately met the vampire driver, who'd followed us in after all. He gave me his usual glower. "Trying to hide something?"

"Trying to look creepy?" I passed him by, half expecting him to reach out and grab my arm. That'd get him stabbed, of course. Which he probably knew.

"We're ready to go," he said, following me.

"I'll see you out." Callie followed behind us, moving a bit slower down the stairs to the main floor.

For a brief moment, I found myself alone at the bottom with the driver.

"What were you talking about?" he asked in a low voice.

"I can still hear you, love." Callie waved, halfway down the steps. "And I am the distance-casting winner in all of Louisiana. Not to mention I always have a spell ready to go. Castration at a moment's notice? No problem. Keep that in mind if you decide to manhandle that girl."

I grinned at the driver.

His eyes narrowed, but he held his tongue.

On the front porch, Dizzy was staring down at something in his hands as Darius looked on. "Callie, look at this. It seems familiar, but I can't place it." Dizzy glanced up and caught sight of me. He smiled. "Oh. I thought you were my wife."

"What's that?" Callie stomped onto the deck, pushing the driver out of the way. The poor guy was not having the best of days. "Where did you get this?" Callie asked with a sharp voice, taking the object from Dizzy. They were looking at one of the casings we'd picked up in the Realm.

I told them and then explained the spells we'd encountered.

Callie's eyes came up slowly, soaked in wariness and fear. She shook her head slowly and angled the casing so she could study it in the porch light. "I've seen one similar to this. Not exact, but similar. Sometimes the police have me look at a crime scene when the Magical Office is befuddled. I found a casing similar to this at one of those scenes." She turned it around in her fingers. "No marking. This mage wants to stay anonymous."

"Ah right, yes. Yes, I remember." Dizzy took the object back. "That was a horrible scene. The skin was peeled off the victim. A human."

"What good would skinning someone do?" Darius asked.

"Why, create a lot of pain, of course. A *lot* of pain." Dizzy tsked. "A mage who could create that kind of spell would also be powerful enough to capture the energy the human exuded. Pain is a great way to amp up adrenaline."

"Adrenaline can be turned into kinetic energy, which can increase power," Callie said. "It is a more extreme version of a dark sacrifice—something used for personal gain rather than good will to the gods."

"Can that power be ingested?" Darius asked.

Dizzy frowned as he studied the casing. It was Callie who answered. "Not to make the magical user stronger and more powerful, no. But if that mage were trying to invoke a stronger spirit to guide and help him, then indirectly, yes."

"A spirit…like a demon?" Darius asked.

"Could be a demon, though they are usually self-serving. An experienced magical person would avoid that route and go with something more…amiable. Something easier to get rid of, like a poltergeist or half-banished banshee, that kind of thing."

"Half-banished banshee?" I asked.

"They're mute, but just as powerful," Callie said. "Happens when the person who's sent in to banish one from its haunting area doesn't do a thorough job. It strips the area of the racket, so if the banisher is quick enough, they can get out of town before the folk realize the banshee is still hanging around."

"Well, that's not so bad. I've heard their wail is the worst part."

"Not so bad? Their whole function is to herald the death of a family member. When business slows down, they've been known to drum up their own business, so to speak. Trust me, you don't want one of them hanging around. A town drops in number pretty quickly."

"Is a demon more powerful?" I knew a few things about demons, but nothing about banshees. "Because this guy is definitely big on power." I thought back to the spells I'd extinguished in the Realm. "And knowledgeable about how to construct his magic."

Callie was shaking her head with a vague look in her eyes. "I seem to recall the police thought the killer was out of state." Her eyes focused again. "But if the styling is similar, it could be the same person. They didn't catch him, I don't think."

"A demon is more powerful?" I asked again.

"A demon is much more powerful, yes, but they don't like to share a body. Oftentimes, they'll start off by sharing, prove to be lovely roommates, and when the body gets complacent, the demon takes over."

"Then what?" Darius asked.

"Well, they find a larger source of power, of course. Demons always crave more power, in themselves and in their masters. It is *always* about power with them, which is why inviting them to the surface is trouble, no matter how insignificant the demon starts out. They can grow and generate more power, and they constantly seek to do so, much like humans."

"So, what if the body had ingested a very potent source of magical power?" I asked, trying to be as vague as possible. "A crazy-days boost of power, we're talking. One that could destroy a magical person as easily as boost them…"

"Then hell would be invited to earth, and the seas would boil in the blood of the lost."

CHAPTER 13

"WELL, THAT WAS a terrifying and horrible end to a lovely visit," I said conversationally as Darius and I drove out of the Garden District.

"Mrs. Banks seemed overly familiar with you when we parted," Darius said in an even tone.

He could say that again. Before releasing me into the car, Callie had given me a fierce hug and a mighty pat on my back, promising me she'd see me again. The warning in her eye said I better not try to get out of it. I was stuck with her, which was a good thing, most likely. If she knew my lineage, she was someone to watch.

Plus, the thought of actually having someone in my life made my middle squishy. My mom's passing had left a gaping hole in my solitary life. I was lonely, whether I would admit it out loud or not. Having a friend, regardless of her age and liberal take on screwing and killing vampires, would be welcomed.

Not like I could tell Darius any of that.

"Yeah," I said in answer to Darius's hinted question. "I told you. I'm likable."

"Moss mentioned that Mrs. Banks muted her conversation with you upstairs."

"Moss?" I turned my focus to the front of the car. I smiled at the dark eyes that flicked up into the rearview mirror. "Is that his real first name?"

The eyes in the mirror narrowed. When I laughed, he glowered.

"Why did she feel the need to keep your conversation private?" Darius asked.

"You'll never know." I entwined my fingers in my lap. "What a strange first name. Moss. Was your mom a hippy?"

Moss's gaze went back to the street. I could barely see the nerve pop out in the side of his jaw from irritation. Why this tickled me, I had no idea.

"Dawn is fast approaching," Darius said. "We will stay in my residence for the day, and tomorrow night will acquire more information."

It turned out his "residence" was a massive corner house in the French Quarter. I hadn't closed my mouth since walking in the front door. Over six thousand square feet of a sort of modern elegance I'd never seen before, let alone actually experienced. Gorgeous furniture graced the well-appointed and spacious rooms. Art like I'd seen in the Dungeon hung on the walls, perfectly accenting other decorations. Fresh flowers sweetened the air. Freshly painted walls hinted at the total makeover this older home must've had in the recent past. It was...extraordinary.

"I am nowhere near classy enough to hang out in this place." I flinched away from the arm of a light-colored sofa. "I'm dirty. Do you have any plastic I can put down before I sit on stuff? Even the floor looks too clean for the likes of me."

"Don't be ridiculous." Darius directed me up a stairway, where I marveled at the textured walls. Strings of flowers periodically draped down from the bannister. They were real, too. Fresh.

"Do they put flowers here every day?" I asked.

"Of course. It is essential to be surrounded by living things. It reminds us of when we were alive, and the wonders of the living. I cherish it."

I grimaced, but refrained from mentioning that the flowers *weren't* alive, not anymore. In essence, he was surrounding himself with *fresh* death.

"Here. A meal prepared for you."

He gestured through an opened door, and when I entered the room, I started laughing. "No." I walked back out. "Don't you have a kitchen I can eat in? At the counter?"

His brow rumpled. "Don't be absurd. You are a guest. You cannot eat at the counter like a servant." He practically spat the last words out.

"Let's not think of me as a guest. Think of me as a

stray cat that you are hesitant to feed lest I stay, but you pity me enough to toss me a few scraps. Seriously. That's the way you should treat this whole situation."

"Do you not want to eat alone, is that the issue?" He studied me.

"Alone is great. I'll just grab a few things and head on down to the kitchen, which is probably still cleaner than I am."

"I am losing my patience. I'll send someone to attend you." His hand on my back wasn't as light as normal, and it became even firmer as he all but shoved me into the large room with a ginormous table that could easily seat twenty people. I knew this, because there were twenty chairs surrounding it.

Twenty chairs.

More could squeeze in, of course. There were another six chairs against the wall, just waiting for go time. A crystal chandelier hung in the middle, bedecked with electric candles. Big, draped curtains closed off the windows, blocking all light, which was weird but probably a necessity, and a large rug stretched beneath all of this.

Did I mention it was all light cream? Walls, chairs, parts of the rug—light cream.

I *did* mention I was dirty. Filthy, actually. I was wearing the clothes in which I'd rolled around in the dirt. Dust was fleeing from me in puffs.

When dust wouldn't even stick to my person, I knew I had no place among cream-colored decorations.

I circled the table, trying to stay on the thin slice of wood floor between the rug and the wall. This became difficult when the extra chairs stood in my way, so I stripped off my boots and gasped at the lines of brown on my socks. Those had to come off, too.

Barefooted, I continued to circle, eyeing the simply wasteful array of food that had been set out. Among the plentiful options was an entire roast beef surrounded by baked potatoes and carrots, a punch bowl of soup with a ladle, a roasted chicken with rice pilaf, a silver tray with crab legs accompanied with melted butter, and shrimp dishes. The spread could feed enough hungry people to fit in all twenty-six chairs, plus a few stowaways besides.

I blew out a breath as I eyed the lone plate at the head of the table.

He'd had all this prepared for one person. Me. What a nincompoop.

"Well..." I sighed. "I better try to eat it all, or he'll think I'm rude."

"What was that?"

I jumped and my hand shot to my sword as a beautiful woman entered the room. Brown hair tumbled over her shoulders in loose curls, and she wore a strapless dress with a sparkly sort of bodice leading down into flowing silk. With a face that would make cupid sport a boner, she was a knockout. I wasn't into girls, but even I wanted to stare at her and drool.

"You're Darius's girlfriend, then?" I asked. Because that seemed to fit. Handsome guy, hot chick, A-list friends. What tabloid *hadn't* I seen that in?

She drifted into the room like a poltergeist and waited beside a chair next to the head of the table. I hurried forward and pulled the chair out for her. Logic said it wasn't my job, but my motor skills seemed to think otherwise.

She lowered herself into it like a queen and folded her hands in her lap.

I hovered around my chair like a gobshite, dopey and clumsy. "You really don't have to hang out with me," I said. My stomach growled.

Why didn't you say that before *you pulled her chair out, idiot? Now she thinks you secretly* do *want her to hang out with you.*

"I'm okay on my own," I added.

Why am I sitting?

"I'm usually on my own, actually." I laughed awkwardly. In fact, there wasn't much about that moment I hadn't made awkward.

I folded my hands in my lap like she was doing. It was like my brain was on complete hiatus. Was this what guys felt like in the presence of a beautiful woman? Because if so, forgiven. And also, they were idiots. *I* was an idiot.

A man glided in wearing a tux and carrying another place setting. I hopped out of my chair. "No, no. Honestly. I don't need company."

"Yes, ma'am," he said, but set her place anyway. She didn't smile or thank him when he was done. It should've been weird, but her muteness just added to the mystery, making her even prettier. It wasn't fair.

Next he put his hand to the back of my chair and waited beside it for me to sit.

"Really, I think I'll just grab a plate and head down to the kitchen." I glanced at my shoes, and was suddenly mortified that I was barefoot. Who in their right mind went to a friend's house for dinner and took off their shoes before they sat down to eat? Surely that looked as strange as it sounded.

I took the chair. It was the least awkward option, and that was saying something.

"Would you like something to drink, Ms. Somerset?" He bent slightly at the waist to give me his utmost attention. "Wine, perhaps?"

"Wine would be great, thanks," I blurted.

"Of course. Ms. Beauchene?"

"Goblet of O-negative, freshly poured."

That was gross.

"Of course," he said, as though it was as simple a request as the wine. He exited the room.

"So…" I said, swallowing a little too loudly. "I'll just get this underway, will I? I'd hate to keep you."

She turned to me with a demure expression. "He will serve you." Her voice was deep and sensual, with a thick French accent.

"Right. Yes. Actually, I think I'll just serve myself. I'm used to it. I wouldn't want you to wait on ceremony and…uhm, it would be a pity for your blood to get cold. You know."

I slid from my chair on the opposite side of the table so as to hide my bare feet. Quickly, I scooped heaping portions onto my plate, helping my overall barbarian look, and scurried back to my seat.

I took up my fork and knife, about to dive in, before glancing over at the empty plate in front of her. Suddenly I was at a loss. "Do you eat, or…?"

"I will attend you," she said pleasantly.

Was that a no?

I was too afraid to ask and look even stupider.

Slowly, I put the first bite of food into my mouth and chewed, staring in front of me while kind of hunched over, wondering if I was being incredibly rude or just incredibly weird.

The vampire in the tux entered with drinks. He stood next to me and opened my bottle. He left it to the side and opened a bottle for her.

Apparently getting blood *was* that easy. How, I had

no idea, nor did I want to ask. They might wonder if I was volunteering to be crushed and bottled.

"May I get you some soup, Ms. Somerset?" the man asked.

"Yes, please," I responded.

"Where are my manners?" The very pretty woman set her drink down. "*Je m'appelle* Marie." She lightly touched her fingertips to her chest and smiled.

"Hi, I'm Reagan," I said, nodding. My face flamed in embarrassment, though I had no idea why.

The soup landed in front of me a moment later, at about the same time Darius wandered into the room. "Reagan," he said.

I'd just put a big chunk of meat into my mouth, intent on getting this dinner over with as fast as possible. I raised my eyebrows. "Mhm?"

"I will be heading upstairs for a day slumber. It can be resisted in the Brink, but it is difficult for more than a day at a time. I'd sooner take it now than when I am needed awake." He paused, possibly awaiting my approval.

I threw him a thumbs-up.

"When you are finished," he went on, "Mr. Giles will see you to your room before retiring."

"Mhm." Another thumbs-up.

"I will see you at sundown." He glanced at Marie. Before exiting, he hesitated. "There are other humans in the house who will be given the opportunity to eat when you are finished. Is that acceptable?"

I looked at Marie, waiting for her to answer. After a moment, she switched her gaze from Darius to me, also waiting.

"Oh." I took another sip of really delicious wine to help wash down my more-than-exquisite food. I could get used to this setup. "Sure. Yeah. They can come in now. Wait, why do you have a bunch of humans here?"

"Several of my older children use this as a safe house in which to dine. The humans are easily acquired, and are invited to stay as long as they are useful."

"Sorry I asked. But yeah, whatever. They can come in now, I don't care."

He scoffed, "Don't be ridiculous," and left the room.

Marie gazed at me. It felt expectant, somehow.

"He's a good guy, huh?" I offered, tapping an invisible spot in the air with my fork.

Not waiting for an answer, I went back to my plate. In truth, I didn't think what I'd said was exactly true. Darius was a hospitable guy, surely. A gentleman, definitely. But I had no illusions. He needed me at the moment, and it was in his best interests to keep me alive and happy. *Afterward* was another story. He was a vampire, first and foremost, and they served themselves. Even their protection of the unicorns was self-serving. It was an important distinction to remember.

"One of the best," she said, thankfully not able to read my mind. "I enjoy having him near."

"Did he make you, then?" I asked, hopefully using the right words.

"He did, yes. He's been the most excellent teacher and confidant. One of the best, as I said. I am very lucky."

"Mhm." She got a thumbs-up, too. I was passing them out like business cards.

"What is your involvement with him?"

"Oh. Just working together. On a thing." I nodded, like that was a sufficient answer.

"You have a delicious aroma. Tell me, does Darius find your blood as delectable as it smells?"

"He wouldn't know." I eyed the rest of the food as I scraped my plate clean. I was still hungry, but I didn't want to be in her company any longer.

"No?" she said. "Interesting. I wonder, would he rather that we be the first to taste and judge?"

Had she really just licked her lips?

"You know what?" I put my napkin on the table—then decided better of it, and rose and placed it on my empty chair. "Mr...." I stared at the man in the tux, off to the side. What had Darius called him? "Sir?"

He turned toward me with an air of patience. "Yes, ma'am. Would you like something else?"

"Actually, I think I'll retire and do a little studying

before hitting the hay. Do you think I can just take a plate on the run? Paper plate, maybe. And that wine. I'll just take a plate to go, a cup—plastic is fine—and that whole bottle of wine. That way I can get out of your hair."

"I apologize—was that rude of me?" Marie stood gracefully.

"Oh no, you're fine."

She took a step toward me. I did not like that look of hunger in her eyes.

"Mr. Durant has specified that Ms. Somerset is to have full access to his home," the vampire in the tux said to Marie. "She is not to be touched, and is permitted to take action should she feel threatened in any way."

"Hmm," Marie said, her eyes shining with mischief. The hunger was still there.

"Do you have a paper plate, sir?" I asked, backing toward my boots.

"I will have a plate brought to your quarters. Marie, I will warn you one final time. If you flout Mr. Durant's command, you are liable to find your permanent resting place."

She laughed, a delightful sound. "He has never carried through with one of his punishments, William. You should know better by now."

"I was not warning you on behalf of Mr. Durant.

Something you might pass on." William passed behind her and made his way to the door. "Ms. Somerset, please follow me."

She eyed me like a cat would a wriggling fish: dinner that she planned to play with first. Thankfully, it kept her from noticing the dirty boots and socks in my hand. That was really the biggest deal, after all. I grabbed the neck of the wine bottle and hurried out after William.

"Please accept my apology," William said as he led the way to a staircase in the rear of the house. "She is not used to the word *no.* Not in her human life, and not now. Mr. Durant is much too lenient with her. To her credit, she is good at ascertaining information for Mr. Durant."

"I bet."

"Have no fear. She will not kill you. The worst that could possibly happen is for her to happen upon you suddenly and taste the origin of that del—of your smell. You will be quite safe."

"Our definitions of safe are…somewhat different."

"Mr. Durant assured me that you are proficient in fighting."

"Very."

"Well, then. If she gravely offends you in that manner, kill her."

He said it without emotion. If she crossed the line, he expected me to rectify the situation. I wondered if he lacked loyalty to her specifically, or if many vampires had no loyalty in general.

We passed by a few closed doors before stopping in front of one. He turned the handle, walked through, and stepped out of the way. "These are your rooms."

"Rooms, plural?"

"Yes, of course." He waited for me to enter and, once again, marvel, because I couldn't get used to a house this nice. "There is a hidden passageway that will lead you to Mr. Durant's quarters. He is currently with one of the humans, but afterward, he will be available should you need anything."

"No thanks."

"I apologize." William crossed the room and slid his finger along the side of a picture frame before clicking a hidden button. The frame popped open like a door. "I didn't mean to imply that he hoped you'd join him for feeding or intercourse. Those needs should be sated in a couple hours. No, use this passageway if something should happen, whatever it might be." He paused before continuing. "He must realize the draw you have on us. You are very unique. I have never smelled anything quite like it. The curiosity, in this case, creates a powerful urge. Almost as alluring as if your blood were to taste as good as it smells."

"You're tap-dancing on the line, bro." I put a hand to my stomach, trying unsuccessfully to deaden the growl.

"Of course. I apologize. I am not usually in the presence of humans who do not wish to...entertain our wishes." He paused for a beat. Hoping I'd relent and stick out my neck, perhaps? "I will bring you something to eat. You have the wine bottle there, I see. I'll bring you a glass. Would you like some water?"

I flushed a little at his mention of the bottle, but really, could he blame me? "Water would be fine, thank you."

"Of course." He exited the room with a slight bow.

I had no idea who would want to be an eternal butler, but I knew exactly why Darius would want one.

I pushed the picture frame closed, hoping Darius couldn't get through the other side, and noticed clothes on the end of the bed. Leather pants, a red tank top, sexy underwear...clearly Darius had rifled through my pile of dirty clothing while I slept in his bed in the Dungeon and had his people pick me up some spares. It was hard to care, since the clean clothes were welcomed.

A FEW HOURS before dusk, I was lying on my bed, wide awake. I'd eaten two more plates of food, finished the bottle of wine, showered, and slipped into a food coma that did not last all day. Being that I'd also slept in the Dungeon, I could not make myself go back under.

I looked around the room for the millionth time.

Despite all the finery, there was a complete lack of entertainment. No computer. No TV. Not even a book.

I debated wandering downstairs to find a library, of which I was certain there was one, but my gaze fell on the heavily curtained windows. Without another thought, I hopped up and got dressed. No sense wasting time waiting for Darius—I could get some information while he slept off his blood and/or sex coma.

The house was silent as I made my way down the stairs and then out the front door. Clouds rolled overhead, dark with warning. I walked briskly along the sidewalk, knowing I should take off my weapons, since it was daylight, but also that I had nowhere to put them. Speed was my friend, and it had the side benefit of getting me to my destination in no time. Once there, I loitered for a moment, looking around the corner of a building.

Loud jazz music blasted into the street. Pedestrians holding drinks or shopping bags meandered along, peering into the bars or talking to each other. As the bodies shifted and moved, I spied my favorite snitch leaning against the wall, sucking on a cigarette.

He kept randomly looking my way, probably waiting for someone. I circled around the block and walked toward him from the opposite direction. Hiding behind a wide man who bobbed and swayed like he was on a ship deck, I kept my head down and out of sight. At the last moment, I stepped out from behind the man, wrapped my arm around Red, put one hand to the side of his face, and applied my thumb to the hollow at the base of his jaw, just below his ear.

Applying pressure, I leaned in. "Let's do this calm-like."

His hands flew up, but he relaxed into the pain shortly thereafter. We'd been down this road before, after all. He knew that if he didn't struggle, I wouldn't hurt him.

"You're choosing the wrong time for this," he warned.

I always did, as far as he was concerned.

I marched him into the closest bar. He staggered, the difference in the light hard on his eyes. Mine adjusted immediately. I led him to the back and into a booth.

"Have you been drinking?" he asked as he fell onto the seat. He rubbed at the offending spot under his jaw.

"It's been, like…a whole day since I finished the bottle. I hardly think that counts. Which reminds me, time for a top-up. Stay here."

I got myself a beer from the bar, and one for him. I drained half of both of them. Props were good.

After setting his beer in front of him, I kept a handle on mine. "Got a question."

"You always *got* a question." He peered down at his

bottle. "They'll know you set that in front of me, Reagan. Everyone knows I don't drink."

"They'll wonder if you started again, and have a moment of worry." I had no idea who *they* were, but his expression darkened. "See how smart I am? Now, I'm looking for a really powerful mage." I dug the casing out of my pocket and showed it to him. "Do you recognize this?"

"How would I recognize that? I don't use those."

I rolled my eyes. "Has anyone mentioned anything?"

"About a casing? No. About a mage? Yes. But it sounds like they're in the same boat you are." He looked at the bar door. He was definitely waiting for someone. Probably a shifter, but I was here on legit business, so it didn't matter.

I had to keep reminding myself of that fact.

"What boat is that?" I asked, putting the casing back into my pocket.

"Not the booze cruise, at any rate. Your teeth are red."

I leaned forward, losing patience.

He read the writing on the wall. "Okay, okay." He put his hands on the table and glanced at the door again. "That guy you picked up the other night?" I nodded. "I asked around about him, out of curiosity. I wanted to know why the vampires were after him.

That's newsworthy, right?" He waited for my nod. "He was selling a sort of drug. It came in the form of blood."

He stared at me, clearly waiting for a reaction.

"Go on," I said.

His lips tightened. "We think it must have been vamp blood, and it certainly wasn't taken with approval, because they ended up killing him."

"Vamp blood? Maybe." I wanted him to think I didn't know the real source of the blood. "It's pretty hard to trap a vampire. Maybe while he was sleeping, but it would take some extreme presence of mind to pull that off without getting killed before you reached the door."

"That's what we're thinking. It doesn't quite add up."

"*We* being the shifters?" I asked.

He looked toward the door again. "Yeah. So we've been looking for any other explanation."

"And you heard about a mage," I surmised.

A troubled look crossed his face. He ran his finger down the sweating bottle of beer. "I've heard about a few, actually. All of a sudden, it seems like mages in this area have gotten really powerful. Like…one can create hellfire." He shook his head. "He went missing a couple days ago, but they say he does that often. He disappears for a while, but he always comes back, usually with some spells."

That sounded like the guy I'd taken out, though the spell he'd thrown at me hadn't been hellfire. Close, but it wouldn't have killed a vampire. It hadn't been hot enough. "Where does he disappear to?"

Red shrugged, glanced at the door, and lowered his voice. "The witch who was telling me was really drunk. He didn't think it was the Realm, but he wasn't sure where else the mage would go. Maybe he disappeared to re-up his supply of the blood?"

"That's all you've got?"

His eyes turned shifty. "Yeah."

He was the worst liar. I said as much.

"That's it. He's been gone a while." Red fidgeted.

"You guys killed him, then?" I tried, watching closely. His head jerked, like he stopped himself saying no, and his shoulder ticked upward, like a shrug in process, but there was no surprise or defensiveness in his expression.

The shifters knew the mage was dead, but they didn't know I'd killed him. Huh. Captain Lox was keeping his secrets, and so were the mage's neighbors. That was good.

"What else?" I asked.

Red shifted in his seat. He licked his lips and eyed the door.

"What else?" I repeated before upending the bottle and gulping down the liquid. For some reason, my heavy drinking scared him more than an out-and-out threat.

"The rumor is, there are a few mages involved," he said in a shaky voice. "They're selling the blood, but that's just a monetary scheme. They're also trying to amass power."

I rolled my eyes. "They are always trying to amass power. Is this all you've got?"

"No!" He scooted toward me. When the man had information, he hated to be disbelieved. Hence the shifters keeping most of the juicy bits from him. "Rumor has it, they've enlisted a few covens of witches for their army. Those witches have somehow turned into full-scale mages. Their power has doubled. *Doubled.* Now, the witch who told me was drunk, as I said, so he could've exaggerated, but still...a witch who couldn't even get into the Realm, suddenly talking about it as a second home?"

That *was* something.

I leaned back, not liking that news at all.

"Exactly," he said, matching my lean. "Exactly. We're a little worried about what this might mean. And even more worried that the vampires will stumble onto all this, and try to bring the leader into their fold. Can you imagine if the vampires suddenly had access to this much power? They could easily use the mages to force us out of the Brink...and, eventually, maybe even take on the elves."

I couldn't hold back a dark look as I remembered what Darius had said: "We won't bow forever."

Red had a point. My job had started as a bounty hunter gig, but now it seemed like I'd be leading them to a large source of power with an amassing army. Not to mention, I had a lot of power myself. Once I found the mage in charge, the vampires would have both of us in the same place, ripe for capture. I was pretty sure this hadn't started as a setup, but if the shifters had made this connection, I could damn well bet it had occurred to Vlad and Darius.

"Not good," I mumbled.

Before Red could reply, a burly man walked through the door. Stacked with muscle that didn't steal any of his grace, complete with a barrel chest and heavy tree-trunk arms, he held himself like he owned the world and everything breathing within it. I groaned when I caught sight of his eye color. One blue and one green.

The most powerful of the shifters in North America had just walked into the bar. My day couldn't get worse if I intentionally sabotaged it.

CHAPTER 14

"HEY, ROGER. NICE to see you. I was just leaving." I got out of my seat as he stalked up.

"Sit," he barked. Full of power and force and intensity, his words demanded obedience. Red quailed and stooped in his seat. If he were in dog form, he would've rolled over and showed his belly.

"Gotta go. I'm working." I took a step away from the table, shamefully ready to run. Downing a guy like Roger would not be easy. Maybe not possible, even for me. I was lucky he couldn't change into shifter form in front of all the humans. Still, if it came to a fight, the whole bar would be taken out.

"Working. Is that what you call constantly badgering my employee for information you are not entitled to?" He stepped in my path.

"Yes. Why, what do you call it?"

Roger's face was a terrible mask of violence. Shivers of apprehension worked up my spine. "This ends, now," he snarled.

Fire sparked in my gut, my automatic response to

bullying. Logic told me to run, but my contrariness had always been stronger than my logic. I sometimes hated that part of myself. "You can't be here all the time, Roger."

His eyes flashed. "I don't need to be here all the time. I can find you anywhere."

"And do what? Hump my leg?" I smirked, the fire spreading through my middle and tingling my fingers.

"I should drag you out of here right now." He took a step toward me. "You've caused a lot of problems for my people."

"I haven't done dick to your people. You hang around like gremlins, hoping I'll slip up so you can haul me into the Realm and get someone to check out my funky smell. I have a legit job, you harassing douche. Spoiler alert: that job doesn't answer to you. You have no power in the Brink magical law enforcement. You are *allowed* to work here because you help them with a few of the outliers. Start messing with their employees, and that might not be the case anymore."

He stared at me, and though he was about my height, it felt like he was looking down at me. Lava replaced the heat in my body—survival mode. It was about to get real, I could tell. Shifters didn't reprimand with words; they did it with actions. They battled to get to the top of their hierarchy. He was ruthless, vicious, and at the top of his game. Quite possibly, I was in over my head on this one.

I wonder how fast he can run...

Roger's tone lowered into not much more than a growl. The small hairs rose all over my body. "I will only say this one more time, Reagan Somerset. Keep my employee out of your schemes, or I will be forced to make good on my warning."

"I didn't remember hearing a warning in your dull sermon." Darius strolled into the bar with a calm expression, all infallible confidence.

I jumped, only then noticing full night had fallen. Roger stiffened and turned around extremely slowly, coiled and ready to strike. Green shimmered around his body, a shifter's magic, making their form change possible. The power of it stung my eyes.

Red hunched so low in his chair that I could barely see his head above the table.

Darius tsked. A little smile played across his lips as he crossed much too closely to the fuming shifter and took his place by my side. "Careful there, little doggie. You wouldn't want the humans to know how furry you can get. That might get you in some trouble. You'd be on the other end of the law, then, would you not?"

"An elder among us. How did I get so lucky?" Roger grinned, a terrifying sight filled with violent promise.

"You turn into an animal. You didn't," Darius replied with nonchalance.

"Given your other form, you probably shouldn't throw stones regarding what he turns into," I murmured.

"You openly feed on human blood," Roger said quietly, his voice muted by the jazz music. "I am authorized to take you down. Do you want a head start?"

Darius laughed. "My, my. Full of ourselves, aren't we? Tell me, when have you ever taken down an elder by yourself?"

Roger's unwavering stare beat into Darius's face. "We're not solitary monsters like you are, hiding in the shadows and preying on the weak. We run in packs. We share the euphoria of a good kill."

"For a species that hunts us, you know very little about our true habits. I find that interesting. Or maybe you trick yourself into thinking we are solitary beings so that when you prey on a lone vampire, you can still call yourself mighty?"

Roger's jaw clenched.

"Food for thought," I said, and cleared my throat. We were wasting the night. Those mages had to know they were being hunted by now, and they possibly knew by whom. They'd be putting up defenses, and if they were gaining power quickly, I'd soon be no match for them. "Anyway, Roger, we are on official business. His faction"—I nodded at Darius—"has posted a bounty, and we are investigating. He has a legal right to be in the

Brink."

"He has a legal right *if* he abstains from taking human blood or revealing his true identity." Roger's stare had not left Darius's eyes, and vice versa.

"I have not taken human blood while on official business," he lied.

"And when you need to?"

"Shifters don't count as humans..."

A more prominent cloud of green shimmered around Roger. He was having a hard time controlling his wolf, which was not usual for someone in his position. Darius obviously recognized this, judging by the taunting smile curling his lips. He wasn't fooling me anymore, though. Darius's body had tensed and the sharp tips of claws were poking me in the back where his hand rested. He was ready to fight, just like Roger was.

"He'll take it from me," I blurted.

Both men blinked and looked at me.

My mouth went dry. I didn't want to say it again. So I dodged. "He won't have to take it from a human, because he is super old, and elders don't need blood as often. Which you know, Roger. He was full up when I met him in the Realm, in anticipation of being in the Brink on this bounty, and that was only a couple days ago—"

"Five days," Darius said, his pupils dilating in a sexual sort of hunger. His hand now splayed across my back possessively.

That probably wasn't good. At least I knew what day it was, though.

Wait…what day was it?

I shook my head, getting back on track. "Right. Five days. And I'll close this in no time. I always do. So there's nothing to worry about. But *if* he needs it, I can supply it. I don't count as human, so that sidesteps your jurisdiction."

Roger's eyes narrowed. If I was on the "shifter watch list" before, I probably had a star next to my name now.

"So let's go." I flung Darius's hand off my back and pushed him so he'd walk around Roger. He did so grudgingly, that hunger now burning bright.

Definitely not good.

"Oh, and…" I tapped on the table, drawing Red's wide eyes, two orbs right above the table edge. While he didn't deserve a favor—after all, he passed on loads of my information to others—I wasn't the type of girl to get a guy in trouble with his boss. "I didn't get a chance to reciprocate knowledge, what with your boss throwing his dick around and all." I saw Roger stiffen out of the corner of my eye. He was really easy to bait when Darius was on the scene. "I killed that mage. The one who disappeared for a while? He's not coming back. His friends are after me now, too. So I've got that going for me. Unlike shifters and vampires, I *am* solitary, so if you want to watch me a little more closely after I take down the festering group of power seekers, that'd be just fine. And it would be preferable if you'd intercede before they kill me."

I switched my glance to Roger, whose brow had furrowed. He hadn't expected that, I wagered. "I'm working with vampires because they stole a mark, and with it, my livelihood. They posted a bounty through the Magical Law Enforcement office. I am not working with them; I'm working for myself while adhering to the terms of the bounty. I have no loyalty to them outside of this particular job."

It was Darius's turn to stiffen. I was making solid friendships that would stand the test of time, as was normal.

"Why are you telling me this?" he asked, clearly confused.

"Because, while I think your people are extremely annoying, I am not choosing a side. I am not your enemy."

Though Roger didn't so much as glance at Darius, I had the feeling he was uncomfortable with the vampire's continued presence. "Noted. The job offer is still on the table. As is the warning for harassing Red."

Roger had offered me a job several times, delivered by his people. The terms were simple—tell the shifters what and who I really was, let them categorize my magic, and then I could help them bring down vampires and occasionally demons for a moderate monthly income. In other words, choose one side, hunt the other side, and let someone control me with knowledge and money.

Nope.

"Declined and, respectfully, declined." I bowed with a flourish. "I'll stick with no ties, if you don't mind. Friends are as dangerous as enemies around here. But thanks for asking and delivering."

"Reagan," Darius said in a soft tone, letting me know it was time to go. It was just as commanding as Roger's barked words, pun not completely intended.

"Are you sure you are working for yourself?" Roger asked as I stepped away.

"No, and it isn't sitting well," I responded as I joined Darius.

"I was not pleased to have awoken and found you missing," Darius said as we stepped out into the sticky New Orleans night. The clouds above hadn't broken open and poured down onto the street yet, but the extra moisture in the air clung to my body like a wet, lightly heated blanket. I loved it for reasons I couldn't explain, like the city itself. It was a living, breathing thing that either took root in a person and brought them to life, or turned them cold and pushed them away. I was the former, and the pulse of my surroundings thrilled me, filled with danger and intrigue, history, and tradition. There was no place like this place, and I felt the pleasure of it drumming through my veins.

"Reagan?" Darius prompted.

"Sorry, the city was talking to me, and I like it better than you." I gave him a grin to say I was joking. "I can go out in daylight, Darius. So when I can't sleep, I might as well work, no?"

"It isn't safe for you to go alone. As you told the shifter, the mages will know of you by now, and they will try to take you down."

"They'll try to take you down, too, O Wise One. And yet you wandered around the city looking for me. Double standards, much?"

He scowled, leading me God knew where, but it happened to be in the direction I was going, so I didn't say anything. "You are a human female. It isn't safe," he repeated.

"That's what I meant by—Never mind. Look, don't worry about me. I'm better equipped at dealing with mages than you are. If a pack of vampires comes after me and I need to walk around at night, you can gallantly stalk me then. How does that sound?"

"I get the feeling you are poking fun at me, Reagan."

"I sure hope so. I'm laying it on pretty thick. Anyway, how'd you find me?"

"One of the humans on my payroll saw you. He kept tabs on you and awaited my call."

"Wow. You really were stalking me. That is horribly uncool."

I gestured him right. He resisted for a moment, but when I stepped around him and went on my merry way, he caught up immediately. He didn't ask where I was going.

I enjoyed that he wouldn't admit to his ignorance—it really made things easy on me.

"I got some disturbing information," I said.

I told him what I'd learned from Red, stopping in front of the brewery on Decatur. I had wanted to watch his reaction. I should've known he wouldn't have one. He was much too controlled for that.

When I was finished, he studied my face. "We haven't much time to find him, or his power might soon exceed yours."

"Yeah. I came to the same conclusion."

"We can try another of my contacts. I did not get the feeling Mrs. Banks was withholding anything."

"She wasn't, but if you'd just talked to her husband, you wouldn't have gotten what we did. Your other vendors might be the same way. Not many people want to get mixed up in vampire politics."

"This is hardly politics."

"Everything with you guys is politics." I watched his

face again, but still got nothing.

I sighed and threw up my hand for a coming cab. Seeing it was a female driver, I shoved Darius toward the street. "Stick your hand up!"

"I do not lower myself to jumping around like a fool to hail a taxi. I will simply call—"

I flung his hand up and shoved him forward again, making him take a step. The cab flashed its lights and pulled into the public parking area.

I hastened Darius that way. "This is faster."

"You engage in life like a simpleton."

"Engage in life? You need to go back to studying how the people of this time speak. That was a big failure, right there." I reached for the door handle, but suddenly his hand was there. He scoffed and pulled it open. I was pretty sure he was thinking *simpleton* again.

I rattled off the address as Darius got in. He smoothed his tight black shirt over firm pecs. This had to be his "dressed down, I might have to fight" look. Some people wore sweats; this too-handsome vampire wore cotton with a designer label and stylish jeans.

"How do you expect to move in those jeans?" I asked.

"How do you expect to move in leather?" he replied, not looking at me.

"With aplomb." I smiled. He didn't notice.

After a moment of sitting in traffic, he asked, "Why

did you seek out the dog?"

"You mean Red?"

Darius turned his flat stare on me, something I was now realizing indicated confusion. "Mr. Nevin."

"Is that Red's last name?"

His brow lowered. "Roger."

"*Oh.*" I laughed. "Hurts to say his first name, huh? Afraid that will imply you're friends?" His expression darkened. "What is up with you two?"

After a moment of staring at me silently, jaw clenched, he lowered his voice and leaned toward me. "Since he became alpha, an unusually large amount of my children have been killed. It is a widespread problem. That is why I now have a safe house. American police are unaware that I am not human; they only know that I own the property. Anyone caught breaking and entering will be apprehended. The human world's judicial system comes in handy, especially when the perpetrators mostly live in that world."

"Why don't you kill them when you see them? It seems like you just wait for them to kill you."

"Your magical law enforcement does not mind our presence so long as we play nice. That is easy to do most times. It is only when we are caught..." He paused as the song changed on the radio, not wanting his voice to be heard in the silence. "Feeding," he continued, "that there is the problem."

"With houses, how could they catch you?"

"I am surprised at the lack of common knowledge about us, given how long we have been around. I hope it continues this way." He gave me a warning look.

I rolled my eyes. Knowing about their habits was nothing compared to knowing about unicorns. I was already under the informational thumb.

"Large-scale changes are becoming more common, given our dwindling numbers," he continued. That was when they created new vampires, I knew. "There is more power in numbers, as you can guess—and less chance of an ambush that would cripple us. Mr. Nevin is very organized, however, unlike his predecessor, and he has been more effective than we would like."

He paused for a moment, looking out into the night. "Then there are the newborns. It takes a lot to quench their thirst, and it is hard to control them for the first few decades. They make a great many mistakes and are often caught in the act. Mr. Nevin has trained and nurtured extremely capable employees. We need to make some changes. Give them something else to do."

The way his voice changed, and his eyes darkened, gave me warning shivers. I was right not to choose the side of the shifters. I had every reason to believe the vampires had something in the works, and whatever it was, I didn't want to be anywhere near it.

I hoped I wouldn't be anywhere near it, anyway.

After what Red had said, I was a smidgen concerned.

"Okay, then. Well, I wasn't there to see Roger. I was there to see Red, the guy who was cowering in the booth. He's great for information. And before you ask, I told him what I did just to help him out. He's a good guy but very low status, so he's dumped on a lot. Besides, they seemed like they already knew the guy was dead."

The cab driver's eyes widened and flicked up to the rearview mirror. Her fingers tightened on the steering wheel.

"Which movie was that?" Darius asked smoothly.

My mind went blank. "'Thriller'?"

"I believe that is a song… Or did you mean the music video, perhaps?"

"Yes?"

"Here," the cab driver said as the car stopped on the familiar street. Darius drew out a wad of money, peeled off a bill and handed it over. The lady grabbed it, barely looking, before turning back in disdain. "Do you got anything smaller?"

"What'd you give her?" Peering around the seat, I spied a hundred-dollar bill.

With his thumb, he flicked off bill after bill. Hundreds kept flashing by. Rolling my eyes, I dug out a twenty I'd found lying around Darius's house. They would never have noticed it missing. Clearly. "Here.

Keep the change." I handed over the money and captured the hundred. Without flinching, I stuffed it into my pocket. "Let's go."

Out on the sidewalk, I paused in front of the familiar house before feeling my body go rigid. I stooped, peering through the partially opened door from a distance, and then started walking. No magic surrounded the outside this time, but the residual feel vibrated off the house like a swarm of bees.

I kicked the door open. It tore off the heat-warped hinges and half crumbled onto the floor. The house I had been inside five days ago was no longer a house. It was a shell. Someone had magically burned out the inside until there was nothing left.

CHAPTER 15

"HOW IS THE roof still intact?" Darius asked as he filed in behind me. "And the walls?"

I reached around and tapped my back. He took hold of my belt, which was close enough. I stepped forward, heard the moan of the badly charred floor, and felt it give a little. It didn't break. I took another step, pausing when he was forced to follow me. It held under his weight, too.

"This was a well-contained magical fire," I said, running my hand along the wall. Black flaked away.

"Hellfire?" he asked through a tight throat. "The dog said that the mage you killed could do hellfire."

I scowled back at him, a knee-jerk reaction, since he hadn't shown up in the bar—at least not publically—until *after* Red had told me that.

My focus snapped back in front of me. "Not hellfire, no. That rumor is false. He didn't have the power. How long were you there for that conversation?"

He didn't respond. Then I remembered his stalking human friend, who must have followed me into the bar and kept the text messages rolling. How annoying.

"He could create fire, though," I said. "That's what burned away my eyebrows, in case you haven't made the connection. It seems someone else has the same ability."

I scuffed the ground with my toe. The carpet had been largely burned away and parts of the wooden floor beneath were blackened. In a small spot near the wall, a hole had burrowed.

"The floor should be worse off. Magical fire can easily be contained from rising, but it has to sit somewhere. There are very few who can suspend fire in midair. Very, very few, and none, that I know of, are human." It was only a half lie.

"Those who can do hellfire can also suspend it?"

There wasn't much Darius was scared of, but clearly hellfire was high on that short list.

"As far as I know, those who work with hellfire can only blast it, not control it. Think of an extremely powerful flamethrower with three settings—destruction, massive destruction, and total destruction. It gushes out, along with the conjurer's power and energy, eats everything in its path, and then goes out. If that were the case here, we'd see melted walls from the blast radius." I shook my head, noticing the fire pattern winged up in some places to form a V. "No, this is a normal kind of fire, created with magic instead of sticks and matches. This fire was kept on a tight leash."

I traced the fire patterns in the air with my fingertip, noticing how the burn marks stopped at the same place near the ceiling on all the walls. I ducked and ran my fingers along the floor before knocking. "Heat weakened the properties of the wood, but it didn't ignite. It was not an efficient fire."

"What does that mean?" Darius asked, following me to the doorway of the room that had held the book. The floor in this room had been destroyed, and remnants of the framework and the ground below showed through. A picture was starting to form.

"An efficient fire is one without much smoke. It is mostly flame. You see, smoke is actually fuel for the fire, in gas form. If a fire isn't efficient, that means it's creating a lot of fuel in the air. Here, the floor's smoke-damaged but mostly intact, which suggests an inefficient fire. But these walls say otherwise."

The living room was about the same, with the right side of the room worse off. Warning shivers raced across my skin. I did not like the look of this one bit.

I worked toward the kitchen at the back of the house. "When fire is burning wood, the actual wood is not aflame. Rather, it's the air right at the surface. There is the tiniest gap. If you see a burning log, the outside might be charred, but if you stop the fire, the middle of the log will be fine. In essence, it's the smoke that's burning. The heat changes the wood's properties, which creates chemical gas, which then fuels the fire. The more heat, the faster the burn. Long story short, the massive amount of heat in this house should've burned the floor as badly as it did the walls. But the floor is fine in some places, and not in others. Our very tricky mage could float fire. He kept it off the ground in some places, but let it burrow in others. How? Why?"

I let out a breath as I broke out in a cold sweat.

"He controlled all this magically?" Darius asked. I felt a tug on my belt as the floor bowed under my feet. It didn't break, though.

I touched Darius's hand attached to my belt just to assure myself I wouldn't fall in. "This belt better be quality, Darius."

We edged forward another few feet, and I answered his question. "Yes. He controlled it very well, or else…" I cut myself off as a light bulb snapped on in my head. Air filled my lungs in relief. "He must've laid down a type of magical floor. I've never seen one used as fire retardant, but it could work, I suppose. The floor's probably messed up in a couple of places because the mage didn't root the spell." I scratched my head. "I should've asked Callie about mages who don't root spells. Usually that's a rookie mistake. The one in the Realm wasn't rooted, either, though that one had some power behind it. Strange."

I rubbed my temple, thinking this through. I couldn't do these spells on my own, but my magical encyclopedia was extensive. If it hadn't been, I'd be dead twenty times over by now. "So he creates the magic buffer first, protecting the ceiling. The layer for the floor comes next, but that spell can't be interrupted by walking through it, so he'd have to do this room by room. The fire seems moderately controlled, which is hard for a human to do. It would take the highest level of power. Or…" I tapped my chin in thought.

"Or?" Darius asked, a captive audience.

"Or it would take the right knowledge and a boost of power. The unicorn blood is the boost. The knowledge and sustained increase in power could come from a demon. Is our tricky mage playing host to a demon? Curious minds want to know."

I saw the hole from which I'd retrieved the sack of spells. Not burned.

I turned back toward the living room, more pieces of the puzzle fitting into place. "I bet he was in here looking for something"—the book of spells, most likely—"and whatever he wanted wasn't there, so he freaked out."

I stepped too far into the living room. The sound of cracking wood made me flinch, but it was too late. The floor gave way. My foot went down.

My hands came up to protect my face. Gravity

ripped at my body, but my backward fall was cut off abruptly—pain cinched my stomach and air greeted the crack of my ass.

Darius held me in the air by my belt.

"Once again, this strange form of security has proven effective," he said. He didn't sound taxed. "And Reagan, you should know that I only buy the best quality."

"It seems so, yes. Fancy putting me down?"

I appreciated that he set me down gently. I *didn't* appreciate the smile on his face.

"Suddenly you gain a sense of humor?" I dusted myself off out of habit.

"I have always enjoyed circus performers."

"Lovely."

Back to analyzing the hole in this room, it seemed I had missed an item hidden in the floor—why else would another cubbyhole exist? Judging by the lesser destruction in this room versus the other, I'd taken the most valuable prize. That was good to know. "Our mage has a rage problem. He wanted something that wasn't here, so he fried the place. Childish."

"Possibly that was the demon at work."

Who had taken the item from this room?

Another light bulb went off.

"Could be," I answered Darius, marching toward the door. His reflexes were as fast as ever, thankfully, and I didn't have to rip out of his grip, or pull him behind me. "Depends on the demon. With all the mage's power, though, that demon must be constantly trying to take over." Outside, I swung my gaze to the side. No curtains moved. "I bet the mage is playing the dangerous game of demon pack and play."

"What is that?" Darius followed me across the dead grass and to the neighbor's house, my original destination.

"He creates a spell to contain the demon in a circle of some kind, one that can coerce the demon into giving information or power at the mage's behest. Those spells are extremely complex, require a *lot* of power, and unwavering confidence and focus to maintain control. When the mage needs to take the power on the road, like he clearly did here, he performs a forced possession, pulling the demon into his body. At the end of his errand, he uses an exorcism to put it back into the circle. There are a few very dangerous points. Getting the demon into the body without it escaping, getting the demon out of the body and back into the circle, and keeping the demon from overtaking the body while the possession is in progress. Lots of work, but our mage clearly thinks it's worth the crazy power boost. It's just a matter of time before one of those three issues goes wrong."

"Or else the circle falters."

"Or that, sure. The demon could eat away at the circle over time, and if our mage is primarily concerned about the more dangerous situations, maybe he gets complacent with the finer details and upkeep. But wow. A true demonic possession for power. I haven't seen this in a while. It totally fits, though."

I felt the wards protecting the property, paltry things designed by a hack.

Or maybe playing with the powerful mage had made me forget what lower-level magic looked like.

"You have magic, you know all about magic..." Darius paused beside me, watching me feel my way around the spell. "Reagan, I have never heard a mage speak like this. The Banks are at the top of the power spectrum in the area, and they have never sounded this confident and insightful. In addition to being extremely aroused, I am certain you could be the best mage I have ever met."

"My mother thought the same thing. Had she lived longer, she would've taught me more. But her time was cut short."

"I hear the sadness in your voice. I would like to revisit this conversation in a quieter time. But for now, why don't you learn magic?"

I stood, whipped out my sword, and sliced through the spell. Immediately I felt the small tug of the sword, asking for a little bit more power to keep it completely stocked. I resisted, to see what would happen. After a moment, the feeling died away.

"I really like this sword. Thank you." I tried to step forward, but felt his hand on my shoulder, stopping me. "You want to soak in the moment of me thanking you, huh?"

"You've cut a ward. Usually some sort of defensive measure happens afterward."

"Yes, professor, that is true. So why are we standing still, waiting for it?"

His hand disappeared from my shoulder.

I stalked forward, waiting for the ball to drop. "I am learning to be a mage, after a fashion. Did you not hear me in that mage's house? I study spells and incantations, but there's a lot of information, not to mention tons of spells that are virtually the same other than their names. A spell that shocks people can be performed in ten different ways, did you know that? *Ten!*"

"Pick one and then you can shock a person."

"Yes. That is the logical conclusion. The problem is, I'm a perfectionist when it comes to magic. Maybe one is better than the other. Maybe the versions are different because of climate or environmental differences. I don't want to try each one, because I'm also cautious. I've seen what happens when an idiot with too much power tampers with unknown spells. So then I look up each variation and try to figure out why it's different from the others. All that takes time."

"I assume you are the idiot with too much power?"

"I am *not* the idiot with too much power because I'm not tampering with spells I don't understand. But thanks for the finger pointing, ass."

He smiled again as we made it to the three steps that led up to a modest porch. No defensive spells had come, or even vibrated from within the house. It was then I remembered what we were dealing with: a community.

"Move!" I shoved Darius to the side and ran the other way.

Not a moment too soon.

A wash of magic rolled through the yard from behind us, churning the air with heat. It bounced against the porch and stopped. I'd seen that spell before—it was supposed to contain blue fire. This one contained a glowing blue orb instead. The caster had sent it in the right direction, but not with nearly enough power.

"This is what I'm talking about. Step in here." I walked into the spell and closed my eyes in bliss. It was a lovely dry heat, like a sauna. "Comfy."

Darius lightly grabbed my arm. He was reaching in instead of walking in. "It is too hot for my liking. I will not be grieved by my inability to take a bath with you."

"You won't be grieved because vampires in water smell like rotting flesh, or because you realize I'm not into dead things and you don't want to embarrass yourself?"

"You have consented to let me feed from you. It is only a matter of time before you desire to feel me, skin on skin."

"I consented to let you feed if you absolutely had to. But you've fed. A lot, actually, considering you just did so again last night after only a week or whatever. You have to be stuffed. We'll have killed the mage or died trying long before you need to feed again."

"Something about you makes me thirsty beyond my control, Reagan. The human last night did nothing to curb the insatiable need that you inspire within me. It made me want you more. I will not last as long as you believe."

"That is an extremely poetic way of saying *you're screwed,* isn't it?"

"I will screw you, yes. Very softly at first, until you are mewling and writhing. Then, when you beg me just right, I will screw you hard, deeply, until you are screaming for holy damnation. I will be the only thing you think about for the rest of your life."

"Sounds horrible. Remind me—did you like getting shot in the leg, or no?"

His hand left the bubble of the spell.

"That's what I thought." I let my own heat coat my body, fire not quite realized, dissolving the spell. "This neighborhood must be a coven, but their combined power is nothing. Pooled together, they would barely get through to the Realm. What were they doing with a powerful mage living among them?"

"You know about magic, but you do not know the culture of mages and witches?" Darius turned as a deadbolt clicked over. "The house is now unlocked."

"Thanks for actually doing something. Other than pissing off a powerful alpha and hanging me in the air by my butt, that is."

"I have also made sexually explicit verbal advances on you."

"Inappropriate sexually explicit verbal advances, at that. That's a mouthful of awful, is what that is." I walked up the steps as the deadbolt clicked over again. I sighed and cocked a hip in annoyance. "Really, Darius?"

"That wasn't me. The human must be by the door."

"Ah. Which means she knows a vampire is outside. That's got to be terrifying." I knocked. "It's me from the other day," I called. "The girl who took out that mage."

I heard heavy footsteps before a curtain in the window at the front of the house shook. I stepped down two steps so she could better see me.

After squinting in the window for a moment, her face disappeared. The porch light blazed down on us and Darius flinched away before he could stop himself. Margaret's face appeared in the window again. Her eyes shone in recognition as she scrutinized Darius. A moment later, the deadbolt clicked over and the door shimmied open. As if on cue, the sound of more locks clicking and doors opening drifted over the quiet street. All the neighbors were up and watching the intruders.

"The spell woke them," Darius muttered as he looked behind.

I nodded, though he couldn't see, and resumed my place on the porch.

"What are you doing here in the dead of night?" Margaret asked me in a hushed, disapproving voice. "You gave me a huge fright."

"I'm working. You have a minute?" I took a step closer.

"In the middle of the night? Absolutely not! Come back in the daytime, young lady. You ought to be—" She cut herself off as Darius appeared beside me.

"You are being rude," he said in that cultivated and eloquent voice, clearly displaying his own disapproval. We might be pushing ourselves on her in the middle of the night, but his tone was so convincing, he made *her* seem like the barbarian in this situation.

It seemed to work. Half sputtering, she backed up out of the way and held the door for us, her face pink. As we entered, her gaze shot past us, to the people obviously watching.

"You can invite some of your friends, if that would make you feel more comfortable," Darius offered gracefully.

"Yes, of course," she said, as though she hadn't meant to. "I'll just…do that."

"Maybe first you would prefer to show us to our seats and inquire after refreshments? Reagan would probably love some coffee."

Margaret stared at Darius like he had two heads. "Sure. Yes."

"You're laying it on a little thick," I murmured to Darius as Margaret ushered us into her home and planted us on the fluffy couch in her living room. The layout was very similar to the mage's house next door.

"While she is probably an excellent hostess, given the strange crotched items—"

"Those are doilies," I supplied.

"—and full tea set, she is frightened and displaying signs of guilt. She is not at her best. I am merely shepherding her."

"I see," I said as she stood in front of us, wringing her hands.

"Can I get you something to drink?" she asked.

"I would love tea, please," Darius said pleasantly.

"Actually, we won't take up much of your—"

"Tea would be fine, thank you." Darius used his soft though forceful voice to cut me off. Margaret disappeared with a sigh of relief.

"You see?" he said, crossing an ankle over his knee. "She is already relaxing. The act of doing something habitual and expected calms humans' nerves."

"Had a lot of experience calming humans down, have you?" I asked.

"Yes I have, unfortunately. It is necessary to get the best results during negotiations."

"I always thought predators liked the thrill of the hunt."

"I am not talking about feeding, Reagan." His gaze found my face. I felt a strange shiver at the unidentified look in his eyes. "In that, you are mostly right. The chase is one of my favorite things. Trying to best my prey. Dominating." Hunger flashed. "But when she is caught, and under my control, force becomes cohesion. Passion is ignited. Fire. It is absolutely exquisite, Reagan, as good for the human as it is for me."

"What happens when you find a woman who doesn't like to be dominated?"

"Such as yourself?" A smile curled his lips. "That makes the hunt so much more thrilling. The complexity of a strong woman is intoxicating. I enjoy it immensely."

"So it's a one-way street? She gets dominated, or you keep trying?"

"You have not been listening. Once she submits, so do I. We form a bond, for a time. Pleasure is shared between us, as is power. The two components wrap us up and block out our surroundings, heightening the feeling. The taste." I watched, mesmerized, as his tongue slid across his lower lip. "When the feeding is done, the bond will fade. Unless that bond is solidified." His voice had softened. His eyes delved into mine, the fire and desire burning brightly.

"How do you create a permanent bond?" I whispered. Staring at his lips. Wondering how they tasted. What they would feel like skimming over my body.

He leaned toward me slowly. The air between us started to sizzle, electrified. "First, I—"

"Here we—Oh!" Margaret stopped next to the couch, tea tray in hand.

Reality punched me in the face, something that happened only *after* I did something stupid in Darius's presence. I jerked back. "NO, YOU AREN'T INTERRUPTING ANYTHING!" My volume control was broken at the moment.

"She didn't ask if she was, Reagan," Darius said, entwining his fingers in his lap.

I nearly punched that stupid smirk off his face.

I jumped up and shook myself out, seeking sweet, *fresh* air. Wishing it were much colder in the room. "That was not what it looked like," I said, swatting my arms to rid them of the shivers. I'd have done the same to my nether regions, to rid them of the uncomfortable pounding, but it would have looked odd.

Not like hopping around the room slapping myself

was exactly normal…

"They are beguiling, vampires," Margaret said as she set the tray down on the coffee table. "Though often lovely…"

"No, I'm just an idiot." I wiped my forehead and sat on the love seat at the end of the table instead of returning to the couch. "I wanted to ask you a couple questions, Margaret, if you don't mind."

She cleared her throat. "Do you take milk and sugar?"

"One sugar and no milk for me, thank you," Darius said.

She'd brought both of us tea, so I said, "Same as that," not really caring. I didn't plan on drinking it, but Darius would insist that I take a cup.

He leaned forward for his tea, his face once again closing down into a flat expression. The arousal must've been wearing away, thank God. I took my cup and waited patiently until Margaret sat down in the recliner across from me.

"I have a couple people coming over," Margaret said, raising her chin as though she expected defiance.

"Fine." I deposited my untasted tea on the table in front of me. "First things first: what did you take from that house?" I raised my finger. "You know that Darius is a vampire. He can tell if you're lying."

I had no idea if that was true, but *I* would know. I

could read a liar from a mile away.

She took a sip of her tea, clearly trying to appear unaffected. It would've worked much better had she not kept darting her eyes to the archway into the room. "I don't know what you mean..." Her hands were shaking.

I braced my elbows on my knees, studying her. The shaking got worse. She wasn't just lying—she was afraid of admitting the truth. "Did you happen to catch me standing in your defensive spell?"

Her cup clattered as she put it on the tray. She didn't respond.

"You worked that out with the neighborhood, right?" I intentionally used a badgering tone. Usually I would start with more of a friendly demeanor, trying to get the person to talk to see if anything useful slipped out. This time, though, I needed exact answers, and I needed them quickly. I'd throw my weight around to get the job done. If she hated me after—well, I didn't have any friends anyway. No big deal.

Her lips tightened. She was trying to prevent herself from talking.

I stood and crossed to the mantelpiece. "Look, Margaret, I know something was taken from that mage's house. Based on the spell your neighborhood cast at a tenth of the necessary power, I'd say it was a book of spells, or notes of some kind. Am I right?"

Her front door opened. I heard footsteps echoing

down the hallway. Margaret straightened, finding some courage. A moment later, a man and a woman entered the room, both in their late fifties and dressed in yoga attire. The rings said they were both married, and the closeness of their bodies said it was to each other.

"Welcome," I said, stepping forward with an outstretched hand, asserting my control over the room. I was the boss here. "I'm Reagan. You are?"

"Tamara Evans. This is Rodney." She gestured at her husband, who wore a stern expression and followed it up with a stern handshake. He stepped a little behind her, a protective position signifying backup. He was the muscle. His wife was the talent.

"Hello. Please, have a seat." I gestured them to the couch. Darius quickly moved to the window, giving me space. He was a good partner when he wanted to be. *Thank God.* "Would you like some tea?"

"Oh. Y-yes, please..." The woman, ruddy-faced and with light burns on her hands, looked at Margaret in confusion.

I cocked my head and closed my eyes for a moment, feeling residual magic. Also an echo of power. I'd never felt something quite like it. I couldn't tell if it was from spell working within the neighborhood coven, or if the power was individual to one or both of them.

I lifted my eyebrows at Rodney, silently repeating myself.

"Sure," he said in something like a grunt, playing Mr. Tough Guy.

He had no idea what a real Mr. Tough Guy sounded like, I could tell.

"Fantastic. Margaret, if you would?" I waited for her to start on the tea before continuing. "I was just asking Margaret what she took from the mage's house."

"She seems to think—"

"I just told them what I think," I said to Margaret, planting myself on the other side of the coffee table, staring down at the newcomers. "You will note that I did not ask *if* you took something. I asked *what* it was. Oh! Forgive me my rudeness." I shoved my hand through the air at Darius, careful to keep my movements coarse. "This is my vampire friend. He's hungry. Being that we saw Roger, the alpha shifter, earlier, and he didn't detain Darius, you can be comforted by the knowledge that we are authorized to conduct business in the Brink."

Rodney swallowed, and his hand jerked toward his wife before he stilled it. He heard the threat loud and clear: *We can and will kill you to get this information, and we'll be operating within magical law.*

Naive people under pressure were largely stupid creatures.

"What did you take?" I repeated.

"It was just a basic-level book of spells." Tamara

shrugged. "It wasn't worth anything."

"*Just* a book of spells?" I crossed my arms over my chest, studying her, noticing the tightness around her eyes and the thinning lips. Quarter-truths were the same as lying in these circumstances. "Get it. And before you do"—I put out a cautioning finger—"know that I am familiar with the defensive spell you cast as a collective. A few books have that spell, but none of them make it roll like that. So this book that you get should have some pretty high-level notes marking up the pages."

Tamara's spine went rigid and her expression set in defiance. She opened her mouth to refuse, but Darius turned into a blur that ended in her dangling from the air by her neck. She flailed. Her husband started, his eyes widening.

"Don't make her ask again," Darius said softly. The small hairs rose on my body.

"Hey!" Rodney shouted, struggling to get up. Margaret clutched her throat, a defensive reaction that wasn't helping anyone.

"Don't—" Tamara wheezed out of a constricted throat. Clearly he wasn't cutting off all her air, somehow. "Don't tell them."

Rodney hesitated.

They must've known someone would come calling for the book, and they were prepared for that someone to use violence to drag the information out.

I sighed, because that would just make all this take longer.

Darius must've recognized it, too, because he changed tactics. "Thank you for this lovely meal." He lowered her to the ground and opened his mouth, revealing his fangs.

"Don't tell them!" Tamara said through clenched teeth.

They must've thought the book was only safe within their coven. Given the spell they'd tried, probably one of the few they could actually do with their power level, that book was a good find. Which made the one I'd taken a great find.

Why would they assume that a bunch of lower-powered witches could keep a book like that safe?

Like a flash of lightning, it hit me. "He was one of you, wasn't he?" I snapped, walking toward the window to think. "He was at your power level, but he got hooked up with the more powerful mages, and they gave him a way to increase his power. Once he reached a certain level, he was allotted some learning material. I bet that book has sacrifices and possessions and…" I trailed off as confusion rolled across two faces. The third had a sort of dreamy look and a firm grip on Darius's flexed biceps. He hadn't even bitten her; he was just whispering into her ear while slowly stroking the skin over her vein with his thumb. The guy was good.

"So then, just higher-level spells, I gather?" I saw affirmation in their expressions. "You want to keep the book to prevent other people from gaining a bunch of power and turning into a whack job, like your former friend and neighbor did. I see."

Darius pulled his head away from Tamara's in order to glance at me. There was no hunger or arousal in his eyes; he was playing a strange sort of bad cop. Or a good cop on ecstasy. That worked, too.

"Trust me, it is way safer in my hands than it could ever be in yours," I said. "I already have that much power. I won't go crazy, trust me."

"Don't give in," Tamara said, her hands now rubbing up and down Darius's arms. He might've been applying a bit too much charm.

"I want that book." I leaned against the wall. "He'll bite her to get it."

"Don't give in," Tamara said again, licking her lips. Her eyes fluttered closed as Darius ran his lips against her skin. Rodney shifted from side to side. His hands flexed and un-flexed. He did not like what was going on, but had no idea what to do.

"You guys didn't prepare for this kind of torture, I'd bet," I said, waiting patiently. This was way easier than busting heads and striking fear into their hearts. "Take notes, Rodney. All he's using right now are words. Clearly you need to up your game in the bedroom. She's probably bored out of her mind..."

Insulting his prowess did it. Rodney cracked. "He did go crazy," he said in a thick voice, watching as his wife traced the hard chest of a vampire. "He got hooked up with that crew, forgot we even existed, and the next thing we knew, he was plaguing the neighborhood with heinous spells. He called them practice spells. He had to be taken out."

"I get that. I took him out for you. You're welcome. But Randy, I need that book."

"It's Rodney," Darius said. He traced a fang down the vein in Tamara's neck. She moaned and slid her hands over his shoulders, trying to pull him in.

Right! Rodney.

"This is getting awkward, Rodney. You should probably do something." I waited, but he wasn't breaking. "Might I remind you, Rodney, that Mr.…." Damn it! I couldn't remember Darius's last name. The name thing was a huge problem in my line of work. "That Mr. Darius is a *vampire.* If he bites her, he'll change *her* into a vampire. She'll die. And become a vampire. And then the shifters will kill you all."

I could barely see Darius shaking his head. I tried to hold back the silent laughter.

Rodney licked his lips. He bounced from foot to foot, not sure what to do.

"Bite her, Darius," I ordered.

CHAPTER 16

THE WHOLE ROOM paused. I'd been certain the threat would be enough to spur Rodney into action, but no one said a word.

"What the hell is up with you people?" I stepped forward and grabbed Rodney by the throat. His eyes widened in surprise. "You'll let your wife take a beating, but will you?" I threw him against the wall. "Keeping that book is just asking for someone to come and take it, moron. You are doing the magical world a disservice by not giving it to someone who has the power to keep it safe."

I advanced on him, grabbed him by the shirt front, and lifted him into the air. His mouth gaped.

"Yeah, I'm strong." I shook him for effect. "Can you imagine what a punch feels like?"

"It's in my house. In someplace safe," Rodney blubbered. "Please don't hurt me."

"What do I look like, your slave? Go and get it." I tossed Rodney toward the archway. He crumpled to the floor like a doll and sobbed. "Good grief, man, it wasn't that bad. You're not hurt. Go get the book." He dragged himself up like a wounded puppy and dramatically limped out of sight.

"This is not at all how I saw this meeting playing out…" I said with a sigh.

"Will he come back?" Darius asked, releasing Tamara.

"Hmm. Go ahead and bite. I've always wondered what it feels like." Tamara reached for Darius.

"And the crazy keeps rolling." I scratched my nose, willing my frustration to simmer down. "Can you put her outside or something? She's making me uncomfortable."

He took a card out of his wallet and handed it to her. "If you would really like to know, call that number. One of my people will get in contact with you."

"Tamara, we've talked about that," Margaret said disapprovingly. "It's a dangerous road."

"It is quite safe, I assure you," Darius said, directing Tamara out of the room. "Beneficial to all parties."

"Will you be there?" I heard her ask.

"Decidedly not." The door closed and he appeared in the room again, looking calm as usual.

"Definitely not how I saw all this going," I repeated. "One minute, serious questions, talk of torture, and a run-of-mill scare tactics. Next minute, crazy vampire lust from a middle-aged married person looking to get bitten by a walking corpse."

"That is offensive." Darius poured himself some more tea.

"Margaret," I said, drawing her attention my way. "You need to break up this neighborhood. It's gotten weird, sweetie. The witch next door was clearly insane before he elevated to mage, your neighbor is looking for thrills while her husband stands by, you're dabbling in spells way above your pay grade…" I touched her arm. "The first step is admitting you have a problem."

She blinked at me for a moment, her face white. "Please don't bite me. Or hurt me."

"Good. A normal response. Thank you." I went to the window and pulled back the curtain. Rodney was on the sidewalk, and he and Tamara looked to be in an argument. He had something tucked under his arm.

Another light-bulb moment. "Darius, go get that book." He was out the door in a moment. "Margaret, you need to watch Tamara. I bet she's looking for a way to power up too. She'll follow in your neighbor's footsteps when she realizes getting bitten by vampires doesn't help."

"No, she won't," Margaret said, setting her cup and saucer aside. "They wouldn't take her."

I turned around slowly, pretty sure I had an *oh my God!* expression. Out of the corner of my eye I saw Darius walking up the stairs with the book. He was moving slowly, studying it. That was probably bad, but right now, this took precedence.

I lightly tapped the window and waved my hand, indicating he should stay out there. I was in friend mode right now, letting her talk. Telling me things I hadn't known to ask about.

"They have criteria on who they take?" I asked, playing it cool, pretending I knew who *they* were. Just a couple of girls gossiping, that was what we were.

Darius continued toward the house. He was going to come in anyway, which was probably good, because his memory was better than mine. I just hoped he did it in stealth.

"Yes. John, the…" She swallowed and nodded in the direction of the house next door. "He had the highest level of power in our community. We all have a little spark of natural magic, but he had quite a bit more."

"Could he get into the Realm?"

She shook her head. "He could see the gate, but it hurt him really bad when he tried to enter. Everyone said he'd die if he went through."

I nodded, because that was correct. The pain was a warning. Some kept pushing through it. A dead body emerged on the other side.

"I guess he had enough magic for the high mage, though." Margaret rose and moved toward the door. I was about to throw a question at her to stop her, but before I did, she asked, "Do you want something stronger to drink?"

I released my breath with a laugh. "I sure do. I'll help you."

That was code for: *I don't want to let you out of my sight for fear you'll stop talking.*

Darius stood by the door, quiet and still. Margaret didn't notice.

"I told John not to join," she said, moving down the hall. "A few of us did, but the others, Rodney and Tamara included, thought maybe he should check it out. That maybe he could learn something and pass it on. I should've pushed. I should've tried to drown out Rodney's goading."

"Why did Rodney goad John?"

We entered the kitchen. "Well, you know, he and John never really got along on account of Tamara and John's affair a while back. And because John had more power. That made a few people jealous. So Rodney didn't care if it was dangerous. He probably hoped it was." She shook her head sadly, and I felt my mouth drop open. This coven definitely needed to split up. "John gave in. Then all it took was the first meeting and he was hooked. We saw his power boost right before our eyes. That's when Rodney and Tamara tried to join. A couple others in the neighborhood, too. I begged them not to, since I could already see John changing for the worst. Thankfully, they weren't allowed. Not enough power."

"But in the end, Rodney still got rid of John," I said softly, the wheels spinning.

"I guess so. Since you had to…" She gulped.

"Kill him, yes." I didn't mention that next Rodney would have to contend with a bunch of vampires, which would be much harder competition than a mediocre-powered mage. "So this high mage *can* boost people's power, then?"

She shot me a strange look before pulling down a bottle filled with brown liquid. "The high mage didn't recruit you?" she asked.

"I don't do magic."

Confusion surfaced on her face. "Then…they let you go?"

"Huh?"

"Huh?" she repeated.

I accepted the glass, holding up my hand to stop the crazy. "Why would you assume I was captured? Or even approached?"

Her face closed down into a look of remorse, and worse, guilt.

"Margaret, what did you do?"

"We'd already lost John," she babbled. "We couldn't lose anyone else. They would've killed us to get that book."

I hunched a little. "So when they came looking for John's goodies, you told them I'd found what was in the kitchen, and you pointed them my way."

"I figured they'd think I was too low-power to find anything myself, so…"

"They didn't even bother looking through this neighborhood, they went straight to me." I nodded, because I should've assumed that. "When was this?"

"Yesterday night. He was in John's house all evening. I saw flashes and fire through the windows, but didn't hear anything. Nothing caught fire outside."

"*He* was… Just one?"

"The high mage. He was alone. B-but, I think he has a few people he sends out to recruit or to assert his will. I'm not sure how many."

I huffed out a laugh at her choice of words. The high mage was definitely on a power trip with that title and all this will assertion he was doing. "What does the high mage look like?"

"You mean, besides the mask? You don't know?" She took a shaky sip of her drink.

"I was gone when they—or some other mages—arrived at my house. I didn't bother going in after them."

"And the spells you got out of the kitchen?"

"They're in a safe place."

She shook her head. "They're not safe from the high

mage. He'll blast through your house with fire to find them."

My heart sank. "Fire won't work on my safety holds." No one, not even my father himself, could break into those. I had a spicy blend of magic and history protecting my most valuable assets. The problem was, my house and all my furniture was wood. I would lose everything I called home. Maybe I already had. "Sometimes I really hate my job."

I felt Darius's comforting hand on my shoulder a moment before he asked, "What do you know about him?" Clearly he wanted to hurry this along.

Margaret huffed. "What *don't* I know? After he recruited John, I started asking around. I'm friendly with witches all over the city. From what I can gather, he is power hungry. More so than most mages. He used to target witches like John—ones who were on the cusp of being mages, desperate for the power boost that would get them there. Word is, he's shifted his attention to those with a higher level of power. They're selling blood of some sort to witches and other mages, trying to enlist them. No one knows what kind of blood it is, though. They've been very quiet on the subject.

"The rumor is that it's vampire blood." Her face turned red as she glanced at Darius. "But I don't think that's it. I've looked into it, and vampire blood gives humans an energy and ability boost, but not necessarily magical people. And this stuff gives only magical people a boost, I've heard. Like magical PCP. It doesn't last, but…"

"This explains some things," I said. This confirmed the theory that had started to take shape in John's burned-out house. A power boost would certainly help the high mage run his demon-pack-and-play gig. It would amplify his spells and allow him to refill his store of magic more quickly. In the slump between boosts, he'd have the demon to give him power.

"How did he start this venture, though?" I wondered. "How did he get that strange blood in the first place? Torture it out of a vampire?" I looked at Darius, hoping he knew I meant torture the *information* out of a vampire.

Darius was staring at the wall, not moving. Thinking.

"If they're in league with vampires, then you're a faction divided," I said to him, watching his expression for any hint as to what he was thinking. I wasn't getting anything. "Someone killed those vampires in the Realm, after all. Then there's John, who I am pretty sure was bonded to a vampire."

Darius's head snapped around, and he scrutinized me. "How do you know?"

"He could see in the dark. No magical spell can do that. That I know of, anyway. What else?"

"There probably is a way. John had access to a lot of advanced spells," Margaret said.

"So do I." I was still looking at Darius.

"Well…now…I've never seen a vampire hanging around his house," Margaret said, tapping her fingers on the counter. "He did disappear for a few days at a time, though. Spread out all my feelers in the city, and I still couldn't find him. But I've only heard about the blood, not any vampires helping him." Margaret made a duck bill with her mouth.

"How often did he disappear?" Darius asked.

"Oh…" The duck bill turned into lip gymnastics. "Every two to three weeks."

"How long has this been going on?" I asked.

"John was approached four months ago or more, but he only started getting really bad in the last couple. That's about when he started disappearing as well."

"That could be a girl, though." I leaned against the wall, my mind trying to fit everything together. "You'd think a vampire would visit his house when he or she needed blood."

"What girl would have him?" Margaret scoffed. "The high mage hasn't approached any female witches or mages, as far as I've heard. And no girl went to John's house. No, that can't be it."

"Do you know where the self-proclaimed high mage is located?" I asked.

"He moves around all the time." A troubled expression came over her face. "I've heard of a couple places, but he knows people are after him. Or will be, if they aren't now." If he was killing vampires and dabbling in unicorn blood, that made sense. "The one thing he does constantly, though, is meet with his disciples—that's what he calls his followers. They go to the same place every week. John used to sneer when he mentioned the meetings, like the high mage was all-powerful. Like no one in their right mind would challenge them when they were all together."

"It sounds to me like a bunch of grade schoolers in a pillow fort praising an older boy wearing a paper crown," I said, feeling the familiar fire of a challenge. "They don't have anything I haven't seen before, I guarantee it." I made a sign like I was writing in the air. "I need that address, please."

Darius started out of his reverie. He looked at me with a straight face. "I need to go to the lair. There is some information I must acquire."

"What are you thinking?"

"Don't go after them alone," he said, ignoring my question. "Wait for my return."

I stared at him incredulously. "You're going to keep me in the dark about what you're doing?"

"Here." He handed me the book, ignoring me again. "Keep that. Go to my residence. They will protect you.

Don't go by your house—he is surely waiting for you. Find out when and where they meet, and I'll—"

"I have that right here, plus a couple of the old addresses I have for him." Margaret held up the notepad. "The meeting is every Tuesday. A lot of witches know about it, even though they weren't invited. But I really don't think that is a great time to go after him. He's got a couple dozen people firmly under his control."

"Two dozen barely trained yet volatile mages who have probably forgotten a bullet will kill them more handily than a spell," I said to Margaret while still staring at Darius's blank face. "They'll be so certain they're the kings of the world, and protected by numbers, they won't realize that very thinking makes them extremely vulnerable and unprepared. Tuesday is the perfect time to go. And I will be going."

He stared at me for a moment, reading me as I was trying to do him. I kept my face just as blank.

"I will return at sundown tomorrow," he said curtly. "Stay away from this until then, or I will consider it a breach of contract."

"Are you seriously not going to tell me what—" He was gone before I could finish my sentence.

I blinked at the empty spot where he'd just stood, taken aback by the sudden shift in power. One moment I had been leading the charge. The next, I'd been ordered to seek protection in Darius's home, where I would surely be monitored by his people, and keep my nose out of the investigation. All this while the big man left to take care of secretive business.

What the hell was that about a breach of contract, anyway? That was not how these things worked.

Anger heated my cheeks and tightened my grip on the leather-bound book. “That’s a load of bullshit, right there.”

Margaret’s lips thinned and her eyebrows rose—silent judgment. She tilted her head down in a half nod, as if to say, *Yes, that is some bullshit, you are right.*

“What day is today?” I asked.

“The third.”

“No, like, the day of the week.”

She shook her head—another silent judgment. “This is why you shouldn’t hang out with vampires,” she said. “I know he is incredibly handsome, and it’s hard to think around him, but as a rule, they run out when they are needed the most.”

“I can think around him perfectly fine, Margaret. I’m only working with the vampires because I’m poor and they offered me a job, which has nothing to do with what day of the week it is…”

She sniffed. “Desperation. That’s how it always starts…”

“No, it starts with biting and canoodling. What do you think I am, a novice? *What day is today?*”

"Sunday."

I tapped each of my weapons, a check to make sure they were there while I mentally got ready to go out on my own again. Damned if I would check into a hidey-hole with a bunch of curious vampires I couldn't trust while Darius went off to do some secret handshakes, or whatever he was doing.

"I know he said he'd come back, Reagan," Margaret said, analyzing me. "But vampires are only your best friends when they need something. As soon as they get what they're after, you're expendable. You should never trust a vampire."

I sighed. She was like a broken record.

"So what are you going to do?" she asked, clearly seeing my decision to ignore her.

"First I'm going to borrow a satchel off you, because this book will be cumbersome. After that, I'm going to collect a bunch of spells for a helluva magical battle. I've got a mark to capture and then use to barter for the money I'm owed. There is no way a vampire is going to dupe me out of a mark a second time. No way in hell."

CHAPTER 17

ARMED WITH A very bad attitude and a handful of spells Margaret had given me, I walked down the street while pulling up the ride-share app. My phone was charged up, thanks to the stay at Darius's house, but my bank account was nearly dry. I planned to rectify that.

After the big, bearded driver picked me up and brought me to my first destination, I made him wait while I thumped on Darius's front door. The poor guy had commented favorably on my sword, but he'd gone white at the sight of my gun. It must've dawned on him that those items weren't for show. He was probably afraid to refuse service, since I'd already gotten in the car.

I thumped on Darius's door again. Out of patience, I stepped back with the intent to kick it in. The lock flipped.

"About time," I said, straightening out.

A handsome man stood in the doorway. Six two, shirtless, and sporting lots of defined muscle, he was human.

Confused for a moment, I backed up and checked the house. Yep, it was the right one.

I shooed him out of the door. "I need to see William."

"William is busy at the moment," the man said in a raspy voice. I noticed three small gashes spread across his torso, in the stages of bionic healing from vampire saliva.

"What were you, the appetizer or the main course?" I pushed him out of the way.

"Hey!" he said, staggering back.

"Where's William? Or another rich vamp. I need money."

"They don't just give us money, you know that."

Not allowing myself to flinch as I stalked across a cream-colored rug in my grimy shoes, I took the stairs. "You should work out a better deal," I told the guy, who was now following me.

I peeked into the dining room and found a couple humans hunched over sandwiches. Clearly Darius hadn't been in charge of organizing *this* dinner.

"Where is William?" I asked the built guy again.

"He's in the east wing."

I rolled my eyes. "This place is a big square. There are no wings. Lead me to him."

Frowning at me, he did as he was told, bringing me

up a floor and into a plush room with plenty of places to lounge. William was sitting beside another vampire, a different gorgeous woman than Marie, both in a state of sublime relaxation.

"It's almost as if you didn't know a crazy, powerful mage was running your benefactor ragged," I said. They looked at me lazily, like two people might after a Thanksgiving dinner. They didn't speak.

I stuck out my hand. "I need money."

"Where is Darius?" William asked, making a half-hearted attempt to sit up.

"Were you giving blood, or taking it? I'm confused why you're this slow." I reached down and patted his pocket. Nothing there. "Money. Where is it?"

"We do not give out money, human," the woman said around a mouthful of fangs.

"Ew. Put those things away," I said.

"I am off duty and pleasantly relaxed." William draped his arm over the arm of the sofa.

"Off duty? Looks like Darius made sure to keep you informed." That was sarcasm. They didn't seem to notice. "Whatever. Give me money."

"William, get rid of this annoying pest, would you? Her smell is making me nauseated." The woman waved her hand in front of her face.

"Stop breathing. Easy solution." I reached down to William's exposed chest, grabbed hair, and pulled. "Up we get."

His eyes cleared before sparking with anger. An instant later, he was standing in front of me, arms flared at his sides, ready to battle. "You are protected now. You won't be protected forever."

I laughed and motioned him on. "Same goes for you. Let's go. The sooner you give me what I want, the sooner you can go back to being useless while I protect the future of your species. No, no. Don't thank me. It's all in a day's work."

His glower didn't stop him from moving out of the room and toward the stairs. We ended up in a large room with a tussled bed, thankfully empty. He opened a ceramic pot with a lid—either a poorly designed vase or an urn—and extracted a wad of money. Before he could leaf off a few bills, all twenties, I snatched it out of his hand.

"Thanks," I said, already walking.

"Darius will be hearing of this." William trailed me. "Your days as his honored guest are numbered."

"You were so nice yesterday. What happened?" I jogged down the stairs, passing the buff human who'd disappeared from behind me somewhere along the way, and headed out the front door. "Have a lovely evening." I closed the door in William's face, not an easy feat from the outside. Timing was on my side.

Surprisingly, the driver was still there.

"Boy are you getting a big tip," I said as I climbed in.

"Just remember to review," he said sheepishly, waiting for me to input the next destination.

"Five stars, all the way. There you go, the destination is loaded."

He checked the new route, and away we went.

I tapped my fingers against my knees as silence descended. I thought back to that woman vamp who'd said I smelled bad. From what little I'd seen of her, I couldn't guess at her age, but I wondered if younger vamps were repulsed by my smell, while the older ones were attracted to it. It seemed to fit, but I had never heard of that happening. There were a few magical creatures that vampires couldn't get enough of, but none that I knew of had a dual effect.

I shrugged to myself and glanced around as the driver slowly crawled through the French Quarter. Even so late and with a light haze of rain finally deciding to fall, people wandered around with their drinks, talking and guffawing, staggering or standing in doorways.

"What happened to the door?" the driver asked a while later as we pulled up outside my house.

My brow lowered in confusion.

The front door, which had already been busted, now leaned against the doorframe to mostly cover the entrance. The screen, which I'd left in the yard, had been placed on my porch, tucked behind my chairs.

"The cat got to it," I told the driver as I got out.

I'd expected the door to be in bits, or at least knocked more to the side. Maybe the high mage hadn't been my visitor after all.

The optimistic feeling was short-lived.

My heart dropped as I moved the slab of wood and got my first peek inside.

Charred to hell was the first thought that rolled through my head.

The floor creaked as I stepped on it. I paused and listened. Shuffling sounded outside, the slide of a shoe. I glanced over my shoulder, making eye contact with the man from down the way. He gave me a stiff nod as he trudged by, his glance taking in my front yard before darting into the house. I wasn't sure what that was about, but he made looking creepy an art.

I took another few steps, gauging the floor. Similar to the mage's house, it was charred but mostly solid. I could walk on it to check out the crime scene, but I couldn't live on it without some serious repairs.

There goes my deposit.

Pressure squeezed my chest as I looked around my living room, a blackened, twisted mess. My couch was a pile of char. Same for my chair. The glass from my coffee table littered the blackened ground. All the little things I'd gathered over the years were destroyed. My physical memories, gone.

Rage and sadness choked me in turns as I checked out my kitchen. Unusable. It would have to be gutted and redone. The weird porcelain cow my mother had given me before she died was nowhere to be found. The blown glass I'd bought off a street vendor lay in black shards.

I blinked away tears. I'd been on the receiving end of grudge attacks before, but this was, by far, the worst penance I'd ever received from doing my job. This was hitting me on an extremely personal level.

In a daze, I continued on, noting that the hallway entrance was in the same state of disrepair. Halfway through, though, the destruction began to fade. The deep black of the walls lightened, and then disappeared entirely as I neared my bedroom.

A shock of fear stole through me. Had the mage stopped his shock and awe campaign because he'd found one or more of my stashes?

I hurried into the spare room, equally as untouched as my bedroom, and slammed open the closet door. Magic pulsed like a heartbeat, strong and comforting. My heartbeat, to be exact.

Quickly, I pulled away a comforter and the board games piled on the floor. The small rug was next to go, revealing a square crack in the floorboards. It was completely undisturbed. No foreign magic loitered around it, and no defense spells had been set in motion.

Something else must have prompted the mage to give up burning my house.

I exited through the back door to check out my shed. The lock was broken and the inside looked ransacked. I waded in and put out my hands, feeling the familiar pulse echoing in my veins.

Another feeling caught me. Something foreign. Probing, almost. Like someone had tried to delve into my unique blend of magic to see how it worked.

Why would the mage do it back here and not inside, where he was less likely to be disturbed?

Unless the person who'd hit the shed wasn't the mage, but someone else who was curious about me, someone who'd recognize both the faint pulse of my heartbeat and the ancient magic I'd used to create this cache.

Possibilities crowded into my head, but there was only one person who came to mind. With his extrasensory hearing, he certainly knew my heartbeat, and he had connections to mages who could study the magic I'd used.

That stalking bastard.

He definitely needed that punch in the face. He was asking for it.

I checked the other caches, found them all unmolested, and returned to the spare bedroom closet. Once there, I pricked my finger. Blood welled up, hot and red.

Turning my other hand palm up, I created a ball of fire, setting it to float in a perfect sphere.

The blood wobbled on my finger before falling through the air. When it touched the fire, a sizzle sent steam twisting upward. I surged my magic in pulses, timed to my heartbeat as I muttered the incantation in Gaelic.

I'd asked my mother, "Why not Latin?" when she'd taught me this spell. Her response: "Gaelic is less used than Latin." I'd thought she was crazy at the time. Some villages in Ireland still spoke Gaelic as their primary language, not to mention the little bit children across the whole island learned in school. Since then, I'd seen so many magical people use Latin, each of them thinking they were so smart, so individual.

The ball of fire froze into a block of ice, which fell to the ground and cracked open. Vapor rose into the form of a skull, turning slowly through the air. Green light shone from its eyes and out of the missing front tooth. After a full circle, I said, "*Droim ar ais.*" Reverse.

Another two circles in the opposite direction and I repeated my command. After yet one more full turn, I said, "*Slainte.*" It literally meant health, short for "to your health," and acted as a toast before drinking. I thought it a fitting sentiment.

The magical lock opened, and I used a knife to take off the cover. A real safe lay inside, fireproof, with a separate spell to be hellfire-proof. My fingerprint opened this one, and finally, after all that, I had access to the book I'd taken from the mage's house.

I glanced at it in the safe's depths, wanting to grab it out and flick through it, but that would be a dumb move. Considering how long it would take to secure it again—and the very real limits on my time—I resisted. Instead, I dropped in the second book and closed it all up. If I lived through the next few days, I would go somewhere quiet and do some learnin'.

As I was getting up, I heard a strange scuffle.

I froze, listening.

Like a live thing, the noise vibrated through my house.

I took out my gun and braced myself near the door to the spare room. Soft movement sounded in the entryway, someone trying to be quiet.

Adrenaline flooded me, heightening my senses and increasing my speed. I swung out into the hallway, gun up, finger on the trigger. A shape loomed large in the doorway, hulking and dangerous.

I sighted and barked, "What do you want?"

The man threw up his hands. *A spell!*

I dove forward and then rolled to the side, coming up on my knee with my gun out, crouching in the doorway to my bathroom. I sighted on the person's head. No words drifted toward me. The hands didn't move.

Finally, I registered the face.

"Oh. Mikey. It's you." I sagged before climbing to my feet. "You could have knocked instead of skulking in."

My neighbor, No-good Mikey, could be one of the meanest sons of bitches in the neighborhood. If he thought you were looking crossways at him on a bad day, he'd charge you like a bull and beat your head against the ground. Or he could be the sweetest man on earth for no reason whatsoever. It was hard to gauge his various moods.

Most people tried to steer clear. Being that he was right next door and my moods could get as black as his, but rarely as sweet, we just tried to give each other a wide berth when one of us was ragey. We didn't talk much.

"How?" he asked, not moving. "You ain't got no door."

I put my hand next to the wall, holding his gaze, and gave three deliberate knocks. "Works on any surface—no door required."

He leaned against the doorframe, squinting in at me. "You're good with that gun. Were you a cop?"

"Yeah, right. Not even dirty cops steal as much as I do." I jammed my gun into its holster and retrieved my spells from the spare room. "What are you doing up this late?"

"Smokey said you came home."

There was that name again. Mince had mentioned him, too. "Is Smokey that guy who was loitering around outside fifteen minutes ago? The creepy-looking dude?"

"Yeah, Smokey. Don't you know your neighborhood?"

"I've seen him around, I just never bothered to ask his name," I muttered.

I flicked a switch, but wasn't surprised when the light refused to shine. I tried again in the hallway. Still nothing. I grabbed a candle from my bedroom—a prop I'd purchased in the silly hope that one day I'd have a romantic reason to use it—lit it with my finger, and brought it out so Mikey wouldn't ask why I was getting around just fine in the dark.

"He's usually up at night, prowling the neighborhood," Mikey said, looking around the place. If he was surprised, he certainly didn't show it. "He's one of those quacks who think vampires and goblins are real. Says he saw a vampire with you the other night. You're on his radar. Watch out." He rolled his eyes.

I wondered if goblins *were* real. They weren't in the Brink if they were.

I didn't think so, anyway. Maybe I should pick Smokey's brain...

"Why'd he wake you?" I asked, kicking the pile that

used to be my couch. I rested my hand on my pocket holding the wad of cash I'd taken from William. It was made up of twenties, not hundreds like Darius carried, and this wad was much smaller. It wouldn't come close to covering repairs for the mess I was standing in. Dare to dream.

"I told him to," Mikey replied.

"Because…?"

"What do you mean, *because*? Look at your house!" He gestured angrily at the walls. "Look at it!"

"I'm standing in it. I see it."

"I know Mince let a couple guys come in here the other day. Heard you left them to it." Suspicion rang in his voice. I had no idea why.

"Yup. I didn't feel like dying."

"You didn't call the cops."

"I don't like cops." That wasn't true, but it was what guys like him needed to hear so they didn't freak out.

"Yeah, well, I heard those guys left without taking nothing. Somethin's not right with that. Somethin's up. So I told ol' Smokey to watch this place. To let me know who was coming and going."

"What's it to you?"

He pushed away from the doorframe, his body going taut. "What's it to me? You're my neighbor, that's what it is to me. I don't gotta get a filthy dog because you're here all the time. Everyone knows there's one person crazier than me in this neck of the woods." He jabbed a thick finger at me. "No one messes with my stuff when you're around."

He basically just called me a crazy, rabid dog. *Awesome.*

He put his hands on his chest. "You got my back." His hands pushed through the air toward me. "I got yours. That's how this shit works."

"Touching," I said dryly.

"Yeah. I'm a goddamned nun."

Okay, then...

"This afternoon," he went on, leaning against the doorframe again, "or yesterday afternoon, technically—another guy showed up. Skinny bastard with his face deep in his hood. I was sitting out on the corner this time, watching. He strolled right past me, not even a nod. In *my* neighborhood." Usually people paid Mikey homage so as not to get their skull cracked. "He walked into your place without even knocking. Walked right on in, like that sonuvabitch owned it."

Mikey took a moment and cracked his neck. A burst of adrenaline filled my body out of nowhere. He was human, but he still wasn't someone I wanted to tumble with. He'd probably conjure up weapons like a magic trick.

"He wasn't worried someone might be in here?" I asked.

"Nah. Just walked on in." Mikey scratched his chin. "He weren't quite right, neither. Muttered to himself like a crack-head. He twitched like a crack-head, too. Far as I know, this ain't no crack house. So that didn't fit." The accusation was soft, but it was there.

"Nope. No crack in here. Not even any weed. I'm naturally this crazy."

Mikey pursed his lips. "That's what I thought. That's why I followed up, just to see what he was up to."

"Let me guess: you didn't call the cops either."

"Hell no, I didn't call the cops! You think I need cops asking me questions? Ain't no one needs cops asking them questions."

"Right." Crime watch was exactly that in this neighborhood—people watching the crime take place. "Can you describe him, at least?"

"Wait a second, I'm not done yet." Mikey held up his hand.

I went into the kitchen to get a second look at the damage. Maybe there was an unmelted fork somewhere.

"You gonna listen to this or am I wasting my time?" he called after me.

"Eyes don't work like ears, in case you haven't realized. I don't actually need to be in the same room to hear you."

I heard a sort of huff, then footsteps. He appeared in the doorway of the kitchen and resumed his lean. "I don't like to yell unless I'm about to bust someone's head."

"Good to know."

"So I walked closer, trying to figure out what the deal was. Before I got there, the door flew away. Blew out like a bomb went off. So I hurried up, then. I got a house right next door. No way do I need my house blown the shit up, know what I'm sayin'?"

"Yes, I'm with you so far."

"Sure enough, that bastard was lightin' fires inside." He blew out a breath and dramatically shook his head, making his body sway from side to side. "Nope." He waved his finger in the air. "*Nope.*"

"Nope, meaning you actually did something, or that you stayed silently angry?"

"I went and got my gun, that's what I fuckin' did. Ain't no motherfucker setting fires in my zone. You think I made it through Katrina to get burned out? Fuck *that*!"

I paused in front of him. He cleared out of the doorway and backed up to the front door, giving me a wide berth. Strangely, it made me relax that much more around him. He was respecting my space.

"Then what happened?" I asked, checking the time. Nearly four in the morning. I needed to get some sleep before I went and bought more spells. After that, it was home invasion time. I wanted to do unto others as they had done unto me.

"I walked into this motherfucker and tried to shoot a bitch, that's what happened."

My mouth dropped open. I blinked a couple times. I hadn't been expecting that response. "That was one way to call the cops," I said.

He chuckled and cracked his knuckles. "Anonymously, yeah. I popped off a couple rounds, made sure that sucker ran so you didn't get your house seized for a murder investigation, then got out myself. I didn't want to be home when the police drove through." He scratched his chin, a sound like rubbing sandpaper. "I mean, I know you rent or whatever, but the way I hear it, you're gettin' a good deal. You don't want to go and mess that up."

"Are you the one who put my door back?"

"Yeah. To keep people from looking inside. I didn't figure you needed questions any more than I do."

I certainly did not, from the police or anyone.

No-good Mikey had saved half my house. I scarcely knew what to say. I'd rarely said more than two words to him at one time, and though I did give him the passing nod, I didn't show him any deference. Him putting his neck out for me, regardless of whether he had a stake in the outcome, was strangely touching.

"Thanks," I said. It didn't seem like enough, but I didn't think he'd appreciate gushing.

He grunted in response.

After a moment of each of us looking around, me at a loss, him taking it all in, he asked, “What are you going to do now?”

My body filled with heat. I couldn’t contain the rage. “See how that house-burning bastard likes it when someone wanders into *his* home and lights shit on fire.”

Mikey started to laugh. “Atta girl. Show that rat bastard that crazy is as crazy does.”

CHAPTER 18

NOT EXACTLY COMFORTABLE with what I was doing, I rang the doorbell and stepped back. Afternoon light filtered down from the partly cloudy sky.

I shifted, still tired from the few scant hours of sleep I'd managed. Then I shifted from side to side in anxiety and thought about leaving. I didn't have many other options, though. So far today, I'd already met with two mages and a witch, trying to flesh out my arsenal of spells with what money I had. I hadn't had great luck. More than half of my shopping list had yet to be crossed off, including many of the essentials. How could I possibly outdo a pack of violent, spell-hurling mages without a distraction of some sort, much less some fierce counterattacks? I couldn't, that was how.

I swallowed my pride and rang the doorbell again. If they wouldn't help me, I'd have to go to the mages who often worked with the shifters. The shifters had some damn good ones. The problem was, like the shifters themselves, those mages were fiercely loyal, and might not help me out of pure bullheadedness.

The lock disengaged and the door swung open. Before me stood Callie, clad in a pink velvet sweat suit. She had a sweatband around her head, containing a mess of frizzy curls. Her red face shone with moisture.

At the sight of me, her eyes lit up and a smile took over her face. "Reagan! I should've known it was you. No one who knows better would interfere with my workouts. Come in, come in." She waved me in before turning, showing me the hot-pink "Juicy" spread across her butt.

There were so many sarcastic things I wanted to say that my mind froze up and I couldn't get any of them out.

"Tea or coffee?" she asked. I saw her check her watch as she led me through the house. "What am I thinking? It's well past noon. Beer, wine, or whiskey?"

"A beer would be great, thanks."

"Have plans tonight, huh?" We entered the kitchen, and she gestured me toward the high chairs on one side of the island. "Grab a seat."

"I can't stay long." I pulled out a chair.

"The beer told me that." She grabbed a walkie-talkie off the wall and brought it to her lips. "T-Rex, come in."

I wrinkled my nose. I didn't like knowing the pet names of married people.

She repeated the words before lowering the walkie-talkie. "He's working on a dinosaur distraction spell, trying to get it into a casing that will hold it. If I don't use the type of spell he's working on, he doesn't hear my voice at all. Trust me, it took me *years* before I figured that out."

"What do you need?" came Dizzy's voice, annoyed.

"Reagan has come for a visit. She's working tonight. Over."

"Oh! I'll be right in. I have another sword for her to try."

"That's why I was calling," Callie muttered to herself. She squeezed the talk button. "She won't be here long. Over."

Silence.

Her brow lowered. "Are you coming now? Over."

More silence.

Callie scowled and set the walkie-talkie on the counter. "No matter how many times I tell him, he doesn't use the proper speech. Half the time he's finished the conversation and I'm waiting on the other end, like a fool, wondering why it's taking him so long to answer."

"What's the proper speech?" I asked as she moved to the fridge.

"Over. Out. Sometimes he takes a long pause, I think he's done, go to answer, and we end up pushing the button at the same time." She popped the top off a beer with a little too much force. "It's a small problem, yes, but it's annoying as all hell."

"Got it." I took the beer. "Thanks."

She poured herself a coffee.

"Coffee? Really?" I asked. "My mother must not have rubbed off on you."

Callie took the whiskey out of the cupboard. I laughed. "Ah."

"She wasn't the one who rubbed off on me." Callie poured a generous helping into her coffee. "It was the other way around. My parents were from Ireland. Why do you think she used Gaelic in her incantations?"

A door opened somewhere in the house, followed by a heavy tread.

"But you use Latin," I said.

"For the household stuff, yes. It's like buying a Mercedes. You're showing your prestige and status more than getting something worth the price. Gaelic is reserved for my personal collection."

"I don't understand."

"No. You wouldn't. It's not logical." She took a sip as Dizzy stomped into the kitchen, leaving a trail of mud and flower petals in his wake. Callie's lips thinned and she leaned more heavily against the counter. She didn't say a word.

A moment later, I saw that she didn't have to.

"I'll clean it up later, Callie, this is important." Dizzy put a sword down on the island and peered at me. "Any feedback about the one you have?"

"No. It's perfect."

He nodded and pointed. "Try this one. Callie tweaked a few things, and I honed it down."

"Do you guys always work on everything together?" I asked, holding my hand above the blade. A sort of song and spice filtered through me as the warming hum vibrated through my hand. "That's nice."

"Good. Yes, good." Dizzy went to the cabinet at the side of the kitchen. "We'll alter the one you currently use, since that's the sword Callie's friend foretold of. This will be a good backup."

"That whack job is not my friend." Callie shook her head at her husband before turning back to me. "We work on all the more powerful and important items together. I am the big-picture worker, and he is the finesse. Separately we are both powerful, adept mages. Together we are the best in the state. It's very rare for two mages to come together in perfect harmony. Usually the balance of power is not quite right. When we got together, society said men should hold all the power in our everyday lives. Men tried to apply that to magic, and women either let them or fought them. Either way, it disrupted the balance. When a magical pair bends their relationship to fit the will of their so-called peers, they tarnish what is pure. They upset the natural flow of energy. Only if they fully trust each other, and themselves, can they benefit from a boost in power. That's why dual mages, the yin and yang of magic, are very rare."

"You keep saying women and men. What about same sex?" I asked, knowing I should be getting down to business, but I couldn't help myself. No one had described dual mages like this to me before.

"That's a reflection on the period as well. A long time ago, there were many same-sex partnerships. From what I've read, some were sexual partners, but most were female besties or men with a bromance. Witches have held that standard through time, working together to boost their power. But when the Mages' Guild formed, things started to change for us. The shift was slow, and incredibly damaging. Now dual mages are mostly heterosexual married people. I'm sure I don't have to impress upon you how hard that is. Keeping a marriage together is hard enough, but not strangling your partner when he repeatedly ruins your flowerbeds and tracks mud all through the kitchen…"

"Look at what I'm doing. I'm fixing it!" Dizzy said as he set upon the clumps of mud with a broom and dustpan.

Callie took another sip of her Irish coffee.

"Right. So he has the shed, and you have your ridiculous sweats," I said.

"I told her," Dizzy said, grinning as he worked.

Callie glowered. "It's ridiculous to tell me I can or can't wear something because of my age. I will not yield to a twenty-year-old trying to bully me!"

"No one, not a teen, a twenty-something, an old lady, or an old man, for that matter, should wear pink velvet sweats with 'Juicy' written on the ass. There is no age where that looks good."

Callie turned around and pointed at her butt. "You stand corrected."

Dizzy looked her way, rolled his eyes dramatically, and bent down to the next pile of dirt. I couldn't help giggling like an idiot, especially since Dizzy hadn't taken off his filthy shoes.

"So, what do you need?" Callie said, leaning on the counter and sipping her drink.

The atmosphere in the kitchen changed from light and fun to somber and pressurized in an instant. I took a slug of my beer and gently set it down on the granite.

"I need to buy some spells," I said, staring at the bottle.

"What kind of spells?"

I reached into my pouch and pulled out my list. Without a word, I slid it across the counter.

She unfolded it. Her gaze traveled down the page before she shifted and held it out to the side. Dizzy walked over, creating a fresh trail of dirt, and took it.

Callie's gaze returned to my face. "Those that were

crossed off?"

"I have them, obviously."

"From who?"

"From *whom*, honey," Dizzy muttered, looking the list over.

"A couple different sources," I said, resting my hand on my pouch. I still didn't have enough spells to warrant a satchel.

"Some of these require some real experience," Dizzy said, poking the page with his finger.

"Names," Callie said. She took another sip, seeming casual, but the keenness in her gaze told another story.

"Allen from the French Quarter—he's a witch—and Julie and Toss, who are mages."

"Oh no, they aren't worth buying from," Dizzy said, wandering to the counter and pulling out a drawer. He started rifling through it without looking. "They aren't even competition."

"I usually don't buy spells." I shrugged. "I have a little money now, but I don't have the hookups. I didn't know where else to go." I shrugged again, this time in embarrassment. I'd only just met them and already I was using their love for my mother to call in a favor. It wasn't right, but I didn't have much choice.

Without a word, Callie poured herself more coffee. Dizzy had found a pen and was now writing on my list, his face very close to the page.

Callie took out the whiskey, poured more, left it on the counter, and leaned down again. Her gaze returned to me. "I need the full story, starting from the beginning. I want to know why you're involved with the vampires, and what they have on you...why you need these spells, and how you're planning on using them. After that, we'll take a look at the things you've crossed out on that list. Only *then* will we make a plan of action. I won't help you until I know the full story."

"I can't tell you the full story," I said, thinking of the unicorns. "Some things you're better not knowing. I don't want your involvement recorded, either. If this goes sour, they might go after anyone who played a part."

Dizzy started to chuckle, still bent over the page. "If I know my wife, she's hoping they do. She's been bored for far too long. The rich life doesn't suit her."

"It suits me a lot more than that shed would," Callie said. She held up a finger to me, got a chair, sat down, and motioned me onward. "Tell me everything except what you absolutely can't."

I did. Like a faucet that wouldn't turn off, I opened my mouth and spilled it all out. Instead of unicorns, I said beasts, and neither talked about their blood nor my near-death experience—not in so many words, anyway—but I gave the gist. When I was done, Dizzy was seated beside his wife, his hand resting on my list.

Silence filled the kitchen and the sun had disappeared from the sky.

"That vampire should be meeting you about now, correct?" Callie asked.

"Yes," I said.

"Do you think he'll find you here?"

"I don't know. I wasn't being followed today, so he'd have to piece together where I was, what I was doing, and where I'd be forced to go."

"He'll know to find you here" Dizzy said, resting his elbow on the counter and his chin on his fist. "Might take a couple hours, but he'll figure it out. He's the smartest, most well-organized vampire I've ever dealt with. Head and shoulders above his minions. There's a reason he's still alive, and you're lucky you hooked up with him."

"How did I not know you were having a love affair with a vampire?" Callie asked.

"Oh no, you're sleeping with him?" Dizzy ran his hand through his thinning hair. "He is one of the best, but I don't advise going that far, Reagan. Vampires have a way of trapping humans with their sensuality. They are predators, after all, and humans are easy to manipulate in that way."

"I meant *you,* you ape." Callie scoffed at her husband, finally dislodging her gaze from me. "Talk about bromance."

"Oh." Dizzy's face turned red. "I respect him."

She gave me an exasperated look perfected by married women the world over. I couldn't help but laugh.

"What happens if he doesn't show?" Callie asked.

"He'll show. He is a man of his word." Dizzy patted the list for some reason.

Callie ignored him and awaited my answer.

"I'll take down their army and claim my mark. I'll store the mage somewhere safe, get information out of him, and then trade him for my money." I leaned more heavily against the counter. "And I'm late for the first leg of my plan."

"Which is?"

I brought out the note with the locations of his past visits, ignoring for now the meeting site. "To check these places out and take down anyone hanging out there."

Callie took a closer look at the note before hauling herself off the chair and leaving the room.

"Why do people keep doing that to me?" I muttered.

"Let's see what you have so far." Dizzy's gaze went to my shoulder. He frowned and looked under the island, only then revealing what he was looking for. "You keep your spells in a fanny pack?"

I gave him a flat stare. Couldn't people see the difference?

"Let me see what's in it," he said, putting out his hand.

"Okay, but some of the spells are volatile. You don't want to shake too hard. Or mess with them too much."

"I am a trained professional, Reagan Somerset," he said disapprovingly. He shook his hand at me. I handed over my leather pouch.

Callie reappeared with a laptop. As Dizzy muttered, sorting through my stuff, she looked up each of the addresses, her frown becoming more pronounced with each one.

"I don't like this," she said, turning the computer so Dizzy could see. She pointed at the screen, the image lost to me because of the way it was turned. "See the way that front yard is set up?"

"Defensive spell paradise." He frowned. "A small opening for the front walk where a lot of power can be rooted for maximum effect."

"Spells can be bound to the earth along this hedge, making it three times as hard to break through." She took her finger away from the screen. "They're all like this. If there isn't a natural hedge, there are wooden stakes beaten into the ground with ivy strung across. This mage knows how to fortify."

"I can cut through," I said. "I know how that mage's power works."

"Not before I have a look, you won't." Callie crossed

to the fridge and took out a bottle of water.

"What's happening?" I asked.

Dizzy folded my list. "We're going with you, obviously."

CHAPTER 19

AN HOUR LATER and teamed with two older mages who would not be dissuaded from extremely reckless behavior, I crouched between two cars with my sword in hand (they hadn't had time to alter it), looking at the largest and most recent hideout. It was about an hour outside of New Orleans, a mile from its nearest neighbors on all sides, and—just as Google Maps had warned us—surrounded by a large hedge with a narrow passageway to the front door.

"Are we really going in without a plan?" Callie asked, bending over beside me wearing night-vision goggles. Dizzy leaned on the other side, both of them clearly sticking out above the car and apparently not caring. Then again, though they were spry and didn't look it at all, they'd revealed they were in their sixties. Jumping up from a crouch was probably not in their arsenal.

"I'm going to cut through that spell, bust into the house, and see what happens." I patted my weapons. They were all present and accounted for.

"That's it? Just take it as it comes?" Callie asked.

"Yup. That's the thing with criminals—when they get cornered they're more violent and largely unpredictable. I'm usually the one who corners them, so..."

"She wasn't knocking your style," Dizzy whispered. "She's excited. I would like to say, however, that I do not like this plan. It's not my style at all."

"Are you ready, Dizzy?" Callie asked.

"No."

"That's his yes." Callie nudged me. "Let's go. We need to analyze that spell as you cut through it. It wouldn't hurt to get more acquainted with your magic, either."

"This is crazy," I said, looking around the empty lane in front of the house. It was deep into the night. "Having you along is crazy."

"Yes," Dizzy affirmed.

"He means no, it's not. C'mon." Callie nudged me again.

"You two have some serious consent issues with each other." Taking a deep breath, I stalked forward and pulled out my sword, staring at the blackened windows, the drawn shades. My pouch was open at my waist, carrying all the spells I could fit in it, including the essentials for which Callie and Dizzy had refused compensation.

"Okay, here we go," I whispered, hoping the other

two could hear me.

The vibration of magic buzzed through my veins as I neared the hedge. Getting closer, I identified two different spells. The walkway to the front door was protected by the same block that had closed off the path to the unicorns' island. This one was weaker in power.

I moved to the hedge, feeling that spell out. Less power still, cast by a different mage lacking finesse and an understanding of the craft. It was piecemeal, almost, like someone not very focused had muddled their way through the incantation.

"These people are still learning their craft," Callie whispered as she walked closer.

"Get back," I seethed, motioning her away. "Someone is liable to jump out. You never know."

"Oh, hush." She pushed me aside and opened her hand, revealing a small handful of herbs. Though she didn't utter any words, the small mixture puffed up purple smoke. It grew into a sort of fog and drifted toward the spell, filling in the narrow opening. She wiped off her hand before digging some leaves out of her satchel. "Crush and blow, dear." She handed them to Dizzy, who'd walked up behind her in a hunch. "Crush and blow."

Dizzy took what was offered and, visibly shaking, crunched up the leaves in his fist. Also without muttering any words, he flung the leaves at the lingering purple haze. The two spells merged and started to circle, the leaves caught in a whirlwind, turning around and around. The swirling haze gradually turned orange, and then violet, before lightening to a pastel pink. A blast of light soundlessly filled the gap in the hedge before rocketing ten feet into the air. Slowly, it fizzled out. The magic within vanished with it, not even leaving a residue.

"Wow. That's handy," I whispered.

"You have the power, you just need the education," Callie said, turning toward the hedge.

"I meant, handy if you aren't me." I grinned and barely stopped myself from powering up my blade. I'd almost forgotten that I didn't have to do that anymore. I stabbed forward, piercing the middle of the other spell. It frayed. Too easy.

"Get back!" I yelled, leaping over the hedge.

The door burst open and a green blast shot out, too far right. Another came right for me. I slashed at it, breaking it apart as though it were paper. He shifted, which was when I saw the staff pointed toward me.

Who was this guy, Gandalf?

I threw on the brakes and dove to the side as a rush of air barely missed my arm. Hopping up, I was readying for the next spell projectile when a bolt of lightning struck down from the sky. It let out a boom as it hit the mage, spitting light and electricity. He convulsed where he stood and dropped the staff, which blasted out another rush of air. It hit the hedge and frosted it over. His body fell, smoke rising from his burning hair.

"Holy sugar tits, Batman," I said, out of breath and looking skyward. When I glanced back, Callie had a huge grin on her face. Dizzy burped like he might be close to throwing up, but he shot me a weary thumbs-up. "It'd be worth learning magic just for that," I muttered.

I eyed the door but ran alongside the house instead. If there were others in that house, they were waiting for my grand entrance.

I stopped down a ways and dug out one of the extremely volatile spells I'd lifted from John. After placing it by the wall, I picked up a rock and threw it on the casing. The spell exploded, releasing darts of red as it did so. Bricks spat out in every direction, melting once they hit the ground. I cut through the aftershock of useless magic unable to take shape—he'd missed the second half of that spell—feeling a disturbing prickle along my skin. Ignoring it, and hoping that decision wasn't a really bad move, I launched into the house, sword in hand.

Two guys were staggering up from beside the front door.

"Surprise!" I yelled as I threw a casing. It hit between the two and roared to life, crackling and sputtering acid. One of the mages jerked away and screamed, the thing in his hand falling to the ground. Whatever it was started clawing up him, freezing his leg in place as it did so.

The other mage already had a casing broken and ready, and he shot a hex toward me. I dropped like a stone, hitting the ground and rolling to the side. The spell splatted against the back wall and ballooned into a bubble before freezing solid.

So, they'd not only expected me, they were trying to capture me.

Fat chance.

I flung out a capsule filled with black powder—I didn't *just* fight with magic. It hit the man and fell uselessly to the ground. He laughed like a moron and dug in his pocket. I threw two more spells, aimed at their feet.

"Women can't do magic," his pal said, cackling. They were both loony-tunes.

The first had another spell out. He crushed it between his fingers, a slick smile on his face. He thought he was really good at this magicking stuff, I could tell.

The house started to rumble. The walls shook.

Crap, maybe he was right.

Like a dart, green shot out from between his fingers. Unfazed, I quickly cut it out of the air and waited for what came next. The structure around me screamed.

Fissure lines cut through the paint on the walls.

The two spells I'd rolled released, purposefully delayed. Flames spurted out, lashing the more active mage's legs with heat. It ignited the black powder, which exploded. His feet flew out from under him as the house roared around us.

Heart in my throat—the power was way greater than this dopey pair should be capable of—I ran out of the hole I'd created in the wall. I had to get Callie and Dizzy to safety before I came back and figured out how to beat this surge of power. There had to be someone else pulling the magical strings.

Bricks ground into each other.

"Get clear," Callie shouted from somewhere behind the hedge.

"You get clear," I yelled back, running at them. "Get out of here. I'll handle it."

A groan sounded right before an enormous crash. The walls blew out the side of the house, and part of it flattened, like a giant hand had swatted it down.

I dove behind the hedge. Bricks flew over and rolled along the ground. I belatedly realized that a wall of magic buffered the hedge, keeping the bricks from shooting through it.

I saw two pairs of lit-up green goggles fifteen feet away—the Bankses. Like usual, they were arguing about something.

"Are you guys okay?" I asked, army-crawling to them.

"Are you okay?" they replied, speaking together.

"Yeah. Thanks for the magical wall." I drew up next to them but didn't rise off my belly. "Duck. Get your head down."

"I told him you'd get clear," Callie said.

"It was too close. We should've told her we were using that one," Dizzy replied angrily.

"We didn't even know we were going to use it; how could we have told her?" Callie said.

I peeked up over the greenery, surveying the ruined residence. That was when what they were saying sank in. Well, that and the fact that the house had been flattened right where the mages were standing.

"You guys did this?" I asked, more than a little in awe. I'd never seen anything like it, not on such a large scale.

Callie's head came around, her state-of-the-art, badass goggles not matching the pink velvet sweats—she'd refused to change, wanting to be comfortable in the battle. "Of course. Now hurry, make sure we got everyone." She turned back to Dizzy. "We gave them far too much warning."

"It's ten square feet of a house!"

"Still, we should—"

I didn't wait around. I hopped up and ran around

the non-flattened area, feeling clunky spells meant to either keep people out or warn of intruders. On the other side, I ran past a shed, waiting for something to surge out after me. Nothing happened. Further on, at the rear portion of the flattened area, I spied two legs sticking out of the rubble. He'd been at a back door, or maybe he'd been trying to get free. Either way, he hadn't made it out.

Good news for me.

Back around the intact area, I put away my sword and snatched out my gun before kicking in a side door. I ducked in, ready to shoot. It was the master bedroom, with a messy bed and dresser. Lived in, but no one was there at present. A quick check under the bed and in the closet cemented that. I checked the bathroom next, and the room next to it. All empty.

House locked down, it was time to see if there were garden tools in that shed, or a mage fighting a demon for control of his body.

Gun in my left hand and sword in my right, I advanced slowly, feeling a pulse of magic. Filthy and violent residual magic lingered within a defensive spell, hinting at the dark deeds that had been done in the shed.

Taking a deep breath, because I had a feeling I knew what awaited me, I put my blade to the spell. I recognized the particular currents as the powerful mage's. I had no way of knowing for sure, but I'd bet this was all him, without the help of a demon. It was far weaker, for one, and more controlled. The spell work didn't seem as erratic as the stronger spells.

"What do you have?" Callie came around the house slowly, with her hands out like feelers. Dizzy was right beside her, studying the ground.

"Not as much power in this spell." I finished slicing through. "You know what would be great? If you guys could design a sword that sucks in the power from the spell and stores that. Is that possible?"

Dizzy's head snapped up. He looked at his wife.

"I have no idea," she said.

"How is this the first time that has occurred to you?" I muttered, grabbing the rusty handle.

"Most people can't use swords like that, remember?" Dizzy said. "But…it's the same principle. Kind of."

"Maybe it could work with her magic," Callie said, looking at Dizzy.

"Here we go." I opened the door slowly, waiting for something horrible to jump out at me. The air was still and stuffy, flavored with a sweet stench. I took a step forward, feeling the clenching of my body that meant something dead and gross was about to enter my world.

Red splatters cut repeatedly across a white chalk line, forming a circle that took up most of the floor space. Within the circle, figures and lines spelled out a complex spell I'd seen in many books. Though the characters lining the edges were different than I remembered, the idea was the same. On one side, nearest the door, there were three more characters just outside the circle. I'd always thought of that as a doorway. My mark was definitely toying with possession, and he'd done it here with a three- or four-level demon. Such a demon was, in essence, middle tier when it came to power, which meant it would give the mage a pretty hefty bump.

At the other end of the shed lay a mangled carcass crawling with maggots. Blood had once oozed from under it, but it had since congealed into a dark, syrupy mess.

"That is super gross." After identifying the animal as a calf, I snapped a picture of the circle with my phone and stepped outside for a breath of fresh air.

"Is it safe?" Callie asked, peering into the shed.

"You have the power to flatten a house, and you're asking *me* if it's safe?" I chuckled and cleared out of the way.

"Just a small portion of a house, actually." Dizzy stood near the door of the shed. "That spell took us a couple months of power storage. This is an entirely different situation. We can't sense power, magic, or spells like you can. You are so much fun to explore with. If it weren't for the danger, I'd love to glue myself by your side. You know what we should do? We should create a magical obstacle course and walk with you as you work your way through it. Wouldn't that be a hoot?"

"Is it safe?" Callie asked again, louder.

"It's safe, but there's a carcass in the corner." I vaguely pointed, trying to scrub the image from my mind. Death was one thing, but a twisted body and splintered bones covered in maggots was entirely different.

A moment later they were discussing the circle and the type of incantations used, commenting on the power and ability of the demon the mage had summoned. I'd catalogued most of that and was now thinking about Darius. Dizzy was certain he would turn up at their house looking for me. Dizzy had left a magical note in Latin, something he said Darius would be able to decode, telling him where we'd gone.

I checked the time. It was edging into the small hours of the morning. If Darius had planned to find me, he would've done so by now.

"He's not naturally powerful," Callie said as she emerged from the shed. "He's less than middle tier."

"How do you know?" I matched her pace as she walked around the house, leaving Dizzy behind. The slow pulse of insects throbbed in the night.

"That circle." She scratched her head. "He had to sacrifice a large animal to reach the power level to use it. I worked backward from there. The ability to pull off the possession confuses me. You're sure he actually took the demon into himself?"

"Positive."

"That circle was calling a level-three demon. There are six power levels, with Lucifer himself being the only one at level six. So three is not too shabby. With the sacrifice, he could get it into the circle. That circle was well made. He's done his homework. Once in the circle, I have every belief he could keep it there."

"You're wondering how he got the power boost to get the demon into his body?" I asked.

"Exactly. Usually a possession is more about opening the body, like providing yourself as a vessel to be filled by the god or goddess who chooses you. *They* choose *you,* not the other way around. The mage's initial progression through the circle was aided by the various herbs and other plants he tossed in with that carcass," she said, vaguely motioning around her. I grimaced, having missed that detail. "But a lower-level mage would need a substantial boost to ingest such a powerful demon. And that higher level would need to be sustained for the duration of the demon's stay. Otherwise, the demon would overtake the body after a single night."

The boost was the unicorn blood. It had to be. But I couldn't tell her that.

"In other words," I said, "as long as he keeps sacrificing and getting that boost, I have a powerful mage to look forward to. And he'd surely do all that before one of his rallies."

"Surely. He has to look like he's all-powerful to attract the power-hungry sheep." She waved that thought away and shook her head. "The boost couldn't be vampire blood. It doesn't work like that."

"I know."

"You know what it is, don't you?"

"I know nothing."

We walked through the hedge and to the car, a beat-up old station wagon that Dizzy referred to as his "company car." I had made a plea to take his aforementioned Cadillac, but Callie hadn't wanted to risk getting it scratched. After seeing what they'd done to the house, I got it.

"It would sure be nice for you to pass on what you know," she said. "But since this guy is being hunted by vampires and a hired gun, I suppose it's better not to know."

"It is definitely better not to know, for a great many reasons."

"Oh yeah, like that helped my burning curiosity. Thanks." She leaned against the car. "If he has that demon in his body, your best bet is to wait him out. Wait until the boost dies down, if it ever does. When he's struggling for control of his own body, or better, kicks the demon out, then you take him down."

"And if he can keep upping his boost?"

She thinned her lips and took off her goggles. "You use our spells, the ones that don't require an elaborate incantation, get close, and stab him."

"You guys don't even use incantations."

"Spells don't have ears. The point of words is to focus the mind of the caster on what they're doing, what they should be feeling, and their expectations of the casting. When witches or mages are trained, they use a combination of words and actions to achieve that focus. Once it becomes second nature, they can go one of two ways. The most common is to continue to use the words and actions, but once that path is forged, it becomes like a rut. Getting out of that rut often takes retraining.

"Dizzy and I, before we'd even met and formed the dual-mage bond, decided to take the harder path. We continued training, first taking away the actions, and then taking away the words. It requires more focus. More patience and practice. But now, we can cast most spells almost instantly—no words and minimal action required."

"Then what was all that talk about Latin and Gaelic? If the words don't really matter, why the different language?"

She shrugged. "We still use words for the harder and more complex spells. It took us nearly a lifetime to get here. There are a handful of incredibly skilled mages who can do it naturally. The rest of us have to go the traditional route and practice constantly. So when we do have to use words, we choose ones others might not understand so no one else will steal our stuff."

"Are those natural mages in the Mages' Guild?"

"Two are, I think. Prized, of course. The others aren't."

"I bet the guild is constantly trying to enlist the ones who aren't."

"Oh yes. One of the naturals constantly disappears, I've heard. He goes off-grid. Wild, that one, not that I blame him. Really handsome, too. If only the fountain of youth were real…" She shook her head and sighed. "You should dump the vampire and seek out that mage. You two would be good together."

"I'm good. Single is a good choice."

"Who said anything about marriage? Good Lord, no. Do yourself a favor: don't move in with him. Then he'll be expecting you to cook and clean—no. Just take him for a spin and return him if he breaks. That's the best bet."

I stifled a laugh.

"Ah. Here comes the light of my life now," Callie

said dryly as Dizzy stepped over the hedge right beside the walkway.

"Don't believe a word she says," Dizzy said, shifting his satchel. "She's mad about me."

"You've got the mad part right." She grinned.

"I took some pictures. Let's get out of here." Dizzy headed toward the driver's side. "This is a crime scene."

"I doubt the cops are going to believe we pulled a house down on top of people." Callie pulled the passenger door open.

"I'd rather not be questioned at all." I slid into the back seat.

The roar of the car cut out the sound of the insects. "To the next house, or home?" Dizzy asked as he pulled away from the ruined house.

"That depends." I watched the houses drift by. "Do you think he'll use those circles multiple times?"

"He won't reuse the one we've just seen." Dizzy rested his hands on his legs and steered with a knee. "That workroom was in disarray. Anyone planning to use a circle as a permanent fixture generally treats the area as sacred. Or at least with respect. It's your protection. It's your container, holding a powerful and purposeful item. You treat it and the area around it like a piece of expensive furniture. He treated it like a necessary, though temporary, area. There's no way he would have left that corpse to rot if he'd planned on coming back. It was a one-off. He's used it and now he's moving on."

"You know a lot about circles…" I let the sentence linger.

"I did a little demon calling in college. Now, that was fun." Dizzy tapped a drumbeat on the steering wheel, though continued to steer with his knee. "Killing animals wasn't as taboo then. We ate it afterward, too, which also wasn't as taboo."

"Yes it was," Callie said.

"Oh. Well, we did it anyway. It was a different time."

"He was a bachelor, is what he really means." Callie adjusted her seatbelt. "He did things without thinking about them."

"That's true enough." Dizzy continued to tap out a beat.

"What about that crime scene you two mentioned the other day?" I asked.

"What about it?" Callie said.

"We didn't find any casings at the house, but I'm positive this is the mage I'm looking for. So this is my guy, but he's doing circles and sacrifices like the mage who skinned that human. Could it be the same mage?" Thinking out loud, I added, "But if he has the gumption to go big, why settle for sacrificing a calf? It doesn't seem to fit with his power hungriness."

"No, it doesn't fit at all," Callie said. "I think we're looking at two different people with the same idea."

"While the circles did have strong similarities, which we should've mentioned before now, I suppose, I agree," Dizzy said. "I would be very surprised if the person who did this circle was the same one who skinned someone to collect their power." He shook his head. "Very surprised. The mage who murdered that person was very controlled. Very diligent. Even the crime scene was well organized."

"This is our problem," Callie said. "That other thing is not. Rule of thumb with mages, Reagan. Don't stick your magical nose where it doesn't belong."

I frowned out the window. Her words were true enough. I had plenty on my plate, and seeing that poor calf had been bad enough.

"So about the other houses," I said, watching homes drift by. They were closer together now. "Let's not bother. The throwaway circle confirms what I heard about his moving habits. He doesn't stay in one place very long—"

"With you and a bunch of vampires after him, do you blame him?" Callie huffed.

"So you're still going to bust in on his gang tomorrow?" Dizzy asked. "Even though a bunch of mages will be there, and the head mage will be carrying around a demon inside his body, you're going to stalk in there, alone, and try to take them all down?"

"When you say it like that, it sounds a little foolish. Besides, Darius might come back to help."

Neither of them commented.

"Not going to sway me either way, huh?" I asked, running my finger along my holster. "Yes, I am. Because if I'm right, their defenses will largely be left to the mages at that meeting, led by Mr. All Powerful. Most of the mages will be scrambling, trying to remember which spell is which, what does what—they'll screw the pooch."

"And Mr. All Powerful?" Callie asked.

"He'll be battling a demon."

"He's used to battling a demon," she said. "He seems to have it under control."

"He's never tried to battle a demon who senses its true master…"

CHAPTER 20

I HAD DIZZY drop me off down the street from my house. The street looked abandoned other than a large figure that was sitting on the front steps of a house. I waved to the dual mages instead of voicing a goodbye, and stood on the cracked sidewalk as they drove away. I looked over at the wall of the graveyard across the street, breathing in the thick air of my neighborhood, relishing the comforting feeling of the humidity coating my skin. *Home.*

"Any news?" I asked, not looking at the figure.

"I've never seen someone leave a house so clean, and come back so filthy. It's a talent."

I glanced down at my leather pants, covered in dirt and grime. Each arm had smears of brown, and I'd ripped a hole in my shirt. I shrugged. "It is what it is."

"It certainly is that." Mikey rested his arm on his knee. "There are a couple knuckleheads running around the graveyard, but other than that, nothing is going on."

"What kind of knuckleheads?"

"Poor kids with grass and leaves 'n' shit. Not worth

robbing, if that's what you were thinking." He dug a pack of cigarettes out of his pocket. "Not worth chasing out, neither. Just some dumb kids who probably got a book on calling the corners or whatever and decided to give it a try."

"What do you know about calling the corners?"

"I know people gather in there and yell at the sky about watchtowers and gods 'n' shit. They wake me up. I'm a light sleeper."

I chuckled. "Okay, then. So you didn't see anyone trying to sneak into my house?"

"Nope. They know better by now."

"No one walking by? That guy Smokey didn't see any vampires or whatever?"

"Smokey said you got two mail deliveries. It was earlier this evening. He said one didn't look right, but the guy didn't go inside. Used the mail slot."

"He used the mail slot in the broken door propped up against the house…"

"Yeah. Where else are they supposed to put your mail?"

I braced my hands on my hips. "That's true, I guess. I'm still surprised the cops haven't shown up yet."

"In this neighborhood?" Mikey heaved himself to his feet. He scratched his stomach then stretched. "Cops don't care about us. Not unless they need a suspect for something gone wrong."

"Half the time I should be a suspect."

"Then you're doing it wrong."

We walked down the street slowly, taking our time. I wasn't sure why, just that when I sped up a little, he fell behind. He was a strolling kind of guy, I guessed.

"You dating that guy Smokey thinks is a vampire?" Mikey asked. "Not that it's any of my business."

"No. Working with him. He was supposed to meet me tonight to do a job tomorrow. Hasn't shown."

Mikey looked behind him before rolling a shoulder. "A partner you can't trust is bad news."

"I know."

He held up his hands. "You don't gotta start with the tone. You ain't no fool. I get it. Just sayin'."

"I've been hearing that warning a lot. I need him to get a payoff, though. I was hoping I wouldn't have to force the issue."

"Trust me, force that bitch. Force it right down his throat. Go hard."

"I plan to."

He dropped his hands and nodded, stopping when we got in front of my house. "I know you do. You're crazy, that's why. You can always count on crazy."

"I don't think that's how the saying goes."

"I don't give a shit how the saying goes. Everyone is crazy. It's the people who go with it, and admit it, that you can trust. So you be crazy, girl. Give that rat bastard hell."

I trudged up onto my first step. "I feel like this conversation has gone a little sideways."

"Yeah. I'm no good at pep talks. Good luck with your thing."

"Thanks for watching my house."

He waved at me and continued walking. He didn't turn into his house, though; he kept going, staring at the wall to the cemetery. I had a feeling he was going to scare the kids out of there after all. That was always a fun time.

I lifted a side of the door and scurried under, not feeling any magic. A few letters sprawled out at my feet, barely inside, given how the door was leaning. I scooped them up and walked back to my bedroom, looking through the house for anyone physically hiding. Nothing.

I plopped down on my bed, feeling strangely hollow. Disappointed. I knew vampires predominantly looked after themselves and their way of life; of course I did. Everyone knew that. And who could blame them? With their humanity eroding away, taking their deeper emotions with it, all they really had was brainpower and boredom. Most of them turned to political intrigues, and as everyone knew, trusting politicians was a bad move. But I had hoped Darius would pull through. I'd hoped he would at least honor the contract, if not our working partnership.

I turned over one of the envelopes and saw that it was a packet of coupons. I tossed it to the bed for a "keep" pile. The way things were going, I'd probably need them. I turned the next letter over. Paper spam. If only there was an *unsubscribe* button for real mail.

The last was a plain envelope addressed to *Reagan Somerset, Bounty Hunter Extraordinaire.* In the sender area was "Your Future Master" with an address below it.

"Oh good, another stalker." I tucked the tip of my finger in a little opening and slid it across, ripping open the envelope. The edge of the paper sliced into my finger.

"You diaper-wearing biscuit handler!" I shook my hand and examined my paper cut. A tiny line in my skin taunted me with stinging pain.

After shaking my hand again, I pulled out the paper and opened it up. A picture fluttered to the ground. Annoyed, I examined the letter.

In large font, the typed message said, *I'll show you mine if you show me yours. Let's make a deal.*

It wasn't signed.

I put it in the trash pile and bent to scoop up what was sure to be a dick pic. Since I wasn't on social media and didn't even have an email address, a few marks turned admirers took to sending me real pictures of their junk. I honestly had no idea why, since I couldn't tell them apart. Yet that didn't stop them from taking part in this strange sort of mating ritual for the hopelessly ignorant.

"C'mere, little willy, time to see the inside of the trash can." My fingers hit off the edge and accidentally flipped it over.

I felt my brow furrow, wondering if it was Photoshop, until I saw the hand scrawled *Darius* and the arrow pointing to clothing filled out like a person wore them, without the person actually pictured.

Much like a vampire wouldn't show up in a photo.

I snatched it up.

Ropes wound around an invisible body, indenting a shirt and pants. Out from the shirt hovered the top of a wooden post. Fire starters, those logs you bought in the store to light a fire, were piled up to mid-calf area on the pant.

That had to be a joke, since fire logs produced a slow smolder, not a proper burn.

I could just make out stone a ways behind the scene, dirty gray. The color and texture matched the Google Maps image of the meeting site. I checked the return address. Yes, the same place.

Darius's clothing was different than when I'd last seen him. If it was him, and I had no reason to assume it wasn't since I wouldn't care about any other vampire, he must've made it to the lair, since I'd gone back to his house that night and he hadn't been there. That didn't tell me if the mage had sought Darius out, or vice versa.

So Mr. All Powerful had trapped Mr. Handsome. That would be fun to rub in Darius's face.

Looking over the picture again, I focused on the rope. No way could normal rope keep a vampire put. He could easily rip out of it in his human form, or change to his monster form for an even easier escape. That rope had to be magical. Or else a spell was keeping him put and the rope was for show. Yes, that fit with the fire logs and the nature of the mage's note. Cute.

I dropped the picture onto the letter and sat for a moment, staring at nothing. Thinking.

I glanced at the window, then the clock by my bedside table, which wasn't working. I checked my phone. Four ten. Dawn wasn't far away. If I stormed the gates now, I'd have a better chance of breaking in before they got all their defenses up. Then again, if they'd dropped off the letter earlier in the night, they were ready for me.

The other problem was that if I went now and got Darius out of there, he'd get fried by the sun. I wasn't sure how exactly that would work with the contract, but killing a high-level vampire probably wouldn't make me any friends, even if I still got paid. I already had one vampire pissed at me for killing a bond-mate—probably; I still didn't have any proof—and I'd rather not make any more enemies.

So that meant tomorrow—or today, rather—evening, sundown.

I had a whole day to obsess. Great.

My mind flitted over the message. *I'll show you mine if you show me yours. Let's make a deal.*

Let's make a deal was clear enough, and I had a feeling it had to do with my power. Maybe he wanted me to stop breaking their spells? Or use my abilities to help them out? Whatever it was, the answer would be no.

What was with the showing-and-telling bit? A dick pic made sense with that line, but a surly vampire tied up to a post, ready to be burned at the stake by logs that didn't do much more than glow?

I tapped my finger against my lips.

Fire.

Somehow, the mage knew I could magically create fire. How, I wondered, and did he know what kind?

I continued to tap my finger against my lips, thinking about the demon the mage was using. Wondering if I'd strayed close to the mage without having known it.

What else could it be?

Unless Margaret had somehow seen my getting John's book, and blabbed when the powerful mage was questioning her…

My finger kept tapping.

The windows were covered. I didn't see how that was possible.

In a sudden movement, I scooped all the paper off my bed, crumpled it up, and threw it in the trash. I didn't know what was going on, but it didn't matter. The mage was cheating in the game of magic, he had a surly vampire I wanted back, if only for the fantastic dinners he put on, and—bottom line—he had my meal ticket to a better, less stress-riddled life. He could light the whole place on fire, shoot hellfire at me, and decorate the building in spells…

I was tired of playing. I was going to get what was mine.

CHAPTER 21

I SLUNG MY stained, frayed-edged, modified satchel over my shoulder and let it drape across my body. It was smaller than the version everyone else used, with an extra strap that kept it close to my side. When the flap was pulled back, there were compartments on the inside for easy grabbing on the run. I used to wear it all the time, but since I stopped being able to fill it with spells, the small leather pouch was a better option. Certainly a nicer-looking option.

My sword warmed my back and my gun was secured to my upper thigh. I buckled a knife to my ankle for overkill, because if the gun didn't work, and the spells didn't work, and my magic didn't work, a knife certainly wouldn't save the day. Still, you never knew.

"Right, then." I took a deep breath and glanced out the window. The dying light put a hard edge on everything. Sundown was right around the corner.

I walked out of my room and down the hall, my head held high and butterflies in my stomach. Usually I went after one person. Occasionally two. I'd never taken on a whole army before. Especially not alone.

This wasn't smart.

I was doing it anyway.

I reached my front door and kicked it. The wood fell away and tumbled down the steps. It felt good. *Destruction!*

A moment later, I hauled the door back to its former glory, leaning it against the gaping hole into my half-burned house. I didn't need anyone telling the landlord on me, if they hadn't already. I'd have to confront him eventually, but I figured I might as well wait, since there was a chance I wouldn't survive.

The cab I'd called pulled up as I finished, ready to go. I climbed in and gave the address, breathing through the anxiety. My stomach flipped and tingles of nervousness radiated through my chest. The breathing wasn't helping.

I thought about all the spells I had and where I'd put them in my satchel. Sometimes all I had was a split second to grab something—I needed to make sure it was the right something.

"You going to a costume party?"

I looked up in confusion, not having expected chatter. The cab driver was looking at me in the rearview mirror.

I glanced down at my leather pants, then touched my leather halter top. Leather covered my lower arms up to my elbows as well, leaving holes for my fingers.

"I work with fire." I looked out the window, a subtle hint that I didn't want to talk.

"You're worried about your arms but not your stomach?"

He had clearly missed the hint.

I could feel the frown creasing my features. "I have hair on my arms, not my stomach."

"What about your head?"

I grabbed the headrest in front of me, anger filling my body. With my finger, I made a circle around my face. "Does this look like the face of a girl who likes small talk?"

His eyes rounded in surprise. He went back to driving. Blessed silence filled the cab.

A half-hour later, I argued with him about where to let me off, finally convincing him that a dodgy side road near my destination was the right spot. He wanted to make sure I got there safely, but he also wanted to keep his nose on his face. The desire for an intact nose finally won out.

My foot crunched on the gravel as I stepped out of the cab. The dull thunk of the car door set my decision in stone—this was happening. Final, final. No turning back unless I wanted a long walk.

The eight hundredth deep breath of the night done, I started on my way, trying not to turn around and yell at the cabbie to come back. The sound of insects replaced the hum of the motor, reminding me that I was on my own. Each footstep was a crunch in the direction of a crap-load of mages who wanted to do me harm.

My father's blood roared in my veins, the key to controlling that demon. My mother's blood sang a song of magic. I was a mutt of excellent pedigree, unlike anything the world had seen before. One of a kind, fated for a throne. I was all by myself, but my ancestors were riding on my shoulders. This had been the way of it my whole life, and I was about to unleash it all on Mr. All Powerful.

He would regret sending that dick pic. He would regret burning my house even more.

The old church came into view, partially hidden behind trees shooting into the sky. Usually buildings and houses around here were wood or brick, but this ramshackle establishment looked like people had painstakingly built it stone by heavy stone, slapping the layers together with mortar and curses. There was an old-world feel about it that didn't seem to fit with the new world of America. It was magical, I had no doubt, and I wondered if humans could even see it.

His chessboard was laid out, and I was about to throw a bowling ball through it. Always trust in crazy.

As I got closer, I could see the structure more closely. An old church, it had a grand entrance front and center with thick wooden doors, and a large square edifice with two rectangles stuck on the sides. I couldn't tell if the building was made up of sections, or if it would be completely open inside.

Large windows, almost gothic in style, dotted the front. Was that a gargoyle? I almost wondered if the whole shebang had disappeared from Europe into the Realm at one time, only to be spat out here. Things like that had been known to happen, close to a gate or not.

As I passed the trees, I did a double take. Wearing a purple velvet sweat suit and night-vision goggles, Callie stood with her hands on her hips like she had been waiting for me. Beside her, wringing his hands and staring at the church, hunched Dizzy, without goggles.

I stopped dead, dread and relief passing through me in turns. "What are you doing here?"

Callie braced her hands on her hips. "What do you mean, 'What are we doing here?' The question is, why didn't you wait for us to pick you up?"

"What?" I glanced at the church, feeling the thrum of magic vibrating off the outside. It was a doozy of a spell, one that would have made me pass out if I had my old weapon. I'd stored magic into both the ugly brooch and my sword. I was ready. Ish.

"I *told* you we'd pick you up at sundown." Callie scowled.

Dizzy poked her. "We need to get going. I don't like the silence. They must be planning something."

"I didn't hear you say that," I replied, not liking the extremely hostile look on Callie's face.

"Honey." Dizzy poked her again.

"I said it when we dropped you off. Did you really think we would let you come here and battle all this *on your own*? Are you *insane*?"

"Honey!" Dizzy nudged her.

"*What?*"

"That's new." He pointed.

A glow flickered under the door. Fire.

Mr. All Powerful was challenging me to a fire walk.

I started laughing and quickly recounted the contents of the letter—and what I thought it meant.

"How would he know?" Callie asked, the anger melting away into concern.

"I don't know." I shook my head, at a loss. "I would've felt a demon if it were close enough to feel me."

"Would Darius have told?" Callie asked.

"Never." Dizzy waved the thought away.

"He doesn't know that side of me. I'm almost certain of it," I replied.

"He wouldn't tell." Dizzy shook his head with a knowing, upside-down smile. "No way. He was a noble in the French Revolution. He risked losing everything to keep his people safe."

"What"—Callie turned to him with an incredulous expression—"does that possibly have to do with him keeping secrets?"

"He would've eternally died instead of giving away secrets! He could have saved himself, but didn't."

"Regardless, I have to go in there." I patted my weapons, feeling the pull of battle. The adrenaline and anticipation.

Dizzy nodded and started pulling things out of his satchel. "Reagan," he said with a tight voice, staring at the church, "the protection spell is going to come down in a hurry. A moment later, I imagine it will be outright war. You'll run in first, and we'll walk quickly to follow. I don't run anymore."

"I understand," I said, bracing myself beside them while watching what they were doing.

"Throw some spells to get everyone ducking for cover," he went on. "Use that to get to some sort of cover for yourself. Don't worry about them throwing spells at you. We'll handle that."

"Got it." I shifted from side to side, ready to run. Eager to meet the challenge.

Dizzy collected more ingredients while Callie palmed a rock and a few blades of grass. "After that, you're on your own."

"If you use your fire," Callie said in a strange, distant voice, "you'll have to kill them all. We can't let that information escape."

"Get ready," Dizzy said.

CHAPTER 22

DIZZY PUT HIS fists around his collection of ingredients and banged them together. Callie rose her rock and grass into the sky, her lips moving but no sound coming out. Dizzy banged his fists again, his lips moving as well, the words no louder than a whisper.

Dizzy started to stomp. Callie joined him. Together they began to chant in Gaelic, their words almost keening, a song of the dead.

Shivers raced up my legs and coated my body. I kept my arms at my sides, fingers lax, no weapons in hand. I didn't know what I'd need. I wanted to keep my options open.

The two reached a sort of wail. A black substance, thicker than smoke, darker than the night sky, pooled around their hands and drifted upward.

Callie changed her language to Latin; Dizzy started to grunt in a rhythmic way. The pair moved their bodies jarringly. The black substance, almost solid, floated higher. It started to roll, twisting and turning, a violent thing. They reached a crescendo in their chanting. Then stopped. The black shot out like a cannonball, heading straight for the church. It hit, splashing across an invisible wall.

I jerked forward, ready to go.

"Wait," Callie said in a wispy voice. "Wait."

Hands opening and closing in furious anticipation, I stood, braced, ready to run, as the black spread out across the barrier of the spell. It sparked in various places, tiny lights.

"Go!" Dizzy yelled.

I took off running like a lion was chasing me. The sparks brightened. Grew larger. Sizzling and covering the front of the church with smoke.

Still I ran, not grabbing my sword. Trusting in Callie and Dizzy. Hoping the warring spells didn't slice me up.

Ten feet away, the brightness of the sparks made me squint. The pulsing of the spell quaked my bones.

Five feet. Brighter still.

I really hoped this didn't melt my face off.

Three feet, and I reached for my sword.

The spells blinked away. The power evaporated.

My face smacked into the door.

I fell backward onto my butt.

"Open the door, you idiot!" Callie yelled.

"Good advice," I grumbled. I'd been so worried about that spell that I'd forgotten about the hard wooden surface in front of me.

I sprang up, grabbed the iron handle, and yanked it open. A flash of red light shot at me immediately. I dropped to the ground while reaching into my satchel. My fingers closed around a volatile spell. I pinched and threw at the same time, quickly crawling to the side.

A blast of cold washed through the room. It was gone in a moment, a terrible casting. Or maybe the spell had reached its expiration date in the casing. Hard to say.

I threw another. A surge of light went up, accompanied by a loud *pop.* The mages flinched. Someone shouted. Another dropped to his belly.

I jumped to my feet and took in the space, taking in the overall shape and positioning of people without registering any specific details. Mostly empty, but with a few wooden bench seats, the airy room was a perfect square. Within that, a dozen or so men were recovering from my distraction, getting ready to cast. Based on the size of the room versus the overall size of the building, the closed doors on the side walls and in the back led to other rooms rather than closets. The problem was that I didn't know where the powerful mage was hiding.

In a quick decision, I broke left, grabbing out volatile spells, pinching and throwing. Red streaked past me, followed by pink. Blue splashed at my feet, unleashing some sort of fog. Whatever the effect, it didn't penetrate my leather pants.

Running, I threw more spells, some lobbed, some hard and toward the ground. Flashes and explosions and one weird monster burst from them, my spells totally unpredictable. Shock and awe. I burst through the side door and quickly slammed it behind me, hoping I wasn't trapping myself.

A large group of chanting women gathered around a cauldron in the middle of the bare room. Liquid bubbled within it, and steam swirled above it, twisting as it reached for the ceiling. As one, they all turned to look at me, their eyes glazed and completely white.

"What the fu—" I paused for a moment in indecision, not knowing what was more dangerous, the strange women or whatever they were brewing. I needed to know what would be chasing me.

My question was answered almost immediately when the chanting quickened, rising in pitch and volume. The steam pulsed red. In the cauldron, blood rose up through the once-clear liquid. The bubbles started popping, spraying the ladies. Their bodies undulated, their arms jerking. The steam drifted in my direction. A figure started to take form within, spindly and clawed—it was definitely some sort of monster.

"Nope." I ripped out my gun and shot the pot. The bullet ricocheted. I snatched a spell next and lobbed it, the throw perfect. The orb plunked into the liquid.

Swish!

The blast went skyward, enveloping most of the steam. A moment later, it imploded, sucking the spell, liquid, and crazy down into itself. The cauldron shook, wobbling on the floor. Screaming drowned out the iron scraping the stone. One of the women ran at me, her hands curved like claws.

"Seriously, what the hell is up with you broads?" I slapped her arms to the sides and punched her in the face. Her feet flew out from under her. She whipped back and landed on the ground, her head thunking.

Cue insanity.

Screaming or gurgling women lurched after me. I ripped out my gun and fired, trying to make nonlethal shots. I hit one in the shoulder. She whipped back, screeching like a bird of prey, but kept coming.

I shot another. She didn't feel it either, ignoring the blood now streaming down her leg.

"What are you ladies?" I asked, backing up.

The door behind me opened.

I whipped out an invisible wall spell, pinched, and threw. The spell engaged a little early, stopping two feet from the man coming through the door. He threw a hex, his lips moving and his brow scrunched in effort. Bright green flew out from his open palm. It hit the invisible wall and reflected. He screamed as his spell ate away his exposed skin.

If I'd needed proof they were trying to kill me, that was it. Green light for the no-holds-barred approach.

A hand grabbed my shoulder. An intense shock dug down and frayed through my body. I jerked out of the woman's grasp, my teeth chattering. I spun and shot. So much for nonlethal. The woman fell. Her eyes changed from white to red, the same color as the potion they'd made.

"You ladies are dabbling in some dark stuff, huh?" I kicked out, my foot connecting with a head. My target staggered, trying to keep her balance. Another woman almost reached me. I shot. She windmilled back, no shock or anything on her face. Just trying to stay upright. That same blood-red color filled her eyes, and her hair changed from brown to a swampy sort of green.

I had no idea what kind of spell would make any of this happen. If there was one, I'd never heard of it before, and that was saying something.

The woman on the ground jerked. Her body bowed backward and she shrieked. I shot another as *Exorcist* lady struggled to her feet. Like a zombie, she convulsed before lurching after me, her arms out, trying to grab.

Zombies.

I groaned. "What kind of a freak show is this mage running?"

I put my gun away and took out my sword. Another

of the women came at me. I slashed, cutting off her head. Killing them was very similar to killing vampires, only easier.

"Dumb move on your part, ladies." I smashed my foot into one woman's knee. It bent sideways. She spilled to the ground, clawing at the stone. "You should not work with spells you are unfamiliar with. Look what happens. You get turned into zombies."

I cut off a head and stomped on a chest. A whizz sounded behind me. The mages were working on the spell I'd thrown.

"Where the hell are Dizzy and Callie?" I chopped off another head, spun, and sliced at a neck. The head lolled to the side, a part still attached.

My stomach swam. That was gross.

I took out the last one as blood started dripping from her mouth. How they could be so stupid as to unknowingly turn themselves into zombies, I had no idea, but it seemed to be par for the course with the type of people the mage had gathered around him.

There were two doors in the back, one to the left and one to the right. Other than their positioning, they looked exactly the same.

I ran to the one on the right until I felt thick, heady magic vibrating from the left. Confused, I jogged that way, palm out. Extremely intricate and wonderfully complex, the pulse of the magic felt pure, comforting.

The power of the spell rivaled even the combined force of Callie and Dizzy. It was a blockade, meant to keep people away.

What was the mage hiding? Himself?

I touched the spell with my sword. A burst of light made me blink, followed by an intense electric shock that violently threw my blade away. My hands followed. I punched myself in the face before I could regain control. I was lucky it wasn't the blade that had hit me…

Taking a step back and breathing heavily, I stared at the door in confusion, knowing my time was bleeding away. I glanced at the door on the right, not pulsing magic. Then back to this one.

There had to be a reason it was protected. I couldn't let that reason remain hidden, especially not when it would probably sneak up behind me later.

A rumble from the other room shook the floor. People shouted. The mage trying to get past my spell at the other door disappeared, yelling instructions. Someone screamed.

That was probably the Callie/Dizzy team. *About time!*

I put away my sword and felt the fire burn through my body, sweet and right. Power and strength. My birthright.

I moved my palm sideways through the air, low,

facing the ground. Flames sprang up and danced at the base of the spell. I lifted my hand, willing the fire to grow. It spread across the surface, and in a moment, the door was covered in living fire, eating away the magic. I kept it slow. I didn't need anything blasting out at my face, and this kind of fire would definitely trigger that reaction if it was burning too hot.

Another rumble shook the room, followed by a different kind of roar. That had to be the T-Rex.

The spell over the door peeled away, though it was still fighting my magic. I'd never seen that reaction. The caster had a solid understanding of his craft, creating something that didn't want to say die.

I didn't take no for an answer.

I held my hand in front of me, clenched it into a fist, and ripped to the side. The fire roared and flew through the air, taking the spell with it. A throb of light announced the defensive trigger I had expected, but there wasn't enough spell left to carry it out.

Grabbing the handle, I whipped the door open before draping the space in front of me with fire. Magic shot out, white-hot. It hit my wall and tried to eat through it. I ripped the blanket of fire away, tossing it to a different part of the room. I yanked out my gun and aimed it, only now seeing a girl about my age hunkered down in the broom closet. *She* was the source.

"I will not join you!" she screeched, her hands digging into a faded blue canvas bag.

"I'm the good guy." I took a step back, recognizing her look of obstinacy teamed with terror as she tried to find something to throw at me. "You dodged a zombie-sized bullet, by the way."

Confusion stole over her face as I turned away. She wasn't the enemy.

"I thought this was a retreat!" she yelled. "They were going to teach me about magic."

"*They* were going to teach *you*?" I laughed, my blood pumping as I squelched the fire and stalked toward the other door. "They aren't even in your league, sweet cheeks. Stay alive and I'll introduce you to someone who isn't a moron. I gotta go now, though. I have to save a vampire from eternal death."

CHAPTER 23

I KEPT THE gun in my hand and pulled out a Weather Beater, a spell that would allow me to make a grand entrance. Pausing at the right-hand door this time, I caught the girl peeping out of the closet, watching me.

"Do you know what's through here?" I asked her.

"A big room. In the middle there's a giant, like, pit thing. Like a long pit from one side to the other."

"How many people?"

"There were only a couple when I was in there. Then I came in here with—What happened to the coven?"

"They came down with a case of the stupids." I rolled my neck. "Here goes nothin'."

I kicked the door as hard as I could. Wood cracked. The hinges broke. The doorjamb broke away.

Kicking doors was one of my favorite things. I was good at it.

Another kick and it came free, tumbling toward the room beyond.

I peeked in to get the lay of the land.

The room was massive, and just as the girl had described it, there was a gap in the middle, running left to right. Ten feet across, so I knew I wouldn't be able to jump it. On my side, a handful of men shifted from side to side, startled into turning my way. They'd be throwing spells in a moment. I didn't have much time.

On the other side, in the left-hand corner, a group of idiots gathered around another bubbling cauldron, probably about to turn themselves into something they couldn't come back from. A circle had been drawn not far from them, with a human crumpled beside it, clearly dead. The right-hand corner held the object of the dick pic, Mr. Dick himself. Darius was still tied to a stake with a pile of store-bought fire logs piled around his feet.

Chuckles bubbled up inside me at the absurdity.

His gaze was pointed my way, but he was completely relaxed, probably pissed off and wanting me to free him so he could go crazy.

Anticipation heated the fire raging within me. I really wanted to see what damage a vampire like him could do. I suspected it would be awesome.

High up in the middle of the far wall was a circular stained-glass window showering blue light onto a podium. Being that it was night, and the stained glass was not blue, I surmised that the window was magical in an annoying, showy way. A thin figure stood at the podium, straight and tall, with a devil's mask on.

"Have you come peacefully?" he asked in a slightly muffled and machine-enhanced voice. He was trying to disguise his identity.

"Are you hoping I'll make fun of you?" I asked. "Because if you keep asking questions like that, it'll be hard not to." I noticed the mages spreading out in front of the gap, most with one or more casings in hand, but some holding items. A couple of those mages looked experienced. That was a bad sign.

The building rumbled, and the Dizzy/Callie team keeping the others busy, taking a really long time to just kill them already.

"You are the uncrowned queen," the mage said, raising his hands. "Bringing you in would grant me a hefty boon."

"Are you getting that from the demon? Because that's just silly. They lie, you know."

He shook, slamming his hands down on the podium. His body went rigid and then he hunched, putting great effort into something. Either the demon was trying to break free, or he was trying to assert his will and smite me somehow. Regardless, it was *go* time.

I threw the Weather Beater. It hit the ground with a tiny *plunk*. The rush of a tornado rose out of it, whipping around and catching a mage. It threw him with force, smashing him against the wall. Lightning rained down, hitting another mage. He convulsed, fried by electricity.

A spell sped toward me a moment later, so pale I could barely see it. I could feel it, though, raising my small hairs.

I stashed my gun and ripped out my sword before slashing through the hex, unraveling it. My sword pulled more power, wanting to stay filled. I let it do its thing while running at the nearest mage. I hacked down, chopping his hand, making him drop his spell. Then I ran him through with my blade and turned for the next, kicking out. My foot clipped his jaw, throwing his head to the side. His body followed.

I grabbed out a spell, pinched, and threw. It burned my fingers before I could get it airborne. It ballooned into a ball of light and fell on a mage. He wriggled and screamed, falling to the ground.

That was probably one of John's spells.

"Take her alive," the powerful mage yelled.

Yeah, right. Like they had the experience to capture someone of my caliber.

I sliced through the next spell, a weak thing badly realized. Lightning struck beside me. I jumped away, much too close to the Weather Beater. It struck someone else. The last two mages standing on my side of the gap raised their hands, focusing.

"Who has two thumbs and brought a gun to a magic fight? This girl!" I stowed my sword before grabbing my gun. I pointed and shot, taking down the nearest mage. Unlike the zombies, he stayed down, clutching his shoulder. I got the other one in the leg, deciding to leave them for Darius. It was good for my karma. Probably.

As the Weather Beater lost its potency, I stalked to the front of the gap, trying to decide how I wanted to handle this. No one had seen my true magic yet other than that girl, and she was shell-shocked. She wouldn't remember correctly. I was still in the clear so far.

Weighing my options, I yelled over at the mage, standing behind his podium on a slightly raised platform. "There won't be a happy ending for you."

The women in the corner started to chant. I rolled my eyes and swung my gun that way, opening fire. They jerked and screeched, most of them falling down. I was a great shot.

Click, click, click.

I also needed to reload.

"This is your last offer. Join me." The mage raised his hands over his head.

"No, thank you. You're too high maintenance."

The women in the corner changed, hunching. Their words slurred. Hair sprang up all over their bodies as their skin began to rip, tearing down their arms and legs. Fangs grew out of their mouths, and their fingers turned into claw-tipped paws. Snarls replaced their groans of pain.

Magically changed werewolves. What idiots.

Unlike the natural shape-shifter werewolves, which had internal magic passed down through bloodlines, the magically changed variety could infect humans with a bite. The full moon ruled them after their first change. They were the beasts feared in fairytales—hunted mercilessly by the shape shifters, and for good reason.

"Roger is not going to like you very much," I said, wondering how far they could jump. "But at least it'll keep him from hounding me. Get it, *hounding*?"

One of the beasts shuddered, opening its mouth. Saliva dripped from dauntingly large fangs.

"Free me," Darius yelled, watching the last of the werewolves change. It seemed only his head was free to move. "Free me to deal with them."

The mage howled in laughter. "And how might she do that?" His hands swung down and in, splayed fingers pointing at me.

A roar of fire burst from between his hands. It shot at me like it would from a massive flamethrower. Feeling the demon within that burst of magic, I stared through the fire as it washed over me, delicious heat tingling my skin.

"So you're letting that demon take control in order to do hellfire, hmm?" I asked. "That *is* a dangerous game."

"What?" he said in a low voice. Then louder: "No!"

I glanced at Darius—nothing more than a flick of my eyes—before firming up my resolution. There was only one way to take down that mage. Only one way to strip that mage of the demon, and then kill the demon so it couldn't head back to the underworld and reveal what I was.

Darius would witness it all, but I had no choice. For now, I had to trust him in order to get out of here alive. I needed him on my side.

"Oh right, about that queen thing—demons don't *always* lie. Just most of the time." I put my gun away and ran my palm through the air. Fire rose from the stone floor in front of me, answering my call. I spread it out around me, covering the ground and licking at the walls. The demon's presence pulsed, a heavy feeling in the air.

"No!" the mage hollered. Clutching the podium with one hand, he threw a spell with the other, shaking madly. The demon was rebelling, hearing the call of a stronger master.

I flicked my fingers. Fire burst in front of the coming spell, enveloping it. Disintegrating it.

Sweet heat raged through my body. I'd never used my power on such a large scale before. It felt so natural. I was meant for this.

Smiling, I spread fire across the walls, growing the flame in size and intensity. It fanned toward Darius, a rescue mission.

"How are you doing this?" the mage screamed. "This is not possible."

"If you think that's cool, get a load of this." I snatched a knife from my ankle, then used it to cut one of my fingers. Blood welled up as I said the incantation to infuse it with fire. When the drop was ready, I threw it into the pit in the middle of the room. "Here, little demon..."

Flame rose from the pit as I lifted my arms.

The werewolves backed away as the first sign of deep orange, almost red, fire licked the air. No smoke; it burned hot and smelled sweet, my calling card.

The mage screamed and writhed, now clutching the podium with two hands. Then he wrestled one of his hands free and dug it into his pocket. He surfaced with a vial, which he snapped open with his thumb and upended into his mouth.

I salivated as I watched it, knowing it was unicorn blood and remembering the taste. Remembering the rush of power and glory that came with it. The call to get to it was strong.

I gritted my teeth and flexed my arms. Power was sucked from my body. Heat intensified. The pit crawled with flame. Fire rose up all around me.

I levitated into the air.

"Leave his body," I commanded, infusing my words with power.

Flame ate away the magic that contained Darius. The werewolves were stalking along the side of the gap, looking across at me. I wanted that mage, but I didn't want to deal with his watchdogs. I probably wouldn't turn into a werewolf if I got bitten, but I wasn't positive. I didn't want to test that theory and be wrong.

"Obey me!" the mage said through clenched teeth. He shoved the podium out of the way. It fell to its side and rolled off the raised platform before tipping into the gap, lost to the flame.

"Leave his body," I commanded again, latching on to the power of the demon and *summoning* it. My blood-fire sang my song, beckoning. The mage had a helluva hold to keep it from answering for so long. "Leave his body."

Fire raced across the ceiling. I stood in a forest of flames. The gap roared, advertising my power but also spreading the aroma of my blood. Darius shook his head before his gaze locked with mine, full of hunger and need and desperation. I couldn't see his eyes at this distance, but I could read every line of his body.

"Focus!" I yelled at him. All I needed was another enemy to add to the demon, mage, and stalking werewolves.

His arms left his sides. The rope ripped away like paper. The spell over his legs, still thankfully holding him in place, was coated in flame.

"Focus!" I yelled again. "Don't be a dick, Darius. I need your help."

He plucked more rope away as the fire worked its way down.

This was not going well.

One thing at a time.

Turning back to the mage, I shouted, "Leave your host!" while infusing my *summoning* with more power.

The mage screamed, curling in on himself, squeezing his hands into fists. The building shook. Dust drifted down from the sky. The blue light from the window died. My blood-fire climbed higher without waiting for me to ask.

I saw the stone floor within that pit, rising to its former height. The mage was closing the gap.

"That's a neat trick," I said, backing up. "Bad timing, though." The vampire's gaze was still on me, and I also had the undivided attention of the stalking werewolves, their eyes glowing sporadically through the row of flame.

A new sort of force rose inside me, coming from my depths and merging with my magic, pumping it higher. Adrenaline sped up my heart, my movements. The thrum of power pushed through my limbs, begging me to use it.

The new presence made itself known. *I am here, master,* it said in my head.

"Oops. That's not what I meant to do." I tore away the blood-fire, lessening the *summoning*. With dexterity that could only be passed down through bloodlines, I pushed the demon from my body and forced it to stand beside me in its original form, a hunched, horned kind of thing with stringy arms and leathery legs.

Darius kicked off the last of the rope and stepped forward, freed. His eyes blackened and his fangs grew, his primal side taking over.

"Not a good time for hunger, Darius," I said, hearing a chorus of growls. In cutting out that fire, I'd also opened myself up for a werewolf attack. "I'm having a bad day."

I blasted a stream of hellfire, Spider-Man-style, pulling the necessary power from my ugly brooch. The corroding flame burned through the air and hit the nearest werewolf. It yelped and stumbled, succumbing to the direct shot even though the magical fire coating the ground hadn't singed it.

Good to know.

Darius rushed me, his pants catching fire almost immediately. I snatched out my gun and shot, belatedly realizing I hadn't reloaded.

Click.

"Shit!" I stuffed it back in the holster and grabbed out my sword. I'd have to reload later.

With the other hand I grabbed a spell, all while pressing my control of the demon so it didn't wriggle away. I wouldn't be able to keep this up for long. Something would have to give.

I threw the spell. Darius batted it away like it was nothing. It exploded off to the side, detonating too late. I braced until he got close, nothing more than a blur, he moved so fast, and struck. My blade barely met flesh before he dodged smoothly. I avoided a hand coming at me and launched, aiming for his middle. He turned to the side, my blade just missing, and kept coming.

"You are really fast." I slashed down, getting part of his arm and not doing much damage.

His body hit me like a pile of bricks. He lifted me up and rushed me backward.

Snarls sounded right behind him. The demon was struggling against my bond.

CHAPTER 24

I PUNCHED HIM just under his armpit and heard him grunt.

"I have very little control right now, Reagan," he said in a rough voice. "It would be nice if you allowed me to protect you. Save the fighting for when we have a bed nearby." I stopped struggling as he put me down near the wall. "I apologize in advance for my appearance."

Before I could ask what he meant, his monster form bubbled out, a kind of pasty-white thing with long, fierce claws and black, stringy hair. Very gross indeed. At least he recognized it.

"Fire," he muttered around his fangs. A claw pointed at the flame curling and flickering across the ground.

I peeled it away from his feet as the demon struggled against my control again.

A werewolf lunged for Darius. He rushed forward to meet it, slashing with his claws. Another ran at him from the side, jumping and wrapping its front legs around his torso. He flung the second against the wall as he slashed the first, opening a nasty, deep gash across its chest.

The thrown werewolf ricocheted off the wall and fell to the ground, baying in pain but not dead. I blasted it with hellfire, silencing it.

Another werewolf went flying, but the angle was such that if I used hellfire I might get Darius accidentally. I reloaded my gun while Darius stuck his claws into the belly of yet another beast. I stepped around him and shot repeatedly, hitting the other werewolf with three slugs.

"Need sh-ilver," Darius slurred through his fangs.

I'd forgotten that. Dang.

"Wait, you're not using silver."

"Magical. Clawsh."

Ah. I didn't have those.

Back to my sword, I chopped at the hindquarters of a werewolf swiping at Darius. The blade sliced through and the beast bayed, falling to the ground.

The sword was a *go*.

I stepped forward and finished it off while Darius took the brunt of the next attack. He slashed and stabbed handily—strength, speed, and power working seamlessly together. The werewolf barely had time to yelp before succumbing to its fate.

There was one left, and it was running at a full sprint toward the back.

"Is there a door back there?" I asked, readying myself for another blast of hellfire.

Darius took three lightning-fast steps in that direction before stopping and looking back at me from a ghastly face. He glanced at the demon next—and then slowly walked back toward me. His monster form melted back into his handsome man form, only he no longer had on any clothes.

I got an eyeful.

"Pants, man! Put on some pants!" I ripped my gaze away. The demon struggled against my control, getting a few steps toward the back door before I caught hold of him. My power was low, though, after all that hellfire.

"Let me join you, master." Its words were sweet and syrupy, echoing through the quietness.

"Join me for what? A game of Parcheesi? Give me a break; everyone knows demons cheat." I handled my sword, letting it pull more power. My legs wobbled.

"Banish the demon." Darius shadowed me. "The mage escaped through the front. We must follow."

"I can't banish it. It'll tell my dad on me. That is a war I do not want to fight."

"Let me worship you, master. I will be your servant in the underworld." A bug crawled out from a crack in its black, gooey skin.

"Ew. No. Don't you have a human form?"

"It's not powerful enough to change form." Darius

put his hand on my shoulder. "If you strike, and you do not have the ability to kill it, there is a good chance it will bleed you of your power. Banish it. If your…creator hears and comes to the surface, we can negotiate."

"He isn't my creator, he's my father, and I don't negotiate with terrorists." I slashed my sword through its middle, its weakest point going by the lack of horns and nobs. My blade ate through flesh. Fire burned up and turned into smoke. My sword sucked more power from me.

I pulled the blade out and stabbed, spearing the demon in the neck. It didn't move to thwart me, but then, it didn't have to. I could chop it up into a hundred pieces, and as long as it still had magic, it would continue living in this world, hoping to find a body to possess.

My head drooped as my diminishing power fought with the demon's. That human sacrifice had allowed him to call a level-three demon, and while before the hellfire and the blood-fire I would've been fine, I surely wasn't fine now.

"Reagan, pull out," Darius said, his voice laced with worry.

"That's what she said." Dizziness came over me, but I let my sword take more. I depleted my ugly brooch. "Almost there."

"Reagan," Darius said again, a plea in his voice.

"How cute that you care," I mumbled, holding on.

Feeling the demon's power sapping. Overcoming the magic that had brought him out of the underworld.

"Here." A warm wrist bumped against my mouth. "This will help. Drink."

I sank to my knees, feeling the blackness coming.

I could do it. I could overcome this demon. But I might have to sacrifice my life to do so.

The alternative was banishing it, easy to do. If I did that, I'd be giving up my freedom.

Banishing it was not an option.

I sucked.

The taste of Darius's blood infused my senses. It wasn't the explosion of unicorn blood, but something about it was almost more appealing. It was like him—smooth, decadent, and silky, winding through my body in a delicious way.

I moaned as my eyes fluttered closed, lust and desire igniting my body. My head turned of its own will, toward him. Wanting his touch on me. Relishing in the sultry taste of his blood.

"Hang on to the sword, Reagan." His other hand drifted down my arm, spreading goosebumps in its wake. His fingers closed over mine, making me hold on. His lips grazed my cheek before slipping down to my neck. "That's right, *mon cherie.* Drink."

Unexpectedly, power surged through me, more savory than the demon's had been. Vampire blood was only supposed to revive magical people, not affect them like it did humans, but it boosted me. I fell into the feeling, pumping magic into the sword, hearing the demon screech and beg in the distance. All I could focus on was Darius's heartbeat pounding in my ears. His touch on my body, like velvet. It felt so good. So *right.*

The blade of my sword fell to the ground, the demon vanishing in a fiery ball followed by billowing smoke.

I barely noticed.

I pushed his wrist away and turned toward him, capturing his face in my hands. His lips pressed against mine. Our tongues entwined. I pushed forward, laying him down and straddling his hips. His hardness pushed against me, large and ready. I slid my hands up his muscular chest and moaned into the kiss. So hot.

"Let me bond you, Reagan," he whispered against my lips. "Become one with me."

It was a terrible idea. Worse than bad. I'd just avoided one form of slavery—I didn't want to embrace another. But oh God, in that moment, I wanted nothing else in the world.

I'd opened my mouth to answer, not quite sure what was going to come out, when I felt soft but insistent hands clamp down on my shoulders. They yanked me back.

Darius was up in an instant, dragging me with him

and shielding me with his body. He hissed out a warning, his fangs and claws elongating, ready to shift to his stronger monster form.

The fresh air away from his heated breath cleared some of the haze. If only my lady bits would calm down. They were throbbing so hard that it was painful.

"Reagan!" Callie braced her fists on her hips. "Have you lost your ever-loving mind? Size isn't everything. He's a vampire!"

Dizzy, standing behind her, blushed and glanced away at the door, probably wishing he were back in the middle of battle rather than standing there.

I knew how he felt. This was more than a bit embarrassing.

I stepped around Darius. "That wasn't what it looked like."

"Well, it looked like you were straddling a naked vampire with the intent of indecent behavior in the middle of a church full of dead werewolves and witches, at the end of a battle that will be extremely damaging to your future should knowledge of your real magic leak out…"

"Okay, it was exactly what it looked like."

I wiped my hand over my face, trying to get back on track. But good-*night,* I felt good. My body was weak, but his blood was singing through my veins, making me feel powerful. Strong. Untouchable. I wanted to climb back on top and ride this feeling to its natural conclusion.

"I'm in a bit of a pickle," I muttered.

"I'll say." Callie pursed her lips.

"Can you at least drape a piece of pant leg over that thing or something?" Dizzy asked in a pained voice. "This is extremely awkward."

"You're not helping, honey." Callie patted his shoulder.

"Focus, everyone, cripes." I scrubbed at my eyes and kept my gaze at eye level. "Here's where we are. The demon has been destroyed, so he can't rat me out to any of the higher-ups downstairs."

"Good." Callie and Dizzy nodded.

"First problem is that we have a magically created werewolf on the loose. It's a danger for the rest of the night, and then with each full moon."

"That is not my problem," Darius said, looking around the ground. Probably for pants. His body was at least starting to…relax, so that was good. Less distracting.

Why won't this pounding go away!

"Right, focus." I huffed out a breath. "The werewolf is a present for Roger, then. Someone should tell him."

"I'll send a gossipy note to a friend who's dating a shifter," Callie said.

"I better do that, hon. They'll know you're just reporting something." Dizzy must've caught my confused look. "She tries to solve problems. No one will gossip with her anymore."

"It's a relief. Such whiners in the magical community." Callie rolled her eyes.

"Then that's taken care of. Kinda." I glanced at the elevated area by the wall, then the burned and broken podium that had been toppled to the floor. "We need to find that mage."

"We got the mage." Dizzy started when Darius and I both beamed our full attention on him.

"You got him?" I asked. Darius stepped toward the door. I threw up a finger. "I am watching you. No stealing my mark this time. I saved your ass. Either I am bringing that mark in, or we're doing it together."

"I saved you. We are even." He took another step.

"You saving me is debatable. We have no proof. Don't you take another step. If you run, I will tackle you."

"Promise?" He grinned at me.

"With a knife, wise guy." I turned back to Dizzy. "Where is he?"

"Trapped in the other room." Dizzy gestured that way. "The mage tried to run when—"

Darius started walking. I ran after him, half staggering as I did so. "Don't you do it, vampire!"

My mouth dropped open when I burst into the other room. All the mages were downed, lying sprawled out across the ground. Black explosive areas dotted various places. Casings lay strewn around, all but a couple opened.

The formally powerful, demon-toting mage stood frozen in the middle of the room, the mask torn off and a look of surprise on her face.

"It's a girl," I exclaimed. "It's *that* girl! What was her name?"

"Tamara." Darius stopped right in front of her, his glare intense. "How do we get her out of that?"

"You know who it is?" Dizzy asked, digging in his bag. "I was surprised it was a woman. I didn't expect that."

"Me either," I said. "I don't get to take down many women. But I'm all for equal opportunity in the crazy department. It's good for business." I wiped a strand of hair out of my face. "She lived across the street from one of the mages. We stood in her neighbor's house and spoke to her. She had that freaking book of John's! I had no idea. She didn't seem very powerful. I had *no* idea!" I put my fingertips to my head and made like my brain was exploding.

"Here." Dizzy blew some powder from his hand and onto Tamara's face.

While she was waking up, I bent to her mask, which had skittered away and bumped against someone's foot.

Sure enough, it had a speaker system in the mouth to distort her voice.

"Did you see her face when she captured you?" I asked Darius. "Also, how did she capture you? That is newsworthy."

His eyes were so hard that they looked like they could punch through walls. "She caught me when I was returning to the Brink. They must've been watching me. The spell was invisible. I didn't know I'd been trapped until it was too late."

"A real ego crusher, huh? Getting caught by a low-level mage…" I smiled tauntingly.

"She took the mask off to bleed me."

Tamara blinked as her head came out of the spell. A look of fear immediately crossed her face when she noticed Darius.

"To bleed you?" A surge of jealousy came out of the blue. I took a step back. "Definitely in a bit of a pickle, here. I might need to be slapped on occasion."

"She wanted to see if my blood would make her more powerful. After that, she tried to force a bond." Darius's eyes didn't waver from her face. A death stare wasn't the best way to get answers, though. Usually questions were more efficient.

"Right." I pointed between Dizzy and Callie. "*Vamoose*, you two. We need to ask some questions you can't know anything about. Check that side room.

There was an extremely powerful mage, one without a demon trapped in her body"—I gave Tamara a *look*—"who was hoping someone would show her how to do magic." Callie flashed me a confused expression. I put up my hands. "I didn't have time to ask any other questions. She was on a retreat. That's all I know."

Callie stomped off, followed shortly after by Dizzy.

I turned to Tamara. "Boy oh boy, are you in a bind. We need some questions answered. First, how did you hear about the unicorns?"

CHAPTER 25

"SHE CRASHED A changing," Darius said, easing into his cool demeanor. It meant bad things for poor Tamara. "She drank the elixir that readies a human for the change. We are more open at changings. Someone clearly shared information they shouldn't have. I have an investigation underway."

"Why would someone crash a changing?" I asked.

"Haven't you ever wanted to be immortal?" Tamara challenged haughtily.

"I am. Or could be, if I wanted to hang out in the Realm. Wait." I held up my hand to Darius. "You're going to give her the special vampire send-off, right?"

"What's the special vampire send-off?" Her eyes shone.

"Death, Tamara. Horrible death." I shook my head. "You should know better than to piss off vampires."

"She will not have a chance to utter your secrets," Darius said.

"Great. So how'd you find out she was at a changing, and then, how'd she get out?"

"The elixir is not designed for magical people," Darius said. "It doesn't react with their blood the same way, and they can stay conscious. They'd die during the change, but a dosed witch or mage would be left with enough presence of mind to leave beforehand. She should've been noticed when the elixir didn't work, but someone was not doing their job. I discovered this when I went back to the lair, dug into our records, and questioned some of our faction. It is being looked into in more depth."

I sat on the ground, dead tired despite Darius's blood still surging through me. If not for him, I'd probably be unconscious. "So she learned of the unicorn blood, which not even newbies usually know about, and figured out how to get more?"

"I reached a stalemate trying to find out where they keep the unicorns," Tamara said. "Luckily, their deal with the demons helped me out."

Fear shot through me. "What deal with the demons?"

"Vlad is working on something." Darius's eyes left Tamara for a moment and landed on me. "I am not a part of it."

"How do the demons know about the unicorns?" I asked. "And, Tamara, why did you need to wipe out the—" It all came together. "You wiped out the footprints because you drew a circle in one of those meeting places. Using a sentry as your sacrifice, you summoned a demon there. You didn't want to leave any more clues than you already had."

"Clever girl." Tamara smirked. "Those serpents in the water are helpful for getting rid of bodies. Then there is my smaller foot size. Everyone always assumes the leader of a movement is male. It has helped me fly under the radar. Even the people in my neighborhood—my own coven—overlooked me. I was a mage in my own right, but they treated me like a witch. They didn't bat an eye when John was supposedly chosen instead of me. Everyone always assumed John had more power because he threw his weight around. He was louder, that was all. I had the most power. *I* should've led. Should've been respected. Not him. I was planning to do away with him, but you took care of it for me. Thanks for that."

"That's what you call sleeping with a black widow, I guess." I grimaced. "But covens aren't about a leader. They're about the unity of combined power. That's what makes witches great. They develop a community and share the bounties. Mages tried that, and the corrupt Mages' Guild is the result."

She analyzed me for a moment. "You and I could rule the world. With your connections and my ability to amass a magical army, we'd be unstoppable."

"You're an idiot and your army is dead." I glanced

up at Darius. "But still, how did the demons know about the unicorns?"

Darius shook his head slowly. "That is a question for Vlad. There must be a leak of information somewhere. It could be disastrous if the demons know how tied we are to the unicorns."

"I bet Vlad is setting himself up to rule," Tamara said. A spark of opportunity lit her eyes as she looked down at me.

"Vlad most certainly is," I said, ignoring the look. She wouldn't be around to use me. Darius, on the other hand… "But not by giving the secret of the unicorns to the demons. Ruling means amassing a larger number of vampires, and losing the unicorns would be detrimental to that need." I rested my hand on my chin, thinking. "You would've created a circle based on the need for information at the start, right?" I asked, looking up at Tamara.

"I don't understand," Darius said.

I slowed down. "Circles don't just call demons. They can be used to call all sorts of things. In this instance, what she really needed was information. So she did a calling based on her need for information, in the form of a demon. That's pretty vague, though. It would call a demon with *any* sort of information that might be useful to her. Clearly she got lucky and called a demon that knew how to get to the unicorns."

"I didn't get lucky at first, except with where to steal those magical books," Tamara said. "I got all sorts of useless information until I found the right demon. Calling a demon is only dangerous if you don't know how to properly set up a circle. And after finding those books, I had that down. Then I found the *right* demon. Another character switch and I was *getting lucky* while I was getting lucky."

"This just got gross." I grimaced. "Demons are asexual until they take on a body, by the way. Just so you know."

"Vlad would have the upper hand in his negotiations if he had you," she said, turning her attention back to me.

I met Darius's eyes. "She's a lunatic, so I'm not worried about her. You, on the other hand, have some very sensitive information that Vlad could definitely use. I will end you if you try to go to him with that very sensitive information." I really should've made that threat when I could stand without assistance.

"If it got out that I helped you defeat a demon, it could upset Vlad's plans," Darius replied. "He is the only one who can destroy me. What you are—what you can do—is safe with me. You need never fear me, Reagan. And if you bond me, I can give you the protection of our entire faction. Your demon creator will think twice about seeking you."

Tamara started to laugh. "You don't get it, do you, vamp? This isn't some incubus demon spawn. This is Lucifer's daughter. *The* Lucifer, master of the underworld. You think a demon spawn can levitate?" She cackled this time. "She's the real thing. She *summoned* the demon from my body to hers, then pushed it out so it materialized on its own. Do you know how much *power* that takes?" She licked her lips. "She has a throne waiting for her for all eternity. Anyone who brings her to Lucifer will receive the highest honors. We can make a deal, vampire. Do you think Vlad is talking directly to Lucifer? No way. He's talking to an assistant, if that. But you could. You could take your place above Vlad. I could get us through the gates of the underworld. With her blood, we'd be granted safe passage. You could speak directly to Lucifer himself."

Darius's eyes widened, then narrowed. "That is preposterous. He is unable to pass on his bloodline."

"That isn't...entirely true." I shifted, uncomfortable. "It would require an ancient bloodline, status as a high priestess, a certain type of magic..." I shrugged. "He was drawn to my mother for a reason, whether he knew it or not."

"How did a lower-level demon know of this when I have never heard of it?" Darius said.

Tamara smirked. "I had the demon in me when I watched the footage from John's house. He was always worried about intruders, so he had a couple hidden cameras trained on his prized possessions. Whenever he disappeared for a rendezvous with his vampire friend, I would let myself in and watch the feeds so I knew what he was up to. He had my books, after all, which allowed me to work intricate spells without the neighborhood questioning. They never questioned him." Her gaze hit me. "I'm going to need those books back, by the way."

I just shook my head. She wasn't getting the grand scheme of things.

"The way she withstood the fire was interesting," she continued. "As was her strength and speed, but her ability to work with fire—my demon knew right away. Only one can do that. Well, now two, I guess, right? He wanted to leave me for her. I had to wrestle him to keep control. Why you're hiding up here in the Brink, I'll never know. You could rule." She stared at me, mystified. "You could have limitless power. Be trained by Lucifer himself!"

"Chained in the underworld with a bunch of demons. No thanks," I said. Darius's stare was starting to make me nervous. "Why all the male mages? Why not invite a girl or two?"

"Men are easier to dominate. A show of power, the promise of greatness—they get in line. Especially the ones craving that next level of power. The trick is making sure they think you are male. Then again, I did bring the women around in the end. So much work, though. They were always asking questions."

"And they turned into zombies and werewolves. I think the moral of the story is that dumb people will follow any whack job, but they'll also eventually land said whack job in the hands of a very unimpressed vampire."

"I wouldn't say he's unimpressed," Tamara said. "He hasn't turned his eyes away from you since he learned the truth. Looks like I'll be getting my ticket out of here after all. Men do love power."

I tried to ignore Darius's assessing stare. "How many more are there?"

"More what?" she asked.

"Mages. There is no way you would have risked bringing them all here. Who else is out there distributing the unicorn blood?"

She sneered. "Like I'm going to tell you."

"I will handle the distribution chain." Something had changed in Darius's eyes. Something I couldn't identify. Tingles of nervousness wormed through me, a reaction that made me edgy because I didn't know why it was happening. "I needed you to bring this to fruition, Reagan. Thank you."

I tore my eyes away, trying desperately to assess. I didn't feel like I was in danger. The opposite, in fact, which didn't make any sense, given the situation. Any at all. Darius was ambitious, and he'd just found a meal ticket. Worse, I was vulnerable—completely drained of strength. His vampire blood was doing wonders for my clarity, but not helping so much with my tired body.

"Did Margaret know about you—" I flinched when Darius ran, a blur of movement, leaving me alone with Tamara. He disappeared through the side door.

"Margaret is a clueless old hag," Tamara said as I stared after Darius. "We can ditch the vampire. He'd just complicate things."

"Tamara, seriously. Let it go."

She spat at me.

"*Really?*" I moved away. "What about your husband?"

"What about him? He's a fool. Making him do as I said was child's play."

"So he knew."

"About this? No way. He'd want to assume control. He was always trying to tear me down. He resents me for my power."

"Sounds like a really healthy marriage."

Dizzy hustled out of the side of the church with a harried expression, followed closely by Darius. "There are plenty of garments out here that you can use. I understand that you don't feel the cold, but have some decency around the women!"

"I will not wear secondhand clothing." Darius motioned Dizzy in our direction. "I need the human freed."

I stood, and all the blood rushed to my head. I swayed, trying to get my bearings. A large hand covered my shoulder, steadying me.

"I'm good." I shrugged Darius off.

"I haven't much time before dawn," he said quietly, too close. I hadn't completely recovered from the whole bloodsucking incident. "I must leave you here."

"I will bring the fire down on your head if you take my mark, Darius. I found her, I caught her—she's mine."

"Here. Get ready to catch her. She'll probably run." Dizzy dropped his mouth to his open palm, where he'd gathered a pile of powder.

I tried to shove Darius out of the way. He didn't budge.

Tamara fell forward, reaching out to catch herself on Dizzy. He contorted his body and dodged away, letting her fall flat on her face.

"That wasn't very nice," I muttered with a smile. "Funny, though."

Darius bent and scooped her up easily. He draped her over his shoulder, shot me a look that may or may not have been apologetic, and took off.

I clapped my hands together, feeling a surge of heat boil through my body as I readied for hellfire. Gritting my teeth, I aimed, and then staggered forward and let my hands fall. The door swung shut behind him.

"It wouldn't have helped my payday to destroy my mark," I said in explanation as I fell to my knees. It sounded like a cop-out, even to me. I let my head hang, panting in fatigue as the fire bubbled inside me.

"Killing that vampire would be a sure way to end your life," Dizzy said, crouching beside me. "He has powerful friends."

"Anyone with powerful friends also has powerful enemies."

"Looks like he just made one. C'mon, let's get out of here. You can come to our house. I'll cook you something, then we can drink whiskey while Callie curses me for the mess I made." Dizzy grabbed my arm and helped me to my feet. "After you heal, you can burn his house to the ground."

"You probably shouldn't hand me revenge ideas, Dizzy. I'm liable to follow through."

"I know. I do like Darius, but it'd serve him right. He must know that you handed him that mark by saving his life." He tsked. "It amazes me she got as far as she did. She wasn't very bright. Or skilled."

"She said that she slipped under the radar. Being grossly underestimated can mess with people, but it can also hide them. In her case, it did both. Her coven didn't even suspect her! That's amazing to me. Although she did have a bigger whack job across the street." I wiped my hair out of my face. "I wonder where she got those books. I should've asked. I bet that was step one. The…boost in magic and energy was step two. From there, amassing a bunch of idiots."

Dizzy guided me through the door to the side room, probably wondering if I would fall on my face. The zombie bodies lay where I'd left them, definitely dead. Callie stood in front of the closed closet door, staring at the woodgrain.

"Someone has locked herself in the closet and we can't get her out." Dizzy headed that way.

"She's powerful, that mage. Told you." When we got to Callie, I sighed and slumped to the ground next to her, peering at her opened satchel. Unlike mine, which was a mess of casings, hers was an orderly combination of casings and raw ingredients. "I used my magic to eat through before. I could do it again, but I'd probably pass out."

"Oh." Callie looked down at me. "You're done with your powwow with the vampire?"

"Yes. He stole my mark and ran out the door."

Callie huffed. "Figures. They only care about—"

"Themselves. Yes, I know. You mentioned it a time or two."

She huffed again and bent down to root through her bag. "How old was that witch?"

"She's a mage, hon." Dizzy dropped his bag to the

ground and opened it, looking at the ingredient side. He extracted a pouch and squeezed it open. A foul smell drifted toward me.

"Until she knows how to work powerful magic properly, she is a witch." Callie grabbed out an herb of some kind and handed it off to Dizzy.

"We are trying to discourage against that form of elitism," Dizzy said. "That's what created this situation in the first place."

"Well then, come up with a different name for it. A mage is trained, plain and simple."

"Leave her in there. Let's go," I said.

"I most certainly will not!" Callie grabbed something else out of her bag and crushed it in her fist. "Any non-trained magic worker who can create a spell like this"—she motioned toward the closet door—"is worth my time in guiding."

"Bullying, she means," Dizzy murmured.

"Fine. Bullying. Whatever." Callie reached into her bag for another item and motioned me up. "If I sit down, I'll never get back up."

"I'm right there with you."

"Quit whining. You're tired, not old. Get up." She motioned me up again, more forcefully this time.

I rose and stood beside her. No way was I getting between her and a spell. It seemed dangerous.

She emptied the contents of her hand over my head,

getting leaves and stuff in my hair. It would be hard to wash out. Next she crushed some other sort of plant, took the pouch from Dizzy, and pinched out wet, gooey stuff that smelled like—

"Please tell me you aren't going to rub poop on me." I winced when she smeared it on my arm. "Did you just wipe poop on me?"

"You'll feel better."

"Eating and sleeping would make me feel better. Smearing poop on me isn't the answer."

"Oh hush. I need you to help me, and for that, you need to be healed. It doesn't smell that bad." She rubbed her hands around a chalky stone.

"Does sense of smell wither with old age? Because it does smell that bad."

"Bullying, see?" Dizzy handed her another leafy plant of some kind.

"I get the job done. Why is that called bullying?" Callie swatted me with the leafy plant. When it hit my skin, a chill spread through my body, making my teeth chatter. I hugged my arms around my torso before yanking my hand away from my arm. Too late—the gooey, foul-smelling stuff was now on my hand.

"Do you have any baby wipes in there?" My body started to shake. "Also, this doesn't feel right."

"I'm counteracting your magic," Callie said as Dizzy handed over a wet wipe. "It will nullify the magic to its full potential much more often. It'll help build up your magical muscles, so to speak. In fact, when I train the new recruit, I should let you sit in. That might help you develop your own abilities."

"We don't know if she'll want to be trained," Dizzy said.

"Of course she'll want to be trained. Who wouldn't?"

"People who hate being bullied?" I asked innocently.

"Would you two stop with the bullying comments?" Callie frowned at me, waiting.

The bite of cold worked its way out of my limbs, tingling my fingertips. Warmth took over, my normal body temperature. The aching was gone, along with the fatigue. I swung my arms, feeling fresh as a daisy.

"It would've been nice if you'd done this before the vampire stole my mark." I tapped my weapons.

"We'll plan your vengeance after we've had some rest. Now." Callie stepped back and pointed at the door.

"I saw you levitating, by the way," Dizzy said as I motioned fire over the spell. "That was really something. I didn't know humans could do that. Can you go anywhere, or just up and down?"

"It was a gift from her father," Callie said. "And I mean gift. There is no spell that can duplicate that. Only fifth-level demons and above can harness that power, and possessing a fifth-level demon and maintaining your sense of self is unheard of. Hollywood glorifies plenty of things, but some demonic possessions are really that extreme. Demons of that magnitude eat a person from the inside out. And yes, she should be able to move from one place to another, though I'm not sure how far she could make it. Amorette saw Reagan's father do it."

"My mom saw him, but she couldn't teach me," I said. "He needs to, or I need to figure it out on my own. Right now, I just can't. I can will it, but I don't move. I might not have enough power."

"You have the power; you just haven't completely grown into it. I think using it more often is the key," Callie said.

"Why don't demons just take their own human shape?" I asked, amping up the magic slowly. It sparked and sputtered as it worked through the woman's defenses. She'd upped her game this time around, altering the spell to withstand another attack from my magic. I wondered if she even knew what she was doing, or if it was unconscious knowledge.

I made everyone take a few steps back, then threw up another fire shield just in case.

"Don't touch that," I said as Dizzy stuck his finger in.

"Ouch!" He yanked his hand back and stuck it in his

mouth.

"It is actual fire. It hurts. Don't touch it." Callie shook her head at him. "Genius."

"Darius went through it! He stood in it," Dizzy shouted back. I was learning that that was his defense against the bullying. It all made sense now. There was a reason they were dual mages.

"Darius won't allow himself to show pain," I said.

"Creating and maintaining a human form takes substantial energy," Callie said, finally answering my question about demons as she watched my magic work. "Crossing out of the underground does, too. When they surface on this side of the boundary, they immediately seek a human body to hibernate in for a time, regaining their strength."

"Here we go." I ripped the shards of the woman's spell away and moved the curtain of fire just in time. The spell exploded, blasting the curtain and sparkling through. "Pretty."

"I don't wish I had your dad, but I do wish I had that ability." Dizzy stared at it.

"I have a book that will teach you how to magically make fire, I think." I stepped up and pulled the door open, quickly swinging to the side as I did so.

A spell streamed out, shooting past Callie and barely missing Dizzy, who jerked too late.

"Whoa, whoa, whoa, we're not here to hurt you!"

Callie put her hands up. "The show is over. All the bad guys are dead."

"Except the escaped werewolf, but don't worry about her." Dizzy smiled in a good-natured way. "She is terrorizing the closest town. We're but a distant memory."

I shook my head and looked at the sky. He wasn't letting the gravity of the situation get to him, I'd give Dizzy that.

"What are you people?" the woman asked, huddled in the closet. She clutched her mostly empty canvas bag.

Callie noticed. "How did you create this spell?" She made a circle in the air with her finger.

The woman's brow furrowed and she drew into herself—a defensive quirk from getting ridiculed often, I'd bet.

"I'm Reagan." I stepped into her line of sight and stuck out my hand. "And they are harmless."

"Penny." She studied my face. "Are you a witch?"

"No. I'm an asshole. It's these two you want to talk to." I hooked a thumb over my shoulder.

"She's not an asshole, she's strong-willed," Dizzy said, stepping up with a smile. He stuck out his hand. "I am Desmond, but my friends call me Dizzy. Nice to meet you. We were about to head to our house for some dinner—would you care to join us?"

"I'm Callie. C'mon, after the night we all had, we

need a stiff drink."

"I don't drink. My mom doesn't think it's ladylike." Penny rose slowly.

"Do you know what's not ladylike?" Callie grunted as she bent to get her satchel and then straightened up stiffly. "Hiding in a closet when there is danger near. That's cowardly. *Real* ladies aren't cowards."

"Take it easy," Dizzy said in a low voice.

"Take it easy, my left foot." Callie stalked for the door. "If she wants any hope of controlling her incredible gift, taking it easy is a waste of time."

I jerked my head toward the dual mages and started walking. Thankfully, Penny fell in step with me. "They are the best in this area, and they don't usually take on apprentices. If I were you, I'd see what they have to say."

She shrugged as we made our way out the door, then stumbled when she saw all the bodies in the outer room. Her eyes got as big as silver dollars.

This probably wasn't the best way to initiate her into her new life.

"This isn't normal for Dizzy and Callie." I waved my hand through the air before picking up the pace. "This is my fault, sadly. I get into skirmishes far more than is healthy."

"This is a skirmish?"

"Well…no. This is a clusterfuck. But you know what I mean." I held the door open for her. "So, what do you say? Fancy some dinner? You can ask questions." It would be an opportunity for me to find out how much she knew without having to ask. I didn't want to let her know my traits were not normal by asking about them.

As we filed into the car, my mind drifted back to Darius and my mark. If he had my wellbeing in mind, he would stop by the Magical Law Enforcement office and check her in, not to mention he could explain what went down in the church so I wouldn't have to. Someone needed to get on cleanup detail. The bounty would be released, and I'd get my money. After that, he could do whatever he wanted.

If he had my wellbeing in mind.

CHAPTER 26

I STALKED INTO the Magical Law Enforcement office with my usual snarl. There'd be no sense in confusing people with a pleasant attitude, which was exactly what I had underneath the carefully cultivated scowl. I'd spent all of yesterday eating, drinking, and sleeping at Dizzy and Callie's house, relishing in their comfortable bed, salivating over their delicious food, and being spoiled with fun and laughter. It was like being with family, something I hadn't experienced in years.

Penny had been dubbed mage-in-training, though she had—so far—refused the actual training. Callie had thrown her weight around, and Penny, with three shots of whiskey in her, had strapped on her new ladylike demeanor and told Callie where to stick it.

I'd laughed so hard that I cried.

Turned out Penny had been approached by a bunch of different mages, all wanting to train her. Finally, she'd agreed to the retreat with the best adjusted of the lot. Her recruiters had turned into zombies and the retreat had turned into a magical bloodbath.

To say the girl was now gun shy was an understatement.

She seemed to like me well enough, though. And while she definitely remembered my affinity with fire, she thought it was magical. Since she could perform magic without all the words and props that the dual mages needed, making her completely natural and one hell of a find, she didn't think I was all that exceptional.

She could live. Yay her.

Now, at midday, seven days after I'd stormed into this office with a chip on my shoulder, I was back again, no mark in hand, really hoping Darius had done the right thing. He did not want me to enact any of the horrendous revenge schemes a bunch of drunk magic people had thought up.

"Stiffed again, I hear." Garret leaned forward in his chair, his elbow braced on the cubicle desk.

Those words didn't bode well.

"Fool you once, shame on you. Fool you twice, and you're an idiot." He laughed. People around him stopped what they were doing and looked my way.

"Taunt me once, shame on you." I stopped in the mouth of his cube in my dirty, battle-stained clothes. I had zombie blood splattered down one side, the whole shebang was covered in scuffs and tears, and I sprinkled dirt as I walked. I could've stayed in the bright pink sweats, three sizes too big, Callie had loaned me, but decided I'd rather be dirty. "Taunt me twice. I dare you."

The joy on his face melted into a guarded wariness. "Yeah, well…"

I continued to stare at him. "I dare you."

His eyebrows fell. He leaned away from me slowly, pulling his elbow off the desk.

"That's what I thought." I continued down the aisle, my good mood evaporating like drizzle on hot cement. I pushed open the captain's door and came to a stop in front of his desk. "Say my mark was checked in."

"Can't. Didn't happen."

Rage blasted through me. I curled my fists, turned, and punched his wall. I enjoyed shows of violence. "What the hell, captain?" I bellowed. "What the bloody hell? *I hate vampires!*"

I punched the metal of the new door, denting it.

"I'll add that to their tab, will I?" The captain entwined his fingers in front of him on the desk. "Quite the bill they're racking up."

"Charge that lying cheat, Darius, the wanker." Fuming, I ripped the door off its hinges. Or tried, anyway. They were a lot stronger than last time. The captain had seen me coming. "Dang it."

"Sorry, kid. You could've been a contender."

I wasn't in the mood for movie quotes.

He must've sensed it, because his face softened.

"What are you going to do?"

"I'm going to get my mark back, drag her annoying ass in here, and get paid. That's what I'm going to do." I clenched my teeth, firming up my resolve. There was no other way. "It's alive or dead, right?"

"Alive. You going into their lair to get her?"

"Gonna have to. *Dang it!*" I braced my hands on my hips and turned to the door, more pissed that Darius would do me like this than about the actual grievance. "He was great at pretending to be a partnership. I actually trusted him to do the right thing."

"Your bad."

I huffed out a laugh. "Tell me about it." I tossed up my hands. "Well then. You know what Woody Allen says: 'Money is better than poverty, if only for financial reasons.'"

The captain chuckled, leaning back. "I can't assign anyone to help you if you don't have your paperwork filled out."

"Yes. We've been through this. Every time I come in, we go through it. Keep wishing on that star."

"You're thickheaded."

"Yup." Shaking my head, I headed out the door. Before I was completely out of the office, though, I turned back. "Put this next thing on their tab, too."

"What next thing?"

I stalked down the aisle, my anger boiling over. I

reached Garret's cube, stepped in, and grabbed his desk. With a show of strength that had everyone gulping, I shook it until it broke away from the cube side, ripped it off, knocking his computer and crap to the ground, and tossed it aside like so much rubbish.

"What the hell?" he hollered.

"Oops." I continued on my way, ignoring his shrieks and everyone else's laughter. One day I would go head to head with that guy, and I'd beat him at the game he thought he was so good at. For today, I'd take Callie's approach—I'd be a lady.

AFTER A FEW too many hours in the bar so I could calm down before heading into the Realm after my mark, and now needing another few hours to return to sobriety, I finally made it to my neighborhood. The sun had waved goodbye to the sky, giving darkness full reign. Mince was standing on my street corner, hands in his pockets, staring toward the graveyard.

"Hey!" I said as I came up behind him.

He jumped and swung around with his hands out, karate-chop style.

I bent as peals of laughter escaped from me. I wished they were girlish giggles, but they were more like deep, body-jerking guffaws. "Really? What's with the karate chop? I thought you were a boxer."

"Holy fats, woman! I didn't hear you walk up. How,

I don't know, with those heavy army boots you got on." He put his hand to his heart. "I nearly pissed myself."

"This is a bad neighborhood, Mince, or so I've been told. You need to watch your back."

"Only from you. Other people make noise." He looked me over, his eyes getting bigger. "What the hell have you been up to? Your house is a mess, your door is broken, Mikey is more terrifying than usual, and here you are, looking like you've been dragged through the gutter. Did you shit yourself, too?" He cocked his head in disbelief. "Tell me you did not shit yourself."

"I *thought* the smell was still there." I looked down at my clothes, which were the only things I hadn't washed at Callie's house. "I'm good. I didn't. I want to go home."

"Okay, but wait." Mince reached out to stop me. I angled so his hand would grasp the air. "Fine." He didn't have to hurry much before catching up to my ambling pace. "Smokey thinks someone is in your house."

"It better be a godforsaken vampire with my money."

"Yeah, I know, Smokey has a screw loose, but he's a good guy."

I picked up the pace. "Where's Mikey?"

"He had to go take care of something in the Garden District. I don't like how much he's been hanging around lately. Watching everything, lurking. That guy is not a man I need looking over my shoulder."

"He won't hurt you."

"No, he won't hurt *you.* He knows you're crazy. Me, though, I'm just trying to go about my day. He hates that."

I wasn't sure if it was because I was drunk, but Mince was not making any sense to me.

I caught sight of Smokey on the other side of the street, creepy as usual, staring at my house. His head jerked in my direction.

"All right, Mince. If I scream, run." I turned up my walkway.

"Holy shit, girl, *are you serious*?" Mince backed away, shaking his head. "Why would you say that? Who are you expecting? *Is that a sword?*"

Mince wasn't cut out for my life.

I pushed my door to the side and stepped in. The door tumbled down my steps and landed halfway down the sidewalk.

Oops.

Darkness and char greeted me, my house still messed up after its visit from that crazy mage and her demon sidekick. My eyes adjusted in time for movement to catch my eye. I took two steps further into my house and quickly crossed the opening of the kitchen. With my back against the wall, I stared at the vampire standing in my living room.

It was not Darius.

"You," I said, recognizing his intense scowl. "You aren't delivering my mark or my money, by any chance, are you?" I had a damn good idea why he was there.

Shapes came out of my bedroom and guest room, three in all. I felt a presence close by, one or more in the kitchen.

"Your contract with Darius is over," said Moss, Darius's driver. "You are no longer under his protection." He walked toward me slowly, all grace and strength. He'd be fast.

I glanced at the others crowding in. They weren't of the same level, but they were still vampires. If I were sober, my chances wouldn't look good. I was nowhere near sober.

"Question." I raised my hand. "Can I phone a friend?"

"Sure. From the afterlife."

"You can't just randomly kill a human," I said, wishing I could back up. There was nowhere to go. "Especially one who just helped your faction. And your boss."

Moss's scowl didn't change. "You aren't human, and by killing a bond-mate, you committed a grave offense to our *faction*. The punishment is death."

"I didn't peg you for the type who'd bond a crazy

person, Moss. You don't have enough humor for that." I eased my sword out of its sheath. It was harder than it should've been. I was way too drunk for this. "I get that you're pissed about John. Look, that was a bounty set up by his neighborhood. I'm not saying they should get your heat, but…they should get your heat. I just go where the money is."

"That will be your undoing."

I laughed, then snorted. I couldn't help the latter. "You're a nerd. But seriously, is that scowl glued on? Do you ever just slip it off just to see how it feels?"

He rushed at me, way faster than I was used to, since I wasn't used to fighting while intoxicated. I stabbed out with my sword, missing entirely. I felt a hand wrap around my neck, coming from the side. It was the vampire from the kitchen. Claws bit into my skin.

Moss reached out, his face a horrifying mask of violence. I slashed at him, catching him weakly on his side. His hand closed around the swampy arm at my neck. Moss ripped it away, and the claws scratched across my skin.

I jabbed at Moss again, catching him in the torso. Until I realized that version of him was not real. My sword cut through empty space.

I closed an eye and tried again, pretty sure I had it right this time. I still missed. He wasn't an elder, but he was an old-ass vamp.

His claws ripped through the chest of the vampire right next to me, yanking out the heart.

"Oh shit. I'm confused." I stopped from attempting to jab Moss as more vampires rushed in from the side.

"Would you be at all helpful?" he said.

"I'm still so confused!" I turned to the oncoming vamps, thankfully much slower. I slashed, missing the one I was aiming for but hitting another. My sword cut through his chest, catching his heart. Lucky.

I hacked at a different one, but hit the wall and stumbled, falling next to the dying, failing vampire and the legs of his living cronies. "Oops." I flipped to my back and hacked away a leg. A vampire stumbled in its monster form. He bent to slash me.

I grabbed my gun, yanked it free with some effort, and fired. The ceiling rained down on me as the claws kept coming. I gulped as I prepared for them to slice into me.

The vampire was ripped away. The other disappeared a moment later.

"Good work, Moss. Team player." I jumped to my feet, staggered, and prepared for more action. I probably should've stayed sober after all.

Darius stood in front of me in a crisp suit, smelling freaking divine. He smoothed back his hair before adjusting a cufflink.

I put my hand to my forehead. "I'm confused again. I think I might be delirious."

Movement by the door drew my eye. Two Mosses waited with their arms crossed.

"So. Wait." I pointed at the Mosses. Then closed an eye so I wasn't looking at two Dariuses. "Was he, or was he not, bonded to John? And who were those other guys? Also, and this is the most important question, who is going to clean up all these gooey, dead vampire bodies?" I held up a finger. "One more. Does anyone have a bottle of whiskey? Mine died in the fire."

"Reagan," Darius said, "why do you still have no eyebrows?"

I felt the area where said eyebrows were pinched together. "They were burned away in the battle and Callie ran out of serum restoring the hair on my head."

"You look hideous." His gaze took me in. "And the state of your house. How can you live like this?"

I struck with my sword, closing my eye to make sure I got the right Darius. He moved away easily. Suddenly, my sword went missing. My gun, which I stuck out next, disappeared from my hand a moment later.

"No problem. About that whiskey…" I lifted my chin, not bothered. I was too drunk for that.

He stepped backward, away from the bodies, and checked his shoes. They were still shiny. "I've come to deliver your earnings," he snapped. Moss came forward with a briefcase, his scowl definitely permanent. "This case holds cash. If you would prefer a check, or to be on payroll, that can also be arranged. Whatever you would like."

"Just turn my mark in." I matched Moss's scowl. "Just turn her in and we'll do this legit-like."

"The mark died before Vlad could question her, unfortunately. Without the demon, she was unable to cross the gate into the Realm, something we did not foresee."

I'd opened my mouth to argue, because that was crap, when it sank in. If she'd been able to talk to Vlad, she would've told him all about me. Darius was trying to protect me.

My mouth snapped shut so hard that my teeth made a gross sound.

"She has been dealt with, the bounty removed and the fines paid. You get a percentage of that, I believe, along with all your expenses paid, no receipt needed. I will turn a blind eye to the way you broke into my house, threatened everyone, and robbed Mr. Giles."

"He deserved it."

"Yes. He is being punished. This is the rest of your fee, as promised." He set the briefcase at my feet, "Along with the contact information for multiple real estate agents I trust so you can choose your new home. We can…fix this one so you don't accrue any financial damages." He stepped back again. "I pay my debts, Reagan. You should never doubt that."

"I can kill you. You should never doubt that."

His lips tweaked upward into a smile. "Not now, you couldn't. Do you have a spell for seclusion?"

I gave him the Evil Eye. "Why?" I wiggled, because my lady bits had roared to life. Drunk and horny were not a good combo. I was liable to launch myself at him.

"I will not touch you." He spread his very large hands out.

"I hate you." I tried to stick my hand into my satchel, only to remember I'd left it with Callie so they could go through my greatly dwindled arsenal. "Also, no. I do not."

He took a step, and suddenly I was in my room with him and his arms were pulling away from me.

"Liar," I mumbled, staggering. "That was fast. Am I that fast when sober? Because I honestly did not think I was this slow when drunk."

He steadied me with a warm hand.

"No," I said. "Just so you're clear. Muffin shop is closed. Come back never."

"Vlad is not a stupid man," he whispered.

I breathed through my mouth, trying not to smell his delicious cologne.

"Eventually, he will figure out what you are. His interest in you is piqued, and while he has not been in the presence of Lucifer yet, I assure you, eventually it will happen. That will be all it takes. If your smell and Lucifer's are in any way similar, or if you look anything alike, or your magic matches in *any* way, he will be on your trail. Eventually, he will learn your true nature."

"My dad is bound to find out I exist. He has been trying for offspring since time began. I'm not the only one he's created, but I am the only one with…my bloodline—the only one who could survive the underworld. I'll have to face him someday, because of Vlad or the next guy. I don't think any parent wants to hear that their child doesn't want to continue the family business. I just don't know if my parent will try to force the issue."

He grabbed my shoulders, staring down into my eyes.

"Are you interested in sex, or"—I ran my hands down his front—"how about whiskey and a lay? I'm in. You?"

His lips quirked upward into a smile again, and his gaze roamed my face. "We will revisit this side of you. I have an important dinner this evening." His expression turned serious again. "If you bond me, you will be protected in our society. You will be mine. Any vampire who wishes to do you harm will have to come through me, even Vlad. That is sacrosanct."

"Nothing with vampires is sacrosanct."

"Unicorns and bonds." He lifted his hand and grazed his thumb against my lips. "Unicorns and you."

"Sir, we are running late," Moss called down the hall.

I snapped my arms up, shoving his away. "Okay, I know no one likes the girl who is all doe-eyed one moment, and cold the next, but seriously, this is your fault. Stop with the whispering and the smell and the handsome. It's annoying."

He lowered his hands, his eyes intense—all four of them. "Think about it."

I would forget by the time I woke up. That was my insurance.

"Okay, but about Moss and the bond and all those vampires…" I let him direct me out of the room.

"A few vampires bonded some of Tamara's mages shortly after this started. They realized, correctly, that something was happening in the magic world, but instead of waiting and seeing which avenue to take, they bonded those they thought were involved—without getting approval from the elders, of course. I believe they hoped the mages and their army would gain power over the magical world. At that time, they would come out on top. The ambition was there; the intelligence was not."

"How'd you know all that if they didn't declare their bonds?"

"Feeding every few weeks speaks of youth. I inquired who went to the Brink to feed and when. Those with serious ambition tend to stay near the lair, trying to learn what they can and use that information. It was easy to figure out."

"So you had Moss bond someone?"

"No, Moss has no bonds. I had him wait at your residence for the vampires who were bonded with John and his allies. Hiding behind his own frustrations—he is not your biggest fan—Moss was able to easily lead the altercation."

"Why didn't you wait instead of him?"

"I had to get ready for the dinner tonight."

I rolled my eyes and looked at the briefcase. "That's everything?"

He walked to the door before checking his watch. "Yes. That is your debt settled. There is also a false identity, should you want it. Can I take you to my residence? This house is not fit to stay in."

"I'm fine. Thanks. You can send food, though. And whiskey. Not to mention a clean up crew."

He turned to go, but stopped and put his hand on the doorframe, facing the street. "It has been a pleasure, Reagan. One I wasn't expecting. I will see you soon."

"Yep. And hey, if you wanted to make up for disgracing me in the Magical Law Enforcement office again, you could run really fast in front of that beady-eyed guy out there. He's convinced you guys are vampires. It'll be fun to give him a little thrill."

Darius turned back, his beautiful eyes holding mine. "You have a strange sense of humor."

"Yeah. I know."

He barely nodded, and then he was gone, a blur of movement. I ran to the door, and a moment later the black Lincoln was leaving the curb and Smokey was pumping his fist in the air in triumph. His gaze hit mine.

I shrank away into the darkness and smiled like a lunatic. It was the little things.

An hour later, a huge feast was delivered to my house, including two bottles of extremely expensive whiskey. Darius had come through. I didn't have to kill him.

With a small smile, I sat to eat, thinking on that false identity Darius had created for me that would allow me to work in the Brink. I could take a stable job at the MLE office without fear of people knowing my true identity. *Finally*, I could show up Garret once and for all.

The End

Printed in the USA
CPSIA information can be obtained
at www.ICGtesting.com
LVHW091830290823
756478LV00001B/5